TOM HORN

Sinnestra's Fury

The Chronicles of Vespia Book 2

Follow Tom at:
https://www.tomhornauthor.com/

Edited by Viv Ainslie

Published by Purple Parrot Publishing
www.purpleparrotpublishing.co.uk

Printed in the United Kingdom
First Printing, 2021
ISBN: Print: 978-1-912677-86-3
          Ebook: 978-1-912677-87-0

Cover art by Ken Dawson of Creative Covers
https://ccovers.co.uk/

Maps created with Inkarnate:
https://inkarnate.com/

Books by Tom Horn

The Chronicles of Vespia:

The Chosen

Sinnestra's Fury

The Hollows:

The Hollows

Witch Moon – published 2022

Acknowledgements

This second volume in *The Chronicles of Vespia* series was written pretty close to the vest; meaning that the size of my Beta Readers was intentionally reduced. Only my Editor, Vivienne Ainslie, and my wife, Dorian knew the secrets it held. Both of these gems have offered sound advice and guidance along the way. Without their assistance this book would not be.

Sinnestra's Fury is far more violent than its predecessor, *The Chosen*, but I felt that it needed to be. The Demoness had been gravely wounded and was slowly dying. This infuriated her. She wanted revenge. The Chosen One, Bekka, had to pay. Sinnestra wanted her to suffer greatly before she killed her.

Lady Rosa had foreseen that a storm was coming at the end of Book 1; and, as we know, she *ees never vrong*! She also knew that it wasn't one that they could all survive.

One death was met with objections. Valid points were made for his survival. Finally, I relented and with extensive rewriting, I saved him.

Through further discussions with my Editor, The Chronicles of Vespia Book 3 was born and is in progress. A fourth book in the series is even a possibility. I am also diligently working on Witch Moon: The Hollows Book 2.

For the time being, I can only hope that you find this book to your liking!

Dedication

This book is dedicated to my lovely wife, Dorian Leigh.
She has always been there for me through every draft,
of every book, offering her support,
her ideas for a better way, her encouragement,
and her undying love.

Dorian – none of this would happen if not for you!

—NNCH!

Contents

Prologue: The Rising Storm 11
Chapter 1: The Coming Danger 17
Chapter 2: Preparations for Departure 27
Chapter 3: Departure 37
Chapter 4: The Road to Freeport 47
Chapter 5: Rebirth 59
Chapter 6: Serendil Brenatis 63
Chapter 7: Troublesome Night 69
Chapter 8: The Vile Forest 75
Chapter 9: Kensington Castle 81
Chapter 10: The Crossing 87
Chapter 11: An Unexpected Welcome 95
Chapter 12: Treachery 99
Chapter 13: Where There's Smoke 105
Chapter 14: Pursuit 109
Chapter 15: The Red Hills 119
Chapter 16: Passion Under the Stars 123
Chapter 17: The Twisted oak 129
Chapter 18: Gwyneth 135
Chapter 19: Return to Kensington Castle 141
Chapter 20: Sinnestra Strikes 143
Chapter 21: Freeport 147
Chapter 22: Graveside Decisions 157
Chapter 23: The Great Library Arcanum 161
Chapter 24: New Friends 167
Chapter 25: De La' Corte's Price 173
Chapter 26: Lost and Found 179
Chapter 27: Trish's Story 187
Chapter 28: Retribution 191
Chapter 29: Discovery 195
Chapter 30: Old Friends Reunited 201
Chapter 31: A Dirty Little Secret 205
Chapter 32: Final Preparations 211
Chapter 33: The Wyndreaver 221
Chapter 34: Dagmarth 229
Chapter 35: Surprising News 239
Chapter 36: Ambush 247

Chapter 37: Tagg Thorun 253
Chapter 38: Darkwater 259
Chapter 39: The Ghostlands 267
Chapter 40: The Winged Galleon 273
Chapter 41: The Stones of Darkwater 277
Chapter 42: The Obsidian Gate 285
Chapter 43: The Bone Yard 289
Chapter 44: Beyond the Gate 295
Chapter 45: Bitterwodd Castle 299
Chapter 46: Blood Oath 303
Chapter 47: Eight-legged Beasties 305
Chapter 48: The Promise 311
Chapter 49: Dragon's Reach 313
Chapter 50: The Darkwater Mines 323
Chapter 51: Preparations 329
Chapter 52: Dragonspawn 331
Chapter 53: My Enemy, My Ally 339
Chapter 54: City in Chaos 347
Chapter 55: Dragon Flight 357
Chapter 56: Tales by the Fireside 361
Chapter 57: An Unexpected Find 369
Chapter 58: The Journey South Begins 379
Chapter 59: Marrene's Generosity 385
Chapter 60: The Vale 389
Chapter 61: Lithania 399
Chapter 62: Rosa's Warning 401
Chapter 63: Breegan Dalmurnin 405
Chapter 64: New Weapons 413
Chapter 65: Betrayal Dawns 425
Chapter 66: Visions of Timestones 431
Chapter 67: The Obsidian Graveyard 439
Chapter 68: The Return to Darkwater 443
Chapter 69: The Demon Spires 449
Chapter 70: An Arduous Journey 463
Chapter 71: Silver Frost Keep 473
Chapter 72: Lithania 483
Epilogue: Midvale 487
Maps: 491
About the Author 499

Prologue
The Rising Storm

The three blind sisters danced about the chamber removing ingredients from dusty shelves and dropping precise amounts into the bubbling cauldron at the room's center. How they managed to avoid one another was uncanny. They twirled and whirled around; their ragged, dingy robes flowing like soft, billowy clouds on lofty breezes. Sinnestra was totally mesmerized by the trio's practiced choreography. Just watching their bewitching dance was almost enough to make the *Demoness of the Dark* forget her troubles—*almost.*

The burning sensation in Sinnestra's left shoulder would not allow her to forget her near-death experience. The grievous wound caused by the Drow weapon known as the *Blade of the Spider's Kiss* had not yet healed. She feared that it was beginning to show signs of infection. The slashing wound was gray and tinged with an angry redness—in complete contrast to her alabaster skin, and it always hurt. Creases furrowed her brow and her jaw was clenched tight. She was obviously in a tremendous amount of pain.

Though the *Chosen One* prophesied to defeat Maragh was not the one to strike her with the Drow blade, Sinnestra still held her responsible for the injury and vowed to make her pay. But first she would make her show her the secret of the *Portal* between worlds. This wondrous world that the Three Sisters had shown her was like nothing that she had ever seen. It seemed so full of hope and promise! Perhaps on the other side she could find a cure.

The priest dropped to his knees and bowed as low as he possibly could without his nose touching the stone floor. A thought flickered through Sinnestra's mind—*how tempting it would be to see how long he could hold this position*—but she quickly lost interest in seeing him grovel. She watched as his entire body began to tremble as he strained to maintain his composure. It was obvious that he was frightened. She could feel fear emanating from him and it excited her. He had good reason to be afraid. He had failed her, and she was in an extremely abhorrent mood. Badly injured, she was consumed by one remaining thought: *Revenge!* After all attempts to heal her had proven unsuccessful, she had sensed her impending demise. It left her feeling angry.

A repugnant stench permeated the air around her. The knife wound in her shoulder was oozing puss at the center of the jagged cut. All efforts to cleanse the lesion had failed. The month-long endeavor had proven fruitless. The agonizing wound refused to be healed. Ancient remedies had done little to hinder the spread of the infection. Even arcane attempts had proven ineffective. The priest claimed that he had never seen such a stubborn affliction. Sinnestra had once seemed invincible to these puny mortals, but now even she knew that she was slowly dying. The *Blade of the Spider's Kiss* had mortally wounded her. It was only a matter of time until it had run its course. *But how much time was left to her?*

She was furious!

Had she not agreed to aid Maragh in his feeble attempt to slay the *Chosen One*, she would still be enjoying a long life. She had been content to rule over the Drow in their world of the *Underdark* fighting a small band of resistance. But Maragh had told her of the world from which the *Chosen One* had come, and it intrigued her. Sinnestra wanted to be a part of that world. It was ripe for the taking! She knew that she could easily conquer it using magic from this side of the *Portal* and then return with its technology to lay waste to all that opposed her. Ultimately she would reign supreme over *both* worlds! She would be revered!

But alas her dreams had been shattered with a single swipe of the enchanted Drow blade. She had received its kiss of death. She was furious at Maragh for getting her involved in his puny mortal dispute, but he could no longer be held accountable. He had been slain by the *Chosen One* just as the Prophecy had foretold. This mere girl was hardly even a warrior. Yet she had gathered unlikely companions and united them to her cause. Sinnestra vowed, gritting her teeth against her pain, to make Rebekka Kensington, *or whatever she called herself*, pay! She would bring the *Chosen One* to her knees. She would show her what it was like to suffer agonizing misery, to know that death is coming, but slowly. She would make the girl watch those she loved endure unthinkable horrors before they died. And then she would leisurely end her life. She would relish the feel of the *Chosen One's* blood upon her chin and the taste of her still beating heart pulsing upon her tongue...

Shaken from her thoughts of retribution, Sinnestra glared at the priest groveling on the floor below her. Her jaw tightened with rage. It was time that she send a message to those who thought her weak, her power waning as her wound continued to fester. He would be that message. She rose from her throne and took each step from the dais slowly, her cloven hooves scraping upon the stone resounded throughout the near empty chamber.

The priest trembled as she descended toward him, dreading the worst. He opened his mouth to plead for his life, but no words would come. Tears formed in his eyes, and he swallowed fearfully. A pool began to form at his knees as he lost control of his bladder. The smell of his piss seemed to bring Sinnestra a moment of pleasure. The man was weak. He was not deserving of her mercy—though it wouldn't have been offered anyway. His fate had already been sealed by his failure.

She knelt before him, smiling tenderly as she caressed his cheek with the fingers of her left hand. "Ssh," Sinnestra spoke softly, like a mother to a small child. "Do not grovel, it only belittles you. Now rise with me." Her voice was gentle, almost soothing. There was no hint of her contempt.

He seemed amazed by her benevolence; she could see it in his tear-filled eyes. He sniffled, wiping his nose upon his sleeve as she helped him to his feet. "I... I thank you Mistress Sinnestra... for your... your understanding. We shall find a cure. I promise!"

She allowed her tender smile to slowly fade; her eyes grew cold as they narrowed shrewdly. In a flash she whirled on him, gripping his jaw tightly in her left hand, she lifted him off the floor bringing his wide, fearful eyes level with her own. "You should not make promises that you cannot keep!" she hissed vehemently. His arms and legs flailed wildly in the air, his attempt at protest only gurgled in his throat.

"*You* have failed me!" she said in a seething voice. "I shall not let your incompetence go unpunished. You will be a message to the others: For as long as I breathe I shall be feared!"

She chanted, her words soft, inviting, elusive.

His eyes grew impossibly wide as he felt her sharpened fingernails dig deep into his chest. She could see the hint of panic flicker in his eyes as he wondered what was happening to him. He felt his flesh giving way, ripping, as her fingers sliced through him effortlessly. *Oh how it burned!* He could hear the splintering of his ribs as her hand penetrated his body. The pain was intolerable. Sinnestra pulled his rapidly thumping heart out of the gaping whole in his torso, and she could see in his eyes that he no longer felt the pain. As she released her grip on his jaw, he fell to the ground unable to move. The cold fingers of death caressed him in their numbing embrace, granting him the mercy that she would not. As life slowly left his eyes the last thing that he saw was the demon's teeth sinking into his still beating heart.

She glared at her royal guardsmen. "Display his corpse for all to see. Let the others know that I will not accept ineptitude any longer. There will be consequences!" She stalked from the Throne Room; her anger echoed with the pound of her hooves upon the flagstones.

Sinnestra closed the door to her private chambers and crossed to the well-lit alcove in the northern wall. She smiled at her reflection in the mirrored glass. Blood covered her chin, and she licked the gore away with her pointed tongue, ignoring the drop or two that had fallen upon the tops of her breasts.

She squeezed what remained of the priest's heart, allowing the blood and bits of tissue to fall into a stone mortar. Her lips curled in a pleasant smile as she swallowed the bloody pulp left in the palm of her hand. She loved the way it slid down her throat effortlessly. Smiling, she began to relax. She added ground vehlwood root and beeswax into the mortar and mixed it with a thin wooden spoon.

With a contented sigh she sat upon a stone bench and took a Griffon haired nailbrush from a jar and began to paint her fingernails with the vibrant red color. She hummed softly to herself, a nearly forgotten tune that her mother taught her when she was young, her eyes glowed brightly. She could feel herself beginning to relax as she plotted her revenge on the *Chosen One*. She smiled at the thought of how sweet her heart would be...

Chapter 1
The Coming Danger

Bekka could hear the voices in the dark. Whispers, really. Like a conversation in another room meant to be kept secret. The deep dark shadows of the night were opaque, making it impossible for her to see her hand in front of her face. In haltingly timid steps she navigated the pitch-black corridor as though she were blind. The smooth flagstones were bitterly cold against her bare feet and she could no longer feel her toes. A chill hung in the air cutting deep into her; she could feel the dull ache in her bones. Already she missed the comfort of her bed, the blankets thick and soft against her skin and the warmth of the cozy security that they offered.

Something inside her warned of impending danger, but her body moved as though it had a will all its own. She must know what the whispers were saying! She *needed* to know! Though she could hear the voices she couldn't quite make out what was being said. She continued onward her arms outstretched before her, hands groping the darkness. She halted suddenly, as though frozen in time and place. An eerie quiet descended upon her. She could feel the tiny hairs on her arms and the back of her neck begin to prickle. Had she made a noise that she alone did not hear in her approach? Had she alerted them to her presence? She was surprised to discover that she was not even breathing.

Soft laughter shattered the fragile silence of the night like massive sheets of dropped glass splintering against hardened stone. Startled, she almost jumped out of her skin, every fiber of her being told her to turn and run, to seek immediate shelter. But *still* her body refused to obey her soundless commands as the whispers renewed. She was drawn to the source of the hushed tones like the Siren's song leads the unwitting sailor to the jagged coastline and his impending demise. She simply had no choice.

As she rounded the bend in the castle corridor Bekka could see the warm glow of torchlight spill into the darkness ahead. Shadows splashed against the walls of stone and seemed to dance in familiar patterns. As the gloom receded she felt her bravado returning. Only now could she discern what was being said.

"...and she won't see it coming!"

More laughter. "She's like completely clueless!"

The last vestiges of Bekka's fear melted away as she stepped into the lighted archway and confronted her friends. An expression of complete shock at seeing her standing before them covered their faces. She had caught them unaware.

Candace Marie Anderson, her absolute best friend in the whole world, or better said, in two worlds, was the first to snap out of it. She bounced excitedly. "Hiya Beks! What are you doing up?" She tried to play it off, to act all innocent. Bekka didn't buy into it because she knew that Candi wasn't *that* good of an actress.

Bekka leaned against the cold stone and crossed her arms over her chest. She glanced from Candi to Valoria, and then back at the blonde. "I could just as easily ask you the same thing."

Candi tilted her head back and squinted at her friend. She swiped at the air between them with one hand. "Don't be silly! Val and I weren't doing anything!"

The problem with her feeble attempt at denial was that Bekka knew Candi better than she did anyone else. After all, they were the best of friends and Bekka knew that all she had to do was wait her out. Eventually Candi would have enough rope and she'd wind up tripping herself up. It was totally impossible for the girl to keep a secret. Bekka arched a brow and kept her silence, knowing it would force Candi's hand and she'd spill the beans.

True to form, Candi stomped her foot and slapped her tightened fists against her hips. "Fine! We were planning a huge surprise for your birthday! But now you've gone and spoiled everything!" Her bottom lip curled outward and she pouted dramatically, completely oblivious to the disbelieving glare that Valoria sent her way.

Bekka pushed off the wall and gave her friend a stern look. "That's really sweet, but you of all people know that I don't like surprises."

Candi placed her hands on her hips and poked out her chest defiantly. "That's just too bad Bekka Kensington! It's not every day that my best friend turns sixteen! Valoria and the rest of us have gone to a lot of trouble to plan this; to make it like *really* special, and you're so *not* gonna ruin it for us!"

Bekka shook her head and rolled her eyes. "But my birthday is still months away."

Candi glared at her. "So? What's that got to do with anything?"

Bekka sighed in defeat, knowing that she couldn't win. She knew that Candi meant well. "Fine. Have it your way. I'm going back to bed!"

"Pleasant dreams!" Their voices combined as one.

Bekka waved a hand in the air. "G'night!"

As far as the pleasant dreams part, Bekka knew that wasn't going to happen. She hadn't had a really good night's sleep in the past eight months. Not since venturing through the *Portal* and coming to this crazy world in the first place; the world of her birth.

Since the defeat of Maragh they'd had time to recover from their wounds and mourn the loss of their friends. But they'd also been living in fear as well. Sinnestra's body had not been found anywhere in the forest. They had hoped she'd been mortally wounded when Lithania struck her with the *Blade of the Spider's Kiss*. The lack of her corpse seemed to disprove the fatality of that incident. Lady Rosa had warned that a terrible storm was heading their way; they were all certain that she was not referring to the weather.

Sinnestra was almost certainly plotting her revenge. The safest thing that they could do was to remain in Maragh's fortress and prepare themselves as best they could. If she caught them in the open, things would not end well. Besides, the castle had reverted to Valoria's control after Maragh was killed. As for the Roma, it was the first real home they'd ever known. It gave them a place to plant their roots. Some of the Romani Elders continued to watch the distant horizon with a longing in their eyes, proof that you cannot take the vagabond spirit out of the Gypsy.

With Sinnestra's apparent defeat, the subterranean realm of the Drow had been reinvigorated. The Spider Queen, not a true spider mind you, had been returned to her throne. Due to the friendship forged between Lithania and Sha'dira during the attack on Sinnestra and the defeat of Maragh, the High Elves of *Serendil Brenatis* and the Drow of *C'el'dihl Ara'k Tali'sharass* had begun a new trade agreement that greatly benefitted both communities. Together they were growing stronger.

As for Kestra and the rest of the orc, they returned to the desert wastelands to carve out a new home free from Maragh's tyranny. Not all prejudices between the orc and the other races had been forgotten. Bad blood still kept them apart, but Bekka was hopeful that they would eventually overcome these differences. The orc remained a proud cultural group; determined to hang onto their warrior spirit at all cost. The orc would need good fortune on their side against the Vortagg. Their future remained uncertain, but if Bekka knew anything about Kestra and her people, she knew that they were determined not only to survive, but to thrive. She was confident that their efforts would meet with success.

Bekka, her friends and her parents had managed to carve out a new life for themselves in their new home, though it wasn't always easy. Robert Kensington had been bringing his *otherworldly* engineering skills into play to update the castle they all called home. Now they had indoor plumbing, at least a version of it, anyway. Though it still had a lot to be desired, it was nothing like they'd had on the other side. It consisted of running water through hollowed out logs; which had been split in half and suspended overhead. It reminded Bekka of the *Swiss Family Robinson*, and maybe that is where her dad had gotten his inspiration. At any rate, Robert seemed determined to furnish them with as much comfort as he could. The Romani, with the exception of Rosa and Vincente, had refused to live inside the castle. Robert helped them to build their own structures near the fields where they worked the land. He also devised a way for them to better water their crops, which had kept everyone fed; and gave them a variety of vegetables to go with their meats and potatoes.

Julia Kensington had her hands full as well. Not only did she become pregnant on this side, she gave birth to a baby boy that she had named Hanzi. Bekka called him Han for short. Rosa claimed that the name meant *God is Gracious* which couldn't be truer where Julia was concerned. On the *other side* of the *Portal* she had been barren, and told by all the doctors that she would never conceive nor carry a child. She and Robert were expecting another baby in the coming year. Lady Rosa swore that this one would be a girl. Most everyone else had decided to take a 'wait and see' attitude, but Rosa insisted she was *never* wrong!

Bekka plopped back into bed but her thoughts continued to wander aimlessly, chasing sleep away. She closed her eyes but she could still hear the whispered voices of her friends down the corridor. With a groan she pulled the blankets up over her head. Sleep remained elusive...

Sometime during what remained of the night she actually did manage to fall asleep; though it wasn't very restful. She couldn't get her mind off Sinnestra. There were three distinct possibilities that she could think of.

One: *The Blade of the Spider's Kiss* had mortally wounded Sinnestra and she had gone off to die. That would certainly explain why she hadn't returned to trouble them in the months since the attack in the woods.

Two: Sinnestra hadn't been killed, but decided that facing them was no longer profitable, especially since they still held the Drow weapon that *could* end her existence.

And Three: She had been wounded very badly, though *not* fatally, and had slipped off to recover while plotting her revenge.

Any one of the three was within the realm of possibility. But only one matched with Rosa's foresight of the coming storm that would prove so disastrous for them all. Bekka needed to talk to Lady Rosa. If the old Gypsy still thought that they were all in danger, they'd have to act. They couldn't allow themselves to become complacent. If suffering Sinnestra's wrath was still a possibility, they had to prepare for her attack. The problem was, they *still* had no idea what the demoness was capable of. Neither the Gypsy's cards nor her crystal ball could tell them that. Frendlestixx had thought that their best bet at discovering that information lay in the coastal city of *Freeport*.

The gnomish wizard had said that anything could be found in the city for a price. The *Great Library Arcanum* of *Freeport* might still be their best chance at learning whatever information there was relating to the demoness. A journey there could be worthwhile. Getting there could be a problem, Bekka mused. Her parents would most certainly object to her going. They were far too overprotective, not that she could blame them. Since crossing through the *Portal* to this side, her life had been in constant jeopardy on numerous occasions, all of them when her parents were nowhere around. They weren't going to like her taking off for a dangerous place like *Freeport*.

Bekka found Lady Rosa waiting patiently in her chambers. She couldn't help but wonder if the Gypsy had known she was coming. She was sitting quietly in a large stuffed chair that dwarfed her, making the old woman appear smaller than she actually was, more fragile if that was even possible. Rosa's eyes were closed. Her hands rested upon her slowly rising chest; clutching a wadded handkerchief tightly. Her mouth was slightly open; a bit of drool threatened to escape one corner of her lips. The acrid smell of incense filled the room and even in the dim light Bekka could see the small gray tendrils of smoke twisting upward in the air, reaching for the darkened recesses of the vaulted ceiling.

She reached out to touch Rosa lightly on the arm but before she even got close, the Gypsy's eyes popped open, giving Bekka a start. After a brief moment of confusion, a smile of recognition lit Rosa's dark eyes. She sat up as best she could and coughed fitfully into the white cloth. She motioned across the table toward the only other chair. "Seet Adara. I 'ave been vaiting for you to come."

Adara Nadja Amador was the name that Bekka had been born with. She smiled, thinking it sweet that Lady Rosa still called her that, she was the only one who still did; everyone else referred to her as 'Bekka.' But to Rosa, she would always be the *Beautiful Hope* of her birth mother and the Romani people. It was quite a lot to live up to, but she seemed to be holding her own, with a little help from her friends.

Bekka sat in the chair and watched with a concerned eye as the old woman struggled through another fit of coughing. Tears filled Rosa's eyes and fell upon her weathered cheeks before they disappeared into the folds of the gray shawl wrapped loosely around her frail shoulders. She waved a wrinkled hand in the air as though it was a natural occurrence. Maybe these days it was, but it hadn't always been so. She cleared her throat before she offered a bit of explanation. "Dis castle ees alvays so damp! I miss de old days! I miss de sun!"

She rarely ventured outside anymore. Not even to tend to her small garden. Candi had kept up with the weeding and the harvesting of the meager crops as they ripened. Looking at Rosa now, Bekka realized that the old woman *needed* to get out more. The castle *was* cold; it must be hard on her bones, tempered as they were with arthritis. Bekka could sympathize. She missed aspirin, central heating, television and even the Internet. She'd do anything for an ice-cold soda and a greasy slice of pepperoni pizza dripping with cheese. She hadn't realized how much she missed home being stuck on this side of the *Portal! Funny the things you take for granted.* She knew they couldn't risk opening the *Portal* and going to the other side, even for supplies. Rosa claimed that Sinnestra might be able to detect any such attempts. Until they learned more about the demoness, they just couldn't risk it; the consequences could be horrific.

Another coughing attack wracked Lady Rosa and stirred Bekka from her reverie. Concerned, Bekka reached out to her but the Gypsy stopped her with a shake of her head and a raised hand. "Eet vill pass," she said as she recovered.

Bekka's look clouded with doubt. She couldn't help but take notice of the dark stains on the white cloth clutched in Rosa's hands, and it frightened her. "Rosa," she spoke in a hoarse whisper rising from her seat. Bekka took her hand and knelt beside her. The Gypsy suppressed another cough, her face turning a deep crimson.

After it passed, she gave Bekka an irritated look. "I vill be fine, child. De sooner dat ve leave, de better." Her breathing seemed raspy.

Bekka shook her head not comprehending what the old woman was saying. How could they go anywhere when she was like this? She needed bed rest; time to regain her health. She couldn't allow Rosa to go, the journey alone might kill her. She'd never forgive herself if anything happened.

Despite Bekka's wishes Lady Rosa placed a hand on her shoulder and used the younger girl to assist her in standing. Her grip was surprisingly strong. "De storm ees no longer an empty threat. Eet ees very real and eet ees on de horizon." The fire of her resolve burned in her dark eyes. Renewed purpose had given the old Gypsy strength.

Bekka's eyes grew wide; she was immobilized by the words. She had been expecting the Gypsy to say something of this nature, but actually hearing it had shocked her to her core. She opened her mouth to speak but was at a total loss; no words came. It was perhaps the first time in her entire life that she'd been speechless. *It was almost a shame that her parents weren't here to witness this.* She blinked in rapid succession as she attempted to kickstart her brain.

She shook her head clearing the cobwebs that had taken hold of her mind. Looking at Rosa, she finally found her voice. "Is Sinnestra coming for us?" She grasped the Gypsy's arm, perhaps a little too tightly, as the old woman squinted in sudden pain. "Please, Rosa! I need to know if we're in danger."

At first it seemed that Lady Rosa was about to have another coughing fit as she took the wadded handkerchief to her lips; but then Bekka heard her strained sobs, muffled by the cloth. The sound was unexpected. Once again Bekka was caught off guard, but this time it was with the old woman's sorrow. Bekka's mouth felt like the sands of the barren wasteland where the Orc and the Vortagg still battled for supremacy. Her tongue seemed unusually thick and dry. She tried to swallow her rising fear, but it was clumped in her throat. "Rosa..." she said breathlessly.

Rosa cried out loudly causing Bekka to jump. She could feel the tiny hairs on her neck and arms rise in response to the chilling sound that had escaped the Gypsy's lips. The truth hung in the cold air that filled the chamber like an ever-darkening cloud. A sense of foreboding enveloped the room. It was strong and palpable to both women. As their eyes met, they knew. *They knew!*

They were in danger!

Rosa indicated that she wanted Bekka to sit again with a wave of her hand. "Eet ees time dat you test yourself, child."

Bekka sat in the chair and lightly shook her head. She had no idea what the old woman was talking about. "Test myself? How?" They didn't have time for this nonsense, but she found herself doing what Lady Rosa asked anyway. She always did, it was impossible to refuse her.

"Close your eyes Adara. Take a deep breath and let eet out slowly..."

Bekka did as she asked, knowing that she could fully trust her. She kept her eyes closed, feeling her body begin to relax as she heard Rosa moving about the chamber, her feet shuffling over the worn flagstones. She sensed that the old woman had returned to her side and she could smell the pungent scent of the incense nearby. As she opened her eyes she saw Rosa holding the burning stick in one hand, and fanning the air with the other. Lady Rosa frowned. "Keep your eyes closed, Adara. Relax. Let de visions come as dey vill."

At first Bekka believed that Rosa was only talking nonsense. She didn't see anything. *But then she did!* She saw the darkness all around her; gray smoke seemed to swirl in the air, twisting tendrils rose up like dancing snakes from seemingly nowhere. A cloaked and hooded figure was kneeling upon the ground in front of her. As she approached cautiously, she reached out and lightly touched the figure's shoulder. The woman spoke to her as she turned her head slowly. "I knew you'd come." Hands that contrasted sharply with the black landscape reached up and pulled back the hood as the figure rose.

Sinnestra towered over her!

Bekka opened her eyes and saw that Rosa was watching her intently. The old woman nodded knowingly. "Good," the Gypsy said simply.

Good? Bekka's mind reeled. How could any of this be good? She was left feeling unsettled, but Lady Rosa seemed to be satisfied. Bekka felt the need to make the Gypsy understand what she had seen. "I... I saw Sinnestra!"

Rosa shrugged her shoulders. "Eet matters not whom you saw. De point ees, dat you vere able to see!" She waved the wadded cloth in the air. "You 'ave de sight; like your mother before you. You do not need de cards nor de crystal," she touched the side of Bekka's head, "You just need to open your mind, and de visions, dey vill come."

Chapter 2
Preparations for Departure

After leaving Lady Rosa to pack the items they would need to take with them on their journey, Bekka went in search of Valoria. If they were going to make the trek to *Freeport* it was imperative that she come along. They had been through nearly everything together and she refused to change that now. There were far too many dangers along the road for Rosa and her to go alone. Though Bekka's proficiency with weapons had vastly improved after months of practice, she was still no match for a highly skilled warrior. The coastal city of *Freeport* had a reputation for attracting a rough crowd; it was going to take level heads and prowess in order to survive.

Though *Freeport* had the reputation for being a dangerous principality, it was governed by harsh rule. The bureaucrat in charge of maintaining the Law was a no-nonsense man known throughout the surrounding lands only as De La'Corte. To uphold his decrees, he employed a band of battle-seasoned orcs that he referred to as *Hellhounds*. Together they retained a tight grip on the seaport; delivering swift justice with an iron fist.

Outside the walls of *Freeport* anything was permissible. De La'Corte and his ruffians had vowed to keep everyone safe within the city proper; they had stated that *whatever* occurred beyond the walls was not their concern. They simply turned a blind eye. Minor feuds that began inside *Freeport* were often settled with bloodshed beyond its boundaries; leaving one or more participants maimed or even dead.

If Julia and Robert Kensington knew how truly dangerous *Freeport* could be, they'd never allow Bekka to go, no matter whom she went with. But Bekka felt that she had no choice at all. It was absolutely *crucial* that they learn all that they could about Sinnestra before she struck. When she attacked all those months ago, they knew only that the *Blade of the Spider's Kiss* could harm her. Fortunately, back then it had been enough to avoid confrontation. But now they needed more than that if they were going to survive. Sinnestra would be coming at them with all that she had, and at the moment, they were not ready. One thought in the back of Bekka's mind continued to nag at her: *they may already be too late.*

Bekka found Valoria with the rest of her friends; Candi, Vincente and Trevor. They were out at the archery field honing their skills. The guys weren't without talent, but the girls were clearly the better marksmen. The reasons were obvious. Valoria was a warrior who had had many years of practice, often when her very life depended on her success. And Candi was an Ace on the *Midvale High's* archery team on the other side of the *Portal*. Ironically, the blonde had kept her talents with a bow hidden because of some crazy fear that it would come between her and Vincente. But after Sinnestra's attack had nearly killed them both, she had discarded that silly notion. Trevor and Vincente were beginners with the bow and arrow, still learning the complexities of the weapon. Despite their lack of experience, they were better than Bekka by far. Bekka doubted that she could hit the side of a barn more than ten feet away from her. She was more likely to pierce her own foot, she was *that* bad. The guys could at least hit the target most of the time, just seldom the bullseye. But that might not be enough to stop their adversary.

Trevor put a finger to his lips and urged Bekka to remain quiet as Candi took aim at a large target crudely painted with red circles some distance away; evidently there was some kind of contest in the works. With a slow, measured breath, the blonde let loose the arrow and it flew true. Candi beamed excitedly as the arrow pierced the heart of the inner circle, dead center of the target. She slapped Trevor with a 'high five'. *"In your face, Val!"*

Her taunt caused Valoria to chuckle softly. She stepped forward and fired two arrows in rapid succession, her movements almost a blur. The first arrow split the shaft of Candi's bullseye; the second neatly splintered the shaft of the first. Everyone's jaw dropped open. Bekka had known that the one-eyed ranger was good; but she'd no clue that Valoria was *that* proficient.

Candi looked at Valoria in astonishment. *"Wow!* That was like totally awesome! You're just as good as Robin Hood!"

Bekka knew the reference was totally lost on her friend, but she could see a blush tinting Valoria's cheeks nonetheless. It didn't really surprise her; the warrior had always been a bit shy and reserved. She had always attributed Valoria's detached manner to the scarring, both physical and emotional, she had received at the hands of Maragh, her own father. When she was very young, he had beat her using leather straps knotted at the ends until her back was a bloodied pulp. Valoria had received this cruel treatment again, when she had tried to stop her father from murdering her baby sister. She had attacked him with a sword, but at that time she lacked any real skill. She had managed to slice open his cheek, but he easily stopped her further aggressions, but not before cutting her across the face, ruining her right eye.

Valoria bore ornate tattooed lines going from her forehead and down her right cheek and neck, disappearing along her shoulder. The tattoo made it difficult to see the thin red scar carved upon her face; and it detracted from the milky whiteness that was all that remained of her right eye.

When Bekka first met Valoria almost nine months ago, the warrior claimed that the scarring was why she had few friends. Evidently people on this side of the *Portal* could be just as judgmental and superficial as on the other. In truth, Bekka believed the decision to limit her friendships was entirely her own making. Almost all the people that she had let get close to her in the past had brought her nothing but pain and sorrow. Since they met, Valoria had begun to open up a bit more. She was learning to trust again, and Bekka couldn't be happier for her friend.

The two were like sisters. They had shared *so* much together; risked their lives for one another on countless occasions. Bekka knew that Valoria would give her life to save her and until she faced Maragh she hadn't been sure that she could do the same. Bekka was truly glad that Valoria and Candi had become such good friends. Both were extremely important to her, and she didn't know what she would do without either of them. She hoped she'd never have to find out. Losing Trish Morgan had been hard enough.

Candi, Trish and Bekka had been together since before they were in kindergarten. They were the best of friends. Bekka had always thought of them as the Yin to her Yang. Trish was the domineering one, the one that *had* to be the leader. She often acted before she thought about what she was doing. She relied on her charm and good looks to get her out of the predicaments she found herself in. Bekka liked to weigh the pros and cons before she acted. She liked playing it safe. With Trish and Candi she didn't always get that opportunity. Bekka was a follower; she was content in that role. She knew it was up to her to look out for her friends, someone had to! Unfortunately, when they went through the *Portal* they had all been separated. She hadn't been there to save Trish... Candi was more of a free spirit than the others. Where Bekka liked things neat and orderly, a trait she attributed to her mother's O.C.D., Candi was totally different. She was excitable, fun loving and approached life with a carefree mindset. Nothing could get her down. She saw the good in everything. She was a Gypsy at heart, it was no wonder she was so at home with the Romani. Vincente and her were a good fit.

As for Trevor and Bekka, they were another story completely. Before going to the carnival out on Miller's Farm they had only shared a class or two together at Midvale High. But there had been a definite attraction. Before going through the *Portal* they were just beginning to explore their feelings. They had even had a pretty heavy make-out session when he had snuck through her bedroom window the night of the carnival. But that was all in the distant past.

So much had happened to both of them since coming to this side of the Portal, and Bekka felt that they had grown apart. After Maragh's defeat they had tried to make things work, but with the fear of Sinnestra lingering, they had never found the time for themselves. And Bekka had sensed that Trevor's thoughts had been on Lithania.

The elven warrior from *Serendil Brenatis* had saved his life on more than one occasion. Her brown, almond-shaped eyes and her softly pointed ears were very exotic. Bekka figured it was awfully hard to compete with something like that, especially if you were merely an average looking human girl, though Trevor had once said that she was the prettiest girl in *Midvale*. The trouble was, *Midvale* was a world away.

Candi shook her head as she turned toward Bekka. "I'm glad that Valoria's on our side!" She rolled her eyes and sighed. "Did you see that shot, Beks? Wasn't it incredible? I could practice for the rest of my life and never be that good."

Vincente looked dismayed. "Don't be silly! Eef you practice every day you vill be just as good! Maybe even better!"

Candi scoffed at him. "No way!" Her face brightened with a huge smile. "But it was nice to hear you say that!" She planted a kiss on his cheek as she threw her arms around his shoulders.

Trevor had to duck beneath the end of her bow as it arced toward him. "Careful with that thing!" They continued to kiss, their lips smacking loudly. Trevor sighed with an exaggerated roll of his eyes. "You guys need to get a room."

"Ve 'ave a room!" Vincente said as he pulled out of Candi's embrace. By the look on his face it was obvious that he didn't have a clue as to Trevor's meaning.

Candi narrowed her eyes giving Trevor a dark look. "Don't go there, Trevor Stevens."

Trevor glanced at Bekka before shaking his head and stalking off. "Whatever."

"Jerk!" Candi called after him.

"Let it go, Candi," Bekka said as she watched him walk away with his shoulders hunched in brooding anger. Trevor was taking long strides; clearly wanting to put as much distance as he could between them. Something was definitely eating at him. By the look he'd given her, Bekka was almost certain that it had to do with the two of them.

Candi turned and faced Bekka. "What has gotten into him lately?"

Bekka shrugged and sighed heavily, not really sure what to say. She had her suspicions but didn't know anything for certain. What she did know was that what had started out with such promise on the other side of the *Portal*, had somehow been thrown off course by the events that had happened to all of them. She doubted that they'd ever find their way back to where they once were. At least not without taking a lot of time to work on it. But *that* was part of the problem. They never seemed to have any time.

Bekka knew what her mom would say. *'You have to make time.'* And her paternal grandpa would always tousle her hair and say, *'Problems don't fix themselves kiddo; they only fester, and then you've got real problems!'* But she knew that already. She just didn't know how to go about fixing them. They seemed to be broken, and she wasn't sure they *could* be fixed. And honestly, she wasn't sure it was what she even wanted anymore. It definitely seemed that it wasn't what Trevor wanted. Whatever was going on between Trevor and her had already begun to decay into a complicated mess. Besides, she had other matters that required her immediate attention.

Bekka believed that Trevor was homesick. He missed his parents and seeing the Kensingtons all together was only making matters worse. After defeating Maragh, Bekka had tried to convince Trevor to go back through the *Portal*, but he had refused. She thought that he was finally regretting that decision.

Candi's face brightened suddenly. "Hey! I know! He just needs to get laid!"

Bekka could feel the heat rising quickly to her cheeks. "Candace Marie!" She couldn't believe the things that came out of her friend's mouth sometimes. She was flabbergasted, maybe even a bit mortified. Trust Candi to say whatever was on her mind. She seldom thought before she spoke, which usually landed her in hot water, but this time Bekka felt the focus shift entirely upon her.

Shocked and dismayed by her sudden realization, Candi gave Bekka's shoulder a quick shove. She actually caused Bekka to stumble back a step or two. "Oh my God! You both do!"

Bekka closed her eyes and lightly shook her head, wishing she were somewhere else; anywhere else. "Candi," she swallowed the lump in her throat, "please just stop!"

Candi threw her arms around her friend's shoulders and gave her a firm hug. She kissed the side of her head. "Sure thing Beks." A huge smile stretched across her face as she released Bekka and grabbed Vincente's hand. "Come on, Vinnie. All this talk of getting laid has given me an idea!"

Bekka shook her head with a surprised chuckle. Candi was beginning to sound more and more like Patricia Morgan. Trish had been the leader of their trio back on the other side of the *Portal*. She had always been a driving force for the friends. Maragh had ruthlessly killed Trish simply because he wanted to. Her death was senseless, and Bekka missed her friend immensely.

A tiny smile curved the corners of Valoria's mouth. "Your friends are something else."

Bekka blew out a long, slow breath. "Don't I know it!" She continued to watch as Candi bounced along with Vincente in tow. Finally, she turned to the warrior and said, "We need to talk about Sinnestra."

She didn't have to say anything more; she could see Valoria stiffen. They had both known that this day was coming for a very long time. Now it was here. Valoria looked toward the horizon and then turned her attention to the girl standing at her side. "What do you have in mind?"

Bekka shrugged. "Frendlestixx had suggested that we go to *Freeport* and learn all that we could about her." She tilted her head and gave Valoria a questioning look. "I was thinking that maybe that would be a good idea. We don't really know much about her other than she had taken over the *Underdark* and imprisoned the Spider Queen. Even Sha'dira could offer us little insight. The demoness remains a mystery. One that we desperately need to solve."

Valoria nodded. "We still have the *Blade of the Spider's Kiss* and we know that it can do her harm, possibly even kill her. The question that I have is: Can anyone wield it besides Lithania? She is the one who struck Sinnestra with it the last time."

But not fatally...

Bekka crossed her arms over her chest and sighed. She looked at the ground and kicked a stone with the toe of her boot. She watched it roll away. "The Drow believed that it was my destiny to slay Sinnestra with it."

Valoria nodded slightly, it was hardly noticeable, but Bekka saw it nonetheless. "It did glow for you when you held it, as I recall; just as it did for Lithania. Maybe *that's* why she wasn't able to kill Sinnestra. Had you wielded the blade maybe she would be dead now."

Bekka shot a questioning glare at Valoria, wondering if she was blaming her for the fact that Sinnestra still lived; she saw no malice in the ranger. "Thanks." Bekka frowned. She had thought the same thing for months. She *still* detested the thought of having to kill anyone, even her enemies. Killing game for food was one thing, killing another person was quite another. "But it glowed for Lithania too when she wielded it against Sinnestra; who knows if it will for anyone else? Anyway, I was thinking that maybe we could send Trevor to *Serendil Brenatis* to bring Litha here. If Sinnestra is going to move against us we might need her here, while we're gone, just in case."

"That sounds like a prudent plan." Valoria said with a meditative nod. "Who goes to *Freeport* then?"

"Well, you and I, certainly. Lady Rosa has already decided that she is going. I don't have the heart to tell her *'no'*, so unless you do, then she'll come with us; but that is about it. We need to keep this place protected."

Valoria inclined her head slightly. "You don't think Candi and Vincente will want to come along?"

Bekka sighed heavily. "Oh, I'm positive that they will. But I'm hoping that I can convince them to stay behind. I don't really want to take a huge entourage into a place like *Freeport.*"

"No. That wouldn't be wise," Val said in agreement. "The fewer we take the less likely we'll encounter unwanted attention, or trouble."

Bekka chuckled. "Oh, you don't know Candi like I do! She *loves* to shop, so she would be running off to God knows where in a heartbeat. And, in case you hadn't noticed, her knack for saying whatever enters her mind can land her in trouble pretty quickly."

"Oh, I have *definitely* noticed," Valoria said with a rueful smile. "That is precisely why I think that it would be wise to leave her behind. Vincente isn't much better, either. He isn't used to big cities; he would wander around with his eyes wide and probably wind up lost or in some predicament that he couldn't get himself out of. Besides, he follows Candi around like a puppy dog. There is no telling what trouble they might stumble into together."

It blew Bekka away when she told her parents about the plan she had set in motion. She had expected them to simply refuse to allow her to go to *Freeport*. But she was impressed by their attitude towards the idea. They sat in silence as they listened to her proposal, even offered suggestions here and there, whenever they thought it was needed; but both completely agreed with her in the end.

They told her not to worry about Candi and Vincente; they would talk to them. They said they knew exactly what to say to make the two of them think it was their idea to stay, which Bekka had no doubt they could do. The only worries that Julia and Robert expressed, concerned Rosa's travelling with them. In the end they agreed with Valoria, it would have to be Lady Rosa's decision and they all knew what that would be. There was absolutely no way she was staying behind.

Chapter 3
Departure

It wasn't easy for Candi to watch her friends leave her behind. Vincente must have noticed her discomfort, and he slipped his hand in hers, giving it an encouraging squeeze. She loved the way their hands just seemed to mesh together so perfectly, and she couldn't help but smile at his affectionate gesture. She looked at him; the corner of her mouth twisting upwards into a seductive grin. He could be so sweet and charming sometimes. She couldn't help but feel all warm and tingly inside! She hadn't had that with any other boy not even Jacob.

The thought of Jacob Williams gave her pause. She hadn't thought of him since learning of his death after coming through the *Portal*. She felt a moment of sadness at his loss. He had been her date at the carnival out on Miller's Farm. They had even kissed. But he didn't make her feel the same way that Vincente did, not even close! She squeezed Vincente's hand, smiling. She had been infatuated with Jake, and she was quite fond of him, but she was in *love* with this Gypsy boy who had stolen her heart from the very beginning.

Lady Rosa seemed so tiny next to the big man sitting beside her on the seat of the wagon. She squinted as she coughed into the ever-present white cloth that she seemed to always carry. Her face contorted as though she were in pain and had turned a deep ruddy color. Candi was worried about her, but she hadn't spoken to anyone else about it, because she didn't want to worry them. But something didn't seem right with the old Gypsy. How could everyone else not have noticed? It was beyond her. She wished that Rosa had stayed behind so that Candi could keep her eye on her. She didn't need to be wandering off right now. She shook her head and sighed heavily.

Candi watched as Armand snapped the reins in his massive hands to start the draft horses moving. He was following behind Bekka and Valoria, who were astride two magnificent looking horses. She could see the big man lean closer to Rosa and speak to her; the old woman nodded, and placed a hand on his arm, with the wadded cloth she motioned with the other. Candi could almost hear her tell him that she was fine and they should just go. But she hadn't said a word, at least none that the blonde could actually hear.

As they rode away, it looked like Bekka was wiping tears from her eyes. 'Good!' Candi thought to herself. She was happy to see that this was hard on her friend, and not just her. She glanced around and scowled darkly as she noticed that Trevor was conspicuously absent. *'Now where the hell is he?'* He could at least say goodbye! She could tell that something was *definitely* going on between the two of them, they just didn't seem the same as before and they were hardly together. They had taken to spending way too much time apart. She was not the only one to notice either. Vincente had mentioned it to her just the other day.

She found Trevor in his room stuffing a burlap knapsack with his belongings. He hadn't noticed her yet, and she kept silent as she watched him go about his task. He seemed to be in a bit of a rush. She crossed her arms over her chest as she leaned against the doorjamb. "You going somewhere, Trev?" Her rising anger seeped into her words. It was almost as if he was attempting to sneak off while no one was looking. It was like a betrayal of Bekka, and that wasn't happening on her watch!

He practically jumped out of his skin. "Geez, Candi! You trying to give me a heart attack or something?"

She arched a brow suddenly recalling something her dad always said. She let him have it. "If you were living right I couldn't have startled you," she said. She had a good mind to punch him. Hard. Like really hard!

His face scrunched up. "What does that even mean?"

Candi pushed off the doorway and waved a hand in the air as she walked toward him. She still thought about slugging him, but she decided against it. "Never mind. It's just something my dad and my gramps used to say like *all* the time." She pointed at his bag. "You still haven't answered my question. Are you planning on going somewhere?"

Trevor blushed. "Bekka wants me to go to *Serendil Brenatis* and bring Lithania back. Apparently Lady Rosa believes that Sinnestra might strike soon; and we may need Lithania to wield the *Blade of the Spider's Kiss* against her." He was barely able to meet Candi's eyes. "So I told her I'd go while they went to *Freeport.*"

"She never said anything to me about it." Candi still had her doubts.

Trevor shrugged. "Not my problem that she doesn't tell you everything."

This time she didn't hold back, she punched his arm, nearly knocking him off balance. Her brows shot up. He was really beginning to piss her off. "You don't have to be such an ass about it."

"Ouch! That hurt!" he said.

"Good! It was supposed to!"

He sighed heavily, running his hand through his hair. "I'm sorry. That wasn't very nice of me."

Candi shook her head. "No. It wasn't." She studied him for a moment. "Why do I get the feeling that you aren't telling me everything?"

He shrugged. "That's about it."

"Bullshit Trevor!" she said. She could tell that there was far more to it than he was letting on. She wasn't going to let him hurt her friend if she could prevent it.

He threw his hands into the air. "What do you want me to say, Candi? Bekka and I just can't make things work for us anymore. We're friends, but that's about it."

Candi felt rocked to her core. "Wow," she said sitting on the edge of his bed, uninvited. She couldn't believe what she was hearing, she didn't *want* to believe it. She had been pulling for the two of them. She knew that if the two of them could make it work then she and Vincente had a real shot at it as well. Now all that was ruined. It was like neither of them even cared to try anymore. They reminded her of her parents, and that had ended disastrously. It made her angry!

She could feel tears roll down her cheeks. "So what happens now?" she asked, feeling the pain of her parent's divorce all over again.

Trevor sat beside her and shrugged. "I don't know."

Candi wiped away at the tracks of her tears and shook her head. "So are you and Litha like together now? Is that it?"

Trevor laughed, but she failed to see any humor in the situation. At her intense glare he quickly sobered and shook his head. "Geez, Candi. I haven't seen Lithania in almost nine whole months, there may not be anything there either. She's probably moved on. Maybe she's forgotten all about me."

Candi shook her head. "You really *don't* know anything about girls, do you? I don't think Elanthor was her type. Besides, I think that Aloena was sweet on him. That doesn't leave Litha with much to 'move on' to. Remember, the elves that we found in that cave were all very young."

She gave him a hard look. "Is Bekka really okay with this?" she asked. She'd know if he tried to lie. Trevor just wasn't a good liar. Why did guys always think they were?

He scratched the side of his head. "It was really kinda her idea. She told me that she had too much on her plate right now to try and make our relationship work, but she wanted me to be happy. It was her idea for me to go to *Serendil Brenatis* and see Lithania. I was planning on making the trip to *Freeport* in case they needed help. We've all heard what kind of place that is."

Candi nodded. He was being honest, she wasn't going to be forced to knock the crap out of him again after all. But as for

Bekka on the other hand... "So, you're heading off to *Serendil Brenatis* all by yourself, huh?"

He smiled, and she noticed his dimples, they were simply to die for. It was easy to see why girls always seemed to find him so attractive. "I'll be fine," he said.

She couldn't help but roll her eyes, it was all she could do to keep from snorting as she chuckled softly. "Trevor, despite the fact that we've been here for almost a year doesn't mean we can survive here on our own. If you think about it, we've had lots of help, people who know this world far better than we can ever hope to, showing us the way; guiding us along, keeping us safe."

Candi could tell immediately that she'd upset him. She could see it in the hard set of his jaw. He went back to packing his knapsack, shoving things in with less care than before. His face flushed with his anger. "I can take care of myself Candi. I don't need a babysitter."

This time she actually did snort when she laughed. "Yeah, you keep telling yourself that, Trev." She sighed, running a hand through her blonde hair. She had to find a way to make him understand without him getting so angry. She couldn't stand the thought of him winding up like Jacob or Cleve. "Look Trevor, all I'm saying is that it's a lot of territory for a person to cover by themselves. What if you like run into a rogue band of hostile Orcs or some of those flesh-eating Vortagg? Wouldn't it be better if you had someone fighting at your side? I don't want to see you get hurt, that's all. I just like worry—about all my friends!"

Candi heard Trevor's little grunt, but he surprised her. He turned toward her and hugged her close but not before she saw the tears clouding his blue eyes. He actually kissed the side of her head.

Trevor said, "I really appreciate the concern, but honestly, I'll be fine. I've studied the maps. I'll follow the Griffin River north. When I get to the base of the Griffin Peaks I'll head northwest to *Serendil Brenatis*. I'll never get close to the Wastelands. So I shouldn't encounter either the Vortagg or the Orc."

Candi pushed him away and wiped the unexpected tears from her eyes. She hadn't anticipated getting emotional. She could feel the heat of the moment rising to her cheeks. "Easy

Peasy," she said. He had thought it all out. What more was there to say?

He chuckled softly. "Easy Peasy."

She didn't know why, but she left Trevor's room feeling saddened. When she found Vincente she collapsed in his arms and began to sob uncontrollably. He was completely at a loss as to what to do with her. She was usually so full of joy; this was not like her. He finally settled on rubbing her back awkwardly. "Tell me, vhat ees vrong? Vhat can I do to make tings better?"

Pressed against his chest, through her muffled sobs all Candi could manage to say was, "Trevor..."

Vincente placed his hands on her biceps and pushed them apart so that he could look into her eyes. An absolute look of fury darkened his face. "I vill keel 'im!" He started for the door, angry.

"Vinnie! No!" she exclaimed in flattered exasperation. "He didn't like do anything to me! He's... he's leaving! He's going to *Serendil Brenatis* to get Lithania and bring her back in case we need her help with Sinnestra."

The sudden grin on Vincente's face was undeniable. "Maybe dat ees a good ting, no?"

"Unbelievable! Why would you even say that?" Candi shook her head. "Guys can be incredibly dumb! I'll never really understand the opposite sex."

He spread his hands. "Vell, he and Bekka seem to be... how you say... dreefting apart. Maybe dey just need some time avay from each other."

"Wow," Candi said, surprised. She flung her arms around his neck and forced him into a prolonged kiss. "When did you get to be so brainy?"

She could feel his smile against her mouth. "Vhen I met you!"

Candi chuckled as she steered him toward the bed, pulling off his shirt. "Good answer!"

After Candi left his room, Trevor shoved the last of his belongings into his knapsack. He scanned the chamber for anything that he may have missed. Seeing nothing, he slung the bag over his shoulder. There wasn't anything left to keep him around. Besides, the sooner that he departed, the quicker he could make it to *Serendil Brenatis* and Lithania.

Just thinking about Litha brought a smile to his lips and admittedly a hint of nervousness. They had had an undeniable connection, but that was almost nine and a half months ago. The elf had literally saved his life on several occasions, but it went beyond that. There was no way he could be certain how the passage of time had affected their relationship. Especially when he wasn't even certain how he felt about her. He scratched his head. How had things become so muddled and confusing?

Almost ten months ago when Litha and he had parted, she was certain that he was in love with Bekka. She was willing to let him go without any strings attached so that they could be together. And, at that point, Trevor thought that was what he had wanted as well. But at the time he also believed that they would all be returning to their own world. And he knew without a doubt that there was no place for Lithania on the other side of the *Portal*. She had known it too. So it had made matters that much easier to accept, at least that is what he had told himself at the time. After having nearly ten months to ponder it all, he had come to the realization that he had simply taken the easy way out. He had been a jerk—Candi had been right. And he needed to make things right.

At the very least Lithania deserved better. So did Bekka. Trevor sighed regretfully as he took one last look around the room. It was time that he man-up. If he didn't, he'd risk losing them both. He was fairly confident that he'd already lost Bekka. They had allowed something to come between them. What had begun with such promise on the other side of the *Portal* had seemed to fizzle and die on this side. They had both changed. They were no longer the same people that they had been.

Initially he had planned on waiting another day and leaving at first light. Now, after his conversation with Candi, he was beginning to feel that it would be best to leave sooner rather than later. He knew that she would try and force Vincente to accompany him. Trevor didn't want that. He felt that this was something that he needed to accomplish on his own. Vincente's presence would only complicate things unnecessarily.

Earlier in the day as Bekka and the others were completing their last-minute packing for their trip to *Freeport*, Trevor had managed to slip unnoticed out of the castle with a horse. He had tethered Jester in the woods where the secret entrance to the dungeon was located. There was plenty of grass nearby for the animal to feed upon, and a good supply of water. His initial plan was to leave through the cell that contained the hidden passage and escape the castle unseen. Candi would be expecting him to depart through the castle's main gate and would most likely have it monitored, she could be so untrusting at times. She wouldn't plan on him being in full-on stealth mode. She was a sharp girl; he needed to be on top of his game in order to sneak something past her.

Over the months since first coming to live in Maragh's castle, Trevor had been carefully spending time excavating the entrance to the secret passage. He had even constructed a wooden door to keep out unwanted pests that might be in the nearby forest foraging for food or a cozy place to call home, he didn't want them to draw inadvertent attention to what he had done. He had the only key for the door. He was pretty confident that everyone else had forgotten the passage even existed. The dungeon was no longer in use. It hadn't been since Maragh's defeat. There had simply been no need for it.

Trevor knelt down in the center of the second cell and with a grunt, moved aside the grating in the floor. He glanced over his shoulder and then dropped into the opening. As quietly as possible he slid the grate back into place. Without a torch, the subterranean passage beneath the dungeon was pitch black. It was times like this that Trevor really missed not having electricity. He had to keep his hands outstretched in front of him so that he wouldn't injure himself by slamming headfirst into solid rock. Where at one time the passage had drastically narrowed, Trevor had spent months chipping away at the stone to make navigating the space quicker. At the time it had seemed like a daunting task that would reap little benefit. Now he was thankful for having done all the hard work. It had definitely paid off. In a matter of minutes he had reached the door.

As he unlocked and opened the door a flood of intensely bright, blinding light momentarily paralyzed him. Regaining his composure, Trevor threw up his hands to block out the morning sun, but still he couldn't help but squint at the glare. God, he missed his Ray Bans! He stepped into the forest as quietly as he could, listening for any sign of potential threat. He didn't hear anything other than Jester munching on grass nearby. He closed the door softly and locked it.

By now his eyes had fully adjusted and he felt himself smile as he breathed in the heavy scent of pine. The underground passage, and the dungeon itself, had smelled dank and musty. He was thankful to be back outside in the fresh air. He crossed to Jester and lovingly patted the side of his neck as he offered the beast a delicious red apple, which the animal accepted gratefully. With a firm tug on the reins Trevor pulled up the stake to which the horse had been tethered and swung up into the saddle. He couldn't help but marvel at how easy riding a horse had become. Nine and a half months ago he had never even ridden a horse, he had actually been afraid of them. Now, he tried to spend a few hours every day on horseback. Jester was certainly enjoying all the attention.

He was a magnificent beast, jet-black in color except for a white patch that ran from his forehead to his muzzle, and white stockings that went about six inches above each hoof. His mane and tail were as black as a starless night. He was well muscled and built for speed. He loved to run. Trevor turned him to the north and prodded him forward. He was eager to put some distance between himself and the castle. Jester seemed just as willing. Perhaps he could sense in Trevor that this was going to differ from their daily routine. Trevor urged him into a full gallop.

Chapter 4
The Road to Freeport

It hadn't been easy riding away from her friends and family, especially not knowing what lay ahead for any of them, but Bekka certainly hadn't expected the tears that welled up in her eyes and blurred her vision. She shook her head and chuckled softly to herself as she wiped them away. It had been far easier for her to leave her old life behind and go through the *Portal* to this strange new world. Then, at least her purpose was clear. And she really hadn't much choice.

All those months ago they had stepped through the *Portal* to try and save their friends and families as well as themselves. They had to stop Maragh and his dogs from killing any more innocents. Ginger Whitney and Scott Thompson were dead simply because Bekka had loaned her jacket to Ginger after dropping a rainbow snow cone all over Ginger's white blouse from the top of the Ferris wheel of the carnival out on Miller's Farm. But countless others, *infants*, had been brutally murdered on this side of the *Portal* all because Maragh feared an ancient and foreboding prophecy, one that Bekka still didn't quite understand.

They had found a way to end Maragh's tyranny freeing several races, but in the process they had made a far more dangerous enemy; one that they knew almost nothing about. Frendlestixx had believed that the *Great Library Arcanum* in *Freeport* gave them the best hope of learning more about the demoness. He, Valoria and Bekka had been heading there when Carlito and his two companions attacked, killing Frendlestixx. Bekka still found herself missing the little gnome wizard and his magical cloud. Though they had their differences, she had found herself liking the gnome; far more than she ever would have admitted to him.

Valoria and Bekka had never talked about what happened on that fog-enshrouded morning. All Bekka knew was that Frendlestixx had been brutally killed and that he had somehow managed to save Valoria before he died. Valoria wouldn't talk about the circumstances. Bekka knew all too well how painful some memories could be, but she also knew how they could fester, like a poisoned wound, if you kept them inside. Sometimes it really did help to talk things out. Wisdom from her mother!

They were traveling in a slight northwesterly direction heading for the narrow pass between the gulf coast and the *Griffin Peaks*. Despite their need for urgency, their progress remained slow. They had to keep pace with the wagon that followed along. They couldn't afford to leave Rosa and Armand behind.

Thoughts of Lady Rosa caused Bekka's brows to furrow in anxiety as she sat astride her horse. Her health was of great concern. She seemed so frail lately. It was almost as if she had been wasting away within the castle walls. The struggle with Maragh and the long months of worry afterwards had taken their toll on the old Gypsy. Bekka glanced over at Valoria, she seemed deep in thought as well. Bekka knew she was concerned about Rosa too.

They had been riding side by side ever since they left home. They could hear the jingle of the harnesses and the creaking of the wagon, as it followed along over the rough terrain. The two teams of horses hitched to the Gypsy box wagon were huge draft horses, bred for their strength and stamina in pulling heavy loads, but still they were having a time of it. They weren't following any road and they were headed slightly uphill. Once they got to more level ground the going would be easier, for both man and beast.

Bekka noticed that Valoria kept turning in her saddle to glance back at the wagon. She was riding with the ranger on her left, which meant that she could only see her ruined eye. Her face remained passive, almost as though chiseled from granite. Bekka couldn't tell what she was even remotely thinking, but she had her suspicions. Val was worried about Lady Rosa. They had all been witness to her declining health. "I wish she'd stayed behind," Bekka offered.

Valoria squinted as she turned to face her, making it much more difficult for Bekka to read anything in her good eye. "There was never a chance of that happening," Valoria said with a hint of humor. "But I do wish she would at least rest in the back of the wagon. The bed would be less of a strain. That hard bench seat cannot be comfortable."

Bekka nodded in agreement. "Especially the way the wagon is jostling around. I suggested that she ride in back before we left. She wouldn't hear it. She said the fresh air would do her even more good, and she wanted to feel the warm sun on her face." She grew silent for a minute before continuing. "She spends too much time cooped up in her room these days. She doesn't get out anymore. She used to love tending to her little garden." She couldn't help but smile at the thought of Rosa's joy when she saw whatever she'd planted begin to sprout. Her face had lit up and her eyes had sparkled with delight.

Valoria turned around in the saddle and watched the wagon bounce its occupants along. She was worried. Bekka silently wished there was something she could say to ease her concerns, but there wasn't. Rosa was like a mother to Val. She was practically the *only* friend she'd had among the Roma for a very long time. Carlito had managed to turn the Romani people against Valoria on several occasions—but *not* Rosa. The old woman *never* wavered in her love and support. In many ways Bekka was certain that the old Gypsy considered Valoria her daughter.

Bekka reached out a hand and placed it on Valoria's arm. "She's stronger than she seems."

Valoria turned back to her and smiled.

They rode along in silence, each returning to their own thoughts. Bekka closed her eyes, tilting her head back, allowing the sunlight to warm her face; she found it comforting. A vision was starting to form in her head. She could see the bustling streets of a city; Freeport? She could hear the sounds all around her, and oddly, even the smells. Though she had never been there before, she somehow knew it was the seaport. But how could she possibly know that? It didn't make sense.

The face of a young man filled her thoughts. He had dark brown hair, slightly curly that ended just above his broad shoulders. He was smiling at a young Romani woman. Obviously the two were smitten with one another. He told her to turn around, and she readily complied, smiling, Bekka's smile, as she lifted up the back of her hair, exposing her neck. He fastened a thin golden chain around her neck. A small charm fell between her breasts, glistening in the sunlight. Bekka gasped sharply. It was the same necklace that she wore around her own neck!

Bekka's eyes flew open and her hand went to her chest. She could feel the charm underneath her blouse. Startled, she had very nearly fallen from her horse. Valoria flashed her a look of concern. "Are you all right?" she asked. Bekka could see a knowing smile starting to curve the corners of her friend's mouth.

She could feel the color rushing to her cheeks. "I must've fallen asleep." What the heck was going on? Where were these visions coming from? More importantly, she wondered, what did they mean? Had she just seen a vision of her biological parents? Could that really be possible? She needed to talk with Rosa.

Bekka glanced at Valoria. "Perhaps we need to stop for a bit. You know, stretch our legs. It might be good for Rosa to get a little exercise too."

Valoria nodded. "I'll ride up a bit further and see if I can find a good spot for us to stop." She reached out and touched Bekka's arm. "Are you sure you're alright?"

Bekka waved a hand dismissively. "Yeah. Sure. Why wouldn't I be? I'll let Armand and Rosa know that we'll be stopping soon." She reined her horse in and waited for the wagon to catch up to her as Valoria galloped on ahead.

Before the big Gypsy could halt the wagon, Bekka started her horse slowly moving again. Both he and Rosa gave her a curious look. She offered them a warm smile. "We're going to stop for a little rest to give everyone a chance to stretch their legs, and maybe get a bite to eat."

The prospect of food obviously pleased Armand. He grinned, giving his head a nod. "Dat vill be good. De horses could use a leetle vater. And I need to check on one of dem, I tink dat she may 'ave thrown a shoe."

Bekka studied Rosa for a minute. "How are you doing?" she asked. She was afraid to let on that she was overly concerned with her wellbeing. She didn't want to anger the old woman. When Rosa was angry she was not good company.

Rosa smiled, her eyes twinkling brightly. "I am fine child. Do not concern yourself vith me. De air and de sun are doing vonders for me, eet ees good to be away from dat drafty old place. I 'ave missed being out on de open road."

Bekka nodded thoughtfully. Rosa seemed to be in much better spirits.

By the time that they caught up to where Valoria had set up a makeshift camp, they were all ready to dismount. Bekka could feel an ache in her hip, she was not used to being in the saddle for such a long time. She tethered her horse to the picket that Valoria had driven into the ground and then turned back to the others. Lady Rosa was sitting upon a log, drawing her shawl around her shoulders. Armand was tending to the big draft horses, giving them much needed water, and a juicy apple, along with soothing words of encouragement.

Somehow, Valoria had already managed to catch and skin a couple of rabbits. She had them on spits above a crackling fire. Bekka was amazed by her friend's prowess. She watched as Valoria gathered her bow and quiver of arrows. She was clearly not intending to remain with the group. Bekka touched her elbow. "Is there something wrong?"

Valoria shook her head. "Not at all. I am just a little stiff from sitting in the saddle. I figured I'd do a little scouting while the rabbits cook." Her face softened with a smile. "I'll be back shortly."

Bekka gave her friend a look of skepticism. "You're sure that's all?"

Valoria chuckled. "Yes little sister! Everything is perfectly fine. My hip aches and I just need to walk a bit. We've got a long journey ahead of us. I won't be any good if I cramp up." She inclined her head toward the fire. "Don't let the rabbit burn."

Bekka nodded. "I completely understand about the pain." She could still feel the aching of her own wounds. She had been witness to the damage Maragh had done to Valoria, it was a wonder the woman could still walk; though she did so with a slight limp. "Armand says that one of the horses seems to have thrown a shoe. Perhaps it would be best if we camped here and get a fresh start in the morning."

Valoria took a measured breath. "I trust his judgement with the horses. It wouldn't do to allow the horse to go lame. We will need all the horses to pull Rosa's wagon. We'll stop here for the remainder of the day. Besides, everyone looks a little worn by the day's travel."

Bekka smiled ruefully. "We're just not used to the activity." She let Valoria slip away without further delay and returned to the camp. "We'll spend the night here."

Armand clapped his hand together as he stood. "Good. Eet veel geeve me time to re-shoe de horses. I noticed another dat ees bad." With that, he headed off and was soon busy with his task.

Bekka smiled as she watched Lady Rosa turn the rabbits on the spit above the fire. "Clearly this isn't your first rodeo." At the Gypsy's confused look she blushed and quickly amended, "I just mean that you've obviously done this before."

Rosa's eyes sparkled in the flickering light of the fire as she nodded. "I do not know dis..." her eyes crinkled, "...vhat you say... rodeo? But I know 'ow to keep dinner from burning." After a moment she patted the log beside her. "Seet vith me child."

As Bekka took a seat beside the old woman, Rosa put her

arm in hers and pulled her close so that their bodies shared their warmth. "So, 'ave you 'ad any more visions since ve left?"

Bekka's eyes went wide in surprise. How did she know that? "I have! I think I saw my parents, my biological parents, I mean." She pulled the medallion from her blouse. "I think I was seeing the moment when my father gave this to my mother. They both looked so happy."

Rosa nodded. "Dey vere very much in love, de two of dem. Much like Candi and Vincente, eet vas very hard to keep de two apart." She chuckled softly at a distant memory. "Your grandmother vas so distraught. She did not know vhat to do vith her daughter. She tried her best to keep dem apart, but young love alvays seems to find eet's own vay."

"Why did she want to keep them apart?" Bekka couldn't resist the chance to learn more about the parents she'd never known.

"Your father, he vas not one of us. Your grandmother knew dat he vould not leave 'is life behind and walk de path of de Roma. She vas afraid dat she vould lose her daughter to de life dat he could offer her. Geeve her all de tings dat her heart could vant. Your grandmother vas afraid of being left all alone."

"That's so sad." Bekka could understand her grandmother's fear, certainly. "So, what happened?"

Rosa shrugged. "Fate 'ad other plans. Your mother was a very beautiful girl. She caught de eyes of many men. Der vas one other dat vanted to geeve her tings dat vould make her happy in life. Vhen he saw dat your mother and father vould not allow anyone to come between dem, he moved against your father. Eef he could not 'ave your mother, den he vas determined dat no one vould. He 'ad vays of making men disappear like a puff of smoke in de vind."

Bekka stiffened. Swallowing, she said, "What did he do?"

Rosa had a sad look in her dark eyes. "Eet vas never truly known. But your mother's heart vas broke. Your grandmother tried to comfort her as best she could. She told her dat she vould find another to love in time. But your mother knew dat vould never 'appen and she vas already vith 'is child."

"Who was this other man? Did he kill my father?"

Rosa gave her a dark look. "Perhaps eet vould be best eef you let de past alone. Some tings are best left to de shadows."

Bekka squeezed her arm tightly. "Rosa... I want the man's name."

Tears fell from the old Gypsy's tear-filled eyes. "De man's name ees not important. Vhat 'appened vas a long time ago, before you vere even born."

Bekka looked at her pleadingly. "Why won't you tell me, Rosa? What harm can it possibly do now?"

"Vhat good vould it do?" Rosa said with a light shrug.

"Rosa, please..."

"Der ees no point in eet." She shook her head. "I am tired. I tink dat I vill lay down in de wagon for a bit. Don't let de rabbit burn child."

Hours later, after they had all eaten their fill of rabbit, Lady Rosa pulled her shawl tightly around her shoulders. Her eyes were bright as she stared at the yellow tendrils of flame rising up out of the campfire. "Dey say dat you should never stare into de flames because eet geeves you de night blindness." The corners of her mouth curved upward. "But de crackle of de pine and de soothing glow of de fire pull de eyes in anyvay. Eet offers comfort to de veary bones and makes de eyes grow heavy, and I love de vay dat de warmth of de flames feels on my face." She shrugged. "So who cares?"

Bekka watched in silence, content to see the firelight reflected in Rosa's dark eyes, the snap and pop of the pine the only other sounds. She too could feel the warmth of the flames as they danced in the firepit, reaching toward the star-filled night sky. It was very relaxing. Rosa coughed into her handkerchief, drawing Bekka out of her relaxed stupor.

Rosa continued. "My own mother used to tell me dat eef I continued to stare at de flames dat de Fire God vould claim me for all eternity. She said dat eef I looked close enough into de fire I vould see 'im." She spat into the flames, causing a small hisss of sound. "I 'ave looked, but I 'ave not seen 'im. But something ees der. But I do not believe eet ees de evil ting dat my mother varned me of."

Armand turned his head to the side and spat forcefully. He shook his head as he stared across the flames at Rosa. "De Fire God ees real! I 'ave seen vhat he does to dose dat scorn 'im." He glanced around, catching everyone's eyes. "De Fire God casts a spell upon de non-believers so dat dey do not fear de fire, I 'ave seen dem valk into de flames and die horrible deaths." He shivered. "I can steel hear der screams!"

"Bah!" Rosa scoffed. "Dey vere fools!"

Armand slapped his massive hands upon the tops of his thighs as he stood abruptly. "No! No dey vere not! Dey vere good men!" His face was a deep shade of crimson. "I vill hear no more of dis nonsense!" He stomped off, preferring the company of the horses.

Rosa cackled as she watched him go. She cupped a hand beneath her chin in defiance. A moment later she waved a hand into the air. "Men can be such babies!"

Valoria shook her head and sighed. "Why do you insist on teasing him so?"

"Eet ees fun," the old woman said simply. She coughed into the wad of cloth that she held in her right fist.

Bekka laughed. "All this fresh air is making her fiesty."

Valoria smiled as she crossed her arms and arched a brow. "So it would seem." She stood. "I am going to take the first watch. I suggest you all try and get some sleep. Tomorrow promises to be another long day."

Bekka waited patiently for Valoria to leave the campfire. As she stepped off into the darkness, Bekka jumped to her feet and moved quickly to Rosa's side. She placed her hand on the old Gypsy's arm. "Rosa, I need you to tell me who this other man was that came between my mother and father. Something tells me that it is important that I know. I can't explain it."

Rosa looked into the girl's eyes with growing sadness. She could tell that there was no point in keeping the information from her any longer. She would find out on her own soon enough. Perhaps it was better she knew the truth now, so that she could be better prepared. The old woman looked into the flames, poking the burning logs with a stick, causing tiny sparks to rise up into the night. "De man's name vas De La'Corte."

Bekka felt her body stiffen. "Wait. What? De La'Corte? The *same* De La'Corte that is in charge of *Freeport*? That De La'Corte?"

Rosa nodded. "I believe dat de are one and de same, yes.

But back den he vas not so beeg, though he alvays 'ad beeg plans." She put a hand over Bekka's. "He 'as alvays been a very dangerous man."

Bekka swallowed. "Did he kill my father?"

Rosa shrugged. "I cannot say. But he met vith your father; dat much I do know." Her eyes grew dark as though she were suddenly very sad. "Ve never saw 'im again, your father. Your mother vas heart broken."

Bekka shivered, recalling the skeletal remains locked within the cell in Maragh's dungeon. Had her birth father suffered a similar fate? Had he been simply locked away somewhere and forgotten, left to die a solitary death? Or had the man that vied with him for her mother's love simply killed him? There was only one person living who knew the truth. De La'Corte…

Lady Rosa pulled her shawl tightly about her shoulders. "Ve should listen to Valoria and turn in for de night." She coughed into her wadded handkerchief. Bekka could see the spots of blood even though the old Gypsy tried to hide it from her. It seemed to be getting worse.

Bekka wanted to say something to her about what she'd seen but was truly at a loss as to what should be said. It wasn't as though they could really do anything about it out here in the middle of nowhere. Maybe once they got to *Freeport* they could seek some aid. But even then Bekka was deeply concerned. It wasn't like the other side of the *Portal.* There were no emergency rooms, no urgent care clinics, no real doctors to help. But she refused to give up hope. There had to be something that could be done. She smiled at Rosa as she took her arm and helped her to her feet. She refused to let the old woman see how worried she was. That wouldn't do either of them any good.

Rosa patted her hand and smiled. "You are such a good child, Adara; alvays tinking of others. You are stronger den you know." She gave Bekka's hand a firm squeeze. "Valoria ees lucky to 'ave you vith her. De poor girl has 'ad a hard life, few true friends. She ees head strong and does not alvays tink before she acts. She lets her emotions guide her all too often. You vill need to be der for her. She vill need de strength and visdom dat you can geeve her. And she vill be der for you as vell. Eet ees good dat de two of you are like seesters."

Bekka chuckled softly. "We have your counsel to keep us in check. It is from you that we get our strength."

Rosa stopped and gripped Bekka's arm tightly. She coughed into the handkerchief for several long seconds. When she recovered she looked into Bekka's eyes with steely resolve. "In de coming days you vill need to fill dat role, Adara." She shook her head slowly. "I vill not alvays be around"

Bekka felt a chill go down her spine. What was Rosa saying? She was thankful that they had reached the back of the wagon. It gave her a moment to gather her thoughts as she opened the door for Rosa. As she helped the Gypsy woman into the wagon she tried her best to smile. She didn't want Rosa to see how concerned and worried she truly was.

Lady Rosa seemed tired and weak as she moved to the bed and plopped down. She turned to Bekka and sighed. "Dis body ees feeling eet's age."

Bekka raised her brows. "It's been a rough trip so far, but it will get better soon. I hope."

Rosa chuckled. "Eet eesn't dis trip, eet ees all of de miles dat I 'ave covered over de years. Eet 'as been a long journey, eet vill be good to rest."

"Get some sleep Rosa. You'll feel better in the morning." Bekka turned to go.

"Adara," Rosa said from the growing shadows.

"Yes?"

Rosa coughed. "Tell me, 'ave you 'ad more visions?"

"A few." Bekka toyed with the medallion she wore around her neck. The images of her parents sprang to mind; they had been so much in love.

"Good," Rosa said. "You need to practice de art. De visions vill not alvays come on der own. Sometimes you need to help dem to come. Eet ees an art. Eet needs practice to grow stronger. You do not require de crystal ball nor de cards to see vhat lies ahead and dat ees a good ting. You cannot alvays pull dem out vhen dey are needed. De more dat you practice calling de visions forth, de stronger you vill become at eet. Eet ees your gift."

Chapter 5
Rebirth

The young girl trembled as she stood before Sinnestra, cowering at the foot of the dais as the demoness sat high upon the throne. She was frightened, terrified for her very life. Sinnestra could smell her fear. The guards that flanked both sides of the girl, Gwyneth, offered no compassion as they tore her robes from her, leaving her naked and uncertain. She tried covering herself but there was very little she could do. The air in the chamber was cold upon her bare skin; she could feel the goosebumps rise across her flesh. The Dark Priest that had accompanied them glanced up at the demoness for approval. With a flick of her fingers, Sinnestra sent the guards away, leaving only the frightened girl and the Priest.

She descended from the throne slowly, keeping her eyes upon the girl. She was perfect. Flawless. The resounding *clop* of Sinnestra's hooves upon the cold stone of the dais' steps echoed through the chamber. The girl flinched with each downward step that Sinnestra took. She tucked her chin against her chest and closed her eyes tightly, praying it was only a dream, a nightmare from which she could awaken. Her entire body trembled, either from fear or the chill in the air, or both. Tears escaped her eyes and rolled down her soft cheeks.

Sinnestra touched the girl's chin with a long, painted red nail, coaxing her to raise her head. She spoke in soft, reassuring tones. "Ssh little one. Do not be afraid. I offer you immortality." Her words seemed to allay the girl's insecurities. Their eyes met, unwavering, hopeful and trusting...

Sinnestra smiled as she glanced at the Dark Priest. At her nod, he called upon his disciples, two thin creatures clad only in loincloths moved in her peripheral vision. They held aloft golden thuribles that swung upon chains in slow circles, enshrouding all with swirling smoke from the incense that burned within. The Dark Priest was chanting in a language that only he knew, his words making no sense to anyone else.

Sinnestra caressed Gwyneth's cheeks with her fingertips. "Are you frightened?" she asked in a gentle whisper, smiling.

Gwyneth tried to answer, but found her mouth was too dry to speak. She swallowed and nodded as more tears escaped her eyes.

Sinnestra kissed Gwyneth on the forehead as she wiped away the girl's tears. "Do not be, there is nothing for you to fear. You will live forever through me, child," she cooed.

"Breathe little one," Sinnestra coaxed softly. Gwyneth's eyes sparkled as she complied without hesitation. The demoness could see the tendrils of smoke enter the girl's mouth and nostrils; her eyes grew suddenly wide as she witnessed the fire in Sinnestra's own ignite. Sinnestra inhaled deeply and then blew the smoke into Gwyneth's face, she took it in and just as quickly Sinnestra could see her eyes beginning to glow with a blue-white light. Gwyneth gasped sharply as Sinnestra drove her fingers into her chest, reaching for her heart.

As Gwyneth's flesh began to grow old and shriveled, Sinnestra sucked in her dying breath. She pulled the girl's still beating heart from her chest, and Gwyneth fell upon the flagstones; only a dried husk of what she once had been. Sinnestra put Gwyneth's heart into her mouth, still feeling its rapid beating as she swallowed it whole. She was only vaguely aware of the Dark

Priest's rising crescendo as he continued to chant. Sinnestra dropped to her knees, feeling fire course through her very being. The smoky incense billowed around her until she could see nothing else. Her eyelids fluttered heavily as her eyes rolled up into her head...

When Sinnestra awoke she felt incredibly strange. Her eyes seemed to burn and her throat was dry, too much of the incense! She was still upon the cold stone floor, but she had no idea how long she had been left there. Glancing around, she could see that she was alone, there was no sign of the Dark Priest anywhere, the dead girl was gone; her shriveled corpse removed. Sinnestra arose awkwardly, almost falling as she stumbled forward. A wave of dizziness washed over her. Everything seemed different somehow. Her throne seemed higher than she remembered, the stone steps of the dais larger but how was that even possible? What did it all mean?

She walked toward her bedchamber and stopped suddenly. Something was definitely amiss! She could not hear her hooves plod upon the flagstones. Glancing down, Sinnestra did not see her cloven hooves; instead she saw the delicate feet of a young girl! She quickly placed her hands upon the sides of her head, searching for what was no longer there. Her horns too, were gone!

It had worked!

Sinnestra slapped a hand to her shoulder and immediately cried out in unexpected pain. The lesion was still there, tender and pus-filled. Unchanged. She could hear movement to her right. It was the Dark Priest.

"The spell that I cast was never meant to heal your wound," he said softly. "But it will enable you to move among those whom have wronged you. You can seek your vengeance unfettered by your physical appearance, as we discussed." She could hear the fear and uncertainty in his voice.

Sinnestra nodded slowly. It was a bitter pill to swallow. She had hoped that the incantation would restore her completely, but she had known that was not its purpose. She could feel the fire burn in the depths of her being. "I will make them all pay!"

Chapter 6
Serendil Brenatis

The Healer of the High Elves always believed that there was a shining place in the sun for his people. That they were destined for far greater things, but only if they worked toward that end. He had been a man of abundant wisdom but he could not persuade the Council of Elders to share his views. They thought he was a dreamer. When the Healer told them that they needed to mingle with the other races of *Vespia*, to share knowledge and coexist, they thought him a fool and scoffed at him. Had they listened to his counsel things might have turned out differently for them. Certainly more High Elves would have survived.

Lithania had often questioned the wisdom of returning to their home in the trees. The attack on *Serendil Brenatis* nearly ten months ago by the Deceivers had very nearly destroyed everything. Less than two dozen High Elves remained, most were under eighteen summers old. Aloena, Elanthor and Lithania were now the eldest of their society.

When Lithania had stayed to face Maragh and Sinnestra,

she had directed Aloe and Elan to see to the safety of the surviving elves. They had done a splendid job rising to the tasks set before them. They had proven to be the leaders that the next generation of High Elves needed moving forward. The two of them had learned to work together harmoniously and Elanthor had seen the wisdom of following Aloena's lead. She had a good head on her shoulders and had always been able to grasp situations quickly, solving complex problems in a timely fashion. Working with the Healer had given her the strength and clarity that she needed. Aloena and Elanthor were fortunate that they had one another. Lithania could see that their love had grown. Aloe seemed truly happy in her role, and Elanthor was smiling more. Both were content.

After Maragh's defeat, Lithania seemed lost. Leaving her new companions behind and returning to Serendil Brenatis had been extremely difficult. Having to walk away from Trevor had left a huge hole in her heart. But she had known it was the right thing to do. She did not belong in his world, a place where no elves existed; and she could not ask him to remain in hers. How could she ask him to abandon his family, even though she had lost hers? Besides, his heart belonged to Bekka Kensington. She had had no choice but to give him up.

The threat that had very nearly destroyed her species still remained. The Deceivers knew where to find them. Eventually they would come again, and Lithania doubted that they would be as fortunate a second time. She believed the Deceivers to be horrible blights upon the land. She could not allow them to continue. They haunted her dreams. Even awake, she found them at the forefront of her thoughts. Something had to be done. She had made her decision. She would strike at the core of the Deceivers and remove their threat once and for all.

Or die trying.

Lithania waited until darkness fell and all were sleeping soundly with the exception of those on guard duty. She eased herself from her bed soundlessly. After strapping on her sword, she then gathered her bow and two quivers of arrows. She walked lightly across the floor of her quarters and eased open the door. She checked over her shoulder to ensure that the others were still sleeping undisturbed; they were. She slipped outside, quiet as a whisper, and pulled the door silently closed behind her. She paused a moment, listening to the sounds of the slumbering city. The leaves rustled in a light breeze that wasn't strong enough to bend the limbs. Everything was peaceful within *Serendil Brenatis*, not a soul was stirring upon the boardwalks.

She avoided the central tree lift and made her way along the wooden platform to the northern most corner of the city. She knelt beside the trapdoor in the flooring and took one last look around before she opened the hatch. She lowered the coiled rope secured to a nearby post, as quietly as possible. She could feel the burn in her biceps as the weight of the heavy rope took its toll. When the last of the rope was played out, she took a moment to catch her breath. She glanced toward where she knew Aloena was sleeping and whispered softly to the night. "Forgive me, Aloe."

Without further hesitation Lithania lowered herself down the knotted rope. The descent was not easy and it caused beads of sweat to form on her brow, as well as her arms and shoulders. Finally, after what seemed an eternity, she dropped down upon the forest ground and paused without moving. She studied her surroundings as she caught her breath. She nodded silently, knowing that she had thus far gone undetected. She smiled. It felt good to have the ground beneath her feet. Lithania had been spending far too much time in the trees. With long, quiet strides she slipped through the trees heading northward toward the *Vile Forest*.

Despite her protests, both Aloena and Elanthor had insisted on restoring *Serendil Brenatis* among the trees untouched by the fires when the Deceivers attacked all those months ago. Lithania was against it. She agreed with the teachings of her father, but they had remained steadfast in their decision. They insisted that the younger elves needed that familiarity to feel safer. Litha wanted a fresh start, but they simply wanted to rebuild. It was a battle that she could not win. Now she knew what her father had experienced when he approached the High Council with his concerns. He too had been outnumbered. His acquiescence had cost him his life, and the lives of so many others. Yet he had planned well. He had stocked the Caves and Highwatch Tower for the inevitable. Like her father, she refused to just sit back and accept her situation. She would not allow history to repeat itself, especially with the same enemy. If she could not convince Aloe and the others to build a new life upon the ground, then she would do all that she could to ensure that they remained safe in the trees. She would take the fight to the Deceivers.

She had a plan. If she were successful Aloe and the others would have nothing to worry about where the Deceivers were concerned; they would be eradicated and a threat no more. The chances of her surviving were minimal at best. The odds were horribly stacked against her. But she had decided that her sacrifice was a worthy cause if it meant that her people could live without fear. In the end she did not want to die, but she knew it was a very real possibility; one that she had considered long and hard. There was a chance that she could pull it off and still make it back safely. Like the Healer always said, *'When one's will is strong enough, anything is possible!'*

As Lithania moved through the forest the thoughts of her father brought tears to her eyes and a smile of fond remembrance to her lips. She hoped that he was proud of all that she had accomplished thus far with the help of Aloe and Elanthor. They had brought their race from the edge of extinction and given them a true chance to thrive in the world. Their alliance with the Romani and the Drow had brought new trade to *Serendil Brenatis* that had not been there before. Though they still chose to remain in the treetops they had allowed a lot of the old ways to remain in the past as they forged a newer, brighter future. Once the orc had things under control in the *Wastelands* with the Vortagg they too would seek to join the alliance. The races of *Vespia* were finally getting along, learning to live harmoniously, just as the Healer had always hoped. He had said it was possible, but the Council of Elders said it would never happen. Yet, it was happening! Or at least it was beginning to.

Lithania knew that Aloena would not be pleased to discover that she had gone. She would likely rush after her and stop her from the path she had chosen, given the opportunity. In the end, Litha knew that her friend would dissuade her from taking the action necessary, Aloe could be very persuasive. That was a course of action that was best with a sizable force—not a lone elf. Yet she *had* to try. She felt out of place in the trees though

Serendil Brenatis had always been her home. Lithania felt like she no longer belonged; she was a stranger among her people.

After Maragh's death she had returned but found that everything had changed. It no longer felt like home to her. She could not get over the feeling that she no longer had a place in the treetops. But where could she go? Trevor had likely gone back through the *Portal* to his own world; she resigned herself to never seeing him again. Those that remained behind in Maragh's fortress were more like strangers to her—and constant reminders of the man she had loved and ultimately lost. She decided that she would leave *Serendil Brenatis* behind and take up the life of an adventurer. There was much of *Vespia* that she had never seen.

But before she left, Lithania vowed to make life safer for Aloe and the others. She would do all that she could to destroy the Deceivers, even at the cost of her own life.

Chapter 7
Troublesome Night

Trevor was having difficulty keeping his eyes open as the horse plodded along the northern trail. He was about to give in to sleep when he felt the muscles in Jester's back stiffen beneath him and the horse's head jerked up with an agitated snort; ears alert and eyes wide. It was all Trevor could do to keep from being thrown from the frightened beast. "Whoa boy!" he patted the horse's neck soothingly as he searched for whatever had alarmed Jester.

He saw movement up in the trees ahead. The silhouette of a mountain lion could just barely be seen in the leaves of the limb on which it rested, waiting to pounce on an unsuspecting passerby. Trevor pulled on the reins, jerking them hard to the right. He prodded the horse with his heals. Jester was all too happy to comply.

Trevor strained to hear signs of pursuit and was relieved when he heard nothing coming from behind them. Evidently the big cat was content to wait on easier prey; not wanting to give up its perch. It was times like this that Trevor longed for his hunting rifle for simple protection more than anything else. He was far better with a gun than he was with a sword or bow.

Jester was in the mood to run. Trevor couldn't really blame him. They galloped along the trail, heading northward, leaving their troubles behind them...

Candi could tell that something was bothering Vincente as he crawled into bed beside her. He was frowning darkly and troubled lines creased his forehead. "What's wrong, Vinnie?" she asked softly, placing a hand upon his chest.

He sighed heavily. "Eet ees nothing. Go to sleep." He slugged his pillow with his fist, not once, but twice.

"Vinnie," Candi said as she propped herself up on an elbow. "Something has gotten you all worked up. Talk to me, I can help."

He exhaled in frustration. "Some of de men are talking about leaving. Dey say dat de Roma are not meant to live like dis."

"That's nonsense!" Candi said. She thought that everyone had been happy here. It shocked her to learn that many of the Romani were not.

"I told dem dat dey vere crazy, but dey vouldn't listen to me. Dey said dat I vas too young to understand vhat eet meant to be a true Romani. Dey said dat ve vere meant to be out in de open country not trapped vithin de valls of dis keep like domesticated animals."

Candi pulled the blankets aside and sat up. "We need to let Mr. and Mrs. K know about this. They might be able to talk some sense into everyone."

Vincente placed a hand on her arm. His eyes twinkled brightly. "I tink dat I 'ave managed to change der minds at least until Rosa returns. Dey 'ave agreed to listen to her counsel before dey leave."

"Well," Candi said as she relaxed somewhat. "I suppose it can wait until morning then."

He nodded. "I tink dat vould be best."

Armand was on watch while the others slept. He could hear Rosa muttering from within the Gypsy box wagon; it was as though she was highly agitated. He could take no more. He touched Valoria's shoulder, and she was instantly awake. "Someting ees vrong vith Rosa. She 'as been coughing and now she seems to be troubled."

Valoria could hear the old Gypsy and knew something was wrong. Usually Lady Rosa slept quietly through the night, but lately she was coughing more and more. And there was blood...

Moving toward the back of the wagon, Valoria glanced over her shoulder. "Wake Bekka."

Armand was only too happy to comply with the simple request. It was far better than an offer to assist with the ailing Gypsy woman. He knelt and touched Bekka's shoulder. She didn't awaken quite so easily; he had to shake her. "Eet ees Rosa. She ees not vell."

Bekka glanced briefly to where Valoria had slept. She wasted no time wiping the sleep from her eyes. She had been having a terrible nightmare with Lady Rosa as the prominent figure. Now she could only wonder if it had been a dream at all or was it perhaps another vision, a premonition?

Valoria's eyes grew wide as she knelt beside Rosa. The old Gypsy's chin was coated in blood and beads of sweat soaked the old woman. Her skin was clammy to the touch. "Rosa?" she spoke softly. "It's Valoria. I'm here to help you."

Rosa's eyes sprang open and for a moment she had trouble focusing, and then her eyes locked with Valoria's. "De boy Trevor, he ees in danger!" She swallowed, her hand grasping Valoria's arm tightly. "De... de Deceivers... dey... dey..." A fit of coughing forced the handkerchief to her lips. She swallowed again, tears forming at the corners of her eyes. "Must varn Adara...! She... she cannot trust..." She swallowed and tried to speak, but nothing would come. Her body shook and then went limp. The intensity left her eyes as her last breath escaped her lips.

As Bekka opened the door at the back of the wagon she froze. She could tell that she was too late to do any good. Valoria was weeping over the old Gypsy as she held her lifeless body close to her chest. She was gently rocking her back and forth as she sobbed. "Rest easy now, Rosa," she said as she cried.

Bekka could feel her own tears well up in her eyes and

flow down her cheeks. She climbed into the wagon and put a comforting hand to Valoria's back. "I'm so sorry, Valoria." Together they wept until they could cry no more.

Just after sunrise they buried Rosa on a hilltop not far from where they had made camp. Bekka had suggested that her body be returned to the castle for a proper service, but Valoria declined that almost immediately. "Rosa would prefer to be buried out in the open, not surrounded by castle walls. She was always a free spirit. That is how the Roma lived."

Armand had taken a shovel and dug the grave without complaint. They wrapped Rosa's body in thick sheets and placed her into her final resting place. Bekka hugged her friend close as Armand filled the grave back in. "I'll never forget her," she said. "She taught me so much. Her humor and her grace never left her." Tears of sorrow and remembrance rolled down her cheeks. She brushed them away with her fingertips, but it was a futile effort, as more simply replaced them.

Valoria smiled. "I can barely even recall my own mother. But Rosa was always there for me when I needed her." A choking sob escaped her as tears sprang from her eyes and down her face. Her bottom lip quivered. "Rosa took me in when no one else would. She . . . she could tell that I desperately needed her." Valoria paused to wipe her nose with the back of her hand. The anguish she felt at the old Gypsy's passing was profound. "When I started to keep company with Carlito she cautioned me that it would be a dark path if I chose to follow it." She shook her head, "But I wouldn't listen. I was in love with him. I thought that he loved me, too."

She laughed suddenly. "Even when Carlito started doing things that I felt were wrong, I went along with him. She tried telling me that I was better than that. Rosa, she never gave up on me. She would just give me a needed hug when he would break my heart. She always seemed to know me better than I knew myself." Valoria wiped away the tears from her eyes. "She was the mother I always wanted." Her shoulders shook with her grief. "I will miss her terribly."

Armand stopped shoveling dirt and nodded. "Rosa vas a strong voman. Der vere not many dat vould cross her. I too, vill miss her." He smiled suddenly. "I remember the stories she told vhen I vas very young. Dey alvays 'ad some hidden meaning and

I knew dat eef I listened carefully, everyting dat was troubling me vould go avay. She vas a very vise voman!"

Bekka wrapped her arm around Valoria and pulled her close. She could feel her friend's body shake as she sobbed uncontrollably. "Rosa was a remarkable woman," she said softly. She wiped her own tears away with the heel of her free hand. "Had she not helped me find my way I wouldn't have survived long. She guided me to the strength that was hidden inside of me. I didn't even know I had it. But somehow she did. She was amazing!"

They spent a good part of the day stacking rocks that Armand had gathered upon the mound of dirt, a small cairn to mark Rosa's final resting place. Valoria had carved Rosa's name upon a marker and placed it at the head of the grave. They stood in silence as the site was completed.

Finally, Armand cleared his throat. "Now ve continue to *Freeport*?"

Valoria glanced at Bekka and then shook her head. "No. Bekka and I will continue on to *Freeport*. You can take the wagon back to the castle and let them know about Rosa's passing. There are those that need to know."

He started to object. "But..."

"Val's right." Bekka said. "Besides, they might need the wagon and the draft horses. There's no sense taking them to *Freeport*. We can travel faster if we don't have to wait on you. The sooner we get the information we seek, the sooner we can get back home and prepare for Sinnestra's attack."

Armand shook his head adamantly. "De vagon must be burned!"

Bekka looked shocked. "Why? It's a perfectly good wagon."

Armand spat upon the ground. *"Marimé! De vagon must be burned!"*

Bekka started to object, but Valoria put a hand on her arm. "Armand says it is contaminated. The Roma believe that if the dead's possessions are not burned they can return as a *muló*—a type of undead. Bad luck and many more deaths will follow."

"You're kidding, right?" Bekka said.

Valoria shook her head. "No, Armand is dead serious. We need to burn the wagon."

As they stood on the crest of the hill where Rosa was buried they watched the flames rising high in the air as the fire consumed the Gypsy wagon. Bekka's brow was furrowed as she looked at her friend. "It seems like such a waste. You don't seriously believe all that mumbo jumbo do you?"

Valoria shrugged. "I have lived most of my life among the Romani. During that time I have seen a lot of things that I could not explain. Things that were simply accepted as a fact of life." She shook her head. "But I don't truly know what to believe." She inclined her head to where Armand was gathering the horses. "He believes it. Isn't that enough?"

Bekka sighed. Maybe it was.

Chapter 8
The Vile Forest

Lithania could remember a time when *Brighte Wood Forest* extended farther south encompassing what is now the *Vile Forest*; a time before the Deceivers scrambled from the depths of the earth, like a plague upon the land. An idyllic village known as *Stosshire* inhabited by peaceful folk once lay at the heart of *Brighte Wood*. Though she had never been permitted to travel so far from her home in the trees, she had heard stories about the humankind that lived there. They respected the land and the abundance of life within the forest. But then it all changed one winter. The Deceivers crawled from the darkest pits of Hell and destroyed half the forest, only the earth magic of the Elves and the Fae prevented them from consuming the entire wood. She had skirted the edge of the *Vile Forest* so that she could more easily come upon the ruined village of *Stosshire* where she believed the Deceivers to be.

Now that she stood at the edge of *Brighte Wood* and the *Vile Forest* she found her breath stolen away. Though the two had once been a single forest, now they were truly separate, the division between the two was as night and day, death and life. *Brighte Wood* was warm and vibrant, alive, while the *Vile Forest* was cold and drab and cadaverous, rotting away.

In *Brighte Wood*, Lithania could smell the thick scent of pine, the sweet fragrance of flowers and the rich earthiness of the soil; but as she stepped into the desecrated forest all that was lost to her, immediately replaced by the pungent odor of rot and decay. She hadn't expected the difference to be so profoundly disturbing; even though it had been visually, it was more so on her other senses once she entered the *Vile Forest*.

A weighty sadness bore down upon her that she could not explain. The sense of loss was overwhelming. Hopelessness threatened her resolve, causing her eyes to tear. *Could she truly make a difference here? Or was she simply fooling herself? Was she enough, alone, to end this blight upon the land of the living?*

She had to be enough.

Her father, the former Healer of *Serendil Brenatis*, had been a wise man. There was much he knew about the Deceivers and he had kept detailed notes in several journals. The weathered journal that she carried held a rudimentary map showing the location of the ruins of the human village of *Stosshire*. That was where her friends had found the remains of Cleveland Montgomery, one of Trevor's friends from the other side of the *Portal*. The Deceivers had stripped his life from him, literally stolen it. When she first met Cleve, she sensed something was not right with the boy. He had given off a strange *energy* that Trevor did not. Her father had told her how to expose the Deceiver and she had done as he instructed. It had been shocking for everyone to witness the boy morph back into the creature that he truly was.

Lithania was convinced that the northern path that led through the forest would be the easiest route into the village. That was why she hadn't entered the *Vile Forest* from the south. She hadn't wanted to make her presence known any sooner than she had to.

The *Vile Forest* was extremely impoverished. It was depleted of all moisture despite the recent rainfall that had soaked it and the neighboring *Brighte Wood* only days ago. It was a wonder that lightning hadn't already struck and sent the forest ablaze. The pine needles crunched and crackled beneath her feet. She tried her best to walk as softly and as soundlessly as possible, but it wasn't going to be easy, it was like walking on eggshells; everything seemed dry and brittle underfoot.

How could anyone *not* hear her? She nocked an arrow onto her bow and held it ready as she continued through the trees. Enemy territory, better to be prepared.

She found a path that cut through the forest that was relatively clear of rubble. It seemed to be going in the direction she wanted to go, so she decided to follow it. There were scattered pine needles here and there, but she was able to avoid most of them with ease. She could move faster now and much more stealthily.

She travelled deeper into the forest following the faint path. She was starting to lose her bearings. There were no clear landmarks within the *Vile Forest* and everything was beginning to look the same. The shrubs and trees were all a dull gray color with hints of dark brown, almost blackened, limbs that seemed to bend in gnarly twists giving them a ghastly appearance.

This repugnant forest seemed even more hideous due to the lack of sunlight that filtered through its contorted limbs. The forest was dark and foreboding, it seemed as though it were almost twilight. Lithania could only wonder what it would be like when the sun actually went down. Hopefully she could accomplish her goals quickly and get out. She really didn't want to spend any more time in this forsaken forest than was absolutely necessary.

She stopped and pulled out her father's journal, consulting the crude map that had been drawn upon the worn pages. She could only guess where she was now. The path had twisted its way through the trees so many times that she had lost her sense of direction. She returned the book to her pouch, she had to be getting close.

Lithania froze. She could see the shrubs move up ahead where the path took another turn to the right. She quickly raised her bow and fired an arrow at her unseen target. With amazing speed she nocked another arrow and was prepared to fire again. She heard something slump to the ground just up ahead; clearly she had scored a hit. Normally she was not one to fire on an unseen target, a dangerous undertaking. But there were no allies in this forest, no innocents, just the Deceivers, and they were all her enemy.

Cautiously she moved forward, all of her senses alert for impending danger. As she drew closer to the bend in the path and the shrubbery into which she had fired an arrow, she was overwhelmed by the smell of putrid flesh. It was as though someone, *or something*, had died and lay out in the hot sun for days on end. Lithania had to fight the urge to gag. She grimaced and continued onward.

Finally, at the edge of the foliage she could see what lay beyond. It was a Deceiver that she had felled. The arrow had struck the Deceiver just off-center of its forehead. Black ooze seeped from around the arrow shaft. Lithania parted the shrubs and knelt beside her victim, eying it with a raised brow.

When she had exposed Cleve as a Deceiver, she had had little time to actually *look* at him. Once disclosed, the creature had quickly made its escape. Then, when the Deceivers had returned to attack *Serendil Brenatis*, complete chaos had ensued, leaving no time for her to really get a detailed look at their assailants. But now she had the lifeless body of a Deceiver mere inches away, literally at her feet.

The Deceiver's skin was a mixture of gray and pink tones, almost a marbling affect. Portions of bone were exposed where rotted skin had either fallen off or had been torn away. How the Deceiver even lived with missing chunks of flesh was beyond her comprehension. She could see shoulder bone, ribs and on this creature, parts of the tibia. Most of the Deceiver's teeth were lacking; it still had one or two yellowed stubs visible in its gaping mouth. Its tongue was black and freckled with bits of pink. The Deceiver had no nose to speak of, just two holes that weren't quite round.

She placed her bow on the ground and took a large piece of cloth from her pouch and tied it over her nose and mouth, hoping it would help against the rancid stench coming from the dead Deceiver. It helped a little. As she pried the arrow from the Deceiver's head, she saw a flash of movement in her periphery and the rustle of foliage. She had to lean in close to the corpse in order to avoid the attack from this new threat. Still, it managed a glancing blow to her left shoulder. She could feel the biting sting of her own torn flesh.

As she rolled away from the corpse, she could see another Deceiver flying through the air towards her. She had little time to react. Still clutching the arrow she had pulled from the dead, she managed to thrust it upward, driving it into the flesh just beneath the chin and jawbone of her oncoming assailant. The full weight of the Deceiver collapsed on top of her, and it took a while for her to scramble from beneath it by pushing its lifeless body off her.

She was breathing hard as she collected her bow from the ground. She silently berated herself for getting so caught up in her examination of the Deceiver's corpse. She had been so absorbed, *so fascinated*, by what she was seeing that she lost focus on her surroundings. The attack from behind could have been fatal. She was fortunate that it wasn't.

The strap of one quiver was almost torn through and her shoulder was beginning to throb painfully. She looked down at the Deceiver responsible for the damage and saw long, savage looking gray claws. They were coated with her newly torn flesh and fresh blood. It looked like one nail had actually broken off. That had happened only recently.

Lithania gingerly probed her shoulder with her fingertips. She found something hard imbedded in the wound. She grasped it between the tips of thumb and forefinger and pulled quickly. Her breath caught in her throat as she felt the sudden tug and the acute pain that it summoned. With a furrowed brow she stared at the cracked fingernail that was now resting in the palm of her left hand. The underside of it was covered with blood, flesh and caked on grime. She cast it aside with a flourish of revulsion. She barely had time to lift her bandana out of the way as she quickly vomited.

Chapter 9
Kensington Castle

Kensington Castle had become a refuge of sorts since the defeat of the tyrant Maragh. Though Valoria inherited the keep from her dead father, she disavowed ownership. Since Maragh had murdered her infant sister, the castle had never been her home. She wanted little to do with it now, save for a place to rest her head and even then she preferred to sleep outdoors.

Since leaving Castle Maragh as a young child, she had hoped never to return. But it drew her back to help Bekka fulfill her role in the *Prophecy*. When the Kensington's opted to stay on this side of the *Portal* due to Julia's pregnancy, they needed a place to live, a safe haven. Valoria offered the castle to them, demanding only that they change the name by which it was referred.

Bekka had suggested they call it 'Castle Valor' in honor of her friend, but Valoria adamantly objected, stating she'd rather see it burned to the ground. In the end, they settled on 'Kensington Castle' which seemed only fitting.

After Maragh's defeat, many of his former soldiers fled the castle and began to live as brigands. Due to their continued atrocities, numerous local inhabitants sought refuge at the castle. The Kensingtons didn't have the heart to send anyone away. They vowed to do all that they could to make their corner of the world a better place. This included employing some former members of Maragh's army but only those willing to redeem themselves and atone for their evil doings.

Eventually the migration to Kensington Castle for sanctuary grew less and less. Primarily due to the fact that the outlaws were seeking more prosperous endeavors elsewhere. Occasionally one or two displaced citizens would find their way to the castle.

Some would choose to remain, others would move on after their bellies were full, searching for another place to call home

Julia Kensington stood on the outer curtain wall, just above the front gate of the keep, as she watched a horse-drawn cart approach. The horse looked like it had been through some rough country and was about to collapse. The driver of the small wagon looked equally forlorn. It appeared like something or someone, was lying in the back of the cart.

The foot soldier that stood guard outside the gate looked over his shoulder and motioned for someone to join him. A moment later Julia could see Candi and Vincente saunter over to the cart. Evidently the two teens were alarmed by what they found; she could see it in their reactions. Vincente climbed up beside the driver and took over the reins as Candi climbed into the back of the cart.

As the wagon went through the gate Julia could see that savage claw marks were gouged in the horse's right shoulder and down its flank. The driver had scrapes as well, but the girl in the back seemed far worse off. Fear drove Julia down to the castle courtyard.

The driver offered a weak smile as Julia approached. "Good day to you, m'lady. My name is Brother Dinurés. I have travelled from the city of *Freeport*, where my brethren and I have cared for this poor child. She has been badly inflicted with a horrible wound that I fear has become quite infected. We have done all that we can for her, and nothing seems to be working. The High Priest, Brother Enetarés, said that the *Chosen One* might be able to offer a cure. That is why I have brought her to you." He swallowed, leaning heavily against the cart for support. "I fear she has little time."

Julia looked at Candi as she listened to Brother Dinurés speak. Candi had been inspecting the girl's wounded shoulder. She touched her arm. "How is she, Candace?"

Candi grimaced and then looked at Julia. "Honestly, it doesn't look good at all. It is badly infected and needs to be properly cleansed and redressed. I wish we had some strong antibiotics on hand. That may be the only way to stop the infection from spreading."

Julia nodded. "Let's get her inside." She turned back to the priest. "You look like you could use some attention as well, Brother...?"

He smiled wearily. "Dinurés, but you can call me Jon if it is easier, m'lady."

She smiled sweetly. "Very well, Jon. And please, call me Julia."

Robert Kensington handed Brother Dinurés a pewter cup of mead. They were sitting at a table in the Great Hall. "It isn't much, but it should help to energize you somewhat." He smiled. "At the very least, it'll quench your thirst." He sat across from him, drumming the tabletop with the tips of his fingers. "Julia says that you came here from *Freeport*."

Dinurés nodded as he took a healthy sip of the drink. "Yes, m'lord, that is correct."

"We don't stand much on formalities here. Call me Robert."

"Jon, then." He raised the cup. "Not bad at all."

Robert smiled. "I suppose it'll do." He cleared his throat. "Since you came from *Freeport* perhaps you encountered my daughter and her companions along the way? They were travelling to the city."

Jon shook his head and took a slow sip of mead. "No, I am afraid we didn't. We had ventured further to the south following the coastline after leaving *Schiff's Crossing* behind. The salt air seemed to help the girl breathe more easily. We didn't see anyone on our journey. I wish we had followed the more traditional route; it might have saved us from the attack by the orc raiders that we encountered. Their barrage nearly cost us all our lives. Brother Belgrid was killed, but his sacrifice allowed me to escape with the girl."

Robert could easily understand. Though this world was still relatively new to him, he was well aware of the dangers it possessed, having experienced much of it. He cocked his head to the side. "This girl…?"

"Gwyneth is the name she gave when she came to us," Dinurés said.

Robert nodded. "How did Gwyneth sustain her wounds?"

"Obviously she was attacked quite viciously." He shrugged. "How, exactly I can't say. She came to us already badly injured. Her wound was showing signs of infection. We tried healing draughts on her wound, both internally and externally; neither worked." He sighed heavily. "But those are most effective when applied immediately after receiving the lesion. She had been several days, maybe weeks, before seeking care from us."

"Why so long?" Robert asked, curious.

Brother Dinurés took a sip of his mead. "Who can say? It was all that we could do to keep her alive. She has been in and out of consciousness, and quite feverish. We were fortunate to learn her name."

Robert sighed. "That sounds so sad."

"Indeed."

"And this High Priest of yours, Father Enetarés, he thought we might be able to help her when you could not?"

Dinurés nodded. "That was the hope. Word had come to him that the *Chosen One* came through a mystical portal of some kind. It was said that she came from a wondrous land where many miraculous things were possible. We hoped that perhaps you had brought a cure for this infection with you."

Robert shook his head and chuckled softly. "I wish that we had been that farsighted. Our journey through the *Portal* to this side was rather abrupt and unexpected. We hadn't planned on coming. Our hope was to prevent our daughter from even coming here; we didn't bring anything with us, except the clothes on our backs." His thoughts momentarily wandered to the comforts that they had left behind, the little things that made life easier.

Dinurés rubbed his chin. "Perhaps Gwyneth could be taken

through this Portal to the other side and cured. It would be a shame if she were allowed to simply die when there is hope for recovery."

Robert raised his brows. "I'm not even certain that there is a way back. If there is, I certainly don't know of it. Perhaps Lady Rosa would know. But she is on her way to Freeport with my daughter."

"I see." The priest finished the last of his mead and then placed both hands on the table beside the empty pewter cup. "Perhaps they will all return in time."

Julia eased the door closed behind her, leaving Candi to tend to the wounded girl. She hadn't regained consciousness since coming to the castle. Julia's brow was creased with lines of worry. The girl's shoulder did not look promising even after cleansing the deep lesion as best they could and the smell was horrible! They had to find a way to rid her of the infection, but even then, the girl would be lucky to survive. Her complexion was pasty; she was weak and had lost a lot of blood. She wondered what had caused the girl's wound.

She smiled as her husband approached. He put his arm around her and kissed her on the forehead. She leaned into him, relishing the comfort his strong embrace offered. "That poor girl," she said.

"Her name is Gwyneth," Robert offered. "How's she doing?"

Julia shook her head. "Not good, I'm afraid. Candi and I cleaned the wound as best we could, but it isn't nearly enough. The infection is pretty severe. We could use some strong antibiotics; but even then, it might be too late. The poison from the infection has likely already spread through her system."

"Jon says that they tried everything they could think of to no avail. The High Priest suggested they bring her here, claiming the *Chosen One* was her only remaining hope."

"Bekka?" Julia pulled out of Robert's embrace looking skeptical. "How can she possibly help her?"

Robert raised his brows and shook his head. "I don't know. They seem to think that Bekka can go through the *Portal* with the girl and get her treatment on the other side, and then return."

"You're kidding, right?"

He chuckled. "Those were Jon's words, more or less."

"They have to understand the dangers involved with that. Sinnestra is probably hoping that we'll use the *Portal* so that she can swoop in and gain access to it. We can't allow that to happen. We simply cannot release a demon like her back on an unsuspecting world."

"I agree," Robert said. "If that were to happen Rosa claims the loss of life on *both* sides of the *Portal* would be devastating. We can't risk it until we defeat Sinnestra once and for all."

Julia gave her husband a worried look. "Do you really think they'll find a way to defeat her?"

"I certainly hope so."

Chapter 10
The Crossing

Valoria and Bekka had been riding through the night to avoid having to travel through the blistering heat of the day. The northern breezes had blown through the *Wastelands* carrying along an arid sultriness that was unbearable unless you were accustomed to such stringent temperatures like the Vortagg were, and maybe even the Orc.

Valoria reined her mount in and reached a hand out for Bekka to do the same. "Whoa," she spoke soothingly to the horse.

Bekka could sense that something was not quite right up ahead. Rising up in her saddle she strained to see what had alarmed her companion. Everything appeared as it should; she saw nothing amiss. "What is it?"

"Something is wrong. Usually Schiff has a pennant flying from sunup to sundown. His flagpole is bare."

Bekka shrugged. "Maybe he simply forgot."

Valoria gave her friend a pointed look. "Marren Schiff *never* forgets. He is a stickler for routine almost to the point of being obsessive about it."

Bekka sighed, smiling. She knew *several* people who suffered from OCD, so she knew *exactly* what her friend was saying. Still, she felt compelled to offer another scenario. "Maybe the flag was torn and needed to be replaced. Just because it's not flying doesn't necessarily mean that something is wrong." She was tired of being in the saddle; Valoria had promised that they would spend a relaxing day at the *Crossing*, and now that was in jeopardy.

The ranger shook her head. "Schiff does things mundanely. If his pennant is not flapping in the sunlight, then something is definitely wrong. Had it been ripped he would have repaired it after taking it down."

"Maybe he was tired."

"He wouldn't let that stop him."

"So, what's the plan?"

Valoria grinned. "Follow my lead."

Bekka raised her brows and smiled. "Always."

At one time, two rivers flowed into *Schiff's Crossing* and further south to the *Sea of Vespin*. The eastern most river, known as the *Dead River*, had flowed out of the *Wastelands* and had never really amounted to much. The *Stebin River's* source was high up in the *Stone Pike Mountains*. It was wide and rough and in comparison, the *Dead River* was nothing but a creek when it had any water in it at all, which was rarely. The running joke was that you didn't want to get stuck up *Schiff's Creek* with a paddle, it simply would do you no good. Marren's humor was just as dry as the land from which the *Dead River* sometimes flowed.

Marren Schiff and his three sons settled in the spot just north of where both rivers dumped into the sea. They saw profit to be made in ferrying travelers across the swiftly flowing *Stebin River* by raft. Thick ropes were anchored on either side of the river and a raft was pulled along the rope. Initially, the river was too swift for this process to be safely manipulated, and the first raft was carried into the *Sea of Vespin* completely destroyed, prompting the Schiff's to come up with a more impervious method. They built a dam up river, not to stop the river's flow, but to slow it down so that the crossing was more manageable.

In the early days of *Schiff's Crossing* there was only one building, the home of the Schiff clan. Now there were several buildings making up the fledgling hamlet. A tavern known as the *Stubborn Goat*, a trading post and a smithy, not to mention several shacks that served as homes for the *Crossing's* residents had all been added over time.

Marren Schiff stepped out onto his porch as Valoria and Bekka began to dismount. His right arm was in a makeshift sling and the hand was covered in a haphazard wad of cloth serving as a bandage. He had a nasty abrasion on his forehead and along his left cheek, ending at the corner of his mouth. He looked like he had been badly beaten. "If you're lookin' to cross I'm afraid I'll have to turn you away. The raft took a beatin' last week. My boys have gone to *Freeport* for supplies an' it'll be another couple of weeks before we're up and running again. I suggest you go a bit farther north to cross the *Stebin*."

Valoria frowned. "I've heard there are some rogue Orcs to the north, maybe even some Vortagg Raiders. Sounds a bit too dangerous for my companion and I. She isn't much of a fighter."

Marren Schiff swallowed as a bead of sweat ran down the side of his head. "Don't know nothin' about the troubles to the north." He inclined his head backwards and to the side, the movement was barely noticeable. "We've had troubles of our own."

Valoria nodded. "These are tough times to be sure. I guess my companion and I will head north. We need to save as much of our *gold* as we can. We have business in *Freeport*."

"Where you coming from?" Schiff asked.

"Kensington Castle. We need to buy some supplies and enough livestock to build a hearty stock. Figured that *Freeport* would be out best bet."

"Aye," Schiff said with a nod. "That it would. I wish you the best of luck."

"We'll be back soon," Valoria said, pointedly.

Marren Schiff winked. "We'll be ready for ye." He snapped the fingers of his good hand. "Take care in your travels. I hear those damned brigands run in bands of five."

Valoria smiled. "Understood."

Schiff winked again.

Valoria looked at Bekka. "Let's head further north, then. We'll make camp near the *Stebin River* due east of *Freeport*. That should help us to avoid the *Red Hills* altogether."

"Aye," Marren Schiff said. "The *Red Hills* are where the outlaws are calling their home these days. Best if you steer clear."

Bekka and Valoria mounted their horses and said goodbye to Schiff as they turned toward the north in silence. After they had gotten out of earshot Bekka looked at her friend curiously. "Why do I get the feeling that the two of you exchanged a ton of information back there?"

A sly grin crept upon Valoria's face. "Because we did."

"And?" Bekka asked.

"Well, for starters, we know that there are five brigands holding *Schiff's Crossing* hostage. I told them that we were carrying quite a bit of gold so that we could resupply Kensington Castle with stores and livestock. And, I told them *precisely* where we were going to make our camp."

"We're not carrying any gold to speak of," Bekka said pointedly.

Valoria chuckled. "Cheese for the rats."

Bekka arched both brows. "So you *want* the bandits to come for the gold we don't have. You set a trap!"

"Schiff and I are old friends. We go back a long way. I owe him more than I can ever hope to repay. This'll be a small repayment that is past due."

Bekka wasn't overly pleased with Valoria's plan to trap the bandits. Like most traps, it required bait of some kind, and for this one in particular, *she* was the bait. After setting up her empty bedroll to appear that she was fast asleep, Valoria had slipped off into the darkness leaving Bekka all alone to stand watch and tend the fire.

The night was growing colder. Bekka yawned and shook her head trying to chase the pull of sleep away that relentlessly tugged at her. It had been a long day in the saddle and she was feeling tired and sore. She stood up and added some of the twigs that she had gathered earlier and stoked the fire, her eyes drawn to the hungry tendrils of flame by reflex. She immediately cursed herself as she stared into the darkness that surrounded the camp. She was blinded by the firelight and the blackness of the night sky was thick and seemingly impenetrable.

She heard movement behind her and she whirled around, trying to unsheathe her sword in the same motion. It was too late. A big burly orc wrapped his beefy arms around her and practically lifted her off the ground. "Rhal," growled a human voice, "grab her legs!"

Rhal slapped her feet away as she tried to kick him as he approached. She was quickly and efficiently subdued.

Two others attacked the bedroll where it appeared the ranger was still sleeping. Their eyes grew wide as they realized that they had been fooled. A large human scanned the darkness at the edge of the camp, searching for the missing warrior; he saw two of the orcs drop as arrows penetrated their skulls. One of them fell across the campfire sending burning embers and sparks flying into the air.

Rhal dropped Bekka's legs and pulled an axe from his belt. He had a wild look in his eyes as he glared at her angrily. Bekka jerked back against the big orc that still had her arms pinned as an arrow struck Rhal in the forehead, splattering her with tiny droplets of blood. His eyes rolled upward as though he were trying to see what had hit him. He fell over backwards, dead.

Bekka kicked at the shins of the orc that held her tightly, to no avail. He turned his body in an attempt to place Bekka in between himself and the unseen assailant that was still firing arrows with deadly accuracy.

"Dralgor! One more arrow comes into the camp, kill the girl!" the human bandit roared. Bekka could instantly feel the cold steel pressed against her neck; she was almost afraid to swallow for fear of being cut by the sharp blade.

Valoria entered the edge of the camp. She still had an arrow nocked on her bow, but it was pointed down in front of her. "Let the girl go, and I'll let you live."

The human ruffian chuckled and spat. "Nah, I think we'd best not." The warrior had already proven her proficiency with the bow. He had no doubts that she could fire two more arrows with deadly precision before they could stop her.

Valoria seemed to consider her options. There weren't many. "It would seem that we are at an impasse."

Confusion seemed to cloud the man's eyes. He shook his head. "I don't know what that means." He indicated her bow with a nod in her direction. "I suggest you drop that before Dralgor decides to slit your friend's dainty little throat. He just *loves* the feel of warm blood coursing through his fat fingers."

Bekka could feel the orc nod as he chuckled in her ear. "They're gonna kill me anyway, Val. Don't listen to them. Take them out."

The human looked dumbstruck. "That just ain't so! We wouldn't kill you pretty ladies, not until we've enjoyed your company first." He glared at Valoria. "Drop your weapons and surrender or your friend dies. Right now!" His bravado was returning.

Valoria eased the arrow from the bow and then dropped both of them to the ground. "Fine. You win. Take the gold and our horses but spare us. We're more trouble than we're worth, I promise you."

The man's eyes sparkled with cruel enthusiasm. When he grinned, she couldn't help but notice that he was missing two of his upper front teeth. "Ooh... I'm countin' on it!" He chuckled, drooling all over his chin. "We *like* it rough."

"Good!" Bekka said as she slammed her head back into the orc's face. Her hands had been forced behind her and she found his crotch. She grabbed what she could and squeezed with all she had. The orc loosened his grip and howled in pain at both actions; the knife moved from her throat. She quickly seized the opportunity and bent her knees upward toward her chest, and then slammed her feet downward and back as hard as she could.

The orc grunted.

She was free!

When Dralgor released his hold on her, Bekka dropped to the ground landing on her hands and knees in front of what was left of the smoldering corpse of the orc that Valoria had skewered with her first volley of arrows. He had managed to climb out of the fire for the most part, despite the arrow to his skull. He was dead; his lower limbs were still feeding the flames.

Bekka cringed at the sickening smell of his burning flesh.

Their human assailant had flung himself at Valoria as Bekka dealt with her captor. She could see the two of them struggling to gain the upper hand over one another. At this point it could go either way. Bekka feared for her friend, the mere size of her opponent was positively daunting.

He swung a massive fist that connected with Valoria's jaw, sending her sprawling upon the ground. She could feel darkness threatening to close in. Blinking frantically, she grasped desperately for a weapon but he quickly kicked at her. She grabbed a handful of dirt and sand and flung it upward into his eyes. He staggered backward, momentarily blinded.

Dralgor had sufficiently recovered enough to where he could move without much constraint. He grasped the human brigand by his shoulders and guided him away from the camp. By the time Valoria had recovered her bow and nocked an arrow they had disappeared into the darkness. A moment later the sound of their horses were heard moving rapidly westward.

Bekka's hands were shaking as the adrenaline wore off. She looked at her friend as Valoria stepped back into the firelight. "Are you okay?"

Valoria nodded, her jaw clenched tight in anger. "I'm fine. I just wish they hadn't gotten away."

Bekka was glad that they had. The two survivors were monstrous in size. She had been deathly afraid of what they might have done to the two of them. She swallowed, pushing the dark thoughts from her mind. She surveyed the camp, worry in her eyes. "Now what?"

Valoria started gathering up her bedroll. "We shouldn't stay here. I don't really think they'll return, but I'd rather go back to *Schiff's Crossing.*"

Relief flooded over Bekka. She knelt and began to roll up her bedding.

Chapter 11
An Unexpected Welcome

Trevor could see the glow of the hooded lanterns high up in the trees of *Serendil Brenatis* as he rode slowly through the forest. Signs of life stirred upon the raised platforms built into the trees. He couldn't help but smile. The last time he had been here was when the Deceivers had attacked and nearly destroyed everything. He was glad to see that much of the *Elven Tree City* still remained. Repairs had obviously been made to what had been damaged. But in all honesty, he was surprised that the elves decided to return to the treetops.

Lithania had said that the Deceiver's attack had pointed out their vulnerabilities. And how another attack by their enemies might wipe them out entirely. Already their numbers were nearing extinction levels. But here they were, back up in the trees. Trevor shook his head. Old habits are hard to break. Still, he would have thought that Lithania could have convinced them to live in a better-suited place.

The hoot of an owl somewhere up above him, caused him to look back up into the trees. The limbs were thick, and he could scarcely see the orange tinge of sunlight in the sky as dawn spread over the forest.

He could sense that he was being watched. He had no doubt that there were several sentries posted throughout the forest and that they had already seen his approach. He reined Jester to a halt and lovingly slapped his hand on the horse's neck. "Easy boy," he said soothingly as Jester snorted, ears twitching nervously. Even Jester could sense that they were not alone. "Easy," he repeated softly.

Trevor waited, his hands resting on the pommel of his saddle, unthreatening. A moment later several young elves stepped out of the trees and surrounded him; all were holding bows with arrows nocked and ready. He grinned. Raising his hands slowly into the air he said, "Don't shoot. I am a friend."

Trevor stood at the base of a wide staircase that rose from the ground, followed a curve of the massive tree trunk to which it was attached and disappeared in the limbs and leaves of the tall trees. He was glad to see that they no longer relied solely on the elaborate elevator that had been so vulnerable to the Deceiver's attack. It had cost the elves many lives.

He smiled as he saw a pair of familiar faces coming down the steps toward him. He was glad to see both Aloena and Elanthor, though he had hoped that Lithania would be the one to greet him. *Did she even know that he was here? Did she care?* He swallowed the lump of fear that was caught in his throat, unsure if he truly wanted to know the answer.

Aloena smiled brightly as she wrapped her arms around Trevor's shoulders and pulled him into a tight embrace. *"Veluin, mon querichère armino'ele,"* she whispered softly. [Greetings, my dear friend.]

Trevor kissed the side of her head. "It is good to see you again, Aloe." He could see the corner of Elanthor's mouth turned up in a knowing smile. It was good to see that he had come to terms with their friendship at long last. He pulled from Aloena's embrace and firmly shook hands with Elanthor by gripping the other's forearm in the traditional manner.

The tall elf surprised him by pulling him into a bear hug. "It is good to see you, my friend. I had hoped that we would meet again."

Trevor looked from Elanthor to Aloena unable to keep the surprise from his face. Aloena chuckled as she entwined her arm with Elanthor's. "Much has changed since we parted ways back at the cave refuge. Elan has come to view humans as friends. He has begun to grow into his role of leadership. Together we are building a stronger people."

Elanthor nodded. "Yes, I was wrong to treat you with such distrust, I see that now. I hope we can put the past behind us and allow our friendship to grow."

Trevor smiled as he put a firm hand on Elanthor's shoulder. "I see no reason why we can't. I value your friendship."

Aloena touched Trevor's arm, her eyes filled with concern. "Litha is not here. I think she went to the *Vile Forest* to deal with the Deceivers before they mount another attack against us."

Trevor stopped. He looked from Elanthor to Aloena. "You didn't try and stop her?"

Elanthor's brow shot up as he shook his head. "We did not know of her plans until after she had already gone."

A lone tear escaped Aloena's eye. "She left during the night and avoided our sentries. We found a note she had left for us only this morning. She will be greatly outnumbered. I do not know what she was thinking. An act this foolish is unlike her."

Trevor turned. "I'll go and bring her back before she does something stupid."

Elanthor sighed. "I fear she has already done that by going to face them alone. We are not strong enough to go up against the Deceivers. As you know we have mostly children here in *Serendil Brenatis*."

"I'm going to need my horse," Trevor said.

Aloena motioned for Trevor's escorts to bring his horse back around. "What can you hope to do?"

Trevor shrugged. "I don't know, honestly. But I can't let her face them alone. If nothing else I might be able to get her out of there before she gets into serious trouble."

Tears streamed down Aloena's face. Her heart was heavy with fear and sadness. She had the agonizing feeling that she would never see Trevor or Lithania again. "I wish I could do more."

A young elven warrior ran up to them, he was clearly out of breath. "There is smoke coming from the north! I think that the *Vile Forest* is burning!"

Elanthor nodded. "Lithania."

Trevor took the reins for Jester and quickly mounted. "Wish me luck!"

Aloena placed a hand on the horse's shoulder. "I wish you good fortune and Godspeed!"

As Trevor rode away from *Serendil Brenatis* his heart was pounding inside his chest. *What was Lithania thinking? She couldn't possibly hope to survive this insane attack against the Deceivers!* She was likely to get them both killed in the process. He didn't really have a plan as he urged Jester into a run.

He could only hope that he would get to her in time.

Chapter 12
Treachery

Julia Kensington dabbed a cool, damp cloth across Gwyneth's forehead. The girl's eyes fluttered open. "How are you doing, Sweetie?" Julia asked with a tentative smile; the girl looked weak and utterly exhausted.

"Could I," she swallowed, "have some water, please?"

Julia blushed, embarrassed by her lack of foresight. She should've known that the girl would be dying of thirst. She reached for the ewer on the bedside table and poured the pewter cup halfway. "Of course you can." She put the cup to the girl's lips and helped her to drink.

Gwyneth nodded gratefully. "Thank you." Her brows furrowed suddenly as her eyes began to dart around the room. "Where am I? Where is Brother Dinurés?" She seemed worried, fearful.

"He is with my husband. You are at *Kensington Castle*. You are safe. We're doing all that we can for you." Julia smiled, hoping to alleviate the girl's anxiety as best she could.

The girl seemed to relax. *"Kensington Castle?"* She smiled. "Then the *Chosen One* will help me? She will take me through the *Portal* and cure me?"

Julia offered the girl a sorrowful look. "I'm afraid that isn't going to be possible. There is a powerful demoness that is just waiting for us to use the *Portal* so that she can pass through it as well. If that were to happen then two worlds would be in very grave danger." She shook her head, her eyes starting to water. "We cannot allow that to happen. I'm sorry."

Gwyneth nodded slowly. "I understand." She licked her dry lips, before she spoke again. "Am I going to die?" Her voice sounded resigned to that fact.

Julia was genuinely surprised by the question. She hadn't really considered that possibility, not seriously, anyway. There was no fear in the girl's eyes. They reminded her of Bekka's, a pristine blue like the waters of the Caribbean. "We won't let that happen Gwyn."

"Candi says that where she is from, where the *Chosen One* is from, they can easily treat this infection. It need not be fatal." Gwyneth swallowed. "But there is nothing here that can save me, is there?" Tears stung at her eyes and her bottom lip quivered. "I don't want to die."

Julia felt the tug at her heart. This girl was so brave, yet so fragile. She didn't want her to die, either. There was a chance that she could still be saved; but that meant either going through the *Portal* or possibly making their own version of penicillin. It had been a long time since Julia had taken either Science of Health classes in school. Perhaps Candi or Bekka would know how to apply the penicillin so that Gwyneth's wound could be healed. There *had* to be way. They were running out of options.

Brother Dinurés closed the door softly behind him and listened intently to see if anyone were passing by in the corridor. Satisfied, he turned toward the sleeping form lying in the bed. "Mistress?" he asked delicately, not wanting to incur her wrath.

Gwyneth's eyes popped open and she immediately sat up, casting the covers off of her. "It took you long enough!" she hissed.

He swallowed the fear in his throat. "It was necessary. Robert

Kensington seemed reluctant to allow me to leave his company. The man is trying to learn to cope with a new world, a new way of living." He smiled. "I think he saw me as someone he could talk to."

Gwyneth rolled her eyes. "I do not care about him, or anybody in this place! What I care about is the *Portal*!" She took a deep breath. "It is clear that they refuse to use the *Portal* even to save the life of a perceived innocent; so we must force their hand."

He took a timid step forward. "And how do you suggest that we do that, my Queen?"

Her lip curled slightly. "Perhaps if their infant son is taken, and then I am the *only* one who knows where you have absconded to with the child, they might be compelled to save me, for my cooperation."

Dinurés nodded. "That is indeed a possibility."

Dinurés could hear the hungry cries echo down the corridor as the baby began to demand his feeding. He hid in the shadows, knowing that someone would be along to tend to the wailing infant. He didn't have long to wait. He could see Julia Kensington enter the baby's nursery from an adjoining room. He watched as she bent over the crib, cooing softly.

"Let's get you changed, and then we'll get you fed. Yes we will," the mother said with an overabundance of sweetness. The baby seemed to respond, calming slightly.

He stepped into the room. "Such a sweet boy you have there!"

Julia straightened, startled by his unexpected approach. She put a hand to her breast and smiled. "Oh my, you startled me!"

He chuckled. "I am truly sorry. That was not my intent." He wrinkled his nose. "Oh my goodness, he seems to have soiled himself!"

Julia laughed. "That's what babies do."

Dinurés reached for the infant. "May I? It has been a while since I changed a diaper, allow me to do this for you."

Julia was touched by the priest's offer to help. "That is very kind of you, but it won't be necessary. I need to feed him afterwards."

He waved a hand in the air as he eyed her extended belly. "I can take care of the child. You need your rest."

Julia grinned. "Alright, you can change his diaper, but you can't feed him. He is still being breastfed."

Dinurés blushed slightly. "Oh, of course. After I clean him up, I'll bring him to you." He shooed her away with a wave of his hand. "Go. Sit. Relax for a moment."

Julia hesitated for a moment. She smiled tentatively. "I'll be in the next room." Truthfully, she could use the rest, if even for a short while. Hanzi was still getting up at all hours of the night. Some things she simply had to do herself, she refused to use a wet nurse.

Dinurés bent over the boy and began to remove his soiled diaper. "I'll have him suckling at your breast in short order."

Julia stepped into her bedchamber for a moment and placed a hand to her stomach and caressed lovingly. She smiled. She would take help where she could get it. She crossed to the bed and began propping pillows. There were no sounds coming from the nursery. "Brother Dinurés?" she called softly.

There was no answer.

"Jon?" she stepped into the nursery and saw the priest stepping into the corridor. She glanced at the crib, but Hanzi wasn't there. She ran to the doorway as quickly as she could. She could see Dinurés making his way hastily toward the steps. He held the baby against his chest.

"Brother Dinurés stop! Give me back my baby!" She ran toward him.

He paused at the top of the stone steps and turned to face her. She reached him and held out her arms for the baby. "Give him to me!" she insisted harshly. She was absolutely infuriated. How could the priest be doing this? She had trusted him!

He grasped her shoulder with his free hand and jerked her toward the steps. Her eyes went wide. "What are you doing?" She fought to regain her balance, and just as she thought she had, he shoved her roughly from behind. Julia Kensington fell down the stone steps, tumbling head over heels.

Dinurés took the steps two at a time and stepped over Julia's unconscious body when he reached the landing. He shoved

Candi backwards as she ran and knelt to check on Julia, knocking her over. Her eyes went wide as she saw the baby clutched in his arm. He ran down the empty corridor as quickly as he could, not looking back.

Candi screamed for help.

Chapter 13
Where There's Smoke

Lithania fired another burning arrow into the last untouched building that still stood in the ruined village of *Stosshire*; she wanted there to be no place for the Deceivers to hide. What remained of the structure was already falling down; gaping holes remained in the outer walls, its thatched roof partially collapsed inward. The hungry flames took hold and quickly spread.

A Deceiver raced toward her from the burning forest, flames nipping at its heels. She fired another arrow, striking the creature's forehead, causing it to fall backward as its feet flew out from under it.

She quickly nocked another arrow and looked around for another target. She could feel the heat of the flames as the fire burned all around her. A breeze picked up, scattering burning embers everywhere, lighting fires anew. If she was going to survive this, she needed to keep moving. The neckerchief covering her mouth and nose was inadequate; searing heat was making it difficult to breathe, and the thick smoke was blinding. She stumbled through the *Vile Forest* trying desperately to stay ahead of the fire.

She stopped suddenly as she found herself confronted by several Deceivers. They swayed as they turned to face her, or perhaps it was only the heat waves shimmering in the air that made them appear that way. She swallowed as she fired an arrow at the closest one. Her aim was off; she struck it in the shoulder. The Deceiver grabbed the shaft of the arrow and snapped it off, casting it to the ground at its feet. Lithania reached for another arrow but grasped at air. The quiver was empty. She swung her bow at the wounded Deceiver and struck it on the side of the head, it stumbled sideways, snatching her bow out of her hand.

Breathing heavily, Lithania drew her sword, tears stinging at her eyes from the smoke and flames.

Trevor tied Jester's reins loosely to the dried stump. He had never seen the *Vile Forest* before, but his friends had described it to him in great detail. It was *exactly* as he had imagined it would be: *Hauntingly beautiful.* He shook his head, his lip curving in amusement. The horse snorted and stamped its hoof nervously. Clearly Jester wasn't happy about being left alone.

Trevor reached into his pouch and pulled out an apple and offered it to the horse. Jester took the fruit but was still not happy. Trevor patted the horse's neck. "It'll be alright." As he turned and entered the dead forest he swallowed the lump of uncertainty in his throat. *'Who am I kidding?'* He unsheathed his sword, liking the way the hilt felt in his hand. Black smoke drifted toward him through the gray trees of the *Vile Forest*, he could see the flickering orange glow of the dancing fires up ahead. He sighed heavily as he turned back to the horse and untied the reins. "Go!" he commanded. Jester didn't hesitate as a strong whiff of burning wood flared his nostrils. The horse turned and ran. Trevor hated seeing the horse go, but it was better this way. He turned back toward the smoldering forest. Squinting, his eyes burned as he walked forward, weaving through the dry trees and foliage that had not yet caught fire.

Burning embers floated in the air around him, sparking new fires among the dry leaves of the already dead forest. Some landed on his arm, burning holes in his thin leather sleeve; he felt their biting sting. He quickened his pace. He knew he couldn't afford to waste too much time in this growing conflagration. He had to find Lithania before it was too late.

He had lost track of time. He was no longer certain he was even going the right way. He had spent so much effort trying to avoid the raging inferno that seemed to have a mind of its own. He even had to backtrack more times than he could count due to the out of control wildfire. As the flames consumed one dry timber, then quickly jumped to the next; there seemed to be no end. *"What have you done, Litha?"* he muttered to himself.

The heat was growing in intensity. He didn't know how much more he could take. With every breath he inhaled more smoke; his childhood fascination of being a daring Firefighter evaporated in an instant. Now all he wanted to do was find Lithania and survive.

As if in answer to a prayer, he saw a lone figure lying in a small clearing, as yet untouched by the fire. Smoke was wafting in from all directions. As he drew closer he could see that it was Lithania. He had found her! But she wasn't alone. Two Deceivers appeared in the thick smoke, moving toward her.

They hadn't seen him yet. If he acted fast he might be able to save her from certain death. Wasting no time, Trevor roared a battle cry and lifted his sword as he ran toward them. His yell had startled them, and as the first turned in his direction, Trevor swung his sword with both hands. The head of his victim flew off, disappearing into the swirling smoke.

His swing had left Trevor off balance, and he stumbled forward, falling in front of the other Deceiver. He rolled to his left and thrust his sword up, with all he was worth. He felt the blade cut skin, the tip striking bone as it splintered the Deceiver's spine. Trevor lost his grip on his sword and it fell to the ground still imbedded in the Deceiver's gut. Trevor scrambled to his feet, coughing as he whirled around, half expecting to find another enemy nearby. He saw none.

Turning, Trevor dropped to his knees beside Lithania and rolled her over. The smoke burned the back of his throat and he coughed as though he were about to hack up a lung. He wiped the tears from his eyes and peered down at the elf maiden. Her face was covered with soot and dirt. Tear tracks had cut muddied pathways down her cheeks; he had no doubt his face was similar to hers.

Lithania's eyes fluttered open and she smiled. "Trevor?" she asked softly in disbelief.

She was alive!

"Yes! It's me, Litha!" His heart soared with joy. He looked her over quickly. "Are you hurt?" She had minor cuts, but nothing seemed to be too serious.

She shook her head. "I... I don't think so. The smoke... I... I just could not breathe anymore."

Trevor nodded as tears blurred his vision. "We need to get out of here. Can you walk?"

Lithania coughed and then nodded. "With your assistance I think I can manage."

He helped her to her feet and she pressed her body against his. He wrapped his arm around her waist and together they walked to the only clear path available to them, eastward.

Chapter 14
Pursuit

Robert Kensington had never seen his wife so battered and bruised. The fall she took down the stairs had caused her to miscarry; she was sporting a nasty abrasion along her right temple, and scrapes on her nose, mouth, cheek and chin. She was lucky to be alive. He sat beside her on the bed, gingerly holding her hand, as her entire body seemed to shake with remorse at having lost their unborn child.

"You have to go, Robert," she said softly, weakly. "That man has kidnapped our son. There's no telling what he might do."

Tears rolled down his cheeks and he nodded. He was torn. Stay with his wife—or pursue the priest and hope to save their son? He felt indecisive. But he knew what he must do. Candi would nurse his wife back to health. He was certain of that. He had no other choice but to go for his son. Hanzi needed him. He would not allow Brother Dinurés to harm their son!

Candi stepped into the bedchamber. "Vincente has the horses ready," she said as she approached the bed.

Robert nodded. He leaned in and kissed his wife on the forehead. "You get some rest. Listen to Candi, she's the boss!"

Julia tried to smile; her split lip made it difficult. "Don't make me laugh, it hurts too much." She swallowed. "Bring our son back Robert." She reached out and squeezed his hand tightly. "Do what you have to do."

Robert sighed wearily. He glanced at the blonde who was already tending to his wife with such compassion and tenderness. "Take care of her."

Candi nodded. "I will."

Vincente handed the reins to Robert with a somber look on his face. "De priest vas last seen heading to de vest. He ees most likely heading for *Freeport*, der are many vays for a man to geet lost der."

Robert mounted his horse and turned toward the gate. "Then we have to stop him before he gets there." Vincente quickly mounted his horse and followed along.

They didn't have time to talk about what their plans were. It was really pretty simple as far as Robert Kensington was concerned. They *had* to catch up with the priest as quickly as they could before they lost his trail completely. He shook his head trying to figure out *why* the man had taken his son; he hadn't a clue. It wasn't for ransom, they didn't have enough gold to warrant such an action. They had been nothing but kind to the priest and the injured girl since they had arrived. It just didn't make any sense! And, to top it all off, he was worried about Julia. He was thankful that she had regained consciousness. She had taken a pretty good spill down the stone stairs. Robert's jaw tightened. She had lost their baby girl that she was carrying. Brother Jon Dinurés was responsible for murdering his unborn daughter. Robert vowed to make the man pay.

The trail they were pursuing was easy enough to follow until they reached the hard-packed ground, where their prey's horse scarcely made a print across the smooth stone. They were forced to slow down. Robert glanced over at Vincente. "Are you certain that he'll head for *Freeport*?" He wished that they had taken the time to question Gwyneth about Dinurés, but they had been desperate to catch the priest.

Vincente arched a brow as he seemed to consider other options. "No, I truly tink dat he vill go to *Freeport*. Dat ees vhere he ees from, after all. He could easily lose us der. He has dose dat vill help 'im to escape." Vincente nodded. "He vill go to *Freeport*," he said with certainty.

"Why couldn't he head north?"

Vincente batted the air with a hand. "Nah. He vill go to *Freeport*, of dat I am certain. Eef he geets der den ve may never see him again. He could geet lost in a city dat beeg. He could geet on a boat and go anyvhere. Der ees not much to de north. I feel he ees travelling vith a purpose. Dat means he knows vhere he ees going." He nodded again. "*Freeport* ees our best chance."

Robert just hated the idea that the man might slip away from them by heading to another location other than what was expected of him. But what could he do? Vincente made sense, there was no disputing that. Still, it was like finding a needle in a haystack. They had to catch up with him before they lost him completely. If he made it into *Freeport* Hanzi might be lost forever. That would kill his wife.

They had been riding at a quickened pace for several hours, but still the priest eluded them; the trail he left behind continued to head northwest. "Ve need to stop and make camp. Eet ees geeting too dark to see de hoof preents," Vincente said hesitantly. He swallowed as Robert glared at him with an angry look in his eyes. He quickly added, "Ve can geet an early start in de morning, and de horses vill be fresh."

Robert sighed dejectedly; he hated the idea of stopping. If the priest continued on and they didn't, they would be allowing him to slip further away. But if they stayed in pursuit and *he* stopped, they might miss him in the darkness. Either way Robert felt like it was a no-win scenario. He nodded. "Alright, Vincente. We can stop. But I want to get back on the trail before dawn. We have to catch Dinurés," he reminded.

Vincente quickly agreed. "Ve vill. I promise."

Robert could only hope that Hanzi wasn't making things easy on the priest. That might be their *only* hope.

It was an hour or so before dawn. Robert was dreading getting back on the horse, but he knew he had little choice in the matter if they wanted to catch Dinurés. He was moving about stiffly, his entire body ached; but his hips were the worst. He watched Vincente with undeniable envy; the young man seemed unfazed by the rigorous pursuit of the day before. They had ridden hard, but the lad wasn't showing *any* discomfort.

With fresh horses and fresh eyes, the trail left by Dinurés seemed easier to follow. They quickly found where the priest had stopped and made camp. Both men were pleased to see that the coals of his campfire were still warm. He couldn't be that far ahead of them!

They remounted and headed off at a gallop following the trail that led them westward. Two hours later Vincente reached out a hand and grabbed the reins to Robert's horse. "Whoa!" he said bringing both mounts to a halt. At Robert's harsh glare he shook his head grimly. "Ve cannot go into de *Vasteland*! Der are bad tings in der. Ve should turn back, maybe geet more men."

Robert snatched the reins out of Vincente's hand angrily. "He has my son!" He scowled darkly as he wiped the sweat forming on his brow. They were so close; he just couldn't turn back now. "If you want to turn back, go right ahead. I'll pursue that bastard to the ends of the Earth if that's what it takes to get my boy back."

Vincente sighed heavily. He couldn't allow Robert to continue without him. It was far too dangerous to allow the man to go on alone. Candi would never forgive him if something were to happen to her best friend's father. He shook his head. "I vill go vith you, but der are *very* bad tings out der." He shivered as a sense of dread swept through him; leaving a cold, empty feeling in the pit of his stomach. He had heard stories about the Vortagg Desert Runners, and despite having made friends with Kestra and Captain Krugg from the Band of Steel; he knew that there were orcs out there that were not friendly toward humans. They would be lucky if they didn't encounter either of these.

The priest that had taken Robert's infant son had not bothered to try and hide the trail he left behind; hoof prints of his mount were clearly evident in the sand. It made Vincente question whether or not it was intentional. Could it be that the priest *wanted* them to follow him into the *Wasteland*? Was he perhaps leading them into some sort of trap? It was certainly plausible. Vincente shook his head. Candi would tell him it was in his nature to be suspicious. Perhaps it was. The Romani were not well liked and were often shunned by society in general, but their distrust of others had been hard earned.

Robert's horse suddenly rose up on its hind legs and kicked at the air with its front hooves as it snorted in fear. It had come dangerously close to stepping on a rattlesnake. The snake coiled itself up and shook its tail fiercely in warning. The horse continued to rear up and stomp wildly, causing Robert to lose his grip on the reins. He fell at an awkward angle and Vincente could hear the snap of his leg as it twisted beneath him on the red rocks at the desert's edge. His horse bolted off across the dry terrain; the snake seemed to be attached to its lower right leg, at first Vincente feared Robert had fallen on the reptile, which would have compounded his injuries even further.

Vincente quickly dismounted and knelt beside Robert. "Are you okay?"

Robert Kensington winced in pain. He was reaching for his left leg. "I think I may have broken my leg." He hissed angrily. "Damnit! Of all the things that could go wrong!"

Vincente eyed Robert's left calf and swallowed the lump of fear that lodged in his throat. The cloth was already coated in blood and something, perhaps a bone, jutted outward, causing the pant leg to bulge. He took out his knife. "I need to see 'ow badly eet ees."

Robert nodded knowingly. His forehead was coated in sweat. "I've a feeling that it's pretty bad." He chuckled humorlessly. "It already hurts like Hell."

Vincente grasped the hem of the pant leg in his left hand and lifted it slightly as he poked the tip of the knife into the opening. "Eet ees going to hurt a lot more."

Robert howled in pain as Vincente cut the fabric and then tore it up past the knee, exposing the bone. The tibia was broken and the jagged edges had ripped his skin open. Vincente gasped. He hadn't expected it to be *this* bad.

Robert was sweating profusely. He felt incredibly weak and he was sure he was going to be ill, but he managed to swallow back the bile rising in his throat. He looked at the young man and gave him a wobbly smile. "You're gonna have to bandage it for me."

Vincente's eyes grew wide. "Vhat?" He shook his head rapidly. "I cannot do dis! Ve need to go back. Geet you some real help! I cannot do dis!" he repeated.

Robert shook his head and chuckled. "There's no time. It *has* to be you."

Vincente swallowed. "But I do not know vhat to do." He waved his hands at the wound, palms up. "I do not even 'ave any bandages." Vincente wished that Candi was here, she would know *exactly* what to do!

Robert closed his eyes at the pain coursing through his leg. He nodded. "Use the sleeve of my shirt. Wrap it around the wound as tightly as you can." He took a deep breath; his head was spinning. He felt like he was going to pass out—or get sick; he wasn't really sure. "But before you cover it with the bandage you are going to have to push the bone back in."

Vincente went pale. For a minute Robert thought the boy would faint on him, but to his credit, he simply nodded his understanding. Robert smiled. "You can do this."

Vincente used his knife to rip a small hole in the seam of his own shirt, just at the shoulder. His shirt was cleaner than Robert's after the spill he took from his horse. Satisfied with the rip, he stuck two fingers in the tear and pulled; the fabric tore rather easily. He swallowed as his hands hovered over the wound in Robert's leg. He wiped the sweat from his brow, took a deep breath and then blew it out in a huff. He nodded. "Okay. I am ready to do dis."

Robert took Vincente's knife and bit down on the wooden shaft. He nodded. He was as prepared as he could be.

Vincente pressed his left hand onto the jagged bone protruding from Robert's leg. The pain was excruciating and Robert screamed as he bit down upon the hilt of the knife; he was covered in sweat. Tears of compassion fell from the young Romani's eyes as he fought to get the bandage secured over the wound; but Robert's thrashing wasn't making it easy.

Finally, mercifully, Robert lost consciousness, making Vincente's task much more manageable. He wished he had some wood to make a splint to better support the leg, but the surrounding area was completely barren.

Vincente clutched his sword in one hand and his knife in the other. The snarls that set him on edge seemed to be coming from *every* direction, all at once. He had no doubt that they were in *serious* trouble. The Vortagg were pack hunters and it sounded like they now had them completely surrounded. He only wished that Robert were awake so that he could help with their defense, but he hadn't regained consciousness yet. He knew the guttural sounds could only belong to the Vortagg. They were carnivores that preferred to eat their prey while they still struggled. His thoughts turned to his older brother, Carlito had been killed by the Desert Runners; it seemed he was about to meet the same fate.

Carlito had once been a good man. However, he became obsessed with power, and he began to force his will upon others, to bully them. He and his cohorts used their strength to intimidate the elder Romani and force them to their way of thinking. He had managed to turn everyone against Valoria when she would no longer follow him. He was willing to let her die simply because she refused to see things his way, to blindly follow along. In the end, he fell prey to the Vortagg and Valoria survived. He suspected that Valoria had somehow doomed his brother, but he had no real proof. In the end it didn't really matter to him; Carlito had chosen his own path, and it was a dark one.

His thoughts turned to Candi. She was simply amazing! He didn't know what his life would be like without her in it. She was beautiful and exciting, so unlike other girls that he knew. He was fortunate that she had decided to remain on this side of the *Portal*! A lone tear fell from his eyes as he thought of her. He had promised to return to her, but that seemed unlikely with the Vortagg closing ranks around them. The thought that he may never see her again stirred a fire deep within him. He vowed to fight as hard as he possibly could to survive against his enemies. Candi gave him something worth living for.

Robert awoke with a start. He was still in obvious pain. Vincente's throat felt incredibly dry. "Good. You are avake. Ready your sword, you are going to need eet!" He swallowed his fear as the gravelly snarls of the Vortagg descended upon their makeshift camp.

The Vortagg Desert Runners leapt from the red rock toward Robert Kensington who had somehow managed to sit up and raise a sword. The Vortagg slapped the hand that held the sword, causing the weapon to fly harmlessly through the air. His body slammed into Robert, knocking him back onto the ground. Robert howled as his injured leg banged upon the hardened sand beneath him. He screamed again in shock and sudden agony as the Vortagg sunk his tusks into his forearm and jerked his head viciously from side to side, ripping away a chunk of flesh and muscle.

Robert's eyes went wide as blood spurted from the gaping wound. He scrambled backwards as best he could despite his wounds, trying to put as much distance between the creature and himself as he possibly could. Disastrously, he was moving further away from his sword. He desperately needed a weapon. He saw his assailant swallow, saw the lump slide down his throat, and it sickened him. He knew that the Vortagg had just *eaten* a part of him. He was horrified.

Enraged, Robert frantically tried to rise but his leg wouldn't support him. Mortifed he eyed the Vortagg and then glanced over at his sword lying in the sand three feet from the fire pit. Flames of recognition reflected in the creature's eyes.

They both lunged for the blade.

Miraculously Robert managed to get there first, but before he could bring the sword to bear, the Vortagg was on him. Robert fumbled with the blade, weakened by the bite he'd already received and the wound on his lower leg. His enemy was too close for the longsword to do him much good anyway.

The Vortagg Desert Runner gripped his other arm with both hands and bit down hard. Robert screamed as the intense pain shot through the extremity. His arm numbed and he lost his grip on the sword; it fell harmlessly to the ground beside him, the flat of the blade slapping his injured leg, bringing a new wave of excruciating pain.

Furious now, the adrenalin pumping, Robert managed to bring his arm up, and the Vortagg with it. He could see the weathered flesh of his enemy's neck as he continued to chew on his forearm. Robert's eyes grew wide and his face went ashen. One thought floated through his mind: *'My God! I'm going to* be *eaten alive!'* He knew he didn't have any other option. Tears streaming down from his eyes, he opened his mouth wide and tore into the Vortagg's exposed skin; warm blood washed over his chin as he bit into the artery, ripping out a huge chunk of the Vortagg's leathery skin...

Vincente had his hands full. Two Vortagg were trying their best to flank him. He continued to fight them off with wild swings of his sword and quick jabs with his knife. He managed to cut both of them, but neither one was injured enough to give up the fight. He could see Robert doing his best to fight with a Vortagg on the other side of the campfire. When he saw his friend bite the neck of his adversary, he was shocked and he paused momentarily; it almost cost him dearly. He recovered in time to fend off his enemy's attack, but he lost his knife in the process.

A Vortagg sprang from the shadows at the edge of the encampment and landed on Robert's back as he once again managed to sit up. He sank his tusks into Robert's right shoulder. Another Desert Runner pounced on Robert's knees and forced him to cry out as the creature savagely ripped at his thigh. Two more quickly emerged from the darkness and joined the pile, opening Robert's stomach. Robert thrashed, screaming. He desperately tried to fend his assailants off, but it was hopeless.

Just as Vincente was sure he was about to suffer the same fate of his friend, salvation came. A small warband of orcs joined the fight, dropping two Vortagg with savage swings of battle-axes and broadswords. Two of the Vortagg that were feasting on Robert were shot with arrows, the rest scrambled to escape into the night.

Exhausted, Vincente dropped to his knees as he saw what had become of his friend. The Vortagg had been voracious, very little was left of Robert's abdomen. Blood and bits of shredded skin, muscle and guts were soaking the ground around his body. The look frozen on his face told of the agony he had suffered.

Kestra Àzul helped Vincente to his feet and looked him over with a keen eye. "You are not seriously hurt?" she asked, sounding doubtful; he was covered in blood that was evidently not his own.

Vincente shrugged. "Only a few scratches." He glanced down at Robert and shook his head sadly. "He deserved better dan dis."

Kestra nodded. She motioned for two of her warband to deal with Robert's corpse. "We'll see that he has a proper burial." She studied the encampment. "There were just the two of you?" When she saw Bekka's father she had feared that her friend was here as well, and not seeing her would mean that she was probably already dead somewhere in the desert.

Vincente nodded. "Ve vere pursuing de priest dat stole Robert's eenfant son."

"So where is Bekka?" the orc prodded.

"She vent to *Freeport* to learn more about Sinnestra. Lady Rosa believes dat de demoness vill attack soon."

Kestra stowed her battle-axe and nodded. "Then the Band of Steel will see you safely back to *Kensington Castle*."

Vincente shook his head. "I must keep searching for Hanzi. I cannot go back vithout 'im." He glanced to where Robert had died; the orc had already removed his body, but he could still see the red-stained sand and bits and pieces of his friend's innards scattered upon the ground. "Especially now dat Robert ees gone."

Kestra placed a hand on his arm. "If the priest that kidnapped Bekka's brother went into the *Wastelands* alone, they are probably already dead. The Vortagg Desert Runners have been marauding throughout this area."

Vincente's shoulders slumped as he scowled. "I knew eet vas a mistake to follow dem into de *Vasteland* especially vith just de two of us and now Robert ees dead." He shook his head and slapped his thighs. "I vas such de fool!"

She put a hand to his shoulder and gave him a firm shake. "I am sorry that we delayed our pursuit of this party of Vortagg. Had we kept up with them we might have arrived in time to save him."

Chapter 15
The Red Hills

Bekka bolted up out of her bedroll with her eyes wide and fearful, her hand instinctively drawing her sword from the scabbard beside her. She could feel the cold sweat of fear dampening her hairline. She had heard her father screaming in agonizing pain mixed with the guttural sounds of snarling animals. No, *not* animals. *Vortagg!* She remembered how they sounded when she had been held prisoner by a tribe of the desert carnivores alongside Kestra Àzul several months ago. Their animalistic language had unnerved her; she was not likely to forget it any time soon.

But what did it mean?

Valoria entered the encampment and eyed her thoughtfully. "What is it? Did you hear something?" She hadn't heard anything herself, and doubted that Bekka had, but *something* had obviously startled her.

Bekka shook her head. "It was a dream." Frowning, she ran a hand through her hair as she knelt and picked up the discarded scabbard. She sheathed her sword and strapped the scabbard to her belt.

"I thought it might be," Valoria said as she stowed her weapon. "Do you want to talk about it?" She could see that her friend was troubled, agitated.

Bekka gave Valoria a troubled look. "It doesn't make any sense. I was dreaming that Dad was surrounded by Vortagg; kinda like we had been before we encountered the Drow." She frowned darkly. "They were eating him alive!" She couldn't help but shiver at the thought. It was a terrible way to die, even in a nightmare. Bekka felt a sickening emptiness in her stomach; she was genuinely afraid for her father.

Valoria nodded thoughtfully. "If Rosa were here she would say that it was a vision. That there was some meaning behind it; something to be learned."

Bekka gave her a dark look. "That really isn't helping, Val."

Valoria put a hand to her shoulder and gave it a comforting squeeze. "I know it isn't and I'm sorry. Rosa was just so good with her advice. Her cryptic little sayings always brought an odd sense of comfort, somehow. It was just a nightmare, I'm sure. Your parents are nowhere near any Vortagg. They're both safe and sound back at *Kensington Castle*. No harm will come to them there; certainly not from the Vortagg."

Bekka forced a smile to her lips. Valoria was probably right. Yet, it hadn't *felt* like just a bad dream. It felt more like one of her visions. She had that feeling of unease that tugged at her from somewhere deep inside. It was different than the unsettled feeling of a nightmare, but she couldn't describe exactly how it was. She could hear Rosa's voice in her mind telling her to trust her visions, that they wouldn't steer her wrong.

Did that mean that her father was dead? And what of her mother?

Frowning, Bekka stared off toward the east, toward where she knew *Kensington Castle* to be. A wave of dread swept through her, leaving her unsettled and cold.

Bekka could only hope that it was just a premonition and not a vision of something that had already happened. But, either way, there was very little she could do about it at the moment. If they didn't get to *Freeport* and learn more about Sinnestra, they could all be in very grave danger.

They had spent the previous night in relative comfort at Schiff's Crossing and Marren Schiff had made sure that their bellies were full. He wanted to do more for them, but until his sons returned from Freeport, his supplies were limited. Bekka was amazed at how good the food was, and she had almost forgotten how good it was to sleep in a bed. She had been reluctant to leave, they both had. After a day's ride they made camp on the western edge of the *Red Hills*. With an early start, they could make *Freeport* by nightfall. They ate from the provisions that Marren Schiff had supplied and their conversation soon turned to the coastal city. Increasingly restless and eager to be off, they decided to break camp and ride through the night.

Chapter 16
Passion Under the Stars

Trevor and Lithania made their way out of the *Vile Forest* heading in a southeasterly direction. They had to move quickly, both fire and smoke continued to nip at their heels. Forced to run, they emerged from the burning wood. Finally in fresh air, they sucked in huge gulps, finding it soothing to their damaged throats. They collapsed to their knees, coughing and wanting to puke as tears flowed from their eyes, cutting paths down their soot-covered cheeks.

Trevor looked Lithania over for the hundredth time, still not certain whether she was injured or not. "Are you okay? Are you sure you aren't hurt?"

She smiled at him as she stretched out on her back and gazed up at the stars. Other than the smoke from the fires, the night was unbelievably clear. Stars sparkled brightly in the heavens. "I am surprisingly uninjured," she said softly.

He shook his head lightly. "What were you thinking? You shouldn't have gone in there alone. That was just plain crazy."

She chuckled softly. "And stupid."

He laughed. "Yeah, and *incredibly* stupid!"

She gave him a long, hard look. "Yet you came after me anyway."

Trevor dropped down beside her and stared up at the night sky. A smile crept to his face; it felt *exhilarating* breathing fresh air, to have Lithania by his side, pressed up against him. He rolled onto his side, propping his head up with his hand. He touched her chin and turned her face toward him. He leaned in and kissed her tenderly. "I would follow you anywhere," he said softly.

Lithania placed a hand upon his chest, pushing him away. She rolled to her side, facing him, her eyes searching his. "What are you saying, Trevor?" Hope seemed to sparkle in her brown, almond-shaped eyes.

He caressed her cheek. "Don't you know?"

She swallowed. "Do not tease me Trevor," she warned.

Trevor chuckled. "I'm not, Litha. I missed you. I came to *Serendil Brenatis* to tell you how I feel. I couldn't stop thinking about you ever since you left." He kissed her parted lips.

She pulled back, hesitatingly, causing him to frown. "What about Bekka?" she asked, sounding guarded.

"Bekka and I are just friends. I love *you* Litha."

She wanted to believe him. Desperately. Tears ran down her cheeks as her lips found his. She lay back upon the grass and pulled him to her. They continued to kiss under a blanket of stars until the smoke from the *Vile Forest* began to find its way to them and she began to cough. "I am *so* sick of the smell of burning timber," she said as she rose to her feet. "We *both* smell like charred wood."

Trevor grinned. "Is that a bad thing?" He had always liked the smell of wood smoke, especially when barbequing a nice thick steak.

She crinkled her nose. "Follow me." She started off through the wooded area north of the *Eagle Peaks*.

Trevor quickly got to his feet and trotted to catch up with her. He took her hand in his. "Where are we going?"

Her eyes sparkled with delight. "Patience," she squeezed his hand, "you shall soon see." The path they took was winding among the trees, steadily rising upward through the forest.

Before he knew it they were walking along a small river. He could hear the sound of a waterfall somewhere up ahead. He grinned. "Can't you just tell me where you're taking me?"

"I cannot," she said with a laugh.

"Why so secretive?" he asked, grinning.

Rounding a large outcropping of rock, they broke through the trees and found themselves at a secluded pond. A cascade of water fell from the rocks, higher up, at the far end of the hidden lagoon. The stars could be seen overhead, through the treetops, and so could the silvery crescent of the moon. Trevor was stunned at the beauty of the place. "Wow, this is absolutely stunning!"

"See?" Lithania said as she began stripping off her soot-covered clothes. "I told you it would be worth the wait." Her eyes sparkled with starlight; her lips curved into a pleasing smile.

He watched, stunned, as she peeled out of her leather armor. He was certain his mouth was gaping open. He hadn't expected this. She was slender and graceful but at the same time she was well muscled and absolutely beautiful. He found it difficult to breathe as he watched her.

She chuckled as she stepped in front of him and began to unfasten his belt. She leaned in and nipped his bottom lip with her teeth. She nudged his nose with her own. Her breathing was quickened with desire and hunger. "Do not just stand there, join me!" She turned and dove into the water, scarcely making a splash.

Trevor just stood there, dumbfounded, watching her swim toward the far end of the pond, toward the waterfall. His mouth was incredibly dry, his heart pounded inside his chest, threatening the serenity of the surrounding forest. His fingers fumbled along as he fought with the rest of his clothes. Lithania had already climbed from the pool and was sitting on a flat rock near the cascading water, watching him, as the moonlight glistened over her wet body. Finally, he tossed the last of his clothes to the ground near hers. He was keenly aware of his own arousal as he dove into the water and swam toward the naked elf maiden.

Behind the cascading waterfall was a small grotto. There, after cleansing one another in the plunging water from above, they made love. It was the first time for both of them, and their craving for one another drove them into a frenzy. Afterwards, they collapsed in each other's arms and slept. They awoke just before dawn and were unwilling to move from each other's embrace. Their reluctance led to tender kisses, soft gentle caresses, and more...

Trevor hated to break the peaceful silence that enveloped them, but he felt compelled to say something. He caressed the length of her body, feeling her quiver beneath his fingertips. "We need to go to *Kensington Castle*. Lady Rosa believes that Sinnestra will strike soon. Bekka, Valoria and Rosa have gone to *Freeport* to learn all that they can. In the meantime, Bekka would like you at the castle to wield the *Blade of the Spider's Kiss* in the event that Sinnestra attacks before they return."

Lithania stirred beside him, sitting up. She placed a hand upon his stomach, enjoying the way his hard abs felt against her palm. "Then we should go there as quickly as we can."

Trevor smiled. "We've got time, I think. Besides, I figured we'd go back to *Serendil Brenatis* first, gather your things. I'm sure that Aloe and Elan would like to know that you are all right. They'd want to see you before we go."

Lithania's eyes grew wide for a moment and she shook her head. "No. There is no time to spare. Something tells me that we need to go to *Kensington Castle* right away. Once we have helped your friends deal with Sinnestra we can maybe return to *Serendil Brenatis*."

"Maybe?" he asked softly.

She stared into his eyes. "We can go wherever you would like, it does not have to be there."

He gave her a questioning look. "Are you certain?"

She nodded. "We need to be there if Sinnestra comes, especially since Bekka is not present. She is counting on us to protect her friends and her home. After that, we can decide what is best for us." She pressed her lips to his. "But know this, I will not give you up again."

Trevor nodded. "Well, if you are sure you don't want to see Aloena first, I guess we could head south."

Lithania's eyes narrowed. "Aloe and I have already said our goodbyes. I see no need in doing it again. It would only complicate matters unnecessarily."

He frowned. *Had something happened between the two elven women?* Aloe had seemed worried about Lithania when he had seen her in *Serendil Brenatis*. She had told him that Lithania had left during the night while they were all sleeping. Litha's manner seemed a bit odd. He shook his head doubting he would ever understand women.

Chapter 17
The Twisted Oak

Bekka was tired of being in the saddle. She gave her horse a dark look, and then turned an unpleasant glare to Valoria. "My butt hurts!" she said with a childish pout as they plodded, side by side, along the road that cut through the forest.

Valoria smiled. "And here I was, sure you were going to ask me the question you've asked for the past two and a half hours: *'Are we there yet?'* I must say that I am happy to note that your physical discomfort is a priority." She smirked. "And not to mention the fact that your vernacular is growing."

Bekka grimaced. "You are so funny lately." She had the sneaking suspicion that she was developing a blister in an area of her anatomy that the sun didn't often see. If she were forced to ride a horse much longer, she had no doubt that she wouldn't be able to sit for several days, weeks maybe. She could tell that her mood was becoming a bit surly and even she didn't like it. What she needed was a good meal, something to quench her thirst other than water, and a nice hot, *relaxing* bath followed by a restful night on a bed with a soft, fluffy mattress free of bugs. Her nose crinkled. *Yes! Definitely a bath!* She sighed after a moment of reflection. She could add Secret deodorant to the growing list of things she missed from the other side of the *Portal.*

"There is an inn up ahead," Valoria said indicating the bend in the road with a nod of her head. "We'll stop there and spend the night. It is a good place to learn about the goings on in *Freeport.* They make a pretty good venison stew if I recall correctly, and the beds are mostly flea and tick free."

Bekka shivered. All she *ever* had to worry about on the other side were bedbugs. She absolutely *hated* ticks and fleas, especially the ticks! But at least you didn't feel the bedbugs crawling on you and biting you, at least she hadn't, anyway.

The *Twisted Oak* was nestled in a stand of tall, red oaks, one of which was oddly contorted midway up the trunk, almost as if a giant had tried to wring out any moisture the tree contained. By the looks of this tree alone, it was easy to see how the inn got its name.

They rode to the barn and stabled their horses together in a stall. After seeing their mounts fed and watered, they prepared to go to the inn. Valoria took Bekka's arm and squeezed gently. "This place can be inhabited by troublemakers of all kinds. It can get quite rough, as it is outside the protective sanction of De La'Corte. Stay close to me," she cautioned.

Bekka nodded, she had no intention of straying too far from her friend. Valoria was her protector, she always felt safer when she was nearby. "I'm surprised you remember so much about this place. Weren't you a little girl the last time you were here?"

Valoria smiled. "I wasn't *that* little."

"I thought you were like twelve or something."

"I was seventeen summers old the last time I was here. But I had already been on my own for a longtime by then."

Bekka nodded. She knew bits and pieces about Valoria's past, probably more than anybody other than Rosa. But there was still a lot that she was unaware of. Valoria had led a fascinating life. One of these days she'd have to ask her about it.

The closer they had gotten to *Freeport*, the darker the sky had become; the scent of rain was heavy in the air. Thick, blackened clouds blotted out the stars and the moon. Occasional streaks of lightning had split the darkness, but only momentarily. Thunder rumbled overhead. The storm was upon them. As they left the relative comfort of the stable, the rain assaulted them in heavy sheets that stung their exposed skin. They were completely soaked by the time they reached the inn.

The place was packed. It seemed *everyone* had taken refuge from the storm within the warm, dry confines of the *Twisted Oak Inn*. Due to the inclement weather, no one appeared in a hurry to leave. They were greeted by harsh glares, and someone muttered for them to close the door. Bekka thought she'd heard a gruff voice ask if they'd been born in a barn. That was something she'd heard so often on the other side of the *Portal*. It made her briefly wonder just how old that phrase was.

Menacing glares caused her to blush, and Bekka quickly pulled the door closed and then turned to face the crowd. They seemed to have lost interest in the pair now that the rain was shut out. She gave a nervous glance at Valoria. "I have a bad feeling about this place," she said in a whisper.

Valoria smiled as she looked around the room. Seeing what she wanted, she took hold of Bekka's hand and pushed her way through the standing crowd. "Stick close!"

Twisting and turning through the throng of people, Bekka lost her hold on Valoria's hand. She tried to rejoin her friend but quickly found herself closed off by a massive body. She looked up and her eyes went wide and her mouth gaped open as she inhaled sharply. Dralgor, the orc that had attacked them two nights before, was blocking her path. He had an evil grin on his face.

Dralgor chuckled. "Well look what we got here! The little runt human!"

Bekka dropped her hand to the hilt of her longsword; it made her feel better even though she knew she didn't have the room to draw it in her own defense. "You must have me confused with somebody else," she said with a raise of her chin. "We've never met."

A hand closed on hers from behind. "Is that right?" a voice thick with the hint of ale whispered in her ear. "Dralgor an' I never forget a pretty face. Ain't that right, Dralgor?"

The huge orc nodded at his human friend. He had a crooked grin. "That's right, Reaghar." He grabbed Bekka by the shoulders and lifted her off her feet. "I think we ought to take her upstairs and get *reacquainted*." Slobber ran down his chin.

Bekka kicked with all her might, striking Dralgor in the crotch with both feet. His grip loosened as his eyes rolled up into his skull and his face became scrunched. Bekka fell backwards, off balance. Reaghar's quick reflexes were the only thing that prevented her from falling to the floor. Grabbing her firmly, he pulled her against him and chuckled. "Looks like I'll have you all to myself!" he clamped a grimy hand over her mouth and chuckled.

Bekka bit his fingers and he immediately let go. He pushed her away, shaking his hand. He went to draw his sword but there was no room in the crowded inn for such a weapon to be wielded with any proficiency.

The crowd moved, and he was pushed aside.

Bekka turned and hurriedly made her way through the packed bodies. She found Valoria standing at the bar. "Where have you been?" the warrior asked.

Bekka rolled her eyes. "I ran into some old friends."

"Oh?" Valoria asked, raising a brow. She sounded surprised.

Bekka shook her head. "It was the two guys from the other night." She gripped Val's arm tightly. "They're here!"

Valoria's eyes went wide. "Are you all right? Did they hurt you?" She glanced around the barroom but failed to see either of them. There was something occurring near the center of the huge room that resembled the makings of a brawl, which she fully intended to avoid.

Bekka nodded, beaming proudly. "I'm fine. I can handle myself."

Valoria gave her a smirk. "I am certain that you can."

Bekka accepted the tankard from the barkeep and sniffed it. Her eyes began to water. She gingerly pushed the pewter mug away with the tips of her fingers, wanting no part of the potent brew. "What *is* that stuff, anyway?"

Her companion chuckled. "I was a bit chilled from the soaking rain, I thought something to warm us up from the inside out might be nice." Valoria indicated the mug with an inclination of her head. "You should try it."

Bekka shrugged and slid the tankard toward her and hefted it to her lips. She took a hesitant sip and immediately coughed as the liquid burned its way down her throat. Even with the small taste she felt the fire burn inside her as the brew made its way to her stomach. "Whoa!" she said hoarsely.

Valoria grinned. "Dwarven Firewater," she said as though that should explain everything.

Bekka shook her head as she took another tentative sip. "Never heard of it." The fire in the pit of her stomach was definitely beginning to make her feel warm and toasty. She looked at the tankard in her hand and smiled. "This is really very good."

Valoria eased the tankard out of her hand; Bekka's eyes were developing a glassy sheen. "And you need to drink it slowly."

Bekka snatched the tankard back and quickly drained it, ignoring the red liquid as it coated her chin. She slammed the tankard down and then crossed her arms over her chest in defiance. "Party poop..." she swayed unsteadily, "...pooper!" She stared out at the crowd and blinked several times. It seemed that the patronage had doubled. She put a hand to her mouth. "Oh God, I think I'm gonna be sick!" She turned her head and puked on the man next to her.

That's when the trouble really began...

Chapter 18
Gwyneth

Candi dabbed the damp cloth upon Julia Kensington's forehead; her eyes filled with concern. Julia's skin was ashen and felt clammy to the touch. She was out of her element. She didn't know what to do. She wished Lady Rosa were here. She would know how to treat her. She saw movement out of the corner of her eye and turned. It was Gwyneth leaning against the doorway. "You should be in bed," Candi said with a hint of frustration.

"How is Lady Kensington?" Gwyneth asked softly, her own eyes filled with concern.

Candi started to reply but the words choked in her throat as tears sprang to her eyes. "It doesn't look good, I'm afraid." She swallowed. "You should be in bed," she repeated. Candi was feeling a bit frazzled. Her best friend's mother was in serious trouble, this girl that the priest had brought into their lives was suffering a severe infection that only seemed to be getting worse; Hanzi had been kidnapped by this same priest. *Why? Why was this all happening?* She had no clue how she was going to explain things to Bekka when they returned! She would be livid! And who could blame her?

Gwyneth stood beside the bed and reached out a hand to brush a wisp of hair off Julia's brow. "I am fine. But I am worried about Lady Kensington and her son. I cannot believe that Brother Dinurés would do such a thing! I feel *awful.*"

Candi felt a surge of sudden anger. "How well do you know this priest, anyway? He seems like a very bad man and you seem like such a sweet girl. How did you get involved with him in the first place?"

Gwyneth shook her head. "To be honest, I know very little about him or his Order. I was taken to them while unconscious. They did what they could for me, and only brought me here as a last resort. I honestly have no idea why he would take the infant boy. Perhaps it is for a ritual of some sort." She shrugged, wincing at the pain it caused. "He always seemed nice enough, but now I don't know."

Gwyneth wasn't making Candi feel any better. Dinurés was an *evil* man. Bekka was gonna be so pissed that she had let him take Han on her watch! She prayed that Vincente and Mr. K could get him back sooner rather than later. She frowned.

"Do you think you can help Lady Kensington on this side of the *Portal*?" Gwyneth asked.

What a strange question! Candi thought. She looked at the girl and cocked her head. "What do you mean?"

Gwyneth gave her a steady look. "Brother Dinurés said that he was fairly certain that your side of the *Portal* was far more advanced than we are. Perhaps she needs to be taken back to the other side, for treatment." She paused. "It would be a shame for her to suffer needlessly." She glanced down at the sleeping woman. "It would be horrible if she were to die when she could be so easily saved by crossing over."

Candi nodded silently. *It would.* Gwyneth was making a lot of sense. Hospitals handle falls and miscarriages all the time... "That's something to think about." She looked into the girl's eyes. "Perhaps we could take you along as well, cure your infection."

Gwyneth smiled shyly. "Oh, that is almost too much to hope for! I would be *forever* in your debt!" She grew quiet, her brows furrowing in concern. "I just don't know how long I can continue like this. I feel like I am rotting from the inside." Tears of sorrow fell from her eyes and rolled down her cheeks.

Candi looked at the girl with sympathy, her own eyes beginning to moisten. "I can't imagine how that must feel. But you must hang on to hope. I promise I'll do whatever I can to help you."

"Can you take me through the *Portal*?"

Candi shook her head. She wasn't even certain where the *Portal* even was; let alone how to operate it. When she had passed through from the other side the Gypsy fortuneteller from the carnival out on *Miller's Farm* had taken them to it. All they had to do was enter the strange, swirling mist. She couldn't be sure it would even work the same way. No one truly did. "I'm sorry," she said softly, squeezing Gwyneth's hand in an effort to comfort her, "but I can't do that."

Gwyneth's face tightened. "So, you are content to let this infection kill me then?" She shook her head, fighting back bitter tears. "I thought you said you would do all that you could to help me. It was just another lie." She pulled her hand from Candi's grasp and ran from the room.

Candi watched her go, speechless. She may not know where or even how the Portal worked, but she did take Health and Biology back at *Midvale High*. Perhaps she could put that to some use to help Gwyneth.

She thought for a moment, trying to recall what it was that Mr. Blythe had said in third period... something about growing mold on bread. She remembered him stating that it was best if you used homemade bread because most store-bought, or packaged bread, contained an antifungal agent that could inadvertently sabotage your efforts. That wouldn't be a problem here; the only bread available was freshly made. Once she had moldy bread, she would need to identify the penicillium, of which there were several types and not all of them produced penicillin. That was the trick. The real trouble was that she just couldn't recall what the correct penicillium colony looked like as opposed to aspergillus, which she knew was very similar. Candi sighed in frustration. All she could really remember form Health and Biology class was that it came down to color and the shape. One was fuzzier and straight while the other appeared branched like a fan. She just couldn't remember which the correct one was.

But there was certainly more to it than just that, she recalled. Once she had the correct one identified she would still have to extract the penicillin. Outside of a lab this could be extremely difficult. But once you had it, you could go ahead and make an antibiotic bandage with it, another taxing project. She let out her breath in a long sigh. It would all take time. Candi wasn't certain that Gwyneth had the time it would take, she certainly didn't have the patience!

Julia stirred, her eyes fluttered open. "Candi?" she spoke softly, frowning.

She started to rise but Candi put her hands upon her shoulders and gently forced her back down on the bed. "Easy, Mrs. K," Candi spoke in soothing tones. "You need to take it slow; you had a pretty bad tumble."

Julia blinked; her eyes filling with unshed tears. "The baby. I lost the baby."

Candi nodded as she wiped her own tears from her cheeks. "I'm so sorry! We did all that we could. I... I just didn't know enough. I'm sorry!"

Julia swallowed. "Robert?"

"He and Vinnie went after that prick, Brother Dinurés."

She nodded, seeming to relax. She closed her eyes as she swallowed. She took a deep breath. "Candi," she said softly. "I... don't trust Gwyneth."

Candi was shocked. "Why? She's not done anything wrong, she's an innocent. She can't be held accountable for the priest's actions."

Julia gave her a steady look. "We know nothing about her. She came here with Brother Dinurés..."

Candi couldn't believe what she was hearing. The girl had come to them unconscious, it wasn't as though she had had a choice in the matter. She was just a pawn in the priest's nefarious plans. She was sure of it. "But..."

Julia shook her head. "I don't want her anywhere near me."

Candi kept her silence. There was no sense in getting Mrs. Kensington worked up over such complete nonsense. If she didn't want Gwyneth near her, that was just fine. She would keep the two of them apart. Besides, the girl needed to stay in bed anyway. "Okay, Mrs. K. Whatever you say."

Chapter 19
Return to Kensington Castle

Overjoyed, Candi bounced on her feet and smiled as she stood on the ramparts of *Kensington Castle*. She could see two riders coming up the road from the forest beyond. She could easily recognize Vincente even from this distance, no one else she knew sat upon a horse quite the same way; always seeming to prefer to be afoot rather than on a mount. She thought he was adorable. She frowned after a moment. The second rider was not Robert Kensington; it appeared to be an Orc. She headed for the steps; this couldn't be good.

As she quickly descended the stone steps leading to the courtyard, her mind was racing through the possibilities. *Why was Bekka's dad not returning with Vinnie? Why was Vinnie in the company of an Orc? Was that Kestra Àzul riding alongside him? Why was she coming here?* Something was up, that much she was sure of! *Why else would Vinnie be returning without Mr. Kensington? And what of little Hanzi? Where was he?*

"Open the gates!" Candi demanded impatiently, wringing her hands.

Vincente slid from his horse and quickly embraced Candi, burying his face in her neck. The scent of her hair and the feel of her arms wrapping tightly around his shoulders brought him immense comfort. He had been dreading his return to *Kensington Castle* solely for the news he carried. Now, with Candi by his side, he felt emboldened.

He placed his hands on her shoulders and forced her to arm's length. "I 'ave some very bad news." He took a deep breath, his eyes searching hers. "Ve followed de priest into de *Vastelands*, I deed not vant to go in der, but Robert… he insisted. He fell from his horse and vas badly injured vith a broken leg. De bone vas exposed." He looked at the palm of his hands, remembering them covered with Robert Kensington's blood; his complexion started to pale. "I 'ad to feex 'im using de sleeve of my shirt for a bandage." He swallowed. "Den ve vere attacked by de Vortagg during de night. Robert vas keeled. Dey vere eating 'im. Der vas nothing I could do!" His shoulders began to heave with his grief. "Eef de Orcs 'ad not come, den I vould 'ave been keeled too!" He sobbed.

Candi's eyes immediately filled with tears as she hugged him close, feeling his body tremble with wracking sobs. Her mind was racing for something to say that would give him comfort, but she could think of nothing that would take away this profound pain. "Oh my God, poor Robert!" She squeezed him tightly, wanting to ease his sorrow. "Surely you know that there was nothing that you could have done to save him?" She looked at Kestra and mouthed a *'thank you'* to the Orc.

"Another rider is coming from the northeast; it looks like two on a horse!" came the call from the ramparts.

Candi slipped her hand into Vincente's and together they turned to face the gate, curious to see whom the riders were. She was genuinely surprised to see Lithania and Trevor astride Jester. She couldn't help but notice that Lithania had her arms wrapped around Trevor's waist which was understandable but it looked far more intimate than it should be. Candi wasn't sure how she felt about that.

Chapter 20
Sinnestra Strikes

Gwyneth stood over Julia watching her in peaceful slumber. She reached down and brushed a strand of hair from the sleeping woman's cheek with the tips of her fingers. The look in the girl's eyes was full of hate and loathing. "Julia..." she whispered. "You need to wake up now."

Julia Kensington stirred, her eyes fluttering open. She swallowed. "What?" She tried to focus, but it wasn't easy. "Gwyneth?" she said, uncertain. Panic started to rise within her. "Where's Candi?" she asked, searching around the room. "You shouldn't be here!"

The girl shook her head slowly, her eyes filled with scathing hatred. "No. I am not Gwyneth. I killed her days ago."

Julia pressed her head against the pillow in an attempt to get further away, but there was nowhere to go. "I... I don't understand... Please, Gwyneth, I need to see Candace. Please..."

Gwyneth seemed to shimmer in front of her, flickering from one form into another. And then Gwyneth was gone, replaced by the towering form of a demon. Julia gasped as Sinnestra loomed over her. Her eyes went wide with fear and she screamed but a pillow immediately muffled her, smothering out her futile protests. She grappled with her assailant but she was just too weak.

She couldn't breathe!

Julia struggled to get free but the demoness was stronger than she was. Julia could feel her strength deserting her. She flailed with her arms trying to force Sinnestra away. She clawed with her hands, but she was unable to get free...

Vincente and Candi walked down the long corridor hand in hand. Together they were going to give Julia Kensington the bad news about her husband. Upon learning of Julia's fall and miscarriage, Vincente felt that he could not give her the bad news alone. Candi gave Vincente's hand a loving squeeze. "I want to check in on Gwyneth first. I'll be along in a few minutes."

He nodded. "I vill vait to tell Mrs. Kensington until you are vith me."

Candi smiled. "I won't be but a minute."

He continued slowly down the corridor, taking his time. He really didn't want to see Julia alone. The news he had was heartbreaking and he wasn't sure he could tell her on his own, he'd never get through it without falling apart. He needed Candi's strength. She would know what to say. He stopped outside the door and looked back down the hallway, waiting patiently for Candi to join him.

Vincente heard something that didn't sound quite right coming from beyond the door. Frowning, he put his ear to the door and listened intently, one hand went automatically to the doorknob. *It sounded like a struggle was taking place!* He knocked on the door. "Mrs. Kensington? Are you all right? Ees der someting dat you need?"

He looked back down the corridor and saw the worried expression on Candi's face. "I can't find Gwyneth anywhere! She's not in her room," she said as she left the girl's bedchamber.

Candi could tell that something was bothering Vincente by the worried expression on his face. She felt the hairs on her arms and the back of her neck stand on end as a chill swept quickly from head to toe. She began to run toward him, her heart pounding in her chest. She stretched a hand out in the air toward him. She wanted to tell him to wait for her, but no words would come.

Vincente turned back to the door, frowning. The sounds of thrashing were getting louder, more intense; and then... nothing. Suddenly it was too quiet. He opened the door and froze momentarily. He saw Sinnestra leaning over the bed, holding a thick pillow over Mrs. Kensington's face. Julia's hand flopped outward, knocking the bowl of water from the bedside table; it crashed to the floor, clattering loudly upon the flagstones. The noise snapped him out of his stupor. He focused his attention on Sinnestra; he didn't like what he saw.

Vincente sprang into action, reaching for the sword that wasn't there, as he raced to the bedside. Sinnestra turned, her eyes blazing with fury. She violently flung out her left hand striking Vincente's chest with a loud *THWOP!* Her fingertips pierced his flesh, splintered his ribs, and found his heart in an instant. His eyes went wide as he lost all feeling in his body. His arms fell useless against his sides. His mouth dropped open as he was effortlessly lifted off the floor.

"Oh God no!" Candi screamed as panic suddenly seized her. Julia had expressed concerns about Gwyneth and *she should have listened!* She flew down the corridor. Vincente had seen something terribly wrong and had raced into the room. *What was going on? Was something happening to Julia? Was it Gwyneth?*

Breathlessly Candi stopped in the doorway not believing what she was seeing. *How was this possible?*

Stunned, she fell against the door and slid to the floor as Sinnestra removed her hand from Vincente's chest and his corpse crumpled to the blood-covered flagstones. The demoness glared at her and squeezed her fist tightly, crushing what remained of the heart she had stolen; it splattered in several directions around the chamber with sickening sounds.

Candi wailed as she saw Sinnestra vanish before her eyes in a blinding flash of light.

Chapter 21
Freeport

Bekka awoke startled, unsure of where she was, or how she had gotten there, her head pounding. She sat up, throwing her legs over the side of the bed and felt the room sway with her. She tried to stand, found she could not, and immediately plopped back down on the mattress causing the bed frame to scream in protest, the thin mattress barely even bouncing. Her head felt unusually heavy, and the sunlight filtering into the room from the lone window guarded by a flimsy curtain made it difficult for her to keep her eyes opened beyond narrowed slits. *'What the Hell was I drinking?'* she asked herself.

And then she remembered. Valoria had called it *Dwarven Firewater.* Just thinking about it she felt the burn in her stomach returning. She rubbed her tummy gingerly; wishing she had an antacid tablet, anything to relieve her unsettled belly. The drink was very good, which is why she had drunk so much of it in the first place. But it definitely packed a punch!

She had a bad aftertaste on her tongue and her mouth felt

dry; she desperately wanted some cold water. Her stomach grumbled loudly, not wanting to be left out. She couldn't recall when she had last eaten. She let out a long sigh. She stood and faced the door. When she was certain that she wouldn't fall, she took a timid step forward, followed by another. Her legs felt wobbly at first, but balance prevailed. She wondered where Valoria was; the other bed was empty, but it showed evidence that it had been slept in.

Bekka stepped out into the dimly lit hallway and looked where the corridor continued for a good distance. Two doors could be seen in the deepening shadows at that end of the upper floor, perhaps other guest rooms. There was another door directly across from her. She could hear loud snoring coming from within this room. Two more rooms were located to her right, as well as the stairs descending to the main floor.

The barkeep gave her a steady look as she stepped into the bar area. "So." He said with a smirk, "I see ye 'ave recovered somewhat. T'were those tha' thought ye might sleep the day away."

Bekka nodded somberly. She blushed as she watched the big man wipe the countertop with a clean white cloth. A sudden recollection of her climbing onto the bar and doing a little dance flittered through her mind. *Had she truly done a drunken song and dance?* She swallowed. "I apologize if I caused you any trouble. I hope that I didn't damage anything. If I did, I'd be happy to pay for it."

He chuckled softly. "Ye dinna' do anymore than everyone else. Truth be told, your lil' number t'was good fer business. I reckon I could give ye a lil' somethin' ta break yer fasting, on the house."

Her stomach grumbled. She nodded. "That would be nice. Thank you."

He motioned to a table in the corner. "Take a seat an' I'll bring it right out."

"Have you seen my friend?" Bekka asked.

He grinned. "Which one might tha' be? Ye seemed ta 'ave quite a few last night."

Bekka felt the color returning to her cheeks. "The woman I came in with."

"The one-eyed warrior? Aye, she left early this mornin'. Said she'd be back probably before ye came down. She'll return fer ye, dinna worry."

Bekka sat at the table with her head held in her hands. She closed her eyes and sighed wearily. She was glad that her parents hadn't come along. They would have been mortified by her behavior the night before. She didn't remember everything that she had done, but frightening bits and pieces were starting to return to her. She shook her head, vowing to never again drink so much.

The barkeep placed a pewter platter in front of her. Scrambled eggs and bits of sausage steamed from the plate. A chunk of bread was on the edge. It all smelled so good to her. Her mouth was beginning to water. She smiled meekly at him. "Tarek, can I get a cup of water, please."

He smiled. "So, ye remember my name, then." He sounded surprised.

She felt the color deepen on her skin. "I'm starting to remember a lot more; most of which I'd just as soon forget."

He chuckled softly. "I'll bring ye a mug o' water." He hesitated. "Unless o' course ye'd like a bit o' hair o' the dog?" He winked at the horrified look on her face and chuckled again. "Water it is, then."

Bekka continued to sit at the table long after Tarek had taken the breakfast dishes away. She wondered what was taking Valoria so long; she should have been back by now. *Unless something had happened to her!* She felt the panic sweep through her in a single wave that left the hair on the back of her neck and arms standing on end. *What if something had gone horribly wrong?* What would she do then? She seriously doubted that she could face Sinnestra without Valoria by her side.

She went up to the bar and impatiently drummed her fingertips on the wooden counter, waiting for Tarek to come out of the kitchen. *What was keeping him?* She glanced at her wrist, still unaccustomed to not wearing a wristwatch. She couldn't take it anymore. She walked around the end of the bar and pushed the door to the kitchen open. Only *then* did she hear the soft moans coming from within.

Her eyes widened. She placed a hand over her mouth and

exclaimed, "Oh my God!" She had not expected to walk in on Tarek and his buxom redheaded waitress having sex on the kitchen counter. Mary? No, Mari, she recalled. She hurriedly backed out of the room her eyes squeezed tightly shut. She struck her funny bone on the doorjamb. "Ouch!" she gasped loudly as she clutched at her elbow. It was almost as bad as walking in on her parents—but not quite.

By late afternoon Valoria still hadn't returned to the *Twisted Oak*. Any number of things could have held her up; she could have gone anywhere. But something told Bekka that her friend hadn't simply deserted her. That was way out of character for the warrior. But what could Bekka do? If she went off in search of Valoria, she might miss her, and then they might waste days looking for one another.

But she couldn't just sit around waiting for Valoria to return. It was best if she went on into *Freeport* and found the *Great Library Arcanum* and began to learn all she possibly could about Sinnestra. The demoness certainly wouldn't wait on them to find her weaknesses, if she even had any.

Bekka decided that the sooner she started, the better. As the inn was beginning to fill up with afternoon patrons, she pulled Tarek aside. "If my friend returns could you please let her know that I've gone into *Freeport* to the *Library*. She can join me there."

He nodded. "Aye, I'll pass yer message on should I see her."

Bekka thanked him and gathered her things and left the *Twisted Oak*. She had an uneasy feeling beginning to creep over her. *Something bad had happened to her friend.* And now she was alone.

As Bekka approached the open gate that led into the coastal city of *Freeport*, she was immediately beset by a combination of tantalizing smells all at once. The heavy scent of freshly baked bread and the mouthwatering aroma of roasting meat made her hungry despite the fact that she still had a full belly.

As the crowd slowed to enter the city, she became more aware of other, not so pleasing odors. The rank smell of human sweat was much stronger now, obviously there were more than a few whom needed a good bathing. Bekka did her best to cover her nose and mouth with her hand, and not seem offensive at the same time. Nonetheless she would be pleased when the mass of people thinned out.

Two huge, armored Orcs stood guard outside the gate of the seaport. They seemed to watch everyone that entered with a threatening glare, as if they were daring you to try something. And, knowing the reputation of De La'Corte's *Hellhounds*, they were probably doing just that.

When one of them met Bekka's eye, she quickly looked away, blushing. She could see him whisper something to his burly companion, who in turn, glared at her menacingly.

She silently cursed herself for even acting guilty. Now she had only drawn more attention to herself than she needed. The second Orc stepped away from his companion and moved in her direction. Fortunately, there was a fairly large group trying to gain access to the city at the moment. Bekka ducked her head and did her best to disappear within the crowd of pedestrians.

The *Hellhound* was not going to be so easily dismissed. He began to force his way through the throng of people attempting to gain access to the city, by roughly pushing them aside. He was relentless in his pursuit of Bekka. She found herself pinned against the wall as the crowd suddenly stopped moving.

Certain she was going to be, at the very least, detained by the *Hellhound*, she quickly tried to come up with a plausible reason for visiting the seaport; one that wouldn't invite more questioning. Problem was, she wasn't a very good liar, and she knew it.

She felt a hand grasp her wrist and pull, almost jerking her completely off balance. "Follow me!" she heard the whisper in her ear. Bekka didn't really have a choice at this point. Either she followed this mysterious stranger, or she risked being detained by the scary looking *Hellhound* that was continuing to move toward her. She chose the former.

All she could see of this enigmatic newcomer was black leather and a face hidden within the shadows of a hood. He led her through the crowd, twisting and turning, even backtracking to avoid their pursuer. It seemed to be working. They had stepped into a side alley and watched as the *Hellhound* walked by, his eyes searching the crowd ahead.

The noxious smell of human excrement and urine jumped

out at her from the depths of the alley; Bekka cringed, squinting her eyes and scrunching her nose at the pungent stench. Still, the alley was preferable to the Hellhound.

She pulled her arm out of her savior's grasp. "Mind telling me who you are?"

He chuckled softly. "Hey, I just did you a favor. That *Hellhound* was about to nab you." He seemed oblivious to the stink that permeated the air around them.

Bekka shook her head. "But I've done nothing wrong."

He laughed again. "And you think that really matters? Those guys do what they want, when they want, to whomever they want." He looked her up and down. "You didn't stand a chance against him."

That pissed her off. "Excuse me? Who the Hell do *you* think you are? You don't know what I'm capable of. You don't know anything about me."

He spread his hands in the air placatingly. "Sorry. I didn't mean to anger you. I was only trying to help a damsel in distress, my apologies."

"I don't need your help," she said, crossing her arms over her chest. "And I'm not a damsel in distress!"

He slipped the hood off his head. He had an amused expression on his face as he looked her over. "Again, I'm sorry."

She was surprised to see the cleft in his stubbled chin and the dimples in his cheeks. He reminded her of Trevor. He was quite good looking; he even had the same blue coloring in his sparkling eyes. She swallowed. "My name is Bekka Kensington." She extended her hand toward him.

He quickly took her hand, twisted it slightly, and kissed the back. He then bowed. "I am Darren O'Leary, at your service." He still had a hold of her hand, and he was leaning down to kiss it again.

Bekka withdrew her hand and once again she crossed her arms over her chest. "Do you always come to the aid of those in need?"

His eyes twinkled brightly even with the dim lighting in the alleyway. "Ah, so you admit it, you *did* need my assistance!"

She shook her head and rolled her eyes. "You certainly are

full of yourself, aren't you," it was a statement of fact, not really a question.

He chuckled, spreading his hands in the air. "So, can I assist you any further, m'lady?"

She studied him for a moment. "Perhaps there is something that you can help me with..."

His eyes lit up and he smiled. "Name it."

"I am looking for my friend, we got separated this morning. We were staying at the *Twisted Oak Inn* and she left early and hasn't returned. Perhaps you've seen her?"

He grinned. "Tall woman, dressed in leather, a tattoo and a scar on her face, oh, and a ruined eye?"

Bekka was shocked. "How did you know?"

Darren chuckled. "I saw the two of you together at the *Twisted Oak* last evening. That was quite a dance you did on the bar top."

Bekka blushed. "Really, I..." She sighed dejectedly. "I *may* have had a bit too much of the Dwarven Firewater. Normally I am a bit more reserved."

He raised his brows and chuckled. "I certainly hope so."

Bekka's blush deepened. She hoped she hadn't done anything to be ashamed of. Surely dancing and singing on top of the bar while intoxicated was embarrassing enough, she hated the thought that her character might be called into question. She absolutely did not need to be falsely judged by anyone, especially Darren O'Leary.

She gave him a stern look. "Oh like you have never done something stupid and regretted it the next day!"

He chortled softly and then cleared his throat by coughing into his fist. "Yes, well, we won't go into any of that right now." He gave her a quick wink and a smile. "I would like to hear more about this bullfrog friend of yours, this Jeremiah. You say he's a good friend of yours?"

Bekka sighed heavily, mortified. "Don't knock the song. It's an oldie but a goodie. I hope I did it justice."

He grinned. "I can only say, having never heard the tune sung by any bard before, your rendition was very lively."

Bekka shook her fists in the air. "Yay me!"

He chuckled again. "Let's go find your friend."

As the evening drew near, they weren't any closer to finding Valoria. Bekka sighed, as she looked Darren over; she had been glad of his company. "I really want to thank you for spending your time with me today, and for saving me from that *Hellhound*."

He grinned. "The pleasure was all mine, I assure you, but it doesn't have to end quite so soon. I could take you to dinner or escort you back to the *Twisted Oak* if you're ready to call it a day."

Bekka shook her head. "No thank you. I left word with Tarek Wyndspear to inform Valoria to look for me at the *Great Library Arcanum*." She shrugged. "She may already be there waiting for me."

He reached out and brushed a strand of hair out of her face. He leaned in and pressed his lips against hers, his hand cupping her cheek. Bekka felt a jolt zip through her and was genuinely surprised when her lips responded to him as though they had a life of their own. She stepped back. "What was that for?" She could feel her heartbeat quicken.

Darren grinned, arching an eyebrow as he touched her chin with his fingertips. He shrugged. "I was hoping that we could get to know each other better."

She felt like a schoolgirl again, crushing on the popular jock. She was almost breathless; her mind a jumbled mess as her thoughts began tripping over themselves. She was once again the nerdy teenage girl who was afraid to talk to a boy. *But this was no schoolboy.* He was a young man and he had just kissed her, stirring up feelings that had been long suppressed. She almost felt giddy inside.

Bekka blinked several times, trying to refocus her thoughts. *She didn't have time for this nonsense! She had already wasted too much time with him as it was! She needed to be getting to the Library!* She tightened her hands into fists, her nails digging into her palms. She didn't trust herself. "Look, I really do need to be getting to the *Library Arcanum*. My home is in danger and so are my family and friends. I need to find a way to save them. I've been told that my answers may lie within the tomes located there."

She swallowed. "So if you would kindly show me the way to the library, I'd greatly appreciate it."

He frowned. "I thought that the *Great Library Arcanum* was for mystics and wizards." He gave her the once over and shook his head. "You honestly, don't look like either."

She dropped her hands to her hips as a slight smile hinted at the corners of her lips. "I'm not but that isn't the point. Are you going to help me, or not?"

He chuckled as he scratched at the stubble on his chin. He sighed after a moment. "I suppose I can take you there."

She crossed her arms and glared at him. "Well I wouldn't want to trouble you," she said sarcastically.

Darren shook his head and chortled. "No trouble at all."

They twisted and turned along the streets so many times that Bekka couldn't keep track. She couldn't be sure whether or not he was purposefully trying to get her lost, or if he was taking short cuts. It appeared to her that he was taking the long way.

He pointed off to the south. "That large fortress is the City Keep. That is where you'll find De La'Corte and his not so friendly *Hellhounds*." He seemed to have a smirk on his face. "I always try my best to steer clear of that place." He frowned suddenly. "Though, to be honest, I haven't always been successful." His smile returned. "I highly recommend you stick to other accommodations."

"Is that why we were taking the route we've been on, because you wanted to avoid it?" she asked with an amused lift to her brow.

He nodded. "Most definitely! There are a couple of *Hellhound* patrols that I really need to avoid. I had a little run-in with them a day or two ago. I need to give them a chance to focus on something else, for a while."

"Oh?" Bekka asked. "Care to elaborate?"

Darren chuckled softly and shook his head. "I think I'll decline. Let's just say it wasn't one of my finer moments. I wouldn't want you to think any less of me."

Bekka's eyes sparkled with curiosity. "Now I am intrigued."

He looked up ahead. "That is the library," he pointed. "Stay on this street until you see the gated entrance, and then you should be fine."

"You're not coming with me?" she asked, sounding disappointed.

"I'd better not. There are far too many *Hellhounds* posted at the gate for my comfort."

She gave him a look of mock surprise. "What have you done to warrant so much attention from De La'Corte's *Hellhounds*?"

He grinned. "Honestly, it doesn't take much, believe me. And I've probably done more than most here lately."

He lifted a hand and gave her a little wave. "I'll be seeing you."

She felt her heart flutter in anticipation. She found that the thought of seeing him again rather pleased her. There was something about Darren O'Leary that she found oddly aesthetic. Sure, he was handsome, strong and self-assured, but there was something else about him that attracted her that she couldn't quite put her finger on. He was the typical bad boy that most girls were attracted to on the other side of the *Portal*. Maybe that was it.

Bekka nodded, started to return his little wave, but at the last second she stepped in and kissed his cheek before losing her nerve and stepping back. "I hope so," she said softly.

He touched the spot on his cheek where her lips had been, his mouth dropping open ever so slightly. He was speechless; he could only nod.

She started toward the Great Library but after a dozen or so steps she turned back to say something to him, but he was already gone. She scanned the thinning crowd but saw no sign of him. She shook her head and sighed, hoping that she hadn't seen the last of him.

Darren O'Leary leaned against the corner of the stone building, and from the shadows of the alleyway he watched her go. Still touching his cheek where she had kissed him, he smiled. There was something intriguing about this girl that gave him a moment of pause. No one had ever excited him as much as she did, and that was saying something. He would make a point of keeping his promise to her. *He would see her again.* He turned toward the shadows and began to sing softly as he stepped into the night. *"Jeremiah was a bullfrog! Dun dun a dun! Was a good friend of mine..."*

Chapter 22
Graveside Decisions

Her heart was broken. Candi felt cold and numb as she stood over the two new plots in the graveyard of *Kensington Castle*. Tears streamed down her cheeks as she silently thought of those that were finally resting in peace at her feet. Her best friend's mom, Julia Kensington had always been there for her. She was so easy to confide in, even more so than her own mother had ever been. How could she tell her friend that she hadn't kept her safe? Bekka would be completely devastated!

And then there was Vinnie... He was her soulmate and now he too was gone! She felt an incredible aching in her heart. She doubted that she would ever love again. In just such a very short time he had been her everything. He was her world and he had been brutally stolen from her, *right in front of her!* She had watched Sinnestra kill him; literally snatching his beating heart from his chest!

The list of loved ones she had lost seemed to be growing longer. *How could she have been so duped by Gwyneth—Sinnestra—or whatever her name was?* She shook her head and wiped away the trail of bitter tears but they just wouldn't stop coming.

She felt like she was going to be very ill but she knew she couldn't puke. She felt so incredibly empty inside! She looked up and met Trevor's gaze. "We need to go to Bekka. She needs to know what has happened to us. We need to help her get ready to face that *bitch*."

Trevor nodded. "She should be returning soon."

Candi shook her head, thrusting out her chin. "We need to go to her! Sinnestra is gone from here, I doubt she'll be coming back."

"You don't think Sinnestra will come here for Bekka?" he asked.

She rolled her eyes, aggravated that he could be so stupid. "Sinnestra knows where Bekka has gone. She'll strike at her before Bekka returns with the knowledge of how to defeat her. Bekka needs to know that Sinnestra can take whatever form she desires. We have to warn Bekka. We have to go to *Freeport*."

Trevor sighed. "If you think that's best."

Candi nodded. "I do." She felt her body shaking. "Besides, I can't stay here any longer. If I do, I'm just gonna lose it altogether. All I want to do is just curl up in a ball and die right now. But Bekka needs us. I can't lose anyone else." Her tears streamed down her cheeks in torrents. "I just can't!" Finally, she turned to Lithania. "You should take the *Blade of the Spider's Kiss*. If we meet Sinnestra on the way, she may try and stop us from joining Bekka."

Lithania gave a slight nod in response. "As you wish," she said softly.

Candi glanced over at Kestra. "Will you come with us?"

The Orc grinned, pounding a fist into her palm. "Try and keep me from it! It is the least that I can do in return for all you have done to free my people from our oppressors."

A smile appeared on the blonde girl's face. "I love you, girl!" she said with a chuckle. She turned to the others. "We'll leave at first light."

Candi carried the ornate silver coffer that held the Drow weapon known as the *Blade of the Spider's Kiss*. It was the only weapon that they knew of capable of killing Sinnestra. The first time Lithania had swung the blade she had struck the demoness on the shoulder with only a glancing blow. It hadn't been fatal, but it had grievously wounded her. "I'm trusting you with this."

Trevor took the coffer from Candi and opened it for the elf. The Drow called it *Syc 'd' Ara'k 'und*. It was a finely balanced weapon, larger than a dagger, but much smaller than a shortsword. A dull crystal shard was fixed upon its pommel. A large ruby was cut into the end of the ornate hilt.

Lithania reached in and lightly caressed the weapon. After a moment she lifted it from the coffer and held it out for all to admire. She would gladly take charge of the *Blade of the Spider's Kiss* and wield it against her enemies.

Kestra stood on the balcony outside of her room and gazed up at the night sky. A multitude of stars sparkled in the heavens. The moon was high overhead, shining brightly down with a silvery glow. She frowned darkly, a puzzled look on her face. Something was amiss. *Why hadn't the Blade of the Spider's Kiss glowed like before? Did it only do that when danger was near? She couldn't be sure...*

Chapter 23
The Great Library Arcanum

As Bekka passed through the tall iron gates of the *Great Library Arcanum* she acted like she had every right to be there, hoping that the *Hellhound* sentries would simply ignore her. She held her breath as she walked by, unnoticed.

Relieved, she paused to admire the fountains that were in the library courtyard. Water flowed from books of stone, mounted upon pillars. Someone had said that it symbolized that *'From books, flow Knowledge'*. Bekka smiled. She couldn't have said it any better. It was something she had always believed.

The *Great Library* was absolutely huge. It was larger than its neighbor, the seaport's *Cathedral* and the *City Keep* that Darren had pointed out to her. She hadn't expected it to be so massive. Wide, stone steps led up to a huge portico that ran along the entire front face of the building. Giant circular columns supported the roof covering the extended veranda. Bekka was definitely impressed; it rivaled the great libraries from her side of the *Portal*.

After entering the *Great Library,* Bekka couldn't help but gasp at the stunning beauty before her. Mahogany shelves seemed to glisten in the natural light filtering in through circular windows set high up in the walls. She stopped in her tracks, her eyes growing wide with wonder. "Oh my," she exclaimed reverently at the opulence of the library. A massive round counter constructed of polished mahogany filled the center of the main room. It appeared to be hand carved with ornate designs engraved in the wood. A single librarian was in attendance behind the counter busily attending patrons with various needs.

Tall shelves filled with tomes of all sizes, large and small, thick and thin, rose up toward the high vaulted ceilings, and she briefly wondered how one would manage to obtain a book from the highest tier, let alone know what was even up there to choose from. She saw no ladders, nor stairs making the great works more accessible. *How, then, were they reached?*

She didn't have to wait long for her answer. She saw a massive tome slide from a high shelf all on its own. It glided through the air, passing overhead, causing her to needlessly duck as it flew toward the central counter where she saw a bearded man in green robes waving what appeared to be a wand. The tome landed in front of the librarian without making a sound. This gentleman was completely bald, except for the beard, a bushy mustache and equally prominent eyebrows.

Looking around in confusion, she sighed heavily. *Where to begin?*

After a moment's reflection, Bekka headed for the central counter where the librarian was perched upon a swivel stool. She figured it was her best bet to inquire about Valoria and to get steered in the correct direction for information about Sinnestra. Otherwise she could spend several days, maybe even months, searching through the massive collection of tomes. She knew that the sheer volume of information could easily distract her, and she didn't really have the time to waste. She needed to be getting back to *Kensington Castle.* She was still deeply disturbed about the vision she had seen concerning her father's death.

She stood in front of the librarian and waited for him to acknowledge her presence. When he finally looked at her, a slight frown turned the corner of his mouth. "How might I be of service to you?"

Bekka smiled sweetly. "Good evening, kind sir. I was hoping that you could direct me to where I might find information on the demoness known as Sinnestra. And perhaps you might have seen a friend of mine, she was to meet me here earlier, but due to circumstances beyond my control, I was delayed."

He arched a brow inquisitively. "I can certainly help you with the first; *Demonology* is located in the sub-basement. As to the whereabouts of your friend, I only just came on duty." He offered a thin smile. "You are only the second person that I've talked to today; and I don't think the first was the friend you seek."

Bekka squinted as she looked up at him. "How do you know?"

With a little smirk, he said, "You said *'she'*, the first person I assisted was, most assuredly, a male."

Bekka blushed slightly. "Oh. My bad. *Demonology* is where, exactly?"

He pointed off to his right. "You will find a set of stairs leading to the sub-basement down that corridor."

She gave him a warm smile. "Thank you very much. You've been most helpful."

"Ahem..." he coughed into his fist. "I assume that you have taken the appropriate precautions?"

She had started to walk away but stopped abruptly and faced the librarian. "I'm sorry? What do you mean, appropriate precautions?"

He rolled his eyes. "That is what I thought. When one is researching information about demons, great care must be taken so as not to do a Summoning."

"A Summoning? What do you mean? Do you mean actually calling the demon here?" That was a frightening prospect; one that she hadn't considered.

He had that same smirk fixed upon his face as he nodded slowly. "Precisely."

A moment of panic swept through her. *Was that even possible?* She supposed that it was, when she considered it. "I certainly wouldn't want to do that," she said apprehensively.

"No," he said. "That would be most unwise."

"I just want to learn about Sinnestra, not call her to me." She decided that honesty was the best policy at this point. "She's coming for me and I'm not really ready to face her. I just need to learn how to protect myself. How I can defeat her."

"We have taken pains to prevent random Summonings from harming the library's patrons. *Glyphs of Warding* will prevent the demon from coming out of the sub-basement." He smiled at her. "My advice to you is for you to go to the *Cathedral* and obtain a *Sigil of Protection*."

He shook his head, as he looked her over. "But, alas, I am afraid that their acquisition may be beyond your means. They can be quite pricey."

Bekka swallowed. "I don't have much money."

The librarian's chin rose slightly. He looked at her with what could only be disdain. "That much is clearly evident," he said.

Bekka stuck her own chin out and glared at him through narrowed eyes. His arrogance was starting to get on her nerves. She decided to cut him some slack. "Guess I'll take my chances."

"You will undoubtedly discover that the tomes are arranged alphabetically by *Demonic Planes of Existence*." He consulted a file that he had on hand. "Sinnestra will be on a shelf near the far wall. Look for the tomes with the red spines. She should be referenced in one of those."

Bekka nodded. "Down the corridor, down the steps, on a shelf near the far wall, a red tome. Got it. Thanks."

"I really do wish you good luck. Demonic possession can be quite painful, not to mention deadly."

Bekka felt a chill run down her spine. "Great."

As she walked down the corridor, she couldn't help but notice that it wasn't as well-lit as the rest of the library had been. Nor were there as many patrons in this area. *It gave her an ominous feeling.* She found the narrow set of stone steps in a darkened alcove. A wooden placard on the wall indicated that this was the way to the sub-basement.

Bekka took a deep breath and exhaled it slowly, steeling her nerves. 'I shouldn't be here alone,' she told herself. Didn't something horrible always happen to the lone girl in all those scary movies that she had seen, especially if a demon was involved? She jumped at her own shadow cast upon the rough-hewn wall of stone. Torches burning in the sconces along the wall made it dance grotesquely. *"Stop it!"* she chastised herself. What harm could there really be in reading a stupid book, anyway? She had read plenty of Stephen King novels back in the day! This should be a walk in the park.

As she was about to descend the stairs a hand grabbed her elbow. She let out a blood-curdling scream...

Chapter 24
New Friends

"You shouldn't grab people like that!" Bekka said breathlessly as she stared at the two gnomes that had accosted her on the stairs. "You could've made me slip and fall. I might've broken my neck!"

The two gnomes exchanged looks. The female slapped her male companion's arm. "I told you it wasn't a good idea! We should have announced ourselves first and foremost!"

"Bah!" said the male. He reminded Bekka a lot of Frendlestixx the Great, only a bit chubbier. "I only touched her arm." He glared up at Bekka. "You really should keep the volume down a bit more, this is a library, after all."

"Well excuse me for being startled. You shouldn't go around grabbing people in dark corridors."

He inhaled sharply, tightened his lips, puffed out his cheeks; while turning slightly red in the face, and then blew out the air in frustration. "I... well... I was just trying to stop you from making a huge mistake!"

The female gnome nodded fervently. "A huge mistake of epic proportions!"

He glared at her. "I believe that I said that already. Why don't you ever listen?"

She shook her head. "No you didn't. I clearly heard you say 'huge' whilst I said 'epic'—there is a difference, you know."

The male gnome rolled his eyes and sighed dramatically. "I do not need you to explain to me the difference between 'huge' and 'epic'; I'm not a simpleton. I happen to be a learned scholar, holding various degrees in—"

The female slapped his shoulder. "We do not have time for you to go into all of that, we have work to do."

He growled in frustration. He shook his head. "Be that as it may, the point is rather moot, anyway." He looked at Bekka and admonished her with a shake of his stubby finger. "And you! I cannot believe you were even thinking of going down into the sub-basement without adequate protection! Didn't the librarian sufficiently warn you about the dangers of such an idiotic notion?"

Bekka felt taken aback, she blinked at him. "Uhm, yes he did." She frowned at him, crossing her arms over her chest. "Did you just call me an idiot?"

"Do you have any protection?" he demanded of her.

She shook her head, speechless.

He shrugged. "Well, there you have it."

"Tsk, tsk, tsk!" the female said. "Not good. Not good at all! No siree!"

"And why do you not have said protection?" asked the male pointedly.

Now Bekka was mad. She arched a brow and cocked her head to the side. "Because I am broke. I have no money. That arrogant dweeb of a librarian said that they were terribly expensive. So, I figured 'what the Hell,' I'd take my chances."

He pursed out his lips and shook his head. "Ooh, no, no, no, no! We mustn't do that. That is how one loses their very soul, not just their life!" He tapped his finger against his lips as he contemplated their options. Finally, he said, "If you come along with us, my sister and I will see that you are better prepared for this harrowing journey on which we are all about to depart."

The female nodded her head affirmatively, and with a wave of her hand she indicated that they should return back the way they had all come.

"We?" Bekka said. "What do you mean the *'harrowing journey on which we are all about to depart'*?"

"Oh," he said rather whimsically, "didn't I say? We are going to join you on this Grand Adventure! Besides, we have a mutual friend that needs our help."

"We have a mutual friend?" Bekka asked skeptically.

He frowned darkly. "Must you repeat everything that I say? It's quite annoying to be honest."

His sister rolled her eyes at her brother as she took Bekka by the arm. "Yes we do! Valoria is in grave danger and we must help to free her!"

Together they left the *Great Library Arcanum* and had wound their way along the edge of the Business District and entered the Mage Quarter. Presently they were standing outside of a shop called Oddities and Magicks Emporium. Bekka waited patiently while the male gnome fumbled through a ring of keys. Finally, after trying numerous keys, he found one that turned the lock. He faced her and said pointedly, "I must caution you not to touch anything. Just follow me upstairs and keep your hands to yourself!"

Bekka smirked. "Okay."

They entered the shop and even though there was nothing lit on the main floor, a soft yellow glow filtered down from the second floor, allowing them to see without stumbling into something, or one another. Bekka stopped, seeing a strange contraption on the countertop. It was like nothing she had ever seen before. Her curiosity aroused, she reached out to inspect the device. Before she could, the female gnome reached out and slapped her hand. "Hey! What was that for?" Bekka asked, recoiling at the slight sting.

"You were told by my brother not to touch anything. You were about to touch!" came her reply.

Bekka could feel the heat in her cheeks. "I wasn't going to hurt it," she said defensively. The gnome giggled. "No, but it might have hurt you!"

"What is it?" Bekka asked, looking back at the strange device.

"Ahem. I am waiting..." came the voice of the male gnome from upstairs.

The female gnome batted a hand in the air. "Best you don't worry about that now. We can have a nice chat about it later."

Sitting around the kitchen table Bekka looked at the two gnomes. It was obvious that they were siblings. She hadn't seen their common features earlier, but now after a chance to study them, it was readily apparent. "So, how do you know Valoria?"

"Oh," said the female, "we go back a few years. When she was a little street urchin we used to feed her scraps of food now and again. We absolutely love her!"

Bekka was surprised at the news. It was hard for her to imagine Val as a 'little street urchin,' but it wasn't unbelievable. After all, Valoria had left her home at a very young age. She had to survive, so it only seemed natural that she would make her way to *Freeport* where there were endless possibilities awaiting.

"So you've known Valoria since she was a child."

"Oh, indeed we have!" said the brother. "We have grown quite fond of her. The four of us were like family."

"The four of you?"

"Yes, that's right," he said. "Valoria, Bimini, our brother Frendlestixx, and myself."

Bekka looked over at the female gnome and smiled. "So your name is Bimini?"

Bimini blushed slightly. "Oh! Where are our manners? Yes, but please, I prefer to be called just Bim. *Not* 'Just Bim' mind you. Bim. That will do." She pointed at her brother. "That's Brendlestixx. I believe you had already met Frendlestixx."

Bekka recalled the Great and Powerful Frendlestixx from the *Emerald Forest* with fondness. He had died on their very first adventure together but not before making a huge impression on her. "I am so, so sorry for your loss. Frendlestixx was quite the character. I only wish that I had known him better." It was obvious to her now why they'd both looked so familiar to her when she met them in the library. She glanced over at Brendlestixx. "Were you twins?"

He nodded. "Triplets, actually." He gave his sister a look of admonition. "And I would prefer to be called Brendle, if you please."

Bim giggled hysterically. "I gave them both the addition of *'stixx'* to their name when we were young on account of that twig between their legs! Frendle loved it! He actually preferred to be called 'Frendlestixx the Great' but that was only because his was much bi—"

"That is quite enough!" Brendle said sharply, a red blush coloring his cheeks.

Bekka burst into laughter, but at a glare from Brendle, she sobered quickly. "Okay, then it's Bim and Brendle. I am pleased to meet you both. My name is Bekka Kensington."

Brendle looked at her with a small smile curving the corner of his mouth. "We already know who you are. As I said earlier, we have a mutual friend."

Bekka nodded. "Valoria. You also said she was in serious trouble."

Bim whistled. "That woman has a way about her!"

"I don't understand," Bekka said.

"It would seem," Brendle said, "that she was involved in a minor street ruckus and apprehended along with two gentlemen. De La'Corte's *Hellhounds* immediately arrested all involved. Fortunately, no one was seriously harmed so the death penalty is off the table."

"What?" Bekka couldn't believe what she was hearing.

Bim nodded. "But, if we do not secure her release she will likely be sold into slavery and shipped off on the next ship leaving the port!"

"You've got to be kidding me!" Bekka said.

Brendle and Bim exchanged looks. "Why would we do that?" they said in unison.

Chapter 25
De La'Corte's Price

De La'Corte studied the young woman across from him with a keen eye. She brought back so many memories of his youth that had faded over time, but now they returned to him with a clarity that was sharp and clear. She was so much like the woman he had loved all those years ago. Though this girl's hair was much shorter, it had the same coloring, perhaps a shade or two lighter. Her cheekbones were just as he remembered, the cut of her chin, the same. Her eyes were different. These were not the same dark brown, smoldering eyes of the woman he had loved. These were blue, like the other man's had been!

He could not steal her from him. Though he had tried. *Oh, how he had tried!* Yet in the end she had still refused him. He had promised her the world; riches beyond her wildest imagination, the finest silks, everything a heart could desire. But she did not return his affections. She was in love with him. She carried the other man's baby in her womb. But if he could not have her, then she could not have him either. He got rid of the competition, hoping that his absence would drive her to him. But it hadn't. It only pushed her further away...

He learned of her death months later. He had heard that she had given birth to a girl. However the timing was bad. Maragh was waging his *War Against Infants* and hers had been of the right age. He had always assumed that Maragh had killed the baby as well; but seeing this young woman sitting across from him, he now knew better. She must have survived. She was the spitting image of her mother. It was like seeing a ghost from the past.

She had come before him to plead for her friend's salvation. She had told him of how they had been attacked by these two ruffians and their other three companions near *Schiff's Crossing*. They had killed three but had allowed these two to escape. They were to blame for the trouble in the street, not her friend. She was only defending herself.

"You make a compelling argument," he said. "But the rules exist for a reason. Violence of any kind will not be tolerated. Your friend drew her sword and fought these two men. The lives of the onlookers were placed in jeopardy. It is my job, my sworn duty, to protect those that cannot defend themselves."

Bekka gripped the arms of her chair tightly. She took a calming breath, not wanting her anger to fuel her words; that never seemed to end well. "But these two men accosted me first, the night before, at the *Twisted Oak Inn*! Had they not, Valoria might not have confronted them. Surely you can understand."

He gave her a helpless look. "The *Twisted Oak* is outside my purview."

He waved a hand in the air. "Be glad that no one was killed in this altercation. The existing laws would sentence all involved to public execution. It is so that further acts can be easily discouraged, of course. I loathe violence as a general rule." He smiled thinly. "Your friend is actually getting off lucky."

Bekka slapped the arms of her chair unable to contain her rising anger any longer. She leaned forward, thrusting out her jaw. "You call getting sold into slavery lucky?"

He shrugged. "As I said, she could've been sentenced to death. It doesn't matter what occurred outside the walls of the city. I am only concerned with maintaining order within the city walls. Leave your differences outside, pick them back up after you've left, I don't care." His face took on a sobering look. "I am the law in these parts, make no mistake. I cannot simply change the laws on a whim for anyone who asks. It is my job to enforce them. The citizens of *Freeport* need to feel safe. They need to know that I will protect them at all costs." He smiled. "It is my duty."

Bekka stood and untied the pouch at her belt. She dropped it onto the center of his desk, the gold coins clinking softly. "Then I'll buy her." Brendlestixx and Bimini had already attempted to buy Valoria but had been denied. De La'Corte had cited some obscure law against gnomes, dwarves and elves from owning human slaves, stating something against possible perversion. It was simply ridiculous.

De La'Corte smiled thinly. He eyed the bag for a moment and shook his head. He lifted his glass in the air in a toast offering. "I applaud your attempt, but I must admit that I have been offered better."

Bekka glared at him with a pleading look in her eyes. "I can get more if that isn't enough. Please, sell her to me. She doesn't deserve this. Sell her to me and we'll leave *Freeport*. We won't ever come back. You'll be done with us."

He lifted the bag of coins and judged their weight in the palm of his hand. "I don't want your money," he said as he stood and walked around to the front of the desk. He held the bag out to her. "Besides, it would never be enough."

Bekka's eyes brimmed with sudden tears. "Please," she softly repeated, "sell her to me. I will buy her freedom."

He placed the bag into her hand and folded her fingers around it. "I don't want your gold."

Her eyes met his and she instantly knew the price he was demanding of her. A lone tear fell from each eye and rolled, unstopped down her cheeks. She closed her eyes, allowing more to fall. She nodded. She would pay his price.

Bekka swung her feet over the side of the bed and pushed off the mattress. She felt sore and abused, unsteady. She could still feel his eyes upon her ravaged flesh. She was bruised, she knew. He had not been gentle with her. She felt dirty.

He had a lascivious look in his eyes as he continued to look her over. He pulled back the thin sheet covering him and exposed the bloodstains upon the bottom sheet. "You were a virgin," he said. It sounded as though he were gloating over his conquest.

Bekka nodded stiffly as more tears fell from her eyes. This was not how she'd imagined her first time would be. There were no soft caresses, no nervous kisses, and no tenderness. She could still feel his clawing scratches upon her naked flesh, his bites upon her breasts. He had savagely taken her. It was almost as though he were punishing her. *But for what?*

He had started out gentle enough but when she refused to reciprocate things had turned drastically. He ordered her to become more involved but she couldn't. She refused to pretend she was enjoying any part of this ordeal. That was when he began to get really rough with her.

When Bekka felt she could trust her voice only then did she speak. "When will Valoria be released?"

He eyed her for a moment longer. "It will take time to secure her release. There are forms that need to be filed. After I have seen to them, she will be set free."

"Then I can go?" she asked softly, holding her breath. Fearing the worst.

De La'Corte chuckled. "A deal is a deal. You may go. If I have need of you for anything else, I will be in touch."

She felt a cold shiver run down her spine. She dressed as swiftly as her aching body would allow, all the while feeling his eyes watching her. Afterward, she fled as quickly as she could, afraid he might call her back to him.

Outside in the cool night air the floodgates opened and she couldn't stop her tears. She retched against the side of the stone building and then wiping her mouth, she stumbled to the street. It took her a minute to get her bearings. She turned to her right and headed back to the only place she truly felt safe. *The Oddities and Magicks Emporium* where her friends were awaiting her return.

She wiped the tears from her face with her fingertips and exhaled long and hard. She had survived this ordeal. Brendle and Bim had given her the gold to secure Val's freedom; they would want details. Bekka laughed. She certainly couldn't tell them what had really happened! But their curiosity would definitely be aroused when she handed them back their coins. She would have to tell them something.

As luck would have it, they were waiting for her. She could tell that they had been nervously pacing back and forth. Brendle gave her a concerned look. "We expected you back hours ago. Where have you been? We've been worried sick!" His eyes took on a haunted look when the candle lamplight struck her face. "Did he beat you?" he asked.

Bim looked at her oddly, and then her eyes filled with compassion. She placed a warning hand on Brendle's arm when Bekka returned the pouch of gold coins and started up the stairs.

Brendle was about to question her further but Bim shook her head in silent warning.

Bekka was sitting on the edge of the bed, tears coursing down her cheeks as Bim tended to her wounds with extra tenderness. "We never should have let you go alone," she said with a whisper.

Bekka didn't respond, she just stared straight ahead as the tears continued to fall.

Brendlestixx tossed another log onto the fire. He frowned darkly as he settled back into his plush chair. He glanced over at his sister, "How is she doing?"

Bimini sighed heavily. "She will heal in time. She's just a child, though. She probably had all these romantic notions about what her first time with a man would be like, all young girls do. De La'Corte stole that from her." Her hands knotted into tight, angry fists.

Brendlestixx almost growled. "We never should have let her go to him. It was just asking for trouble."

Bimini nodded. "We knew he was a monster."

Brendlestixx sighed, his eyes beginning to water. "I wish there was something more we could do. Fix things, somehow."

Bimini smiled at her brother as she reached out and patted the back of his hand. "I know you do, Brendle. You are a good man."

Chapter 26
Lost and Found

As the *Hellhound Orc* approached, Bekka stiffened. She had been waiting with Brendle and Bim for over an hour. A slave ship had departed the harbor earlier this morning and Valoria had still not been set free. Bekka had a bad feeling in the pit of her stomach. She was almost certain that she had been double-crossed. She suppressed a shiver. She did not want to see De La'Corte ever again if she could help it but she had to know about Valoria; a week had already gone by with no news. Surely the *paperwork* had been processed by now!

The orc glared at the gnomes with contempt. He glanced at Bekka. "De La'Corte will see you now, alone."

Brendle shook his head as he pointed a finger up at the green-tinged menace. "Now see here!"

The orc shoved his fat finger into the gnome's chest, knocking him backwards several feet. "Just what do you intend to do about it?" He had already drawn his battleaxe and stood ready to use it.

Alarmed, Bekka intervened. "It's okay. I'll see De La'Corte alone."

Bim started to object but Bekka put a hand on her arm. "Bim, it's okay. Really. I'll see him alone. It is the only way we are going to get Valoria released. In the meantime, why don't you and your brother go to the *Cathedral* and procure the *sigils* that we'll need? We've lost enough time as it is."

Reluctantly, Bim agreed. "I don't like the idea of you going to that man alone. Not after what he has already done."

Bekka smiled at the gnome. "I don't like the idea any better."

She was only just beginning to feel like herself again; the nightmares had only recently stopped. But she saw no other way to accomplish her goal. "I'll be fine. Besides, what more can he possibly do?"

She waited outside De La'Corte's office while the orc went in. A moment later he returned and held the door open for her. "The boss will see you now."

Bekka could feel her mouth go suddenly very dry. Her whole body felt strange to her as panic swept through her. She wanted to turn and run before it was too late, but she couldn't. Valoria needed her to be strong. Steeling her nerves, Bekka entered the room and stood in front of the massive desk. She was surprised to see that De La'Corte was not sitting behind it. Instead, he was standing at the window, his back to her. Her hand drifted to the hilt of the dagger on her belt. She could easily see herself stabbing him in the back. *For a brief second she thought she actually had stabbed him, repeatedly. She could feel his warm blood spilling over her hand as she plunged the dagger into his skin, again and again and again!* She dropped her hands to her side, balling them into tight fists as he turned to face her. She could feel beads of sweat dampen her brow.

A smirk twisted his lips, as he looked her over. "I see you are doing much better than the last time I saw you."

She raised her chin, eyes flashing. "Small wonder," she said, raising her right hand with her forefinger and thumb less than an inch apart, "very small."

He gave her an odd look and then shrugged. "Please, have a seat." He motioned at the chair across from him as he took his seat. She refused it.

"I must admit," he said with a charming smile, "I had not expected to see you again."

"We had a deal," Bekka said tightly. She swallowed. "I paid your price, now honor it. Where is my friend?"

He sighed heavily as he looked at her. "There has been a problem with that. You see, your friend, Valoria, I believe, was not released as per my order. It seems that the paperwork mandating her release was inadvertently misplaced."

Bekka's jaw clenched. "Find it."

De La'Corte sighed. "Oh, the paperwork was found. The problem I have is that your friend was on the slave ship that sailed from the harbor this morning." He shrugged. "Unfortunately, there is nothing that I can do for her. She is gone."

Bekka's eyes narrowed as she fought back her tears. Her hands were tightly fisted at her sides. She was furious. She pounded her fists upon his desktop. "We had a deal!"

He chuckled softly. "Yes, well, sorry about that."

Brendlestixx sighed with relief as he saw Bekka walking up the front steps to the *Great Library Arcanum*. Tapping Bimini on the shoulder he pointed in her direction. "There she is!"

Bimini turned and waved at Bekka, a concerned look on her face. "We're here!"

Brendlestixx thumped her arm. "She can see that we are here. You don't have to make such a big deal of things!"

She glared at her brother, rubbing her arm vigorously. "You better stop thumping me or you are going to regret it."

"Will you just relax and get over it. I didn't thump you that hard. Quit being such a baby." He rolled his eyes.

She balled up a fist and slugged his shoulder nearly knocking him backwards. "If you don't want me to punch you again, you'll change your attitude. I'm tired of your surliness. And don't call me a baby," she warned.

He raised his hands in the air in an attempt to placate his sister. "All right, all right. I am sorry. I promise not to do it again."

As Bekka joined them on the veranda, she smiled down at

the pair. "If I were the two of you, I think I'd avoid bickering in public. You don't want to get arrested by a *Hellhound*. The *City Keep* is not where you want to spend any time. Trust me, I know."

Bimini gave her a quick hug. "Good to see you're back. We had hoped you would have Valoria with you."

Brendlestixx was still rubbing his shoulder. "Where is she, anyway?"

Bekka crossed her arms over her chest and scoffed. "That man is an asshat."

Brendlestixx placed a hand on her arm. His brows drew together. "Asshat? What's an asshat?"

Bekka shook her head. "Never mind, it isn't important. We've got bigger problems. De La'Corte claims there was a mix-up. Valoria wasn't released like she was supposed to be. She was on that slave ship that sailed this morning."

Bimini touched Bekka's arm. "You can't be serious?"

Tears filled Bekka's eyes. "I wish I weren't."

"What are we going to do now?" Brendlestixx asked, rubbing his chin.

Bekka sighed as she ran a hand through her hair in frustration. She sighed heavily. "We have to find out where that ship was going. We *have* to get Valoria back!"

Bimini touched a finger to her lips. "I may know someone who can find out where she was taken. I'll meet the two of you in the sub-basement a bit later."

Bekka wiped the tears from her cheeks. "Did you guys manage to get the *sigils*?"

Brendlestixx quickly nodded. "Indeed we did!"

"Good," Bekka said. "Shall we get started?" There was nothing they could do for Valoria at the moment. They still had to find out as much as they could about Sinnestra. Bekka had the feeling that they were running out of time.

"Hmm," Bimini said as she turned another page of the massive tome in front of her. It was about half the size that she was. Bekka had to retrieve it from the shelf so that the gnome could peruse it at a study table. Bimini was standing in a chair, her shoulders barely rising above the open text.

Brendlestixx slid his reading lenses down his nose and gave her a look of irritation. "Must you make so much noise when you read?" he asked. He was standing in a chair across from her looking through another hefty volume. "It really is quite annoying."

She shot him a harsh glare. "You study the way you want, and I will study the way that I want."

He pushed his glasses back into place, which only served to magnify his eyes into frighteningly large orbs. "The way that I would like to study is in complete silence. So if you don't mind, dear sister, keep it down!"

Bekka slammed the cover of the book she had been reading closed and glowered at both of them. "Will the two of you please just stop it? Your constant bickering is driving me crazy."

Brendlestixx slid his glasses back down his nose and looked across at Bim. "A tad bit touchy, wouldn't you say, sister?"

Bimini blinked. "Well, she did just learn that her friend was sold into slavery and was shipped to the Gods only know where! I suppose that would put anyone's nerves on edge, don't you think, brother?"

Brendlestixx nodded with a sigh. "I suppose. But still, it seems kind of rude to be so short tempered with the help."

Bekka pushed herself up from the end of the table and shook her head at the two of them in exasperation. "I think I need a moment or two alone." She couldn't help but smile. She'd had time to adjust to the gnomes' banter. Usually she found that with a little concentration she could ignore them completely, but the way her day was going, her patience was running extremely thin. She stretched her arms as she rolled her head on her shoulders slowly, hearing the popping of cartilage. She stifled a yawn. "This is taking forever!" she groaned. They had already been at it for several hours. By her estimation they were not even halfway completed with their research. At this rate they'd be at it throughout the night.

"Maybe you should take a break," Bimini suggested.

Bekka shook her head. "Nah, there are still a few other books in the back that I'd like to check out. I'll be back in a bit."

Without looking up from his tome, Brendlestixx nodded. "Just make certain that you take your *sigil* with you."

Bekka held the necklace out for him to see; it was a thin tile with a mysterious glyph etched upon the stone, which glowed softly. "I've still got it around my neck."

"Uh huh," he said without looking up, "I see."

Bimini glared at him. "Quiet! I'm trying to concentrate."

"Me?" he said, flabbergasted. "She was the one making all the noise. I just wanted to make certain that she still had her protective *sigil*."

Bekka walked off, shaking her head and smiling. She could still hear the two of them going back and forth, attempting to get in the last word and assign the blame on the other.

They all had been here pouring over tome, after tome, after tome for a better part of the day. They were all tired, achy and getting more than just a little bit cranky. Bekka had to haul the heavy tomes from the shelves and then back again once they had been examined, for each of them; they were just too heavy for the gnomes to handle. She could feel the strain in her neck, arms and legs.

There had been others that had come and gone, but no one stayed long especially once the gnomes started their bickering. There hadn't been anyone else come down the stairs in several hours, leaving them alone with their research.

Bekka pulled a red tome from a shelf and carried it to a nearby table. It was heavier than the last one she had gone through. So as she plopped it onto the tabletop she let out a little sigh. "Let's see what secrets you can tell me," she told the old book. As she opened the cover she felt a tingling sensation at the back of her neck, and a slight breeze seemed to stir her hair lightly.

She started turning the pages of the tome, scanning for any mention of Sinnestra. She noticed the tiny thin hairs on her arms were beginning to prickle as goosebumps formed. She looked up from the massive book and glanced to her right where she caught the glimpse of movement in her periphery. A girl with auburn curls disappeared around a corner. The way she moved seemed oddly familiar. Bekka blinked, her head drawing back slightly in surprise. *"Trish?"* she said in a hushed whisper of shocked disbelief. *How was that even possible?* They had told her that Trish was dead, Maragh had stabbed her in the forest! *Had her parents and Lady Rosa been mistaken? Was Patricia Morgan alive? Or was she just seeing a manifestation of her dead friend conjured up by her overly exhausted mind?*

Bekka had to find out.

She got up from the table and started toward where she had seen the girl a moment ago. As she turned down the aisle of books she didn't see anyone, but she didn't let that stop her; she pressed on. As she reached the end of the shelving she glanced to her right and then to her left. She saw the girl at the far end, rounding another corner. This time she saw her profile fleetingly. She gasped sharply. *It looked like Trish!*

Bekka started to run, hoping to catch up with the girl so that she could know for certain. Her heart thudded in her chest excitedly. "Trish?" she called out breathlessly.

She turned the corner and saw the girl a few feet ahead of her. "Trish? Is that really you?"

The girl stopped and turned. It was Patricia Morgan! *But how could it be? She was supposed to be dead!*

Chapter 27
Trish's Story

Bekka embraced her friend with tear-filled eyes. "How is this even possible? I thought you were dead! Mom and Dad, even Lady Rosa said that you had been murdered by Maragh when he had taken you all prisoner." She held Trish at arm's length, ignoring the tears of joy that continued to fall from her eyes, blurring her vision. She shook her head. "I can't believe it's really you!"

Even Trish's eyes had started to water. She felt herself stiffen at her friend's embrace. Bekka had noticed it too. She released Trish and gave her a questioning look. "Is everything all right?"

Trish stared at her and then smiled. "Sorry. I was taken by surprise. You were like the last person that I thought I'd see here."

Bekka laughed. "Same here! We have so much to catch up on! I'm not sure where to even begin."

They sat at a table and Bekka began filling Trish in on all that had happened. When she was finished, she couldn't help but blush a little in embarrassment. "Look at me, just blabbing away." She reached out a hand and placed it over one of Trish's. "Tell me about you."

Trish sighed. She had been looking at Bekka as her friend spoke, but now she dropped her eyes, unable to keep her friend's gaze. Instead, she focused on their hands clasped together on the tabletop. "Well, as you know, Maragh had us all standing in a line; your parents, Lady Rosa and me. He wanted us to tell him where you were. He threatened to kill us if we didn't. He eventually chose me as his victim, hoping to force the others to give you up." She shook her head. "But we didn't know where you were. After he stabbed me with his sword I was left for dead. They never even bothered to see if I was or not. They just left me there on the forest ground, bleeding out." She quickly looked up into Bekka's eyes, her own brimming with tears. "Not that I blame your parents or even Lady Rosa for that matter; they were prisoners. There was nothing that they could do." She swallowed, tucking a strand of auburn curls behind her ear. "For the longest time I thought I was going to die, I could hear the creak of the harnesses as the horses moved slowly through the forest; the clank of armor, the sobs of Rosa and your mother, and the curses of your father. And then I heard nothing, only silence. I thought that I had died; but if that was so, then why was I still hurting? Shouldn't death take away all of my pain? Where was the peace? It wasn't there, it continued to elude me. Whatever had been growing inside of me wouldn't let me die. It did something to me, so that we both could live!"

Bekka swallowed, her eyes taking on a haunted look. "What are you saying, Trish?"

Trish shook her head; her hand trembled as she covered her mouth. "I'm not the same girl who came through that *Portal*."

"We've all changed since that day," Bekka said. "How could we not?" None of them had been prepared for the dangers that had awaited them in *Vespia*; the horrors that they would be forced to endure. Her thoughts drifted to De La'Corte and she shivered suddenly; still feeling his hands upon her.

Trish gave her a slow smile. It was almost a smirk. Her eyes held an intensity that seemed to bore through her. Bekka felt uneasy as she stared into the deep green of her friend's eyes. Her mouth was incredibly dry. She could feel the hairs on the back of her neck stand on end as the uncertainty rose within her. It was more than just a simple feeling that stole over her—it felt like a premonition. Trish was different. And that difference was frightening!

While the others were preparing dinner, Brendlestixx and Trish were standing outside the *Emporium*. The night air was cool and crisp. The gnome took a long drag on his pipe as he looked at Trish and smiled. "So, you and Bekka have known each other a long time, I hear. That's good. I'm glad that the two of you have been reunited. She really needs someone to talk to that knows her so well. She's been through some terrible things lately, and she hasn't really talked to Bim or I. We both feel like it is slowly eating away at her. De La'Corte did some terrible things to her, promising to release her friend, but in the end, he sold Valoria to the slavers anyway. It's really upset her; she's shaken to the core. Maybe she'll talk to you?"

Trish narrowed her eyes and swallowed. A knowing smirk turned the corners of her lips. "We've both gone through some difficult things since coming to this side of the *Portal*. Maybe I can help her deal with all that has happened to her. I can at least try."

Brendlestixx chewed on the stem of his pipe and nodded slowly. "The two of you seem to have a strong bond, almost like sisters. It may be easier for her to open up to you. What I *do* know is that she cannot keep all of this bottled up inside. She needs to come to terms with it or she'll *never* be able to face Sinnestra."

Trish nodded. "I can see that you really care for her. I am glad that she has had you and Bim by her side. She couldn't have made it through what she has without your support." She gave Brendlestixx a grateful hug. "Together we'll see her through this. She won't ever have to face that man again."

Bekka poked her head out of the door. "Bim says you need to come in before dinner gets cold." She eyed the two of them suspiciously. "What are you two talking about, anyway?"

Brendlestixx shrugged. "We were just getting to know each other a little better."

Trish smiled. "Let's eat, I'm starved!"

Chapter 28
Retribution

A cool breeze ruffled the curtains. De La'Corte pushed passed them and stepped out onto the balcony of his private chambers. He was certain that he had heard something, a whisper of sound, but all was quiet. He emptied the contents of his tankard over the side of the rail, allowing the warm ale to splash upon the cobblestones below. He sighed heavily. He was tired.

Returning to his room he closed the balcony doors behind him. The room was dimly lit, a few candles flickered their dull glow here and there, causing vague shadows to dance. He sat on the edge of his bed and scratched his chin before removing his boots and tossing them aside into a haphazard pile in the corner.

The balcony doors opened and a woman stepped inside.

He stood immediately, angered by this intrusion into his private quarters. "What is the meaning of this?" he demanded of his unexpected caller.

The woman had auburn hair that curled about her shoulders, the glow of the candlelight made it look like bouncing flames. She put a finger to her lips, calling for quiet. "I was just in the mood for a little... company," she whispered seductively. "If you catch my meaning. I didn't mean to frighten you."

He chuckled. "I am afraid of no one; least of all, a woman."

Trish crossed the short distance between them quickly, with a cat-like grace. She pressed her lips against De La'Corte's own, her tongue darted into his mouth playfully, tantalizingly. Teasing him. When he tried to take control and do the same to her, she caught his tongue between her teeth and bit down, drawing forth a small amount of blood. His eyes widened in surprise. He grabbed her roughly by the upper arms and held her away from him. "What the *Hell* do you think you're doing?" he snapped angrily.

She chuckled softly. Reaching out she started to unfasten his belt. "I heard from a friend of a friend that you like it rough." She had a flirtatious little twist to her lips as she bit her bottom lip invitingly. "You do *like* it rough don't you?"

Grinning like the Cheshire Cat, he grabbed his shirt with both hands at the collar and ripped it open. "Rougher than you can handle," he said, his eyes flashing brightly in his renewed excitement.

Trish let out a throaty laugh as she pushed him down upon the bed. "Oh I *seriously* doubt that." Her eyes twinkled brightly.

Before he could bounce twice upon the mattress she pounced on him, straddling him with her thighs spread over his waist. She leaned her face to his and smiled alluringly. Reaching around and sliding her hand into his pants she grabbed him and squeezed, not bothering to be gentle. Her eyes were smoldering with intense desire.

De La'Corte grunted painfully. He grinned with an adolescent excitement. "Give me all you've got, wench!" His mind raced with the thoughts of what he would do to her. He had *never* been this aroused!

Trish opened her mouth and he gasped in surprise; his jaw dropped open but only slightly. A thick, snaking tendril shot past Trish's lips and forced his mouth to open wide in acceptance. His eyes bulged outward, threatening to leave their sockets as the tendril continued down his throat. But that was only the beginning! Two smaller tendrils shot out her nose and slipped into his nostrils. He could no longer breathe! He frantically slapped her thighs in a feeble attempt to let her know he'd had enough. It was no use. Her leg muscles tightened against him, pinning him in place.

Trish could feel a strange energy coursing through the tendrils as his life force was sucked from his body; she could feel it flowing into her own, quenching a thirst she hadn't known existed. She forced his manhood inside of her and rocked her body on top of him. Her hunger rose, but his fear only intensified. De La'Corte wanted desperately to scream, in fact he tried but it only enabled the tendrils to penetrate faster, deeper. His eyes looked at her with undeniable terror, and then the light left them; like the flame of a candle being snuffed out. His body shuddered and then just seemed to collapse, lifeless. The tendrils withdrew all at once, snaking their way back to their host.

Trish stared down at his defeated corpse, her eyes burning bright with triumph. She smiled as she wiped her mouth with the back of her hand. She bent down and kissed his bloodied lips. "Don't *fuck* with my friends." His body seemed to dry up and wither beneath her.

Chapter 29
Discovery

Brendlestixx could hardly contain his excitement as he raced upstairs to the living quarters of the *Oddities and Magicks Emporium*. "Eureka!" he exclaimed, a huge smile contorting his features. "Bim! I think I've found it, the break we've been looking for!"

Bimini rolled her eyes; she hated when her brother got this worked up. Not only was he hard to live with because of his gloating, he just started thinking he was *always* right, about everything!

"Did you find a weakness in Sinnestra that we can exploit?" she asked.

He paused, the smile wavering on his face. "Well... not exactly."

She crossed her arms over her chest and shook her head. "Then why are you getting so excited?"

He shook off his momentary frustration. "I may have discovered where her fortress is located!"

Bim stroked her chin. "Bekka said that Sinnestra had taken up residence with the Drow, and actually overthrew the *Spider Queen*, so if that's what you're referring to, it's old news. Besides, the Drow revolted and the *Spider Queen* has reclaimed her throne."

Brendle swiped a hand in the air. "Bah! Of course that isn't what I was referring to! I mean her *actual* fortress; the seat of *all* her power on this plane."

Bim's face brightened. "That could be big; really big!"

He had a rather smug look on his face. "Exactly!"

"So, where is this fortress of hers located?" Bim asked.

He coughed into his fist. "Well, it is located some distance from here, as it happens. We would have to book passage on a ship, for starters. And then we would have to go through some pretty rough territory." His eyes twinkled. "It would be a grand adventure, to be sure!"

Bim rubbed her hands together excitedly. "I can hardly wait! I'd better get a start on packing right away!" She turned to leave.

Brendle quickly stopped her by placing a hand on her sleeve. "I think it would be best if you were to pack lightly. We cannot afford to be hauling your entire workshop along."

She frowned darkly, her eyes narrowing. "I know that!"

"Biiiimmm..." he said, drawing out her name. "I mean it. We cannot afford to take a bunch of your junk along."

Her eyes grew wide and her cheeks puffed out slightly. "Junk!?" Her face started turning red. "How *dare* you!" Her words were laced with venom.

"Now Bim, you know what I meant."

"I have *never* referred to all of your mystical garbage as junk. Not once!"

His face reddened. "Now see here, Bim! My spell components are absolutely not garbage!"

She shrugged. "Could be. But what do I know?" She gave him a particularly nasty glare. "It certainly smells like garbage to me. All those rotting herbs... disgusting."

"Take it back, Bim!" He shook a finger at her. "I mean it! Take it all back!" His face was beginning to turn beet red.

Bim crossed her arms over her chest. "Make me," she said with a daring smirk.

Brendle began to sputter in his outrage. "Don't think for a minute I won't By heavens I'll take every last one of your *stupid* inventions and throw them out into the street!"

She lowered her hands to her hips, her eyes narrowing menacingly. "My *what*?" She took a step closer to her brother. "Did you just call my inventions *stupid*?"

"Enough!" Bekka said. She couldn't take it anymore. She glared at both of them. "Don't make me separate the two of you."

She turned to Brendlestixx and smiled. "That is good news about Sinnestra's fortress. It could come in handy." She turned to Bimini and arched a brow. "What have you learned about Valoria? Do we know where she was taken?"

Brendlestixx had a smug look as he turned to face his sister. "Yes, what have you learned? Hmm?"

Bim shot her brother a dark look before turning and smiling at Bekka. "As a matter of fact, my source of information should be coming by this evening with all the pertinent details. These things take time, you understand. The information must be verified. We can't afford to be running off on a wild goose chase, now can we?"

The bell jingled above the shop door, someone had just entered the *Emporium*. Bimini gave them all a smile of satisfaction. "That would be him now."

"Him?" Brendle asked incredulously, arching a brow. "Surely not! I don't trust Lightfingers O'Leary as far as I can toss him. He's a two-bit thief and a hustler. Nothing more!"

Bim gave her brother a narrowed gaze. "Lightfingers is completely trustworthy. He always comes through for me." She turned her head toward the stairs. "Up here, Lightfingers," she beckoned.

As Darren O'Leary stepped out of the stairwell Bekka gasped in surprise. *"You're Lightfingers?"*

He smiled with a soft chuckle as he bowed formally. "Well if it isn't my damsel in distress!"

Bim looked from one to the other. "You two know each other?"

Bekka nodded. "He pulled me into a dark alleyway the day I arrived."

Brendle glared at him with sudden anger lighting his eyes. Bim's jaw dropped. She crossed her arms over her chest and said, "Care to explain?"

Lightfingers O'Leary grinned slyly. "In all honesty, I was saving her from one of De La'Corte's *Hellhounds*. She had the misfortune of managing to catch his attention."

Brendle scoffed as he continued to glare at Lightfingers. "You should not be permitted to use the term 'honesty' given your chosen profession."

Bim swatted her brother's arm. "You be nice! Lightfingers is a guest in our home." She turned a flirtatious smile at the thief. "So, did you manage to find out anything useful?"

He nodded. "Indeed I did. It wasn't as difficult as you would think, especially with all the excitement going on at the *City Keep*. Seems like someone broke into the private quarters and managed to kill De La'Corte."

The gnomes glanced at Bekka; it was clear that this news was a surprise to her as well. Brendle perked up. "What? Do they have any idea who the murderer was?"

Bim raised her brows. "I can't say that the old goat didn't have it coming."

Bekka went silent, sitting back in her chair.

"It was pretty gruesome stuff," Lightfingers continued. They found his corpse on the bed, half dressed. His body was pretty much just a dried husk."

"Bah!" Brendle said with a wave of his hand. "Good riddance, I say! The city is better off without his kind."

Bim nodded in agreement. "Well, like I said, he had it coming for a long time. What I want to know is what you managed to find out about Valoria."

Everyone looked at him expectantly.

"It would seem that she was purchased by an intermediary from *Dagmarth*. This agent bought her for a considerable sum for a gentleman named Kaspian Altair."

Brendle had taken a sip of wine and at the mention of the buyer he spit it out in a spray, almost choking in the process. He stared at Lightfingers, wiping his chin with the back of his hand. Did you say Kaspian Altair?"

Lightfingers glanced at Bim and then back at Brendlestixx. "I did. I take it that you know him?"

Brendle shook his head. "Know him? No." He nodded slowly. "Know of him, indeed I do."

Bim frowned. "So are you going to sit there like a knot on a log, or are you going to tell us who he is?"

Brendle gave his sister a haunted look. "Kaspian Altair is a very powerful wizard of some renown. He is what us wizarding folke call a *Dark Mage*." His eyes narrowed as he plucked at his bottom lip with thumb and forefinger. "He is one of the darkest to be sure. Not a man to be taken lightly. Very, very, very dangerous!" He shivered.

"What would a wizard want with someone like Valoria?" Bim asked.

Brendle shook his head, frowning. "Beats me." He glanced at everyone in turn. "But it cannot be good!"

Chapter 30
Old Friends Reunited

Bekka and Trish entered the *Twisted Oak Inn* an hour before the evening crowd usually arrived. The place was nearly deserted. Tarek Wyndspear was wiping the bar top with a clean, damp, cloth. He smiled as he recognized Bekka. "Well ye certainly are looking a lot better than ye were the last time I laid eyes on ye!"

Bekka smiled. "I should hope so."

"What can I get you ladies?" he asked, pausing with his clean up.

Bekka put a hand in the air. "I just came to collect the gear we left behind and to settle the tab that I owe you."

He nodded. "Ye be heading back to *Kensington Castle*, then?"

Bekka wondered how he knew about her home, but decided not to ask. She was afraid that he might let something embarrassing slip in front of Trish. The less she knew of her night at the *Twisted Oak*, the better. She shook her head. "No. We'll be sailing to *Dagmarth* soon."

Tarek scratched the stubble on his chin. "So ye won't be takin' yer horses, then?"

"Do you know of anyone who might be interested in taking them off my hands?"

"Aye," he nodded. "Those are mighty decent lookin' beasties. What say I take 'em off yer hands fer what ye owe me? We call everything square?"

Trish gave him a hard look. "How 'bout you throw in a hot meal and some of your best ale?"

Tarek chuckled softly. "Aye, I'll toss tha' in as well."

Bekka giggled, nudging Trish with her elbow as Tarek headed for the kitchen. "You haven't even seen the horses."

She smiled. "Well, he seemed pretty anxious to get his hands on them, so I figured we could at least wrangle something to eat and drink in the barter."

Bekka nodded. "They are beautiful animals. Valoria's gonna kill me when she finds out I let them go."

Trish shrugged. "What's she gonna do? You couldn't easily take them aboard the ship."

Bekka agreed. "That's certainly true."

They found a table and sat down to wait for their meal. After a few minutes Mari brought out a tray with two large bowls of steaming stew and two hefty chunks of bread. Tarek followed behind her and placed two tankards of ale in front of them. "We're fresh out of the venison; but this is a specialty of mine. Squirrel."

Bekka paused with a spoon halfway to her mouth. "Squirrel?"

Trish had immediately started in on the stew, and then lifted the tankard to her lips and washed it down with a huge gulp. Bekka watched her in astonishment as she shoveled another spoonful of squirrel stew into her mouth. "You act like you haven't eaten in days!"

Trish wiped her mouth with the back of her hand and then tore a chunk of bread and dipped it into the bowl. She shrugged as she took a bite. "You never know when your next meal is coming. After I was left to die in the forest by Maragh and his goons I went several days with very little sustenance." She shook her head as she lifted another spoonful of stew to her mouth. "I'm not doing that again."

Bekka smiled. "I understand completely," she said. She had gone several days with very little herself on her quest to confront Maragh. She watched as her friend continued to enjoy the stew. Finally, she looked at Trish with furrowed brows. "Who do you think murdered De La'Corte?"

Trish paused halfway to her mouth with a chunk of bread. "Who cares? Does it really matter? The guy had it coming. I wasn't gonna give him a chance to hurt anyone else."

Bekka swallowed. "What do you mean you weren't gonna give him a chance to hurt anyone? Did you kill him, Trish?"

Trish swallowed the bread. "No."

Bekka bit at her bottom lip. "You just said that you weren't going to let him hurt anyone—I heard you quite clearly."

Trish took a healthy sip of her ale. After an unladylike belch, she wiped her lips on her sleeve, dipped more bread into the bowl and shoved it into her mouth. "Fine. I killed the bastard. But he hurt you Bekka. He raped you. I had to make him pay!"

Bekka shook her head. "He didn't rape me."

Trish reached out and grasped Bekka's hand. "Yeah, he kinda did, Beks," she said with a nod. "No one hurts my friend and gets away with it. I made sure that he'll never hurt another living soul. Not ever."

Bekka's eyes grew wide as she stared at the bowl of stew in front of her. She placed the spoon down, no longer hungry. "Lightfingers said that De La'Corte's body seemed to be drained. He was nothing but a dried husk." She looked up at her friend. "How did that happen?"

Trish stared at her friend and crossed her arms over her chest. "Do you really want to know?"

Bekka wasn't sure that she did.

"I told you earlier that I am not the same girl that came through that portal. I've changed."

Bekka swallowed her fear. "How?"

Trish rolled her eyes and shook her auburn curls. "God, Beks! What's with the third degree? Can't you just let it go? I took care of it! I'm starting to lose my appetite for Pete's sake."

Bekka sat back in her chair, horrified. She couldn't stop the tears that sprang to her eyes. "Sorry, Trish. I'll stop asking so many questions." She shook her head firmly. "But one of these days you and I are going to have a serious talk."

Trish ate another spoonful of stew. "Fine. When you're ready to hear all the nitty-gritty little details, you just let me know; but I promise you, you won't sleep for weeks!"

The door to the Twisted Oak opened and Bekka glanced in that direction, happy for the distraction. Her jaw dropped open. Candi and Trevor had just come in with Kestra and Lithania. She jumped up from the table and ran to greet them. "Ohmygod! I can't believe you're here!" She hugged the blonde close.

Then she pushed Candi at arm's length. "Wait. What are you guys doing here?"

Candi's eyes began to tear up. "Is that Trish?" she asked, searching Bekka's face.

Bekka broke out into a huge grin and nodded vigorously. "Can you believe it? She's alive! She's been here in Freeport all this time! It was only by accident that I found her!"

Candi hopped up and down excitedly. She hugged Bekka close. "I'll be right back! Don't go anywhere!" They parted, and she ran across the barroom to where Trish was still sitting. She jubilantly flung her arms around the redhead, screaming with excitement, and hugged her tightly. "Trish! Oh my God! I so thought you were dead! How is this even possible?"

Bekka watched the two friends reunite with a smile. Then she turned her attention to the trio standing with her. Feeling awkward being so close to Trevor after so long, especially with Lithania nearby, she smiled tentatively. "So," she said, "What brings you all to Freeport?"

Trevor's eyes seemed clouded with sudden compassion. He pulled Bekka into a tight embrace and said, "Bekka, we've got some terrible news..."

Chapter 31
A Dirty Little Secret

Bekka stood at the window of her bedroom above the *Oddities and Magicks Emporium*, staring out into the night through teary eyes. Candi and Trish were standing at her side, trying to offer what comfort they could; their eyes were equally wet. The street below was nearly deserted, a stray cat seemed to be on the hunt for a mouse, but there was little else going on. It was too late for the locals to be out and about. Since the murder of De La'Corte, a curfew had been in effect. She sniffled and shook her head slowly. "We've all lost so much since we came through the *Portal*. I should never have brought you all through. I should've just come alone."

Candi gave Trish a glance. "No way, Beks! We're in this together. Just like always!"

Trish nodded. "As I recall, you didn't force any of us to come with you. We made that decision on our own." She looked out the window and saw the cat pounce on its prey. You could just hear the terrified *squeak* of the mouse even from this distance.

"Besides, if anyone forced anybody to go through that *Portal* it was me, I kinda forced Cleve. There was no way he would've come through on his own; he only did because of me."

Bekka heaved her shoulders. "I know. But if I had never said anything to any of you, and just came on my own, they'd *all* still be alive. Everyone would've thought that whoever had killed Ginger and Scott had gotten me too."

Candi sighed. "That would've killed your parents."

Trish slapped her arm. "*Candace Marie*! We're supposed to be comforting her. Geez, I can't believe some of the things you say sometimes! Don't you *ever* think before you open that mouth of yours?"

Candi blushed. "Sorry. I didn't mean to say it quite that way. But you know what I mean! Mr. and Mrs. K loved you so much! You were everything to them. That's why they came after you. They couldn't bear the thought of you being in danger without them here to protect you."

Trish glared at their blonde friend. Candi shook her head. "No. You both know I'm right about this. Despite everything we've lost, I don't regret it. Sure, I'm sad that people we love have died, and all. But I am glad that we're all together now. We're better this way. All of us are."

Trish grinned as she looked at Bekka. "She's got a point, you know."

Bekka chuckled softly as new tears fell. They had all been through so much. They had changed since coming through the *Portal* in unbelievable ways; yet some things were the same as they always had been. She took comfort in their dynamic. "I love you guys!"

She wrapped her arms around their shoulders and pulled them to her. "I honestly don't know what I'd do without either of you. You guys are my rock!"

Candi giggled. "Well, now that we're back together, hopefully you'll never have to find out what life's like without us in it!"

Bekka was truly relieved to have both of her friends back with her. She felt like together the three of them could survive just about anything. She had been concerned about Candi since she'd gotten here. The carefree light in her eyes had dimmed, replaced by a profound sadness. She knew that Candi was grieving the loss of Vincente and seeing him die right in front of her, must have been horrific. She gave her friend an extra little squeeze. But Candi was stronger than she had given her credit for. She seemed to have bounced back after all the loss with a grim determination, a new purpose.

She felt Trish stir in her embrace. And what of her? She still seemed to be the same old Trish from their *Midvale* days. But Bekka knew that she wasn't. She had been changed, probably the most, by all that had happened. The look in her eyes disturbed her. There was a *darkness* there that she just couldn't figure out. She *knew* that Trish had changed. The old Trish could not have killed anyone, let alone a dangerous man like De La'Corte. But this *new* Trish had done just that. And she had left a dried husk of the man behind. It made Bekka shiver. She wondered how that was even possible. It just wasn't normal at all. It just wasn't something she thought her friend was even capable of.

Her friends pulled out of her embrace and looked at her. In unison they said, "Are you okay?" And then the three of them giggled like in the old, carefree times.

Finally Bekka nodded. "Yeah, just a little tired. We should get some sleep. Tomorrow promises to be a busy day. Trevor, Lightfingers and Brendlestixx can see about booking passage for all of us on a ship. While in the meantime we can go check with the monks at the *Cathedral* and see what we can learn about this Brother Dinurés. This High Priest that Candi mentioned may be able to give us a bit more insight. He might even know where Dinurés may have gone. That could help us find Sinnestra and my brother. Kestra, Lithania and Bim can see to whatever supplies we might need."

Trish scowled. "I think I'll pass on the *Cathedral*."

Candi blinked, startled. "What about the three of us sticking together?"

Trish rolled her eyes. "You're a big girl now, Candi. You don't need me holding your hand anymore. Besides, those religious types just aren't my thing."

Candi seemed surprised, "Since when?"

Trish glared at her, "Since coming through the portal things have changed; I have changed."

Bekka could see Candi stiffen. She quickly intervened to

diffuse the situation. She took hold of Candi's hand. "It'll be fun. Just the two of us!"

Candi's eyes were clouded with hurt. "Sure."

While everyone else slept, Trish and Lithania slipped outside. They walked around the corner of the *Emporium* and into the alleyway. The elf looked at the redhead appraisingly. "Something on your mind?" she asked, crossing her arms over her chest.

Trish allowed a little smirk to appear on her face. "I just wanted to have a little chat." She smiled at the elf maiden as she placed her hands on her hips. "I *know* your dirty little secret," she said, her eyes twinkling.

Lithania studied her intently, suddenly wary. She dropped her hands to her sides. "Oh? And what *'secret'* is that?" she asked, guarded. She arched a brow, waiting.

Trish giggled as she stepped toward the elf. Tilting her chin up, she whispered. "I know *what* you are."

Lithania shook her head, seeming confused. "I would have thought that the shape of my ears made it rather obvious that I am an elf."

Trish laughed as she walked around the tall elf maiden. "Oh, so we are going to play *that* game, are we?" She came to a stop in front of her and crossed her arms. "Let us not *deceive* one another." Her eyes flashed red, but only for a brief instant.

Surprised, Lithania gasped sharply, her eyes flashed in response. "How did you know?"

Kestra had followed the pair outside, still suspecting that something was not quite right with the elf maiden. She had been deeply troubled ever since the elf had picked up the *Blade of the Spider's Kiss* at *Kensington Castle* and it hadn't glowed. Now, after this exchange between the elf and Trish, her suspicions seemed warranted. But now she knew that Trish was far more than she seemed as well! She staggered backwards, surprised by what she had just witnessed; over the last several months battling Deceivers she had seen the same fiery glow in their eyes. She lost her footing and fell to the ground. Before she could rise, they were on her. She reached for her weapon, but realized that she had left it inside the shop. Kestra growled. She grinned suddenly; there were only two of them. She liked those odds. Her eyes narrowed. "Today is a good day to die!"

Tentacles raced from the mouths of the two women standing over her...

Bekka had hoped that Kestra Àzul would accompany them on their quest to find and free Valoria from slavery, but she understood her concern over her warband. It was the fact that she hadn't bothered to say goodbye before taking off for the *Wastelands* that disappointed Bekka the most.

Trish shrugged. "The Orcs are still fighting a war with the Vortagg. You really can't blame her for wanting to get back to her own people. It was just fortunate that Kestra had taken the time to help Vincente. With all that she has going on it's a bit unfair to expect her to board a ship and just sail away."

Bekka nodded, blushing slightly. "I guess you're right." She sighed.

Trish gave her friend a hug. "Of course I am!"

Chapter 32
Final Preparations

Bekka and Candi were waiting just inside the *Great Cathedral* of *Freeport*. They had mentioned that they needed to speak with Brother Enetarés, but were told that the High Priest was extremely busy and could not make time to see them. Perhaps they should return in a week or two, after events within the city had settled down. The murder of De La'Corte had thrown the city into chaos and the Brotherhood was trying to restore order; but other factions within the coastal city were vying for control as well. Now simply was not a good time to bother the High Priest.

Bekka crossed her arms as she stared at the priest that was denying her request for an audience with his superior. She was not about to be dismissed so easily. "I need to speak with the High Priest concerning Brother Dinurés and the demoness known as Sinnestra." She saw the priest immediately stiffen when she mentioned the names.

He opened his mouth to speak, but closed it again. He cleared his throat. "If you would please follow me." He turned and started down a long, broad corridor that stretched deep into the sanctuary.

They passed wide alcoves along the pristine corridor; in each was a life-size stone statue depicting various Gods and Goddesses that were commonly worshipped by the citizens of *Vespia*; none of which were even remotely familiar to Bekka or Candi. Flanking the alcoves were carved stone murals picturing these Deities performing benevolent deeds for throngs of adoring believers.

The priest stopped in front of two massive double doors. He motioned to his left where a simple marble bench was located. "If you will be seated I will see if the High Priest can see you right away." He opened one of the doors and stepped inside; the door closing behind him.

Candi sat down on the bench and leaned her back against the wall. She crossed her arms over her chest and sighed as she crossed her ankles. "Now we wait," she said in a bored voice. She hated waiting. Sitting idle really was not her strong suit.

Bekka smiled at her friend, knowingly. She was not a fan of sitting around either. She began pacing back and forth. There was still too much to do. She was by no means ready to face Sinnestra. They had no real idea where Valoria had been taken. They only knew for a certainty that the slave ship had sailed for *Dagmarth*, but there was nothing to keep the ship from altering course to a new destination. And there was no way of knowing if Valoria had disembarked once it reached the seaport. It could have sailed away with Valoria still held prisoner aboard. It scared Bekka to even think that the ship may never have docked in *Dagmarth* at all. If it sailed to a different port Valoria could very well be lost to her—forever.

After a few minutes the priest returned and beckoned for both Bekka and Candi to come inside. "The High Priest will see you now."

Candi jumped to her feet with a quickness that seemed to take the priest by surprise. His eyes grew wide and he stepped back. After regaining his composure he held the door open, allowing them access to the inner chamber. To their surprise the man that greeted them was a tall, rather thin looking elven male. His long graying hair was pulled back and tied into a tight ponytail. He wore pristine white robes with thick cuffs and fancy embroidery on the sleeves. He smiled as they entered.

"Hello there, my good ladies. Please, make yourselves comfortable." He indicated the chairs in front of a massive mahogany desk with a sweep of his hand. As he walked to the far side of the desk he took a seat in a high-backed chair, he glanced up at the priest that had escorted them in. "That will be all, Brother Sorren."

Brother Sorren bowed and quickly left the room, closing the door behind him.

The High Priest turned his attention back to the women seated before him. "I am Brother Enetarés. I believe that Brother Sorren mentioned that you had information concerning Brother Dinurés?"

Bekka and Candi exchanged glances. Bekka took a quick breath and then began, "Were you aware that Brother Dinurés was working in collusion with the demoness Sinnestra?"

He frowned, steepling his fingers together as he placed his elbows upon the desktop. "Brother Dinurés left us some months back. I can no longer vouch for either he, or his acquaintances."

Candi leaned forward. "What about Brother Belgrid?"

His eyes narrowed. "As I said, both Brothers Dinurés and Belgrid left our Order several months ago. They began to show an increased interest in matters that went against the collective teachings of the Brotherhood. They were summarily dismissed and no longer welcomed here. Where they went, and with whom they associated themselves, I do not know." He glanced from Candi to Bekka. "Forgive me if I sound a bit harsh, but I truly do not care what they became involved in. After recent events I find that my attentions are needed elsewhere. The city of *Freeport* is falling into a state of anarchy, we must concentrate our efforts to restore order."

Bekka could feel her anger starting to rise. "Brother Dinurés and Brother Belgrid left *Freeport* with a girl who was badly wounded. They said that you sent them to *Kensington Castle*. Bandits near *Schiff's Crossing* supposedly killed Brother Belgrid. Dinurés and the girl went on to *Kensington Castle*. Once there, Brother Dinurés pushed my mother down a set of stairs, kidnapped my baby brother and took off to parts unknown. He seemed to be heading back to *Freeport*. The girl turned out not to be a girl at all; she was the demoness Sinnestra in disguise. Sinnestra murdered my mother and a very dear friend. We intend to avenge them."

The High Priest shook his head sadly. "I am truly sorry for the losses that you have endured. But I assure you that Brother Dinurés will not return to the *Cathedral*. If he returns to the city at all, it would most assuredly be to book passage on a ship. He would find no safe haven here in *Freeport*. Not from the Brotherhood."

"So you can't help us locate either Dinurés nor Sinnestra?" Candi asked.

Bekka added, "Can't or won't?"

He spread his hands in the air, keeping his elbow planted firmly on the desk and sighed. "These are troubled times for us all, I am afraid. The Order must concentrate our attention on what we perceive to be only the most pressing issues; those that directly affect the citizens of *Freeport*. We must restore order." He narrowed his gaze at Bekka. "If you are the *Chosen One* as reported, you are destined to fulfill the ancient prophecies. Sinnestra is to die by your hand." He shook his head slowly. "And if that is truly what you are destined for, then I have absolute faith that Divine Providence will guide you. I cannot help you."

He picked up a silver bell and rang it. A moment later Brother Sorren returned to escort the girls out. Candi could see that her friend was angry. It was sculpted in her posture; the hard set of her jaw and her lips were tightly closed. The look in her eyes was smoldering. Candi thought it best to remain quiet.

They were escorted back the way that they had come in complete silence. Bekka didn't trust herself to speak and Candi seemed to know better. Brother Sorren followed them outside of the *Great Cathedral* and cleared his throat as they descended the steps. The girls exchanged glances and then looked at the priest expectantly; it was clearly obvious he wanted a word.

He turned and looked quickly over his shoulder. "I have heard that Sinnestra has a fortress on the other side of the *Demon Spires*. If she is to be found, I believe it would be there where your best chance would lie."

Bekka narrowed her eyes at the priest, suspicious about

this sudden divulge of information. "Why are you telling us this when the High Priest of your Order has denied us any information?"

A slight smile threatened to turn the corner of his mouth. "Brother Enetarés has authorized me to give you this piece of information. He believes it may prove valuable to your cause. You must understand that the High Priest needs to maintain deniability to his superiors if he is questioned. By allowing me to impart this snippet of information he can do just that, and you can still gain the information that you seek. The High Priest is a good man, but he is a prisoner of the politics within the Order."

Candi looked at Bekka. "Well, as my Gramps used to say, you could knock me over with a feather!"

"I know, right?" Bekka shook her head as she looped her arm around Candi's. "We'd best be heading back to the *Emporium*; everyone else will be arriving back there shortly."

Trevor stared up at the rather large sign that hung above the door of the dockside tavern. It depicted an octopus holding a fork, a spoon and a knife. The remaining tentacles held a mug of either rum or ale; Trevor couldn't be sure which. Above the artwork was the pub's name: *Paddy's Cove*. Brendlestixx gave him an amused look. "Quit your gawking, we haven't the time."

Trevor shook his head. He wasn't too fond of the gnomish wizard. "Take it easy. I was just looking at the sign."

"You had stopped walking and were just standing there like you had nothing better to do. We need to meet with Lightfingers and secure passage to *Dagmarth*."

Trevor sighed, looking around. "Lightfingers isn't even here yet. He went off toward the docks. Who knows when he'll return?"

"That is beside the point, lad. He instructed us to wait here for him." Brendlestixx shook a finger at him. "We needn't waste time when there are better things to do!"

Trevor frowned. "Darren told us to wait *here*," he pointed to the street, "not in *there*," he shifted his finger to point at the pub. "Besides, what are we going to do in there, anyway?"

The gnome sighed in exasperation as he rolled his eyes. "My dear boy, we are about to be stuck aboard a ship for at least a few days. This may very well be our last opportunity to have a decent drink. Trust me, you won't fancy the taste of shipboard grog!"

Trevor chuckled. "Now the truth comes out. This need to hurry is all about you wanting to quench your thirst!"

Brendlestixx grinned. "Let this be our little secret, shall we? What Bim doesn't know, can't hurt me, or you," he winked conspiratorially. "She's quite a handful when she is angry."

Trevor smiled at the gnome. "So, you're afraid of her?"

Brendlestixx's eyes went wide as his brows shot up his forehead. "Oh most definitely! My sister is as sharp as a tack, and her twisted little mind can come up with all sorts of gadgets and gizmos that can make your life absolutely miserable if she sets her mind to it!" He chuckled without humor and shivered suddenly; goosebumps rose on his arms. "She can be quite nasty when she wants to be."

Trevor chuckled softly. "I get it," he said. "So why risk her wrath?"

The gnome patted his arm. "My dear boy, you only live once!"

Trevor shook his head as he held the door for Brendlestixx and they stepped inside. Trevor held the door open longer than he should, and was quickly scolded by a grizzled seaman threatening to keelhaul him if he didn't shut the blasted door. He quickly complied.

The interior of *Paddy's Cove* was quite dark, especially after stepping in from the bright sunlight. There were a few oil lamps scattered throughout the single room, but the light cast from them was dim, due mostly to the dingy, amber colored glass of the lanterns themselves.

After his eyes had adjusted to the shadowy tavern, Trevor could see that there were only a few patrons other than the one that had threatened him with bodily harm; all of them similar in appearance; men hardened by the wind and sea. Brendlestixx paid them no attention as he made his way to a table in the far corner, closest to the bar.

As Trevor followed the gnome to the table, he struck the boot of the seaman that had promised to drag him under the keel of a ship, thereby ripping him to shreds as the barnacles tore his skin. Off balance, Trevor pitched forward striking another seaman sitting at the bar, causing his mug of ale to spill down his grimy shirt.

The sailor stood and grabbed Trevor by the arms. "Watch where yer a goin' laddie!" he said in a gruff, alcohol thickened voice. "Blasted landlubber!"

Trevor swallowed. He could hear the chuckle coming from behind him. He had no doubt that the seaman had purposely tripped him. He was in serious trouble, and he knew it. "I... I'm sorry, sir."

"Sorry says you, eh?" the seaman seemed to sway unsteadily as he still gripped Trevor in a powerful clutch. "Why tha' t'was me last copper tha' bought me tha' mug o' ale, it was."

Brendlestixx cleared his throat, tapping the sailor's massive forearm. "The lad said he was sorry. Perhaps I can make amends by buying you another ale?"

"The clumsy oaf scuffed me boot," the other seaman said as he pushed off from the table. Clearly he had no designs to let the matter drop.

Brendlestixx glanced down at the seaman's worn boot. It was difficult to determine if the scuffs that covered it were old or new. "So he has." He glanced at the barkeep, "How about a mug of ale for the house?" He jabbed a finger into Trevor's stomach. "You need to watch where you are going, lad! Disturbing these fine, hardworking men during their time of well-earned leisure. Disgraceful!" He shook his head and glanced over his shoulder. "It is hard to get good help these days!" He continued to shove Trevor ahead of him, making their way back to the corner table and relative safety.

Trevor's eyes were wide as he quickly took a seat. "This is a pretty rough crowd," he said. It was obvious he was keen to leave. He was willing to take his chances with the shipboard grog. *How bad could it really be?* Besides, he didn't really drink, anyway.

"This isn't so bad, laddie. Not if you keep a somewhat lower profile," Brendlestixx said as he nodded at the barkeep and held up two fingers. A buxom red-haired waitress made her way to the table and placed two mugs of ale in front of them.

Trevor glanced up at her and smiled. "Thank you."

She pinched his cheek and gave it a little jiggle. "Ain't you a polite one!" She giggled as he turned a bright red. "Aw, just a pup, eh?"

As the waitress departed, Brendlestixx took a sip of his ale, leaving a trail of white froth on his upper lip as he returned the mug to the table. "Seems like you've made a new friend," he said with an amused smirk.

Trevor chose to ignore the comment. He took a sip from his tankard. The ale was surprisingly strong with a hint of bitter and sweetness, followed by heat as he swallowed. He found that it left his eyes watering slightly. He peered down into the mug and blinked. He had scarcely taken a sip; he seriously doubted his ability to drink the entire contents. Trevor suspected that if he were successful he'd likely be incapacitated. He sat the mug onto the table and nudged it away with the tips of his fingers.

Brendlestixx grinned at him "Dwarven Firewater isn't for everyone, lad. It's the one thing that those blasted dwarves got right." He finished off his tankard and then pulled Trevor's to him. He cocked his head and smiled. "No sense in letting it go to waste." He lifted the mug to his lips and drained it in three large gulps.

Trevor shook his head. "I think you might want to take it easy with that stuff."

"Bah!" Brendlestixx lifted the empty tankard in the air and waived it at the waitress. His eyes already had a glassy look. He plopped the pewter mug onto the table with a resounding thud and belched loudly. "No tellin' when we'll shee Lightfingersh."

Trevor nodded. "Exactly my point. If you drink much more of that stuff Bimini will be unhappy with the both of us."

The gnome chuckled. "I'd sooner face Bim's wrath than shail aboard a ship shober," he said thickly. He smiled as the serving girl placed two more tankards in front of them. He quickly downed one and as he reached for the other, he pitched forward and face-planted the table.

Much to Trevor's relief, the door opened and Lightfingers stepped inside, quickly closing the door behind him. The thief made his way to the corner table. "What happened to Brendlestixx?" he asked, then shook his head. "Never mind. I can already see." He raised the other mug and drained it himself. "I don't think I want to be completely sober when I haul him back to face Bim." Lightfingers sighed heavily. "Bim'll give us an earful, you can count on that."

Trevor nodded. "He said he'd rather face her than sail sober."

Lightfingers chuckled. "Brendlestixx has never liked sailing; too many things that can swallow him whole if he were to go over the side he claims."

"Did you manage to secure us passage to *Dagmarth*?"

"I did indeed. We depart at high tide aboard the Wyndreaver, which means we need to get our drunken friend back to the *Emporium* and gather the others. We only have a few hours until the 'Reaver sails."

Chapter 33
The Wyndreaver

Bim glared at Lightfingers and Trevor with fury blazing from her eyes as she stood in the doorway of the *Emporium,* watching them approach. Brendlestixx was slung over the thief's shoulder. She had no doubt what that meant. She could almost smell the fumes of the Dwarven Firewater from where she stood. She shook her head, narrowing her eyes. "How could you allow this to happen?"

Lightfingers raised a hand in the air. "I was not present at the time. I was securing us passage aboard the *Wyndreaver.*" He inclined his head toward Trevor as best he could. "The lad had no idea that this would happen."

She took a long breath and slowly let it out. "Of course he didn't." She glared at the thief. Clearly his absence didn't excuse him from what happened. She was furious. Trevor thought it would be best to steer clear of the gnome.

Bim had decided that most of the supplies that they would

need could be found in *Dagmarth*. It didn't make a lot of sense to board the ship with more than they could carry, unless it was something that she felt they absolutely had to have. She was certain that Brendlestixx would need components for his spells; unfortunately he was not in a state to pick and choose after his visit to his favorite haunt, *Paddy's Cove*. She would have to decide for him. She knew him better than anyone else and had a fairly good idea where his preferences lay. If she missed something, he would either have to go without or hope to find it in their next destination. But whatever she packed for him was better than nothing.

Bekka stood on the pier waiting to make her way up the gangplank. She couldn't wait to leave *Freeport* behind; the coastal city had given her more than her fair share of misery. Down at the wharves, the smell was even worse than most of the city's alleyways had been. The scent of fish was heavy in the air as was the salty brine that slapped against the moorings and the hull of the ship. Seagulls hung in the air, ever watchful for a morsel of food that might be tossed their way by fishermen that dipped poles into the water for the chance at catching enough to feed themselves and their families before the sun set on the horizon.

She peered into the murky water and was surprised to see so many ghostly looking jellyfish floating near the surface. At first she wasn't even certain that they were alive, but then she saw several of the umbrella-shaped bells begin to gently pulsate, propelling the gelatinous fish along in an undulating fashion; their tentacles trailing behind. They almost seemed to glow majestically in the darkened sea.

Bekka shook her head, clearing her thoughts as Trish nudged her from behind. "We're gonna miss the boat if you don't start following the others," the red-head said with a twisted grin.

"Sorry," Bekka said with a soft chuckle. "I was entranced by the jellyfish."

Candi shivered. "I hate those things! If they sting you it's like really painful. I had a cousin that got stung by one a few years ago. They had to pee on her to stop it from hurting."

"Eew! Gross!" Bekka and Trish said in unison.

"I know! Right?" Candi said as she reached out and touched

each girl on the arm. "It was the most shocking thing I ever witnessed!"

Bekka's eyes went wide. "Did it work?"

Trish shook her head in disbelief. "Why are you even curious about this? I mean, seriously!"

Bekka shrugged. "I don't know. I've always heard that pee would take away the jellyfish sting. I was just wondering if it was true; that's all."

"Well, I'm here to tell you," Candi said emphatically, "Carla Mae said she immediately felt better!"

Bekka shivered, mortified by the vision stuck in her brain. She quickly turned and started up the gangplank. The smells surrounding the docks were nauseating. The sea filled the air with a heavy tang of salt, and when combined with the stench of gutted fish and stagnant seaweed, it was almost overwhelming. The thought of someone having to pee on her to rid the sting of a jellyfish was almost enough to send her over the edge. She could only hope that once the ship got out of the harbor the air would be fresher. It certainly couldn't be any worse.

The *Wyndreaver* was a three-masted schooner built for speed; its hull was painted a jet black. The figurehead mounted on the ship's bow sent a shiver down Bekka's spine. It was a *Grim Reaper*, complete with a shining scythe held in front of it with skeletal hands of weathered bone. The captain claimed that it enabled the ship to slice through the wind and high seas more efficiently. Her eyes rose to the top of the main mast; she fully expected to see a black flag emblazoned with a skull and crossbones fluttering in the light breeze. She was almost disappointed to see a single red pennant snapping in the wind.

Trevor grinned at her. "Were you expecting to see the *Jolly Roger*?"

Bekka smiled, nodding. "I was." She felt a momentary pull at her heartstrings; he knew her so well! For a brief second she remembered their first kiss high atop the Ferris wheel out on *Miller's Farm* the night of the carnival. It seemed a lifetime ago. She smiled at him; maybe they could still be friends after all.

Lightfingers studied the two for a brief moment. He could tell that there was something going on between them, but he wasn't certain what it was. Trevor and the elf maiden were together; at least he had thought they were. Still, there seemed to be a strong connection between he and Bekka as well. He smiled as he approached them. "The captain recommends that we go to our quarters while the ship gets underway. There will be a flurry of activity and we wouldn't want to be in the way." Turning, he guided them through a hatch, which led below the main deck.

The big sailor pulled on one of the mooring lines as he watched the group go below. He grinned and pushed the tip of his tongue through the gap in his teeth and ran it along his upper lip. Reaghar chuckled to himself. They said the third time was the charm; perhaps he still had a chance for revenge. He nudged the orc beside him and inclined his head toward the hatch where they had disappeared. Dralgor nodded; he had seen them as well; he grinned in anticipation; vengeance could be incredibly sweet!

Bekka felt the tingle run down her spine as her senses warned her of impending danger. She stopped on the steps that led below the main deck and turned. She saw nothing that appeared out of place. The sailors were busy hauling in the mooring lines aboard ship, or casting them over the side; others were scrambling about the deck busy with tasks of their own as the *Wyndreaver* was pushed from the dock. She could hear the First Mate, a grizzled sailor with a wooden leg, shouting orders that she didn't understand, something about readying the sails. She had never had a good grasp of nautical terminology.

Bekka turned away from the flurry of activity and descended the steps. It took a moment for her eyes to adjust to the low lamplight of the narrow passageway. She felt cold and apprehensive. She was stressed and she was tired. Hopefully it was only her imagination getting the best of her and not one of Lady Rosa's premonitions. She couldn't really tell anymore. They didn't come often; they were always just a feeling, a whispering sensation. Sometimes they meant nothing, but other times these glimpses turned into reality.

The movement of the *Wyndreaver* was getting to Bekka as the ship tossed up and down and rocked side to side by wave after assaulting wave. She had gone topside for fresh air, having found the close confines of her shared cabin a bit stifling. The storm had appeared out of nowhere, giving everyone aboard the ship little time to prepare. *"Batten down the hatches!"* roared the captain over the rising gale-force winds. *"Stow the mainsail! Ready the storm sails!"* The commands were echoed by the First Mate. Bekka didn't have a clue as to their meaning. She quickly made her way back below deck, her body haplessly bouncing off of the bulkheads of the narrow passageway. Feeling slightly battered and bruised, she opened the door to her cabin and stumbled to her bed. She scrambled onto the bed just as the ship rolled in the opposite direction. She clutched at the blankets desperately trying to keep from being tossed about the room. She curled up in her bunk, grabbed her knees, and pulled them against her chest, hoping she wouldn't puke.

Candi moaned from across the room as she closed her eyes tightly. "I don't want to die!" she said, near tears.

Bekka swallowed her bile. "We're not going to die. Everything will be fine." She tried to sound confident, but in reality she just couldn't be certain.

"How can you know that for sure?" Candi asked, her eyes rimmed with red; she had obviously been crying.

"It's just a stupid storm, Candi. It will pass!"

The ship rose high upon a massive wave and crashed down into the sea below, rocking the vessel from side to side. Candi cried, "I don't like this!"

Bekka pulled her pillow over her head and drowned out her friend's whimpering. She bit her bottom lip still hoping she wouldn't lose her lunch.

The *Wyndreaver* continued to navigate the rough seas for several more hours. The rocking back and forth seemed to ease somewhat and the gentle motion helped the girls to relax. Eventually sleep claimed them both.

In the early morning hours Bekka awoke to the sounds outside the cabin; heavy boots seemed to scuff along the floorboards, pausing at her door. "Candi, are you awake?" she asked softly.

"Huh? What? What's up?" Candi said as she tried to sit up. She seemed to struggle within her sheets.

"Someone's outside!" Bekka said, her voice full of tension.

"Geez, Bekka, why the big fuss?" Candi said finally freeing her legs from the sheet, "It could be anybody."

Bekka shook her head. She had had a dream, a nightmare really. In the dream both she and Candi had been attacked; it was unclear if they even survived. She didn't think that whomever was outside their door was a friend. "Don't open the door!"

Candi wasn't listening. She was finally free of her sheets and blankets and was heading for the door. In Bekka's dream Candi had opened the door and a cutlass was thrust in her chest. She remembered seeing her friend slump to the deck, eyes wide and lifeless.

Bekka's eyes grew wide as Candi reached for the door. She scrambled to get out of bed and save her friend. She made it to her side just as Candi was opening the door. Bekka could see Reaghar and Dralgor standing in the passageway, weapons drawn. She threw her body against the door, slamming it closed. A flash of forgotten memory glared in her mind like a beacon; she shoved Candi's chest, *hard*, pushing them apart. A second later the steel blade of Dralgor's cutlass penetrated the flimsy door, inches away from their faces.

"Holy shit!" Candi exclaimed, backing away from the door.

Bekka was unable to keep the door closed on her own. The combined weight of Reaghar and Dralgor splintered the weakened door and pushed her back, causing her to sprawl upon the floor.

Reaghar reached for the stunned blonde and grabbed her throat roughly. He pointed toward Bekka. "Get her, Dral!"

The orc was fast. Bekka tried to back pedal away from him, but she struck the bunk before she could escape. He grabbed her legs as she attempted to kick him off of her. She flung her arms wildly, her fingernails finding purchase on his green-tinged face. She clawed for all that she was worth raking deep furrows into his cheek. The last thing she remembered was seeing his massive fist flying towards her face.

Candi struggled but she was having difficulty breathing. Black spots exploded around her vision as she desperately slapped at Reaghar's thick arm. His free hand ripped at her clothing. "Time for some fun!" he said, drool dripped from his chin, the smell of rum thick on his breath.

"Funny," Trish said from the doorway, "I was thinking the exact same thing!"

Candi collapsed upon the wooden deck as Reaghar released his hold on her throat. Red-faced, she coughed, her throat burning as she fought to breathe. She forced her eyes to open wide, desperately fighting back the darkness that threatened to close in. She gasped, finding it difficult to believe what she was seeing.

Snaking tendrils shot from her friend striking the orc and the human with precision. Their screams were stifled almost before they even began. Their bodies seemed to quiver; *were they really being lifted from the floor?* The next moment their massive bodies were hurled against the bulkhead as though they were sacks of grain. They cried out in horror as Trish moved in front of them, legs spread wide, tendrils shooting outward, striking again and again without mercy. Eventually the repeated blows took their toll, the lifeless flesh squishing horrifyingly as their bodies collapsed onto the bloodstained floorboards of the cabin's deck. Candi's eyes fluttered as she lost consciousness.

Chapter 34
Dagmarth

Lightfingers and Trevor wrapped the corpses in canvas and carried them topside. The deadweight made it difficult, but somehow they managed. Brendle joined them as they dropped the bodies onto the deck. He nodded. "The night watch is fast asleep, but they won't be for long."

Lightfingers nodded. "Do your thing," he pointed to the shrouded corpses.

Brendlestixx closed his eyes and began to speak in a language that Trevor couldn't comprehend. The words were foreign and elusive, melodic and mesmerizing. When the gnome stopped chanting, he nodded. "They should be good." He glanced around, making sure they weren't being observed.

The thief grasped the canvas of the first corpse and grunted. He looked at Trevor. "Give me a hand, will you?"

Trevor quickly grabbed the end of the rolled canvas and was surprised by the unexpected weight. He glanced quizzically at Lightfingers.

O'Leary grinned. "Brendle turned them into stone. We can't very well have them floating for all to see. It's best if they sink out of sight quickly." They tossed their burden overboard, the splash barely noticeable over the gusting winds.

Trevor wiped his brow after they tossed the second stone corpse over the side of the ship. "What do you think really happened to them?" He looked from Lightfingers to the gnome; neither answered right away.

Finally Lightfingers shrugged. "They got what they deserved."

Trevor studied the ocean; there was no sign of either corpse. The sea had already claimed them.

Brendlestixx slapped his arm. "Come, lad. We best get below before we are seen."

The storm at sea had actually worked in their favor, speeding them along. Initially the *Wyndreaver* wasn't going to dock pierside until late in the day. Now, as the sun was beginning to reach its zenith, the seaport of *Dagmarth* was coming into view. Dark clouds seemed to hover over the coastline soaking the town in a torrential downpour, giving the port a dark and brooding appearance.

Bekka and Candi were standing in the fo'cs'le of the *Wyndreaver*, the sea breeze blowing through their hair. They had minor cuts and abrasions on their faces after their encounter with Reaghar and his orc companion Dralgor had attacked them in their quarters. Both were sporting split lips which stung, as salt spray dampened their cheeks occasionally as the ship cut through the ocean.

Candi turned and looked aft. She could see Trish's auburn curls blowing in the breeze as she and the others stood on the ship's poop deck. She shook her head, keeping her voice to a whisper, though no one was around to hear. "Trish scares me. She's not the same person that came through the *Portal* with us. I'm not even certain she's even human anymore."

"Don't be silly," Bekka said absently, giving her a dark look. Her focus seemed miles away.

Candi squeezed her friend's arm. "You didn't see what I saw, Beks. If you had, you wouldn't say that. She had these... these *things* that shot out from her." Candi shivered uncontrollably. "It was horrifying!"

Bekka looked toward the stern of the ship. She could see her friends huddled together, smiling, laughing. They seemed to be enjoying the day without a care in the world. She glanced out to the empty sea, her thoughts jumbled. Ever since they had come through the *Portal* they had been in danger. They were ill equipped to handle the rigors that *Vespia* demanded. It was a hard life, one that they might not survive. She glanced toward the shoreline where *Dagmarth* dotted the horizon, wondering what trials and perils awaited them. *'Am I doing the right thing, bringing my friends into this perilous adventure?'* she could only wonder.

Though Bekka had tuned her out, Candi had continued to babble. "...and I'm not sure we can trust her."

Bekka's eyes narrowed thoughtfully as she studied the group of companions at the rear of the ship. A moment later Trish turned and waved, almost as if she could feel eyes upon her. Bekka returned the friendly gesture. She looked back at Candi. "We're all a little different than we were on the other side."

Candi chuckled without any trace of humor. "Oh, I agree. You'll get no argument from me. We've all grown so much since then. But with Trish, it's different. She's different." She shook her head. "She's *something else* entirely. Some kind of *monster*."

Bekka sighed. "Trish is our friend. She's had a rough time on this side of the *Portal*. She was alone for so long, we at least had each other to lean on. Trish had nobody. She's *not* a monster."

Candi squeezed her friend's arm. "Are you so sure about that?"

Bekka bit at her bottom lip, as she seemed to consider it. "Okay. All right. We'll keep an eye on her. We'll give her a chance to prove herself to us. You okay with that?"

Candi nodded. "Sure, Beks. Whatever you think is best."

Bekka placed a hand on her arm and squeezed it reassuringly. "Candi, she *saved* us from those two. Had she not, no telling *what* might've happened." She couldn't very well tell Candi she'd had a vision in which they both died. If she did, Candi wouldn't likely trust her either.

Candi shrugged. "Whatever you wanna do, Bekka. I'm with you."

That was the problem! She wasn't sure what was the best for everyone. She never truly had been. She had simply plunged ahead and hoped for the best. But where had that gotten them? Her parents were dead. So were Cleve, Jacob, Vincente and Lady Rosa. Sinnestra's High Priest had kidnapped her infant brother. And Trish... she was *different* now. She had been altered somehow. Time would tell what that would mean; she was certain of it— but even that fact frightened her. She hated to admit it, but Candi might be right. Trish *might* just be a monster. She had admitted to killing De La'Corte; and if the reports were true, his death had been unusually gruesome. Bekka had seen the ghastly looks on the faces of the guys, they had been horrified by what they found in the cabin. Reaghar's and Dralgor's deaths had been equally *monstrous*.

They walked down the gangplank of the *Wyndreaver* and when they finally stood upon the pier they all seemed to smile. It was good to be back on solid ground. Candi quickly put a hand over her mouth, her fingers stretched up to cover her nose. "Eew! What is that stench?"

Lightfingers chuckled. "That, dear lady, is the smell of *Dagmarth*."

Bim gave her a small, sympathetic smile. "It is the smell of rot from the seaweed clinging to the pillars of the pier and the peat from the nearby swamp. I don't know how anyone can get used to it, but the people hereabouts don't seem to mind it much."

Candi looked as though she were about to be ill. "Well, the sooner we can leave this place, the better."

Beyond the wooden docks Bekka could see the coastal village of *Dagmarth*. Numerous buildings of varying sizes populated the town. Where cobblestones had been the norm within *Freeport*, dirt, or now mud after the heavy rains, constituted the makings of streets here. She could see several murky puddles scattered throughout the seaport. The mud seemed to glisten in the afternoon sunlight, promising a need for sure footing. "Well," she said, "hopefully we can find the information we seek and be on our way. I'm just afraid that if too much time passes it'll be that much harder to find Valoria."

She smiled at Lightfingers, placing a hand upon his arm. "I'd like to be on our way tomorrow, if possible."

He nodded, giving her a two-fingered salute and a small bow. "I will see about securing adequate transportation for us," he glanced at Brendlestixx, "You should see about our accommodations for the night."

Brendle squinted up the street. "I seem to recall a nice tavern with several rooms on the far side of town; it should satisfy our needs."

Bim gave her brother a dark look through narrowed eyes. "Just remember, we need to get an early start tomorrow. We need to find Valoria as quickly as we can, so I don't want you to drink much. In fact, I would suggest that you spend your free time looking over the spells you might need going forward. Make sure you have the necessary components."

Brendle frowned. "You make it sound like I make a habit of drinking too much."

She poked a finger into his chest. "That's because you do!"

He shook his head. "Not when a friend is in need of our help."

Bim crossed her arms over her chest. "Oh? What happened to you in *Paddy's Cove*? Valoria was still in need of our help, yet you got so drunk you couldn't even walk back. You had to be carried home."

Brendle glared at his sister. "That was entirely different. As you well know I am not particularly fond of sailing. I need a drink or two to calm my nerves."

She shook her head and made a *tisking* sound. "It was my understanding that you had more than just a few drinks, dear brother."

He glared at Trevor who was about to come to his defense. "Yes, well..."

She raised a hand in the air, cutting him off. "Save it."

A southern breeze blew, carrying with it the smells of the sea as they walked along the pier. Dark clouds were pushed inland, filled with the promise of more rain. They could smell it in the air and their step quickened. As they left the sure footing of the dock behind, they slowed somewhat, careful not to slip in the already slickened mud. They went their separate ways, determined to accomplish their goals before the weather turned against them.

A group of four men watched them, blending in with the workers of the nearby warehouses that were busy with their daily tasks of moving crates either to or from the ships tied to the piers. They spoke to one another in hushed whispers, their grizzled faces menacing. "Remember," their leader spoke in a thick voice, "Lady Sinnestra will not accept incompetence or failure." Deciding it was safe to follow their prey, they split up, careful to remain unseen.

They gathered in the dining hall of *The Gilded Rose Inn* well after the sun had set. They had had a successful afternoon, securing several rooms for the night, a wagon to transport their belongings, and several horses to ride and a team to pull the wagon. They had also uncovered vital information.

They learned that the slaves from the slave ship had been loaded into a wagon and departed several days ago. They had traveled along the river; their destination was a village known as *Darkwater*, far to the north. This was certainly good news, as far as Bekka was concerned. This validated the belief that they were on the right track to locate Valoria.

The news only got better. Two days before they arrived in *Dagmarth* a man with a small infant had booked a room in the *Gilded Rose*. Another man eventually met him and they all departed soon after. No one fitting the description of either Sinnestra or Gwyneth had been seen. But when they questioned further, it was discovered that this second man had a wounded shoulder that seemed badly infected, refusing to heal. This left little doubt who this man actually was. Obviously Sinnestra was able to shape-shift somehow, but the bite from the *Blade of the Spider's Kiss* always remained.

Bekka could feel the excitement rising within her. They were not that far behind their quarry, and with a little bit of luck they could easily make up some time. "I wish we could start out now," she said as they stood looking at the map that Bim had spread out upon the table.

Bim grinned knowingly. "We'll depart early in the morning, when there is sufficient light to see by. We'll hopefully be able to keep a good pace."

Lightfingers crossed his arms over his chest. "The heavy rains will make it rough going for our wagon. It will likely have slowed the slaver's wagon as well, which should help us some. We could split up and attempt to catch them and then wait for our wagon to join up."

Brendle shook his head. "I don't like the idea of splitting up our merry little band. Not with that demoness out there somewhere, especially since we've no way to know what form she's taken. It would be just like her to attack our weakest link."

Lightfingers frowned. "I wasn't suggesting that we leave the wagon defenseless." His annoyance was clearly evident.

Brendle shook his head again. "I still don't think it is a good idea to split up. We're stronger together."

Bekka sighed. The wagon *would* slow them down, especially if the rain persisted. It would make the road north as bad as the streets of *Dagmarth*. She liked the idea of splitting their forces to make a quick assault on the slaver's wagon; but she knew that the gnome had a valid point. They *were* stronger together. Sinnestra was out there, and everyone knew what she was capable of. They really couldn't afford any more losses; keeping the group as strong as possible was the better plan under the circumstances.

A serving girl dropped off a tray filled with wooden tankards of ale. She gathered the empties and headed off toward the kitchen. Brendle licked his lips and hefted a mug to his lips. Before he could take a sip, Bim took it from him and drained it rather quickly. She wiped her chin with the back of her hand and smiled at him, a gleam of mischief in her eyes. "Thanks, brother."

Anger flashed in Brendle's eyes. "You could've taken one for yourself, you know!"

Bim suddenly scrunched up her face as she took a faltering step sideways. She placed a hand at the base of her neck, her eyes growing wide, bloodshot. Her skin turned pallor as she pitched forward. Bekka was able to grab her and ease her to the floor. Bim convulsed, white froth escaped her lips; and then she lay still, her eyes bulged.

Brendle had taken another tankard from the table and was about to drink, but hesitated as he saw his sister's reaction. Lightfingers knocked the mug out of his hand. "Don't! I think they're all poisoned!"

Trish pushed past them, heading for the kitchen. The barkeep gave her a menacing look as she stepped behind the bar, after seeing the look in her eyes; he did nothing to stop her. She shoved the swinging doors open in time to see the girl exit the back door. She sped through the sparse kitchen and got to the door before it closed.

The girl slipped in the mud and fell to her knees, whimpering, she tried to rise. She froze. Lithania stood above her, sword drawn. The elf smiled at Trish. "Thought she might try to get away. The back door was her only option."

Trish looked around. "We need to question her, but not here." She pointed to a rundown shed some distance away. "That should do."

The *Gilded Rose* was mostly deserted when Trish rejoined the others. Bekka eyed her friend warily as she pulled up a chair next to her. "Were you able to find her? What did she have to say?"

Trish shrugged. "She actually had a lot to say, really. The serving girl was paid to deliver the tankards to the table by a pretty rough looking individual. She had seen him in the pub before, but she didn't know his name. She gave a pretty good description of him. He'll be hard to miss. He has a long scar down his forehead that crosses his crooked nose and continues down his cheek, ending at the point of his chin. He paid her with a silver coin. She swears that she didn't know the ale was poisoned. He told her he was buying a drink for friends."

"Do you believe her?" Bekka asked.

Trish nodded. "I do. She was too frightened to lie."

Bekka studied her for a moment. "You didn't hurt her did you?"

Trish turned to face her friend, giving her a little smirk. "Geez Beks, what do you take me for? I'm not a monster."

After a restless night they prepared to part ways with Brendlestixx just prior to the sun rising over the *Barrier Peaks*. He would accompany them no further, deciding it best to return Bimini home for burial. He would catch the next ship back to Freeport, and then return his sister to their ancestral home in the *Emerald Forest*. Without the gnomes in their company they had no real need for a wagon, most of the gear had been theirs, anyway.

It nearly broke Bekka's heart to see such sadness in Brendle's eyes. Tears streamed down her cheeks as she hugged him close; she had grown quite fond of both brother and sister. "Do what you need to do, we'll manage," she whispered in his ear. She could feel him tremble against her as he croaked a muffled response that she couldn't quite decipher. She gave him another comforting squeeze, hesitant to let him go.

Finally, Brendle grasped her arms and pushed out of her embrace. His eyes were wet with tears. He wiped his runny nose with the back of his hand. "Go, the others are waiting." He quickly turned away and then rushed back inside the *Gilded Rose*.

Bekka watched as the gnome turned to close the door behind him. In the shadows of the doorway she could see that his cheeks were wet with more tears. She wanted to run to him, hug him again, and grieve with him over the senseless loss of Bim; but the others were waiting for her to mount up. They still had a long, hard ride ahead of them. She couldn't afford to waste any more time. There was nothing else that she could do for either of the gnomes. She had to turn her thoughts and her efforts to saving Valoria and Han. With a heavy heart, Bekka turned away and took the reins of her mount from Lightfingers. They rode in silence, leaving the seaport of *Dagmarth* behind, shrouded in a gray, morning mist.

Chapter 35
Surprising News

A storm was beginning to blow up from the sea. Thunder rumbled and the sky grew dark with ominous clouds that blotted out the sun, making it impossible to judge the time of day. Bekka figured it was close to noon, and her stomach growled in confirmation. She was hungry. She hadn't felt much like having any breakfast but she was incredibly thirsty.

As though he could read her mind Lightfingers brought his horse up beside her and handed her a waterskin with the stopper already removed. Bekka accepted it with a grateful smile and took a healthy swig before handing it back. It was cool and refreshing; just what she needed. He took a sip from the skin and slammed the plug back into the top. "We should probably find some form of shelter from the coming storm. It'll be upon us before we know it."

Bekka nodded. She could already feel the air change and smell the promise of rain even before the first few drops splashed in her face. She could see Trevor and Lithania turning off the northern road and leading their mounts into the *Sarn Forest*, opting to get out of the sprinkling rain before it became something more.

The trees that made up the *Sarn Forest* reminded Bekka of the longleaf pine trees that grew around *Midvale*. *Odd*, she reflected, *that these trees would spark such a memory*. She remembered her mom and dad taking her for a hike through the forest when she was a little girl; the strands of pine needles caressing her skin as she passed by; it tickled. She closed her eyes in an attempt to hold onto the memory; the smells of the forest made it seem so real. She didn't want the memory to end. When she opened her eyes she found that she had been crying.

Trish gave her a look. "Everything okay?"

Bekka nodded. "Yeah, sure. Why wouldn't it be?"

Trish shook her auburn curls and chuckled softly. "Oh, I don't know, you seemed to be talking to your mom and dad."

Bekka smiled sheepishly as she wiped the tears from her cheeks. She hadn't realized that she had spoken out loud. "These trees just remind me of happier times. Of home."

Trish reached out and caressed Bekka's arm as they rode side by side. They allowed the sound of the horses plodding along to envelop them. They could hear the wind whisper through the pine needles as the rain began to fall harder. Before long they were completely soaked and miserable.

There was no distinct path that they were following; they wound their way through the tall pines keeping in a northerly direction as best they could. They meandered around thick clumps of trees, boulders and shrubs as they floundered along through the forest. Trevor, Candi and Lithania had stopped ahead of them. Trevor held the reins of the elf's horse; Lithania was nowhere to be seen.

"What's going on? Where's Litha?" Bekka asked, suddenly feeling the urge to pee. "Potty break?" she asked, sounding hopeful.

Candi pointed toward a cluster of rocks that was scarcely visible through a fog of rain. There appeared to be an opening, perhaps a cave of some sort, which might offer a bit of relief from the weather. "Lithania is investigating." She crossed her fingers.

The urge to relieve herself became too strong to ignore. Bekka climbed from her horse and handed the reins to Lightfingers. As she headed for some privacy, Trish and Candi quickly joined her. Trevor shook his head as the sound of girlish laughter erupted from the lush shrubbery.

Lightfingers nudged his mount toward Trevor and handed over his reins. "That doesn't sound like a bad idea, really." He slid from his horse and moved in the opposite direction.

Trevor frowned as he lifted the jumble of reins in the air. "Great. What about me?"

Lithania appeared at his side, she had moved soundlessly through the forest. "What about you?" she asked with a raised brow.

Trevor made a startled sound, completely surprised by her unexpected presence. He glared at her with wide eyes. "Don't do that!"

She cocked her head. "I did not *do* anything."

"You startled me half to death!"

She quickly looked him over. "You appear to be just fine."

Trevor shook his head, rolling his eyes. "You know what I mean."

She smiled at him and took the reins from his hand. "We can take shelter in the cave. There is some grass nearby where I can picket the horses."

Trevor nodded. "Sounds like an excellent idea right after I go take a leak."

"Take a leak?" Lithania questioned with another raise of her brow.

Trevor mimed his meaning, twisting his body to and fro.

Lithania laughed. "Why did you not just say you had to make water?"

He chuckled as he stepped through the trees. "I did!"

The cave was not very big, but it was of sufficient size and depth where they could all fit comfortably. Lightfingers glanced up as Lithania entered the rocky shelter after tending to their horses. "This was a nice find," he smiled.

She smiled at him.

Trevor shivered. "We need a fire."

The elf shook her head. "That would be nice, but unfortunately everything is very wet outside. Even if we could get a fire going it would produce far too much smoke for comfort. We would not be able to breathe in this enclosure and would be driven back out into the rain."

Trevor sighed heavily. "That's a shame."

Trish slugged his arm playfully, nearly knocking him over. "Don't be such a wuss! Toughen up! Litha can't be expected to handle *two* babies."

Lithania visibly tensed. Candi looked from the elf to Trevor, and then to Trish. *"What did you just say?"*

Trish glanced up at the elf and shrugged. "Oops, my bad."

Trevor's jaw dropped as he gazed up at the elf, he was speechless. His eyes were wide with shock as his gaze lowered to her abdomen where a slight bulge was barely noticeable. He plopped back against the rock wall, clearly dazed by this unexpected revelation. He had not expected to discover that he was going to be a father; not quite like this, anyway. He felt woefully unprepared for parenthood.

Lithania knelt beside him and took his hand in hers. "I was planning to tell you when we were alone." She shook her head as she gazed around at everyone watching them closely. "But I never got that chance. I am sorry that you had to find out this way."

He could only nod. His mind was a jumbled mess. He glanced at Bekka and she was just staring at him. After a moment she looked away. *What was going through her mind?* He couldn't help but wonder. Lithania had continued talking to him, but he hadn't heard a word she'd said. Finally she had given up. Standing quickly, she rushed out of the cave, tears filling her eyes.

Candi glared at him angrily. She slapped his leg. "Quit being such a jerk, Trevor Stevens! You need to go after her!"

He blinked. "What?"

She shook her head. "Why are you guys all such idiots? Go after her! She's carrying your child for gosh sakes!" She hit him again, this time much harder than before.

Trevor blinked several times and then pushed himself off of the ground. "Right," he said. He left the cave and stepped out into the rain. Looking around he saw branches swaying back into place; there was no wind. He quickly moved in that direction, following the elf through the forest.

She always seemed to be just out of sight; only the sweep of thin branches guided him along. "Litha! Wait!" he called; a rumble of thunder nearly drowning out his voice. He quickened his pace. Finally catching up to her as she stopped suddenly.

She whirled around, facing him, her dark hair plastered to the side of her face so that he could see the points of her ears. The sorrowful look in her almond-shaped eyes threatening to break his heart. He could see her bottom lip quiver as she started to speak, but no words would come.

He practically threw himself into her, wrapping his arms around her in a fierce hug. "What were you thinking? Why did you run out?"

Her body felt unnaturally stiff in his embrace. "I saw the way you were looking at Bekka. It is obvious that you still love her. I can tell that you are no longer wanting me." She shook her head as a sob escaped her. "I... I... can no longer stay where I am not wanted! I... I feel so... so *humiliated*! I..."

He stepped back and placed a finger to her lips. "Hush. Don't." He shook his head and smiled. "I'm sorry if I upset you, I... I was completely blindsided. Honestly, I had no idea that was coming. I hadn't noticed; but that's entirely on me. It's my fault. It has *nothing* at all to do with Bekka. We are just friends, nothing more. I promise." He chuckled softly. "I just had no clue that you were pregnant. *We're* pregnant!"

Her eyes searched his. "You are not displeased?"

He pulled her against him and kissed her. "No. I'm not. I'm actually quite happy. I love you, Litha!"

Booming thunder shook the tall, slender pines as lightning flashed, filling the spaces between the trees. Another streak raced to the ground, striking a tree about twenty feet away causing it to very nearly explode, the splintering wood crackling loudly. Trevor could feel the ground shudder around him as the smell of ozone filled the air. He could feel the static electricity heighten in the surrounding forest. The wind picked up and splatters of rain began to pelt them from above. "We should be getting back," Trevor said.

Lithania nodded, her eyes locked on the tree that had been destroyed by the lightning strike; the cavernous gash in the trunk of the tree glowed a bright orange as it alone continued to burn. "It is not safe out here," she said softly.

Trevor smiled as he reached out and took her by the hand. He caressed the back of her hand with his thumb. It surprised him how happy he truly was. He had been considering returning to the other side of the *Portal* just a month ago. Things between he and Bekka had soured drastically and they were barely even friends anymore. That was the driving force for him wanting to go to *Serendil Brenatis* to reunite with Lithania. Before he left *Vespia* he had to know if there was something that still drew them together, a reason for him to stay, perhaps. He couldn't leave without being certain; because once he was gone, there would be no coming back.

He had never thought about having kids; he had only just turned sixteen last month. He would still have a couple of years of high school if he had remained in *Midvale*; and then he would've gone to college. Starting a family just hadn't been on the horizon any time soon—eventually maybe. But things were different in *Vespia*. School was a thing of the past. He was going to be a father; the mother was a full-blooded elf. Their child would be a half-elf; it made him wonder if the baby would have pointed ears? Or would the tips be rounded like his; more human? He couldn't help but smile. *Were they going to have a boy or a little girl?*

Candi glared at Trish; sometimes her red-haired friend could be *really* annoying. "You shouldn't have spilled the beans about Lithania that way. You should've considered Bekka's feelings." She shook her head. "You're unbelievable and so not in a good way."

Trish crossed her arms over her chest and cocked her head to one side as her brows shot up her forehead. "What *are* you talking about? How was I supposed to know that you didn't know already? It was really pretty obvious. The signs were there, the way she looked at Trevor, the way she caressed her stomach when she did. How could you not see? You have all known her longer than I have! And why would Bekka care anyway? I thought she was over Trevor."

Candi shook her head. "Still, it *wasn't* your place to say anything! You are *always* getting after me for not thinking before I speak; you should practice what you preach. But why would you? You've never really cared about anyone other than yourself. It has always been your way or the highway." She sighed in frustration. "Frankly, I'm tired of it."

Bekka couldn't take it any longer. "Would the both of you just stop! Seriously, it isn't a big deal. Trevor and I are *just* friends. He can have a baby with whomever he wants! I don't care!"

Trish lowered her chin slightly and stared at Bekka. She chuckled softly. "You're still in love with him."

Color rushed to Bekka's cheeks. "I most certainly am not!"

Trish shook her head and smiled at Candi. "You were right. I never thought about how she might feel about the whole thing. I just assumed that they were no longer an item and she was okay with Trevor being with an elf." She gave Candi's arm a squeeze. "When did you get to be so smart?"

Bekka stomped her foot. "I *don't* have feelings for him. Not anymore. It's not like that. Lithania is a sweet girl. I *like* her."

Trish pulled her friends into a tight group hug. "I've missed you guys!" At first they struggled against her but her embrace only tightened. Eventually they accepted it and just let it happen.

Chapter 36
Ambush

Dawn saw the end of the thunder and lightning, but the rain continued to fall steadily with no real end in sight. No one was looking forward to being out in this kind of weather but Bekka was reluctant to wait out the storm. She felt that those that they sought would only slip further away and they may never find them. She managed to convince the others that they needed to move. After all, the slaver's wagon would make little progress in these conditions; they stood a good chance of catching up with them. Sinnestra and her dark priest were another story altogether; but even they might be slowed down travelling with an infant child.

Bekka's real fear was that Sinnestra would just kill her baby brother and be done with it. There was nothing she could do about that other than to keep pushing forward. She had to concentrate on the trail ahead, it was better than giving in to the panic that threatened to consume her. She just hoped and prayed that they didn't come across Hanzi's tiny corpse along the way. *That would be the straw that broke her.*

They headed west out of the forest and found the northern road that paralleled the *River of Sorrow.* Many huge puddles of murky rainwater gathered in the low spots of the narrow lane almost turning the road into a muddy stream. If the conditions of the road did not improve and they had no reason to think that they would, then the slaver's wagon would find the passage difficult, if not impossible; that gave them hope. They turned their horses northward, trotting at a brisk pace.

Finally, the rain stopped, but they were already thoroughly soaked and miserable. The sun poked through the late morning sky and brought with it a warming breeze that everyone seemed to enjoy. Smiles began to appear on sullen faces and joyful banter sounded as they continued along. Their mood had improved measurably.

They rode alongside the muddy lane in pairs, chatting amiably. Lithania and Trevor were leading the group and they were holding hands as they went. Trish and Candi followed behind them; engaged in a conversation that seemed guarded but not antagonistic. Occasionally Trish would chuckle and shake her head. Bekka and Lightfingers brought up the rear of the procession.

Bekka watched the pair at the front of the column with pursed lips. She was thinking about the conversation that she had had back in the cave with Candi and Trish. *Was it possible that she* still *had feelings for Trevor? Did a part of her* still *love him?* She took a deep breath and sighed, letting it out slowly as she pondered her nagging thoughts. No, she decided. She did not love Trevor. They were really good friends. She was delighted for him. He finally seemed at peace, happy. The dark, brooding mood that he had carried with him for the last few months seemed to be finally lifted. Bekka could feel a sense of relief. She hated seeing any of her friends down in the dumps. With Trevor finally so happy, it gave her one less friend she needed to worry about.

Lightfingers followed her gaze. "They seem happy."

Bekka glanced over at him and smiled. "Yes they do. They look very happy."

He arched a brow as he studied her. "And what about you? Are you happy?"

She chuckled. "I am more content than I have been in a long while, but still I have a ways to go before I can say that I am truly happy. That won't happen until we have rescued Valoria and my brother."

Lightfingers nodded. "Understandable, certainly. But I meant are you happy for them? I know you had feelings for Trevor some time ago. Are you sure that you are ready to move on from him? To let another woman care for him?"

Bekka laughed. "I am."

"That is good to hear," he said with a smile.

She studied him for a moment, a small curve at the corner of her lips. "And why is that, Darren O'Leary?"

He chuckled softly. "Three's a crowd," he said wistfully.

Bekka frowned. "I'm not certain that I'm following you there. Were you referring to Litha, Trevor and I perhaps? Or something else?"

He grinned. "Yes, and no."

She shook her head. "Why can't anyone in this world just say what they mean? Why does everything have to be so cryptic?"

He laughed, leaning in he kissed her on the lips. "Is this better?" he asked with a smile.

Her eyes were wide; she hadn't expected that. She narrowed her eyes at him and fire seemed to smolder within. "Don't do that again," she said tightly.

He blinked, surprised. "I'm sorry. I thought—"

She cut him off. "Well, you thought wrong."

He raised his hands in the air. "Fine. I see that."

Bekka sighed. "Look, I'm sorry. I like you. I really do. It's just that after my encounter with De La'Corte, I just... I'm just not ready." Tears stung at her eyes and she shivered.

"I get it," he said.

Bekka shook her head. She could tell that she'd hurt his feelings. "It's just that I feel as though I'm broken inside. Until I can figure things out, I can't get involved with anyone in that way."

He smiled after a moment. "Fair enough. But, just so you know, it is not in my nature to give up so easily. Rejection only tends to make me work harder. I don't like to lose at anything, especially when I have my heart set on something."

Bekka smiled as she arched a brow. "Oh? So your heart is set on me, is that it?"

He chuckled softly and shrugged. "Could be."

They crested a small hill and stopped. On the other side, at the base of the sloping hill, apparently stuck in the muddy road, was the slaver's wagon. Several bodies could be seen lying about, unmoving. The horses were gone, either they had run off on their own or they had been taken. No life was stirring.

Bekka nudged her horse forward with a prod of her heels, her breath caught in her throat, afraid of what she might discover.

The back wheels of the slaver's box-wagon were sunk deep in the mud. Attempts had been made to pry the wheels free using long, thick branches cut from nearby trees, but it had done little good. They surmised that the guards had been ambushed as they watched the prisoners try to free the wagon. There were bodies of chained prisoners, guards and several dwarves scattered across the scene; Valoria was not among them. Where, then, had she gone? Had those that had ambushed the slave caravan freed her, or was she still a prisoner?

The steady rain had washed away any trace of their departure.

Bekka slammed the heel of her fist against the slaver's wagon. "Damnit!" she said in frustration as she studied their surroundings. "She could be anywhere!" Tears formed in her eyes, it was hard not to give in to despair. They had hoped to catch up to the slaver's wagon before it made its way to its final destination; but not like this.

The hardest part, was wondering whose hands Valoria was now in. Was she still a prisoner? Or was she free? And if she had been inadvertently rescued, what did that mean, and where was she now? They simply did not know. It was extremely frustrating.

Bekka looked at Lightfingers and sighed. "I just don't know what we should do now. She's out there," she waved a hand in the air, "somewhere."

Darren nodded. "That is something. She's not here among

the dead, at least. We can still find her. We just have to keep looking."

"But where do we look? We don't really know anything about what truly happened here. Any clue would be nice." Bekka was beginning to feel disheartened.

He placed a hand on his hip, the other stroked his stubbled chin as he scanned the area. A light sparkled in his eyes. "But we *do* know something," he said with a thin smile. "I've been to *Dagmarth* and seen the slave caravans before. Dwarves are generally not used as guards."

Bekka looked at him. "So you think that the dwarves may have ambushed the slavers?"

He nodded. "I do."

"So?" she asked with a shrug. "What does that mean? We still don't know who has Val."

"True. But I suggest that we continue on to *Darkwater*. Once we are there, we may learn more."

All eyes were on Bekka. She nodded and then mounted her horse. "Then what are we waiting for?"

Chapter 37
Tagg Thorun

They made camp on the northern edge of the *Lake of Tears*, finding a relatively sheltered spot among some massive white oaks. If they got a good night's rest and started fresh just after dawn, they estimated that they'd make it to *Darkwater* by midmorning.

They found a nice grassy area to picket their horses where there was plenty for them to munch upon and fresh water from the lake.

Candi took a knife and set to work removing stems and leaves from narrow tree limbs, and then she tied strings upon the ends. She had made metal hooks back at *Kensington Castle* a month ago and now she fastened these to the end of her line. Satisfied, she took her makeshift fishing poles and headed to the lake. "Wish me luck!"

"Wait for me!" Trish said, scampering off behind her.

Trevor and Lithania had walked off, holding hands, eager for some alone time. Bekka had seen them disappear into a clump of trees. She glanced over at Lightfingers. "Guess that leaves you and me to get the fire going. If I know Candi, she'll bring back plenty of fish." She smiled. "She's been so eager to try out her fishhooks."

He chuckled as he began to gather stones for a firepit. Shortly they had rocks formed in a circle and plenty of wood for the fire. All that remained was the fire itself and something to cook upon it. Lightfingers formed some relatively dry grass into a nest shape. He took a flint rock out of his saddlebag and began to strike at it with the back of his knife blade. Eventually he had enough sparks to get a small fire going in the nest. He lightly blew on the flames to keep them going and then added the burning nest into the firepit. He added twigs until the fire grew to the point that he no longer feared it would go out. He made it look easy but she knew from watching many seasons of Survivor that it was anything but!

Bekka nodded her head. "I'm impressed!"

He chuckled again. "This is not my first time making a fire."

She watched him as he continued to tend the fire. "Can I ask you a question?"

He grinned. "You mean another one?"

Bekka couldn't help but laugh. "Why are you called 'Lightfingers' anyway?"

He pulled her necklace out of his pocket and handed it to her, saying nothing.

Her jaw dropped as she instinctively put a hand to her neck. "When did you take that?"

Darren chuckled. "Remember when I kissed you earlier today as we were riding along?"

She slapped his arm. *"No way!"*

He shrugged. "Sorry. Old habits are hard to break, sometimes. But I like to stay in practice. Helps to keep my fingers nimble."

"I didn't even feel it!" she said as she put the necklace back on. "I was so unprepared for your kiss that it just threw me completely off."

He shook his head. "I wouldn't fret over it; you are not the first lady that I have distracted in that manner. Doubt you'll be the last."

"So," she put her hand on her hips, "do you make a habit of kissing all the girls just to swipe their jewelry?"

He shrugged, a smirk forming on his lips. "A man's got to eat."

She frowned. "So is that why you kissed me? Just to steal my necklace?" She wasn't sure whether or not she should be angry with him. "Was I just a mark?"

He sighed. "Look, I kissed you because I'm attracted to you." He shook his head. "I don't know what it is, but there's just *something* about you that I find *very* appealing." He shrugged. "I guess I took your necklace by reflex. Then when you got angry at me, I just stuck it into my pocket. I didn't want to enrage you any further."

"So," Bekka said as though it only just dawned on her, "you're a common thief."

"Whoa! A thief, yes, but certainly *not* common!" he seemed mildly aggrieved.

"Guess I'll have to keep my eye on you," she said.

"Haloooo the camp!" a gravelly voice sounded from the darkness. "I come in peace. Would ye be so kind as ta share yer fire? Me bones are chilled and me stomach be empty!"

They had been sitting around the campfire enjoying the fish that Trish and Candi had caught. Lightfingers had fried it up and it was quite tasty. They searched the darkness where the voice appeared to be coming from but saw nothing. They began to casually arm themselves; careful not to make any sudden moves. The night air had grown quite cold. They could see their breath hang in the air before it dissipated into nothing. The season was definitely changing.

"Tha' trout *smells* mighty good." The voice was closer now, but still it was difficult to pinpoint its source.

Trevor shook his head. "I don't like this. We should've set a watch."

"Too late to worry about that now," Candi said softly. She eased her knife out of the scabbard tied to her thigh.

Lithania had slipped silently off into the forest. Bekka had no doubt she was readying her bow.

Lightfingers looked over at Bekka, his brow raised. She nodded at him. He spoke loudly, "Come on in friend."

Trevor shot him a startled look. He whispered harshly, "Are you insane? We know *nothing* about this guy! He might not even be alone."

A dwarven male stopped at the edge of the firelight. His hands were raised in the air, even with his belt, non-threateningly. He appeared to have a weapon strapped to his back; they could see a leather-bound handle rising above his shoulders. His dark brown beard was sprinkled throughout with streaks of silvery gray. His hair was long and slightly curled. He had thick black eyebrows that seemed to grow wild upon his forehead which appeared covered in dried blood. He had a wide, bulbous nose. "I come in peace," he said again.

Lithania entered the camp behind him. "He is alone."

He nodded. "Aye, tha' I am," he said in agreement.

Bekka quickly stood and offered him some fried trout on a pewter platter. "Please, eat." He had a kind look in his green eyes. Friendly. Trusting. Non-threatening.

He ravenously complied. "Thank ye lass." He plopped down near the fire. He took their names in with a glance and a nod as Bekka made the introductions. He finished the last of his trout and smiled, licking his fingers clean. "Tha' t'was might good. My compliments ta the cook." He handed the plate back to Bekka with a wink and then placed his thick hands onto his knees and gave them a good wiping before extending them toward the fire. "Mine's Taggarty Thorun. Most just call me Tagg."

"We came across some dwarves south of here," Lightfingers said. "All dead. Were they friends of yours?"

Tagg frowned and his eyes seemed to moisten. He nodded slowly. "Aye, they were. All good men too."

Bekka leaned closer. "I had a friend that was a prisoner in that wagon, a human female; tall, a scar on her face and a ruined right eye that glistens white. Did you happen to see her?" she sounded hopeful.

Tagg's face grew cold. "Aye, I saw the warrior o' whom ye speak." He shook his head. "But she t'weren't no prisoner, t'was an *armed* guard, tha' one! And ruthless like ye wouldna' believe! Killed me brother and two o' me friends! They begged fer mercy, but she wouldna' have none o' it. She murdered them where they lay! T'were no longer a threat ta anybody."

Bekka bolted up, startling everyone. *"That's a lie! Val wouldn't do that!"*

Taggarty got slowly to his feet, keenly aware that several weapons were targeting him. He took great care to make no sudden moves that could be misconstrued as an attack. "I thank ye fer the repast and the warmth o' yer fire. Perhaps I should leave ye now. I misjudged ye. Thought ye might be friendly folk."

"We are," Candi said.

He glanced at her and nodded slightly. "Tha' ye may be, but if tha' woman t'was yer friend then ye canna be mine. We should part *a'for* we become enemies."

Candi looked from the dwarf to Bekka. "There has to be some explanation. Valoria wouldn't murder anyone. Certainly not like that."

Bekka glared at the dwarf. "No, she wouldn't."

Taggarty spread his hands as he backed into the darkness. "Maybe t'was another tha' I saw then. Someone tha' only looked like yer friend. But know this: If I see her again, I plan ta kill her wi' me axe!"

Trish stepped to Bekka's side. "You want me to go after him?"

Bekka shook her head. "No. God no. Just let him go. Hopefully we'll never see him again." She was afraid to turn her friend loose on anybody.

Chapter 38
Darkwater

They awoke with snow covering the ground and more snow falling as the sun attempted to peak through a curtain of gray clouds without much success. The morning air was frigid. Winter was upon them.

Candi sat up and stared around at the deepening snow. "Seriously? I knew it was cold last night, but I wasn't expecting to wake up to all this!" Nobody else was either.

Fortunately, the heat from the fire had kept the snow from accumulating on top of them while they slept, except for a light dusting. The night had been cold and they had all thrown down their bedrolls near the fire for the warmth it offered. It seemed even colder now, as the temperature continued to drop.

They broke camp, moving about stiffly as they gathered their gear. They mounted up in relative silence, even the horses seemed eager to leave. Lithania and Trevor had seen to the firepit, covering it with a mountain of snow that hissed as it quickly melted over the hot coals, but by the time they were done, the fire was out.

As they rode north it was difficult to distinguish where the actual road was. Everything was covered in a blanket of white, including hazardous rocks that they could no longer see. For safety, they were forced to move slowly. They could ill-afford for a wrong step to cripple a horse. But, even proceeding with increased caution, that was still a real possibility. The only sure way was to dismount and simply lead their horses through the snow, which would only impede their progress even more. They chose to remain mounted. The snow continued to fall at an alarming rate.

By noon the snow had lessened some, enabling them to see what was ahead to some degree. They could see gray chimney smoke rising in the distance and dark splotches of buildings and tree trunks on the pearly landscape. Eager to leave the cold and snow behind, they picked up their pace. Thirty minutes later they were on the edge of the tiny hamlet known as *Darkwater*.

"It isn't much," Bekka said as they halted their horses. They hadn't wanted to just ride in without knowing anything about the place. They still had enemies to be concerned about.

Lightfingers nodded. "Honestly, I was hoping for a bit more."

Bekka gave him a little smirk. "I bet you were."

He lowered a brow. "What do you mean by that?"

She shrugged. "I know that you fancy yourself as a *lady's man*; your prospects have got to be limited in a little hamlet the size of this. Whatever will you do?"

His jaw clenched and his face turned a bright shade of red. He sighed heavily, thinking it best not to respond. It seemed she was *trying* to get on his nerves. He raised his shoulders and let them drop. Finally he said, "As a matter of fact, I grew up in a place very similar to this, if not a bit smaller. Once I left it behind, I vowed never to return. This," he indicated the hamlet ahead of them, "makes me feel like I've lied to myself."

"Never say never. That's what my mom always said."

He chuckled. "Sounds like a wise woman."

She turned to face him, wondering if he was being sincere or just a smartass. He looked as though he meant it. She reached out a hand and squeezed his arm. "We won't be here long."

He arched a brow and nudged his horse forward without saying a word.

Bekka stared at his back as he rode away. She had angered him, she knew. She needed to apologize for being so mean; he had done nothing to deserve her rude behavior. But still, she felt it better if he didn't get too close to her; she had too much going on for any of *that* nonsense.

The morning snow was crisp and it crunched loudly beneath their horses' hooves as they plodded, single file, down the slight incline that dropped down into *Darkwater*. The tiny hamlet consisted of six houses, an inn, a smithy and two other shops. If it hadn't been for the smoke rising from the stone chimneys, the place would seem totally deserted. No one had been outside; the snowfall from the night before lay upon the streets, pristine in the midday light.

As they rode past the first two houses, they could feel eyes upon them. When they looked in the direction of the homes, shutters were hastily closed. The inn was situated along a bend in the road, just beyond a baker's shop and a fishery. They could see the barn and the smithy further in just to the east of the *Spilt Tankard Inn*.

They could hear the high-pitched ping of the blacksmith's hammer coming from the smith and headed in that direction to see to the wellbeing of their horses. They could see the blacksmith swing his hammer down upon a glowing horseshoe as he held it against a blackened anvil. He was a big, burly man with broad, muscular shoulders and thick arms. His hair was a dark shade of brown with plenty of silver streaks throughout. He wore it tied at the back of his head to prevent the long strands from getting into his face while he worked; some strands had managed to escape nonetheless. He had on a leather apron covering doeskin pants and a thin white shirt that sported a few holes here and there; his sleeves were rolled up above his elbows. He struck the shoe twice more with the hammer and then held it up to his face scrutinizing his handiwork. Satisfied, he thrust it into a bucket of water that was close at hand. The hot metal caused the water to steam and sizzle.

The smithy glanced over them as they dismounted. "Good day," he said gruffly. He wiped his forehead on his upper arm leaving a trail of black on his dingy sleeve.

"Mind if we stable our horses?" Lightfingers asked.

The smith inclined his head over his shoulder. "Plenty o' stalls ta choose from. Fresh hay and water too. It'll be a copper per horse, per day."

Lightfingers nodded. "Sounds reasonable."

The smith whistled loudly. "My boy'll tend ta yer beasties fer an extra copper if'n ye don't want ta be bothered."

"Fair enough," Lightfingers handed the reins of his horse to the boy that ran out of the barn. He was a much thinner version of his dad, and his hair was fairer by far. He gathered the reins from the group and led the horses to the barn talking gently to them.

"The wife runs the inn. Ye can pay her fer the horses an' anythin' else ye might require. She'll be happy ta take care o' ye." He turned back to his work, pulling another glowing horseshoe from the kiln. Before they could make it to the inn, the sound of the hammer striking the steel shoe shrilled through the crisp, cold air.

The *Spilt Tankard Inn* was deserted, which Carandra Toshe, the proprietor, claimed was normal for this time of year. She was a tall woman with honey-blonde hair neatly tied back and twisted into a bun. She had a kind, weathered face and crow's feet at the corners of her eyes; still she was a remarkably beautiful woman. She had no problems assigning everyone their own rooms despite the fact that it would ultimately mean more work for her. Trevor and Lithania declined separate rooms in the end. Bekka, however, was thrilled to have a room to herself. She needed time to think and to reassess everything.

Tagg Thorun's story about how Valoria had killed the helpless dwarves couldn't be true. There was absolutely no way that her friend could be so heartless, unless of course she herself, felt threatened. In the heat of battle, it was hard to see things with an objective eye. Tagg could be easily mistaken. The dwarves had attacked the slaver's wagon; that much was not in dispute. Some of the slaves had been killed during the assault. Valoria could have been protecting herself and the others from overzealous attackers. She could have been armed by the slavers simply because they were overwhelmed by a stronger force.

Perhaps Valoria had been forced to make a hard choice.

Carandra Toshe placed the last bowl of steaming venison stew in front of Lightfingers. "Will there be anythin' else tha' I can get fer any o' ye?"

Bekka placed her spoon back into the bowl of hot stew, she had been about to take a bite but there was something that she really wanted to ask of Carandra and she didn't want to do it with a mouthful of food. She knew her mother wouldn't approve. "I was wondering, have there been any others that have passed through here fairly recently?"

Carandra had a sweet smile. "As I've mentioned before, we dinna' get many visitors this time o' year, so the ones tha' do come through 'ere, kind o' stick out."

Bekka's eyes widened hopefully. "Could you tell me about them?"

"Well, t'were the soldiers from *Bitterwood Castle* tha' came through a day or so ago." She frowned. "I thought it t'was strange tha' they didna' 'ave their wagon with them; they 'ad prisoners though. Tha's why I thought it ta be peculiar. One o' their horses 'ad thrown a shoe; my Bran 'ad ta reshoe the beastie. They left in quite a hurry as I recall." She shook her head. "Truth be told, t'was glad ta be rid o' the lot o' 'em."

"Why's that?" Lightfingers asked as he shoved stew into his mouth.

Carandra seemed to shiver. She took a look around and then leaned in closer. "They work fer Kaspian Altair. He's a *dark mage* sure enough. Better ta 'ave his ilk gone as quickly as possible, if'n ye catch me meanin'."

"Any others come through here?" Bekka asked.

Carandra nodded. "A family came through a day or two earlier. A man, 'is wife an' their babe; a darlin' li'l boy."

Bekka stiffened. "Do you know where they were heading?"

Carandra shrugged. "They didna' say. My son, Taren, t'was out huntin' deer fer the stew ye be eatin' now. He said he saw 'em headin' ta the nor'east." She shrugged. "Could be they was headin' fer *Dragon's Reach*. They'd be crazy ta try the *Northern*

Pass this time o' year." She gave them a motherly look. "The weather is startin' ta turn fer the worst. I wouldna' recommend anyone travel further north. Better ta be headin' south."

Carandra frowned and gave Bekka an admonishing look. "Ye oughta eat tha' stew a'for it grows too cold." She turned and walked back to the kitchen.

After everyone had had their fill of venison stew, they headed off for their rooms. Trevor gave Lithania a little peck on the cheek and smiled. "I'll be along in a minute or two. I want to talk with Bekka for a bit."

She returned the kiss and smiled. "Do not be too long."

He sighed contentedly as he watched the elf maiden climb the stairs. Bekka interrupted his thoughts as she touched his arm. "Best not keep her waiting," she said with a smile.

Trevor blushed.

"Something on your mind?" she asked.

Trevor stared at her for a moment and then quickly looked away. He seemed to be struggling with what he wanted to say. Finally, flustered, he shoved his hands into his pockets and said, "I've been thinking..." he glanced at the stairs.

Bekka stiffened, knowing *somehow*, what he was going to say. She bit her lip, forcing herself to breathe slowly as she waited for him to continue.

"...about Litha," he swallowed, "and the baby."

Bekka could only nod.

"I have to consider what is best for them." He looked at Bekka and touched her arm. "I was thinking she shouldn't be out here like this, not while she's pregnant. She should be home, back at *Serendil Brenatis*."

Bekka quickly crossed her arms and nodded. "Oh *definitely*. You should go. Take her back where she and the baby will be safe."

"Are you sure?" he asked. He hadn't expected Bekka to be so onboard with this plan of action.

"Yeah." She tried hard to keep the tears from coming to her eyes, but it wasn't easy. "We've got this. Don't worry about a thing!" She forced herself to smile. She quickly indicated the stairs with a nod of her head. "You should go on up. You don't want to keep Litha waiting, she might get the wrong idea."

He gave her a quick hug and then started for the stairs. Halfway up he stopped and looked at her. "Are you okay, Bekka?"

She nodded. "Yeah, I'm fine. You should go up to her."

"Goodnight, Bekka," he said with a smile.

"Night," she said, turning away. She didn't want him to see her cry.

Chapter 39
The Ghostlands

"Trevor, we need you!" Candi said with a stomp of her foot as Trevor led the two horses out of the barn. She found it hard to believe that he and Lithania were actually leaving them and going to the Elven Tree City of *Serendil Brenatis*. She shook her head. *How could he just up and desert them when they needed him most?*

He glanced at her and shook his head. "I need to keep Litha and the baby safe, Candi. The only way I can do that is to take them back to *Serendil Brenatis*. Litha needs to be with her people."

Candi grabbed his arm, feeling a sudden surge of anger. She forced him to face her. "What about *your* people? What about Valoria and Han?"

Trevor pushed her hand off of his arm. "They've got you guys. You don't need Litha and me."

She stepped in front of him putting a hand on his chest. "What about Beks? She needs *you* Trevor! How can you just run off and desert her like this?"

He pushed her aside with a sweep of his arm. "You need to let this go, Candi."

She scooped up a handful of snow and made a quick ball and threw it, hitting him in the back of the head. "You are an asshole, Trevor Stevens! I hope you freeze out there!"

He thrust his chin out angrily. He could feel snow sliding down the back of his neck. "To Hell with you, Candi!" he snarled as he continued to walk away. Another snowball hit him on the shoulder causing him to growl in frustration. *She could be so immature!*

Bekka looked up at Trevor as he and Lithania sat astride their mounts. "So, what's your plan?"

Trevor looked to the south. "We'll go back to *Dagmarth* and catch the next ship heading to *Freeport*. With luck, it shouldn't take us too long."

Bekka nodded. "Good." She glanced over at Lithania and then back at Trevor. "You need to keep your family safe. Don't worry about us."

He put a hand on her shoulder. "Bekka, I..."

She shook her head and took a step back. "You *need* to do this, Trev." She glanced at Candi who was standing beside the others on the porch of the *Spilt Tankard*. "Don't worry about Candi. She'll get over it in time."

Trevor sighed. "I hope she does." He straightened. "What about you guys? What's your plan?"

Bekka chuckled. "I need to get Valoria back as quickly as I can. I think we'll split our remaining forces. Lightfingers and I will head for *Bitterwood*. Trish and Candi can head for *Dragon's Reach*, and hopefully they will be on Sinnestra's trail. Once I have Valoria freed, we'll join them."

He nodded. "Bekka, I really hate that it is going down like this. It was always my plan to be there for you when you needed me. Now I feel like I'm running out on you when you need me most."

She shook her head. "Don't worry about it, Trevor. Our paths are going in different directions now. I just want you to be happy, really I do. If that means you are going to live your life among the elves of *Serendil Brenatis*, so be it."

He sighed after a minute. "You think that's wise, splitting your forces like that?"

She gave him an exasperated look. "What choice do I have?"

Trevor shrugged. "Oh, I don't know. Forget about saving Valoria. Catch up with Sinnestra and get your brother back. You've got the *Blade of the Spider's Kiss* back; you're the only one that can use it to defeat Sinnestra."

Bekka glanced at Lithania and then shook her head. "Don't worry about it; it's not your concern." She turned and walked back toward the inn. She didn't stop until she had joined the others on the porch. She could hear Trevor and Lithania turn their horses toward the south. She ignored her friends and entered the inn without a backwards glance.

Candi glared at Trevor's back as the pair rode away. "Trevor's a real bastard."

Trish chuckled softly. "I wouldn't waste too much breath on him. He'll get what's coming to him soon enough."

Candi glanced at the redhead. "What do you mean by that?"

Trish shrugged and kept her silence as she turned and followed Bekka inside.

"So," Candi asked as she and Trish rode out of *Darkwater* heading northeast, "what are we gonna do if we manage to catch up with Sinnestra?"

Trish gave her friend a condescending look. "What do *you* think we should do?"

"Well," Candi said feeling slightly embarrassed, "it's not like we can actually *kill* her. We'd need the *Blade of the Spider's Kiss* for that. That weapon only glows for Lithania and Bekka."

"Well," Trish said with a wry smile, "neither one of them is here and we don't have the weapon."

"I know," Candi said, "that's what worries me."

Trish chuckled. "Relax, sweetie. I'll keep you safe."

Candi shivered, remembering the two assailants that had threatened Bekka and her on the *Wyndreaver*; that had *not* ended well for either of them. "How are you gonna do that?" She swallowed. She turned a hesitant eye to the auburn-haired girl riding beside her; she wasn't *totally* sure she wanted an answer.

Trish raised both brows and smiled as she studied her friend. "Ah Candi, you are still so naïve." She shook her head. After a moment or two passed, she spoke again. "Do you honestly think that the Drow blade is the only thing that can kill Sinnestra? That is probably just a silly old tale told in the *Underdark*. I mean, look at the *Prophecy of the Chosen One*; everyone believed that Bekka, our Bekka, mind you, was destined to kill Maragh. We both know that she couldn't really hurt a fly." She chuckled. "Bekka gets all squeamish when she steps on a cockroach!"

Candi smiled. "That's true."

"More than one person was responsible for killing Maragh in the end. I believe more than a single weapon can kill Sinnestra too."

"Maragh was just a man," Candi pointed out. "Sinnestra is a freakin' demoness. There's a difference. Like, I mean a *huge* one!"

Trish batted a hand in the air. "Pish posh!" she said with a roll of her eyes. "If she can be wounded, she can be killed. I've seen you shoot a composite bow for the Midvale Archery Team; you could put one of those pointy things straight through that bitch's heart, maybe even two of them."

"You mean an *arrow*?"

Trish nodded. "Yes! One or two of those straight into her heart!"

"So you want *me* to kill her, is that it?" Candi asked.

"You. Me. The two of us together; I don't care. If we get the opportunity to take her out, I say we take it. We both know that Bekka can't kill her. So it *has* to be us. It's up to us to save Bekka from herself. If we rely on her to slay the beast, then it'll be her dying in the end, you know it as well as I do."

Candi pulled on the reins, halting her horse. Trish stopped and turned her horse to face her. "Is there a problem?"

Candi studied her friend. "What *are* you, Trish? I mean, truly?"

Trish laughed, her eyes sparkling brightly. "Ah, finally! The million-dollar question!" She winked. "Let's just say that I am Trish 2.0. New and improved."

"That's not really an answer," Candi said.

The smile left Trish's face. She shrugged. "I guess we'll just have to wait and see." In truth, even she wasn't really sure.

The snow continued to fall in light, swirling flakes as the bitterly cold wind blew from the north. The *Ghostlands* stretched before them, shrouded in a gray fog that was several shades lighter than the heavy clouds that hung overhead. They had wrapped scarves over their faces keeping only narrowed slits to see through. It kept them warm for the most part, but the cold air stung their eyes unmercifully.

"We can't keep going like this, we need to wait out this storm," Trish shouted over the howling wind. Between the fog that hugged the ground and the bright, blinding sunlight reflected across the mounds of snow, seeing where they were going was becoming increasingly more difficult.

"What if it only gets worse?" Candi asked; worry tinged her words, she didn't like traveling in these conditions, but her fear of being trapped in the harsh circumstances was even more frightening.

She heard Trish chuckle. "Then we are definitely screwed!" The redhead stated matter-of-factly.

"How do we know if we are even going in the right direction?" Candi yelled, over the roar of the northern winds. "I haven't been able to see anything for the last hour. We could be going in circles."

They had entered a wooded area that hadn't been on their map that they were following. Bran Toshe had drawn a crude map and he claimed it might not be incredibly accurate. He had been a kid when his father took him through the *Ghostlands* and he had never returned; there was little he remembered.

Candi tried her best to remember the maps she had studied in the *Great Library Arcanum* back in *Freeport*. If memory served her right, they had failed to show this wooded area of the *Ghostlands* too. Fear crept down her spine. Was there such a thing as a *spectral forest*? A place that was there one minute, and gone the next? *What would happen if they entered such a place? Would they be trapped inside when it inexplicably disappeared?* She shivered. Her imagination was getting the better of her. "I don't think I like this place."

They rode on, deeper into the snowy wood.

As darkness fell, they managed to find a small cave large enough to keep them and their horses out of the weather. The wind continued to howl as the snowfall increased and it now seemed to be falling *horizontally*. Trish managed to get a fire going using wooden planks she found half buried inside the cave. It was only then that they discovered that the cave was actually a wooden shelter of some sort.

Chapter 40
The Winged Galleon

Golden sunlight warmed Trish's face as she stepped out of the wooden shelter. The howling storm had passed during the night and now the sky was a cobalt blue. A few wisps of clouds remained, but the morning sky seemed filled with promise. Looking around, she couldn't see any signs of their arrival. More than a foot of snow had fallen during the course of the night, hiding their trail under a blanket of pristine white. As she inhaled the fresh air, she could feel the burn at the back of her throat; it was still quite cold.

Last night, due to the swirling wind and snow, they had been nearly blinded when they had arrived in this uncharted forest. Finding the shelter had been a stroke of luck; it had probably saved their lives. The snow crunched loudly as she walked; it was almost knee-deep. She stopped and turned around, her eyes growing wide in surprise. "What the Hell . . .?"

She was amazed to discover that they had taken refuge from the storm inside the broken hull of a ship. "How did a ship get way out here, so far from water?" she asked herself aloud. She shook her head in wonder.

Candi saw the look of shock and bewilderment etched on her friend's face like it was stone. She stepped out of the shelter and went to her side. "Trish, is everything alright?"

Trish let out a small chuckle. "Look at this!" she pointed behind Candi.

Candi turned. She took a startled step back in disbelief, nearly losing her balance in the deep drift of snow. "No way!" Her jaw dropped open as she looked back at Trish. "Is *that* a ship?"

Trish nodded. "It sure looks like one."

"Well," Candi said, "wait! What? How did a ship get way out here?"

Trish shook her head. "Maybe a hurricane scooped it up and dropped it here?" She could think of no other plausible explanation.

Candi gave her a quizzical look. "You think this place used to be under water?"

Trish pointed at the structure before them. The ship's hull was twisted and broken. The bow of the Galleon was pointing up at a 45° angle. The ship's stern, in which they had camped, was leaning toward them. What appeared to be none other than a large wing jutted out from what was left of the starboard side of the ship. The canvas was ragged and torn, hanging limp. There was no morning breeze. "I think it flew here," Trish said.

"A *flying* ship?" Candi said in fascination, her eyes wide orbs.

Trish pointed off to her right. "Look."

The ship's main mast protruded out of a mound of snow. The crow's nest was in pieces, hanging from its ankle was the body of what looked to be a child. Horrified, they both started walking toward the dangling corpse.

As they drew closer, they could see that it wasn't a child after all. The dead body was certainly no bigger than a child, but they could clearly see that it wasn't. Candi looked at Trish. "You think he's a gnome?"

Trish shook her auburn curls; she didn't think so. "Not a dwarf, either. Reminds me of a hobbit from *Lord of the Rings*, especially with the hair growing on the top of the feet."

Candi pursed her lips. She remembered something that Vincente had told her months ago during one of their talks. He had been trying to make her more familiar with his world. He had mentioned beings that were small, somewhat larger than dwarves and gnomes. "I think he's a *Halfling*," she said.

Trish nodded as she gazed at the corpse. She shook her head. "Whatever." She didn't really care; he was long dead.

Candi looked up at the body that hung overhead; the arms were stretched out, reaching for the ground, the eyes wide open, fixed and unmoving; the corpse's mouth open in a silent scream. She shivered. "How long do you think he's been like that?"

Trish shrugged. "Who knows?"

Candi reached as high as she could but was still not able to get close enough to actually touch the dead man's hand. "It couldn't have been long, surely."

Trish looked at her strangely. "What makes you say that?"

Candi wiggled her fingers as she stood on the tips of her toes, still trying to make contact with the dead man. "The body hasn't started to decompose yet."

Trish laughed. "It's like a damned freezer out here. The body won't start to decay until it thaws out." She shook her head in disbelief. "You're the science nerd! You should have known that!"

Startled out of her morbid fascination with the dead body, Candi pulled her hand back. She sniffled as she felt the biting cold. "You think we should bury him?"

"No, I do not!" Trish snorted loudly. "We'd have a heck of a time cutting him down, and then we'd have to get through all of this snow just to find the frozen ground. Besides, we don't have a shovel."

Candi gave her friend a dark look. Sometimes Trish could be *too* damned practical. It was annoying. But she was right; they'd have a hell of a time getting through the frozen turf even if they managed to get him down. She shrugged, defeated. "Sooo we're just gonna leave him like that?"

"Yup," Trish said as she trudged back to the shelter. "Besides, we need to be moving on if we're gonna find Sinnestra."

"Right. Han," Candi said, having almost forgotten Bekka's little brother.

They packed up their camp and covered the hot coals with snow, causing the slush to sizzle and steam to rise. They tied their bedrolls to the back of their saddles and led the horses back outside. A light breeze had picked up and snow was blowing across the ground in swirls. At the edge of the clearing they could see dark shapes coming toward them from the trees; they were small, like the man hanging above them.

"Shit!" Trish said. "Mount up, we need to move!"

Candi hesitated as the dark shapes lumbered toward them.

"Candace! Move. Now!" Trish said tightly.

The way the figures were walking through the snow reminded Candi of zombies. They certainly weren't *living* beings. The horses snorted nervously, stomping their hooves in the ground. They were eager to leave. Candi mounted her horse and quickly caught up with Trish; her friend was leaving without her.

"Whoa!" Trish reined in her horse. Ahead of them, more of the dead *halflings* were coming out of the forest. Candi stopped beside her. She blew out a deep breath, causing a billowing cloud to form in the air as she tried to calm her nerves; it quickly dissipated.

"What are we going to do?" Candi said as panic rose in her voice. "They've got us surrounded."

Trish swallowed. "I think we ride right through them. Don't stop. Just run them over if they get in your way. If you hesitate at all they will get you. There will be *nothing* I can do to help you."

Candi nodded.

Trish urged her horse forward swiftly. Candi was beside her as they galloped as fast as they dared. The dead *halflings* moved to stop them, arms outstretched. At the last second Candi's horse panicked and reared up. Caught off guard, Candi fell from the horse, striking her head upon the ground. She saw her horse as the *halflings* forced it to the ground. She tried to get up but found it too difficult. Her head was bleeding. A dark shape loomed in front of her...

Chapter 41
The Stones of Darkwater

Lightfingers caressed the side of Bekka's arm, she hadn't said a word after the others had all departed, and now she was busy packing her rucksack. He was worried about her. "Is everything alright?"

The concern in his eyes was touching, but she hardly noticed. After a moment she sighed heavily, running a hand through her hair as though distracted. "Yeah," she said, "I'm fine. I just don't want to forget anything."

He could see that she was struggling with her emotions. It would be so easy for her to falter and spiral completely out of control. That would be dangerous, especially where they were headed. "You know, we don't have to do this." He shook his head. "I'm not even certain that we *can* do this."

Bekka shook her head. She looked at him incredulously, finding it hard to believe that he could even say such a thing. "If we don't do this, then *who* will?" She looked around the *Spilt Tankard* and shrugged. "There's no one else. Valoria is all on her own; it's up to us to save her. I *have* to save her. I have to at least try."

He nodded. "Fine. But what if that old dwarf was right? What if she is a cold-blooded killer?"

Bekka's jaw tightened and she shook her head vigorously. "He's wrong. She's not."

He sighed. "What if we can't save her?"

Bekka slammed her fist on the table. "We *have* to! I need her. I can't face Sinnestra without her."

"Maybe you shouldn't. Maybe it's time to just walk away," he was trying to talk some sense into her. Going up against a demon with only one other warrior on their side was insane.

Bekka stared at him, her mouth dropping open in disbelief. "Sinnestra is responsible for the death of my friends and family. She stole my baby brother! I can't just walk away. He needs me to save him."

He ran his hands over her arms and sighed. "This is crazy, you know. Just you and me against Kaspian Altair and his whole army." He shook his head and chuckled softly. "We don't stand a chance."

"Fine!" Bekka said as she slung her rucksack over her shoulder. "Stay if you want. I'll go alone."

"You wouldn't stand a chance against him; he's too powerful," he said flatly.

She shrugged. "I've lost everyone else; I've really got nothing else to lose."

Lightfingers squeezed her arm. "You'd be throwing away your life. Where's the sense in that?"

Bekka couldn't help but laugh. "Some life."

"Bekka," he sighed heavily, "don't do this. We can go somewhere else. We can start over, just you and I."

She shook her head. "I can't." She stood on the tips of her toes and kissed his cheek. "Stay here. Have a good life, Darren. You don't have to do this. I do."

"Why?" he asked, searching her face.

She smiled. "Because Valoria would do it for me."

Bekka had ridden away from the *Spilt Tankard Inn* alone; but she was absolutely fine with that. She didn't need anybody. She was better off this way. She shook her head. She knew that it was probably a fool's quest and the odds were stacked greatly against her, but she felt that this was the *right* thing to do. She should've come through the *Portal* alone in the very beginning. If she had, Jacob, Cleve and her parents would all still be alive. Her parents might have been worried sick about her, wondering what had happened to her, but at least they would still be alive.

These thoughts forced her eyes to water and tears to run down her face. She was glad that she was alone so that no one would see them. No one would ask if everything was okay. She didn't have to pretend that it was. Wiping her cheeks she rode along, her thoughts drifting to the task before her. *What had she been thinking? How could she—all by herself—hope to rescue Valoria? It was one thing when they had all been together, attacking the slaver's wagon would have been a cakewalk! But this? This was absolutely nuts! She was going up against an army. And even if she managed to slip past them, she would still have to deal with Kaspian Altair.* He was a dark mage; which really meant very little to her. She wouldn't know a dark mage from any other. Only one thing was for certain: she was riding to her death.

The realization didn't frighten her. It would all be over soon. She would join her friends and family in whatever came next. The next great adventure! She frowned suddenly. Was there even a Heaven here on this side of the *Portal*?

She reined her horse in, stopping on the center of the bridge that spanned the *River of Sorrow*. She glanced toward the sky, wondering if her *God* was up there. That thought made her laugh. She giggled uncontrollably. Wasn't she from this side of the *Portal*? Of course *her* God was up there! She just wondered if it was the same God she had prayed to since she was a little girl in *Midvale*.

She closed her eyes trying to *sense* something. Anything. She felt nothing. Suddenly thoughts of Lady Rosa flooded her mind. She could almost *smell* her! Hints of spices assailed her senses. She opened her eyes and smiled. It wasn't really a surprise to her that she *actually* saw the old Gypsy woman standing on the other side of the bridge, in the middle of the road. "Rosa," she said softly, and smiled.

The old Gypsy turned toward her, her dark eyes sparkling in the morning sunlight. She looked around her and shrugged her frail shoulders. "Vhat are you vaiting for? An invitation? Kaspian Altair ees not going to velcome you vith open arms, you know."

Bekka laughed. She slid from the saddle and ran to the Gypsy, hugging her tightly. *She was real! She could actually feel her!* "Oh Rosa! I've missed you so!"

She could hear the plodding of her horse as it moved toward her.

Bekka slipped out of Rosa's embrace and turned. Lightfingers was there, sitting on his horse, holding the reins of hers out for her to take. His face was blank, but a flicker of concern flashed in his eyes. She turned back to the Gypsy, but she was gone. Bekka did a complete circle but there was no sign of Rosa. She put a hand to her head in bewilderment. *How was this even possible?*

They rode along in silence for what seemed an eternity, leaving the tiny hamlet of *Darkwater* far behind. The road twisted and turned as it made its way through a small wooded area at the outer fringe of *Darken Wood*. Finally, Bekka couldn't stand the quiet any longer. "What made you decide to come?"

He shrugged. "No one should die alone."

Bekka shook her head and smiled. "You *do* realize that we probably *are* going to die, don't you? I mean, we're going up against some pretty long odds. He's got an entire army fighting for him, and it's just you and I."

Lightfingers rolled his eyes. "Where have I heard that before? I really don't need you to state the obvious. Yes, we are likely going to get ourselves killed before we ever get anywhere near Kaspian Altair. If what that old dwarf said is true, it'll likely be your friend that kills us."

Bekka couldn't help but laugh. "Wouldn't that be something?"

Lightfingers tugged his reins to the left, leading them off the road and deeper into *Darken Wood*. "Where are we going?" Bekka asked as she rode beside him.

He smiled. "It is probably not the wisest thing for us to do, staying on that road. Kaspian Altair probably has patrols going up and down it fairly often. I'm not so eager to die that I'm just going to hand him my head."

Bekka nodded. "Smart thinking."

He smirked. "While I've still got my head, I might as well use it."

The pine trees of this forest were a darker green than any Bekka had ever seen before. They were tall and slender but still had low hanging branches. They had to twist and turn their way through them fairly regularly. She was glad that Lightfingers had taken the lead; she would probably take them in circles, but he seemed to know what he was doing. She trusted him.

The smell of the pine seemed fresher with the newly fallen snow weighing heavy upon the boughs, but that could simply be her imagination. It was growing colder, and she could feel the light caress of snowflakes upon her face. It was hard to discern whether it was actually snowing again or if these were just flakes swept along in a light breeze.

Eventually they made camp in a slight clearing. They were both feeling the bite of the frosty air and were eager for the warmth of a fire, so they got one going as quick as they could. They huddled close together while they ate the sliced ham and biscuits that Carandra Toshe had prepared.

"By this time tomorrow our fate will be clear," Lightfingers said simply.

Bekka nodded. "It's not too late for you to turn back, you know."

He chuckled. "Nah. Who wants to live forever, anyway?

Bekka laughed. "That's the spirit!"

She smiled at him as she put a hand to his cheek. "I'm glad that you're here." She felt something stir deep within her. He was a *very* good-looking man. She found herself wanting to kiss him. She leaned in, her eyes closing as his head bent to hers.

"Haloooo the camp!" came a familiar call from the shadows of the forest.

Bekka glanced at Lightfingers. "That *can't* be our little friend, can it?"

He had a frustrated look in his eyes as he shrugged. He slipped his sword from its scabbard and said, "Tagg, is that you?"

"Aye laddie, t'is me! Might I share yer fire?"

Lightfingers gave Bekka a questioning look and she nodded her consent. "Come on in and warm your bones," he said.

As the old dwarf stepped into the firelight, he appeared genuinely pleased to see them at first, but then he frowned. "Where be yer companions? I seem ta recall a couple more lassies..."

"We've taken different paths," Bekka said. She saw him eying her biscuit. "Have you eaten?"

He shook his head still eying the biscuit she held. "Not since the trout."

Bekka dug through her rucksack and handed him one of Carandra's biscuits. "You should take better care of yourself, especially out here in the wilderness."

He nodded as he shoved the biscuit into his mouth, leaving a crumb to fall into his beard. "Aye, tha' I should lass. Tha' I should." He chuckled softly as he chewed.

After a minute he glanced back at her rucksack. "Would ye 'appen ta 'ave another one o' those biscuits?" He smiled at her. "Tha' sure t'was good."

She sighed and handed him another. At this rate they would quickly run out before they got very far. "I shouldn't really be feeding you. You're out to kill my friend." A moment of panic swept through her. *Had he already?*

Tagg nodded. "About tha', I'll not be a killin' yer friend. Least ways I'll try me best ta spare her."

"Why the change of heart?" Lightfingers asked.

The dwarf shrugged. "T'is probably na' her fault tha' she killed me friends. I think she may be *bespelled*."

They stared at him and waited for him to elaborate. He seemed not to notice as he finished off his ham and biscuit. Finally, Bekka could take his silence no longer. "What do you mean, bespelled?"

He nodded. "It 'appened ta me brother, Shamus. I found 'im in the woods na' far from this very spot. I was truly happy ta have joined 'is company. Then I noticed he 'ad a strange look in 'is eyes. He damn near took me head off with me own axe!" He looked up at the two of them, his eyes suddenly wet with tears. "I tried na' ta kill 'im, but he wouldna' give me a choice. It came down ta 'im or me." He shook his head in sorrow. "Shamus weren't 'imself."

Tagg wiped his nose on his sleeve. "Been fightin' Kaspian's minions all day." He reached into a pocket and pulled out a handful of small, smooth, dark rocks. "Ye kill the bastards an this be all tha' left o' 'em."

The stones seemed to have a fiery blue glow deep in their center. "What are they?" Bekka asked.

Lightfingers exhaled slowly and pointed at the dwarf's hand. *"Those are the Stones of Darkwater!"* He had thought them only a myth.

Chapter 42
The Obsidian Gate

Sinnestra cradled the infant in her arms and softly cooed to him. He smiled up at her, feeling all warm and safe. His tiny arms flailed in the air. She returned his smile, stroking his chubby cheek with a crimson fingernail. She began to hum a forgotten tune, one that her mother had sung to her a long, long time ago.

Brother Dinurés bowed low before her. He cleared his throat softly, hesitant to disturb her, she seemed so *happy*; the infant was good for her or so it would seem. "Mistress?" he whispered.

She immediately stopped humming and glared at him, her eyes taking on a faint red glow. "What is it?"

He swallowed his fear and continued. "All is as you have requested. I await your pleasure."

She stared at him for a full minute; her eyes softening to a light shade of blue as her anger subsided. She smiled. "You have served me well, Dinurés. I am pleased."

He bowed again; her gratification was all he truly needed. Things had gone poorly for his Mistress since she had been cut with the *Blade of the Spider's Kiss*; but that would all be changing soon.

She would have her revenge.

Sinnestra followed the priest down the long, stone corridor and down the winding steps that led to the depths of her fortress. She continued to make little sounds that the baby found pleasing. He cooed his happy baby sounds, oblivious to the clip-clop of her hooves upon the flagstones.

Jet-black stones formed the arch that stood in the center of the chamber. Torches burned in the wall sconces of the circular room, reflecting flickering orange light upon the obsidian stonework. You could walk completely around the arch; you could even walk *through* the archway without anything happening. But once it was activated, that would change.

The baby wailed hungrily. Sinnestra's lip curled and she slipped a knuckle into the infant's mouth. He immediately seemed to calm. She continued to walk around the arch, humming softly as her hooves clip-clopped loudly. She turned and faced the priest. "What are we waiting for?"

Brother Dinurés nodded. He studied the demoness and the infant for a moment. "Mistress, if I may be so bold?"

Her eyes narrowed as she looked from the baby in her arms to the dark priest. "What is it now, Dinurés?" She could feel her impatience starting to get the better of her. She was growing tired of all the delays, of all the failed attempts to heal her wound, of *everything*. She just wanted vengeance.

He coughed into his fist, uncomfortable. "Time on the other side of the *Gate* passes much faster than it does here," he paused, his eyes going to the wound on her shoulder, "that will only worsen there."

His meaning was all too clear. Sinnestra nodded. "I am aware of that."

"You are also aware that it will bring you closer to your own demise, then?" Surely, she was. But he felt it was his duty to make certain.

She sighed heavily. "I am."

"Perhaps you should remain here. I could take the babe..." He was sincere in his offer. She could await their return in relative comfort. It would ultimately buy her more time.

Sinnestra stomped a cloven hoof. "No! It must be me." She was *not* about to pass up the opportunity to shape the baby's life, to mold him to *her* design. She *would be* his mother!

The priest nodded as he walked to a small table along the wall and drew a ceremonial dagger out of its sheath; the blade was not straight and narrow, but wavy like a viper moving upon the ground. He stepped to the archway and drew the sharp blade across the palm of his hand. He placed his bloodied palm against the obsidian stone where a small handprint seemed carved to receive it. Almost immediately blood seemed to flow up and down the black stone along small grooves that at first were not noticeable. The stonework seemed to glow with a thirst of its own. Glyphs, arcane writings, glowed with a bright blood-red deep in the rock.

The *Obsidian Gate* was open. Swirling flames danced in its center as streaks of blue-white lightning flashed from the stonework joining the fiery inferno. The growing flames totally consumed the arch.

Sinnestra drew herself up and let out a long, slow breath. She smiled down at the baby still sucking at her finger. "Are you ready, my sweet?"

She stepped through the *Gate*, vanishing in an instant, leaving the priest alone in the circular chamber...

They could feel the golden sunlight warm their skin as they left the *Obsidian Gate* behind; the stark coldness of *Silver Frost Keep* departed like a whisper. Birds chirped high up in the trees, a doe raised its head and stared at them for a moment, and then loped off through the pines, unconcerned.

Sinnestra looked down at the babe in her arms and smiled as she walked through the tranquil forest. She brushed through his dark curls with her fingertips and then traced along his chubby jaw line. They stepped into a clearing where a quaint little cottage was surrounded by tall pines and slender aspen. "Welcome home, my son." ·

They would be safe here. As long as neither of them ventured beyond the forest even *he* would not know they were here. She bit at her bottom lip and reflected thoughtfully. If *he* knew that she had returned to this *demon realm* they would be at risk. She would have to teach Han never to stray too far from the cottage. She was not ready to face *him*.

He would demand her fidelity and she would be forced to bend to *his* will. Oh, *he* could take away her pain, to be sure, but *his* cost would be high. *He* would likely demand that she give up her plans for vengeance. But she could not rest until the *Chosen One* was made to pay.

It was best if they remained unnoticed.

Chapter 43
The Bone Yard

Candi awoke with a start. She tried to sit up but found she couldn't. She managed only to prop herself up on her elbows. Her head hurt, throbbing unmercifully. "I'm cold!" she said, pouting.

Trish stirred beside her. "Oh, thank God! I thought I was going to lose you!" She tentatively touched her friend's arm. "How are you feeling, Candi?"

Candi blinked, confusion still muddling her brain. "What happened?"

"You got thrown from your horse, you hit your head pretty hard; must've been a rock under the snow." She studied her closely; her voice was thick with emotion. "There was so much blood. I thought... I thought I was gonna... lose you for a while there." Tears trickled down her cheeks.

"Aw," Candi said with a smile, clearly touched by the emotional response of her friend. "You love me!"

Trish slugged her arm.

"Ow!" Candi said, shocked. "What the heck was *that* for?"

"For scaring me!" Trish said, running a hand through her auburn curls.

Candi shivered. "It's freezing! Why don't you make a fire, or something?"

"No!" Trish said almost too fast. "We can't have a fire. It attracts those things like a moth to a flame. We need to move as quickly as you're able. We're down to only one horse."

"Mine ran off?" Candi said, touching her forehead gingerly. It was still tender. She winced.

Trish shook her head. "No. They ate your horse."

Suddenly Candi remembered the *zombie-halflings* pulling her horse to the ground. The frightened whinny of the horse; she could still hear the sound of their teeth ripping the hide from the terrified beast. She shivered. She remembered Trish fighting the swarm of them that were focused on her. "You saved me."

"Well," Trish said with a smile, "I wasn't gonna let you be eaten."

Candi held her hand out to Trish. "Help me get up?"

Trish pulled her friend to her feet and then hugged her tightly. They stood together for some time, both reluctant to let the other go. Finally, after what seemed forever to Candi, Trish slipped out of her embrace. She moved with purpose, quickly gathering their things. She tied them to the horse and then mounted. She offered Candi her hand and helped the girl swing up on the stallion behind her. "Hang on," she said, urging the horse to a steady canter through the trees.

Candi wrapped her arms around Trish's waist and rested her head on her shoulder. She was still so very tired. "Don't let me fall," she whispered.

Trish smiled clasping a hand over Candi's own. "I won't," she promised.

Somehow, Candi had drifted off to sleep despite the jostling that came with riding a horse. How she had managed to keep her balance was beyond her; it was hard enough when it was just her in the saddle. Trish still had a firm grip on her hand, perhaps that was the secret. She inhaled and placed her chin on Trish's right shoulder. The smell of the evergreens coupled with Trish's familiar scent. She could see golden sunlight slipping through the gaps between the tall pines. Candi was optimistic; they hadn't seen any more of the *zombie-halflings*; she could only hope that they had left them far behind. They had ridden hard for most of the night and now a new day was dawning.

The horse's ears twitched nervously, and then pointed straight back; it snorted loudly, clearly frightened. Trish tried to soothe the beast, patting its long neck reassuringly. *Something* was out there! They could hear a swooshing sound growing louder and louder. *Swoosh, swoosh, swoosh, swiiiiish...* Something dark flew toward them as the sound stopped suddenly, they heard a loud *THUD* as it struck the horse between the eyes, dropping it instantly. Both girls flew over the horse's head and landed on the ground. Fortunately, they both absorbed the shock as their shoulders struck the ground; they rolled with their momentum carrying them forward. Trish was on one knee, sword already in hand.

The edge of the forest was nearby, less than thirty feet away. Whatever had attacked them was determined that they did not leave the woods; it wanted to keep them there.

Wide-eyed and alert, Trish leaned toward Candi and whispered in her ear. "We need to get out of here as quickly as we can."

"But the horse..." Candi was not thinking clearly.

"The horse is dead," Trish said. "We need to move."

Candi looked back and saw the horse on the ground, eyes wide open, its thick tongue sticking out of its open mouth; blood running down the forehead. She could see a bloodied rock near the horse. "Who did this?" she asked.

"Can you run?" Trish pulled on her arm.

Candi blinked, frowning. "What?" she was still dazed and confused.

"Can you run?" Trish asked again, giving her arm a shake. She didn't have time for this. "We need to get out of this damned forest."

Candi put a hand to the side of her head. She nodded. "I think so."

"Good!" Trish said, giving her a shove. "Run, and don't stop!" She could only hope that once they were free of the spectral wood, the *zombie-halflings* would cease their relentless attacks; they were twirling long sticks with a sling attached at the end, firing rocks at their targets.

Candi could hear the *swooshing* sound start up again as she ran toward the forest's edge. She crashed through wet foliage, rustling the leaves behind her. As the sound stopped, she quickly darted to the right. After several long strides she darted to the left, each time she saw a stone zoom past her, narrowly missing her. "Zig-zag!" she called out triumphantly, hoping Trish would hear her.

Candi surged past the last of the foliage and slowed in a thick mound of snow. After another ten feet, she turned and searched for signs of her friend. *Nothing.* Fear gripped Candi. *Had Trish been taken down? Was she even now being eaten like her horse had been?* Relief washed over her as Trish stepped out of the forest a few minutes later; the blade of her sword was coated in gore.

As they walked along Candi kept looking over her shoulder, expecting to find the *zombie-halflings* lumbering after them. She stopped suddenly, reaching out she grabbed Trish's arm. "You *won't* believe this."

Trish turned, her eyes grew wide; the *spectral forest* was gone. It had simply vanished. Candi pinched her arm. *"Ow!"* Trish howled. "What the hell was *that* for?"

Candi shook her head. "Just checking."

"What?" Trish said rubbing the red spot on her lower arm. "You thought we were dreaming?"

Candi shrugged. "It was a thought."

Trish gave her an angry glare. "You do realize that you're *supposed* to pinch yourself, don't you?"

Candi chuckled softly. "That would be just silly."

They continued to walk through the deep snowdrifts for the next hour, seeing nothing but snow after mound of snow. It was getting quite deep, up to mid-thigh which slowed their progress greatly. Both women were getting tired quickly. Occasionally

Candi would stumble and fall, and Trish would have to help her to her feet; ignoring her pleas to just leave her there and to go on without her.

After another hour Candi pointed up ahead and to the left. "Are those *dinosaur bones*?"

Trish shook her head, frowning. "I don't think so."

They looked at one another and said in unison, *"Dragons!"*

The pair quickly forgot their exhaustion and plunged through the snow toward the skeletal dragons, giggling as they went.

They walked among the skeletal remains of the magnificent beasts that littered the ground. Some of them were quite large, clearly able to swallow them whole. It was hard for either of them to believe that such creatures had actually lived. But the proof was undeniable.

"Do you think that there are still dragons?" Candi asked as she placed a hand upon the skeletal snout of a long dead wyvern.

Trish shrugged. "They could be like our dinosaurs."

Candi pouted. "I hope not. That would be just sad."

"Well," Trish said with a shake of her auburn curls, "I certainly haven't seen any and by the size of these things I think I am glad of that!"

A large dragon tooth dwarfed Candi as she looked at her friend. "I know what you mean! How scary would it be having one of these suckers chasing you?" She frowned suddenly. "Do you think any of them really breathed fire?"

"Maybe."

Chapter 44
Beyond the Gate

The boy looked at the only mother he had ever known. *'Why,'* he wondered, *'do I not look like her?'* Not that it truly mattered. She loved him, as he loved her. They were inseparable. But still, he wondered...

She saw the grimace upon his face and she knelt in front of him, touching his cheek. "What troubles you, Han?"

He looked up from his wooden toys and shrugged. "Why are we so different?" He reached out and put his hand upon hers. "Why do we not look the same?"

She smiled at him and ran the fingers of her other hand through his blond curls. His skin was a normal human flesh tone, which stood out against her alabaster complexion. He had no horns protruding from his head, no hooves for feet. He was human in every way; she was not.

"Do you doubt that I am your Mother?" Sinnestra asked softly.

He frowned again, shaking his head. "No. Why would I?"

She smiled. "Remember those very bad people that I told you about?"

He nodded. "The ones that killed Daddy and did that to you?" he indicated her left shoulder where the *Blade of the Spider's Kiss* had cut her.

She smiled at him. He was such a sweet boy. He brought her so much joy. "That's right. They were *very* bad people. They still want to kill Mommy; that is why we are here. We are safe here."

"Why do they want you dead?" he asked with a pout.

"Because I am different. If you were to look like me, they would want you dead too."

His jaw tightened. "I wish that I *did* look like you! I wouldn't care!"

She caressed the side of his head. "I could not bear to lose you, Han. That is why I made you look like them, so that they *won't* hurt you. When I die, you can move among them without fear."

He clenched his jaw tightly and shook his head. "I won't fear *them*, Mommy. *They* should fear me!"

Sinnestra kissed the top of his head. "My dear, sweet boy!"

He grew silent, frowning. She could tell that something else was weighing heavily upon his mind. She smiled, waiting, as she watched him set his toys aside. He was obviously struggling with something. "What is it, Han?" she prodded softly.

He shrugged his tiny shoulders. "Yesterday I was deep in the woods. I could see darkness beyond the trees."

She felt her breath catch in her throat, as panic seized her. She forced a smile to her face, not wanting to frighten him. Sinnestra inhaled and slowly let the air escape past her lips. She reached out and touched his small shoulder, noticing that her fingers trembled slightly. "You mustn't stray so far from the cottage, you know that. I don't know how many times I've told you that it isn't safe. There are *other* enemies out there. Mommy doesn't want you to play in the woods. You are to stay in sight of the cottage at all times."

His frown deepened. "But why?"

She could feel the anger rising within her; she *hated* having her authority questioned. She closed her eyes and took another breath. When she had control over her temper she said softly. "There are beings out in the darkness that would betray us. They would run to *him* and *he* would come for us. *He* would take you from me so that I would be forced to do *his* will."

He looked up at her with wide, curious eyes. "Who is *he*, Mommy? Is *he* a bad man?"

She put a hand upon his dark curls and nodded. "*He is evil incarnate.*"

Chapter 45
Bitterwood Castle

They had made their way to a bluff just above *Bitterwood Castle*. Tagg Thorun pointed through the trees. "Thar be the *Dark Mage's* fortress. We'll likely na' find a safe way inside."

Lightfingers scratched at the stubble that covered his chin. "I don't like it."

Bekka had expected to find an outer curtain wall, similar to the one protecting *Kensington Castle*, surrounding the Keep of Kaspian Altair. Instead, *Bitterwood Castle* was ringed by a fairly wide moat that was filled with unknown horrors; the water was very dark and unnatural looking. It appeared thick, almost ooze-like. The only way across was by a single drawbridge.

"You think they keep the prisoners inside?" Bekka asked, feeling her hopes dashed.

Taggarty shook his head. "Nah. Tha' dark bastard 'as 'is prisoners workin' in the mines fer these blasted stones." He patted his pocket. "It would be a waste o' time ta 'ave ta keep

299

haulin' 'em back and forth. I s'pect he'll 'ave 'em caged closer ta the mines. Yer friend will likely be there guarding the others, or perhaps even in the mountain watchin' 'em dig."

"Do you know where these mines are, then?" Bekka asked, putting a hand to his arm. She much preferred going to the mines over an assault on the castle, especially with their numbers.

The dwarf nodded. "Aye, I do. Tha' be where I found me brother, Shamus." He shook his head. "Or rather he found me. Damned fool was bespelled, I tell ye. Nearly kilt me with me own axe!"

Lightfingers rolled his eyes. "Yes, so you told us."

Taggarty's eyes narrowed as he stroked his beard. "You sayin' I'm lyin' ta ye, laddie?"

Lightfingers chuckled, spreading his hands wide. He didn't want a confrontation with the dwarf. They needed allies badly, not more enemies. "Not at all."

Bekka shook her head. "Really, guys? We don't have time for this macho crap. We need to find Valoria and get her un-bespelled. We still need to meet up with Trish and Candi so that we can go after Sinnestra."

"Sinnestra, eh?" Taggarty sounded surprised. "Didna' know ye were goin' after a demoness too."

"You know about Sinnestra?" Bekka asked. She hadn't expected that he would.

Taggarty chuckled. "Aye, tha' I do. She took o'er the dwarven kingdom o' *Silver Frost Keep* almost a hundred years ago, when I was just a wee lad. Still calls the place hers, I believe, though last I heard she was tormenting the Drow."

"*Silver Frost Keep?*" Bekka asked.

Lightfingers stroked his chin. "Isn't that somewhere in the *Demon Spires?*"

"Aye, t'is tha'," Taggarty said. "On the opposite side from where we be now. Best reached through the *Northern Passage.*" He stroked his chin. "If'n ye can get through all the snow. Spring might be yer best bet."

"We don't have until spring," Bekka said. She gave Lightfingers a steady gaze. "That's where we'll find Sinnestra. We need to make our way there once we have Valoria. It all makes sense; Brendlestixx said he had learned that she had a fortress somewhere in the *Demon Spires*. This confirms it."

Taggarty tucked his thumbs over the top of his wide belt. "Like I said, tha' be far easier said than done." When they both looked at him with raised brows he continued. "This time o' year the pass is dangerous. One could find theyselves completely o'errun by an avalanche, or worse!"

"What could be worse than being trapped by an avalanche?" Lightfingers said. He shivered just thinking about it.

"Well, laddie, ye could be eaten by a vicious snow leopard if'n ye ain't too careful."

"A snow leopard?" Bekka said.

"Indeed," said the dwarf with a wink. "There be a few o' 'em baddies in the *Demon Spires*." He stroked his long beard thoughtfully. "Though, in truth, they be mighty rare. It be the Crystal Dragons tha' ye really gotta be lookin' out fer."

"Crystal Dragons?" All Bekka could imagine was a little crystal figurine like the ones in a store located on Mainstreet back in *Midvale*; those were harmless. The ones that Tagg was referring to were likely not.

"Aye a cunning beastie ta be sure!" Taggarty said. "They be verra hard ta see. If'n they catch ye unawares ye be a gonner fer sure! They breathe an acid spray tha'll eat right through chainmail; the older ones'll spit acid tha'll eat through plate like it t'were a hot knife agoin' through butter. Ye can imagine what it'll do ta a feller's skin."

"I've heard of Crystal Dragons. There are two different kinds, aren't there?" Lightfingers said.

The dwarf nodded. "Aye, thar be the red Crystal and the white. Course, the white be the ones ye 'ave ta be the most concerned with in this country. The reds prefer a much warmer climate."

The thief shivered. "I don't think I want to meet either one."

"Nah," the dwarf said. "Either one t'would likely be the end of ye, lest ye 'ad powerful magic," he shrugged, "and an army o' considerable size." He stroked his beard thoughtfully. "An' ye need a hefty hammer ta boot! Swords an' such tend ta shatter when ye strike the beasties."

"Well," Bekka said with a sigh, "let's not worry over something that may never happen. We need to free Valoria first. That alone may get us all killed."

Chapter 46
Blood Oath

Brother Dinurés turned from the *Obsidian Gate* and walked back to the table. He tore a white cloth into narrow strips and wrapped his still bleeding hand; he had sliced deeper than he had intended. He could almost immediately see a long red spot growing where it covered his palm. He would survive. He glanced back at the archway and sighed.

Mistress Sinnestra was taking a chance with her life. Time did not pass in the same increment on the *other side* of the gateway. Hours were days, maybe months, and possibly even years. He couldn't be certain. She would condition the infant to regard her as his mother; in that, she would undoubtedly succeed. Sinnestra could be *very* persuasive.

Unfortunately, her ultimate success would hasten her own demise. The infection would grow more rapidly there. The infant would quickly become a man instilled with a hatred for those that opposed Sinnestra. Her hope was that she would live long enough to see Han defeat her enemies.

The priest had made a *blood oath* to help him succeed. Failure would mean an agonizing death, so that was not an option. Success however, would guarantee Dinurés more wealth than he could ever hope to amass in numerous lifetimes!

His fingertips caressed the arm of her throne as he walked around the dais. This fortress would ultimately be his. After Han killed his sister and her friends, the *blood oath* would be fulfilled. Then Dinurés would betray and kill him; and he would be Master! He would build an army and ultimately reign supreme.

Dinurés sat upon the throne and smiled; he had endured much in service to Sinnestra. Soon the bite from the *Blade of the Spider's Kiss* would take its toll and she would no longer be a problem for him. Han would slay those that came to 'save' him, and then he would grieve his lost mother. Dinurés would move to comfort him, but instead would slide his jagged blade into his heart. Wealth and power would be his!

Pleased with himself, he began to laugh...

Chapter 47
Eight-legged Beasties

Bekka followed behind Tagg and Lightfingers as they ventured deeper into *Darken Wood*. Every once in a while, the old dwarf would stop, remove his horned helm and scratch his head, grunt and then head off in a new direction. She only hoped that he wasn't getting them *hopelessly* lost. For the most part, he seemed to know where he was going.

"Na' far now," the old dwarf said in a whisper as he wiped his brow.

Looking around, Bekka could see thick cobwebs hanging from several branches of the dark evergreens. The sight alone made her shiver. "I *hate* spiders!" she said with a shudder.

Tagg laughed. "Then ye truly won't be 'appy 'ere. These beasties are just a wee bit bigger than me."

Bekka stopped walking; her eyes went wide. "You're kidding right?"

He chuckled. "I only wish tha' I were."

Lightfingers drew his shortsword. "Stay close to me."

Bekka slowly pulled her longsword from its scabbard. Having the weapon in hand brought her only a little comfort; the thought of giant spiders made her skin crawl. "Maybe you should stick close to me." She said with a smirk, eying his shortsword. "Size *does* matter."

They heard the rustling of shrubbery nearby, almost on cue. Taggarty eased his battleaxe off his back. More stirring came from the undergrowth on their right. A loud *purring* sound came from every direction. Bekka swallowed. "What was that noise?" It reminded her of a contented cat, almost.

Taggarty adjusted the grip on his axe. "Tha' was the beasties. They produce vibrations tha' hit the needles o' the trees causing them ta *tremble*. Tha' way they can git yer location. They be smart beasties fer sure. We need a fire, quick! The beasties don't like fire!"

"Why didn't you say so earlier?" Bekka asked, sounding a bit frantic.

Taggarty shrugged.

After a glimpse at Bekka's longer sword, Lightfingers sheathed his. He quickly dropped to his knees and gathered a bunch of dried pine needles into a pile. He took out his flint and steel and struck them together; tiny sparks appeared, but no flame.

Bekka could see a dark shape lumbering toward them. *"Hurry!"*

Taggarty had been leading the horses and he quickly let go of their reins. He slapped the first horse on the rump; fearing the spiders, the horses bolted through *Darken Wood*, eager to be away.

"What was that for?" Bekka said surprised.

"T'would've killed the horses, this way they'll 'ave a chance," Tagg said.

"Aren't we going to need them, later?" Bekka said, shaking her head.

"Oh," Tagg said. "I suppose tha' we might." He shrugged. "We've got bigger concerns now."

After three more strikes of the flint, Lightfingers had a small fire going. He leaned in and blew, adding more kindling to the rising flame.

"Hurry it up, lad!" Taggarty pleaded. Two more shadowy figures were closing in.

"Where are they all coming from?" Bekka asked.

"The mines used ta be *full* o' 'em lassie!" Taggarty exclaimed as he swung his axe at a shadowy form. "But when Kaspian Altair started workin' the mines, he drove the beasties out into the forest." He grunted as he cleaved the front legs off of a skittering spider. The huge arachnid screeched loudly as green goo squirted from its wound. Tagg swung again, delivering a fatal blow to the creature's head.

Bekka could hear the giant spiders hiss all around them as they tried to surround them. She was breathing heavily, her eyes wide with fear. She was trying to control the panic rising within her.

Lightfingers lit a torch and handed it to Bekka; she immediately brandished it at an approaching spider—the thing was absolutely *huge!* Drawing its front legs up, it backed away with ease, hissing as it went. Bekka could see some silky cocoons that resembled humanoids between the evergreens; they glowed with a ghostly light in the sun. She didn't have to guess their fate if they failed to fight the spiders off.

They all were nearing exhaustion as they battled the giant eight-legged swarm. It was as though the spiders were a pack of wolves attacking from every possible angle, hunting for a weak spot in their defenses. Bekka didn't know how long she could keep it up. Both arms were lowering slightly from the weight of the torch and the sword; she had to give one of them up if she hoped to continue. Finally, she sheathed the blade.

She saw Taggarty touch his burning torch against a cocoon; it burst into flames almost instantly. Screeching spiders sounded all around. Taggarty lit another; it was quickly consumed with crackling fire. "Foller me lead, lassie!" he bellowed.

Nodding, Bekka swung at a spider and then touched a cocoon as the creature retreated out of harm's way; it burst into flames sending thick, black smoke up through the trees. The tactic seemed to be working; the giant spiders ceased their attack for the moment.

Lightfingers grabbed Bekka by the arm. "We need to be going before they come back."

She nodded, blinking. She had been staring at the small burning spiders that spilled from the fiery cocoons. Skeletal remains of humanoids could be seen inside the burning swaddle of silk. She shivered.

"This way!" Taggarty motioned to their right.

A giant spider dropped down from a tree, striking Lightfingers in the back, knocking him to the ground. He struggled to get away but the creature had him pinned. Bekka whirled and thrust her torch into the arachnid's face. It screeched loudly as it struggled to get away from the flame that was quickly consuming it.

Taggarty helped Lightfingers to his feet. "Are ye alright laddie?" He looked at the thief with concern.

Darren nodded. "I'm fine. He just caught me off guard."

They continued through the forest following a fairly worn path, or at least it appeared to be. Soon, they left all signs of the spiders behind. No webbing stretched among the trees and the screeches grew less noticeable. They stopped for a badly needed rest. Taggarty passed around a waterskin.

"How much further to the mines?" Bekka asked. She took a sip of water and then passed it along to Lightfingers. The water tasted slightly stale but it was nonetheless refreshing.

Lightfingers passed the skin back to the dwarf and wiped his mouth with the back of his hand. He was breathing heavily; clearly he had overexerted himself with their recent activity.

Taggarty slammed the stopper in the lip of the waterskin, and then he looped it around his arm and dropped it over his shoulder. He furrowed a brow as he looked at the thief. "Ye sure ye be okay lad?"

Lightfingers nodded. "I'm just a bit winded. Usually my activities are far less strenuous."

"Well," said the dwarf, "we should be gettin' a move on then. Not much farther ta go." He pointed to the northwest. "Just o'er tha' rise be the road leading ta the mines. We oughta be able ta foller it fer a good bit a'for we 'ave ta take greater care."

They reached the road leading to the *Darkwater Mines* in

just under an hour. Going up the 'rise' had been a lot harder than Taggarty had let on. Numerous pine needles covering the ground made the going slick and they were slipping almost constantly. They had abandoned their torches long ago, needing both hands to navigate up the steep incline. It was a lot easier going down the other side.

The road was abandoned. Deep ruts had been cut into the dirt by the passage of heavy carts. Evidently the mines were showing signs of prosperity. Whatever they were taking out of the mountain there was a lot of it. *Could it be those stones that Tagg had shown them? What had Lightfingers called them: the Stones of Darkwater? He had said it with such reverence...* Bekka could only wonder what it all meant.

Chapter 48
The Promise

Han looked at his mother with concern. She was *not* looking well at all. Her alabaster complexion was looking blanched, almost gray. The wound in her shoulder was getting worse, if that were even possible. She was severely weakened. He lifted her from the bed and carried her out into her garden where she could get some sun. It always seemed to help ease her suffering.

Sinnestra sighed heavily as the young man laid her out on the lounger. This part of the garden was her favorite spot. There were roses of assorted colors and numerous marigolds. She smiled weakly as she caressed his cheek tenderly. "My dear, sweet boy."

He blushed. "I am a man now, Mother."

She chuckled softly, giving his cheek a little pat. "You will always be my boy, Han. No matter how old you are, no matter what happens."

His face seemed to harden. He hated being reminded of the

fact that they had so little time remaining. She was going to leave him. She was dying. Her enemies had done this to her. Made her suffer. Made *him* suffer! He took her hand in his and kissed it lovingly. "Stay strong, Mother."

She closed her eyes for a moment. "I am *so* very tired, my love."

Tears formed in his eyes. "I know, Mother. Soon you can rest."

She nodded slowly. "We can spend no more time here, Han. We *must* go back. They will come for me soon. They will..." she swallowed, "they will say things that are not true." She squeezed his arm tightly. "You mustn't allow them to trick you as they did me. They murdered your father. They will want to finish what they started. They might even kill you."

His chin rose slightly as his fists clenched tightly. "I won't let them kill you, Mother. I will fight them. I will kill every last one of them!"

She caressed his cheek again. "My dear, sweet boy. I only want you to be happy. Vengeance leaves such a bitter taste on the tongue."

He stood and glared down at her. "I promise you, Mother. I will make them pay for all that they have done to us! I *will* kill them all even if it is the *last* thing I do"

A small smile curved Sinnestra's lips. Her heart leapt with pride at what she had accomplished. There was more than one way to destroy one's enemies...

Chapter 49
Dragon's Reach

Trish and Candi were in bad shape as they entered the village of *Dragon's Reach*. They hadn't eaten anything in several days; having left their belongings on their dead horse when they fled from the *Spectral Forest* and the *zombie-halflings*. The only thing that had kept them from being totally dehydrated had been the snow that they had consumed; but that had done little to alleviate the rumblings of their stomachs.

They needed something a bit more substantial. Smoke rose high in the air from several buildings, the largest of which was the first that they came across, which as it happened, was a rustic looking inn called the *Dragon's Maw*. Two mammoth teeth framed the doorway of the inn, the tips of the incisors pointed upwards, with a slight inward curve above the door.

Candi shivered, not from the cold. It gave her the sense of being eaten as they entered the *Dragon's Maw*. They found the tavern was fairly crowded and all conversation ceased as they entered. The patronage seemed to be all elves. They turned curious eyes toward them, staring apprehensively with brows arched impossibly high. Obviously they didn't get many visitors. Candi reached a hand out toward Trish, needing contact to still her nerves.

They found a small table perfect for two along the far wall. As they took their seats, they noticed that all eyes continued to watch them; except for one. The serving girl stared at a dark corner of the tavern. She nodded once, and then approached their table. "May I get you some stew?"

Trish smiled up at the girl, and her breath caught in her throat. The girl had the *strangest* eyes she had ever seen in a person, or elf; they were almost cat-like. She had long vertical slits for pupils instead of the normal round. Trish swallowed. "That would be nice, thank you."

The girl nodded and before she walked away she smiled. "I will bring some tea to ward off the cold."

After the server had departed Candi leaned toward Trish and whispered, "Did you see her eyes?"

Trish lightly kicked her with the toe of her boot. "Did you not notice that they all have similar eyes? We should take care not to offend any of them."

"But what do you think it means?" Candi asked.

Trish gave her a warning glare as the barmaid returned with a tray. Two steaming bowls of dark stew with carrots, potatoes and meat were set before them along with two mugs of steaming tea. "If you need anything else, just let me know." She glanced toward the darkened corner of the inn, gave a slight nod, and then walked away.

Candi could see a figure sitting in the darkness, all alone. She wasn't able to discern any relevant details. She couldn't help but shiver slightly. She picked up the mug and sniffed. It had a pleasing aroma, familiar, somehow. Taking a sip, she licked her lips. "Is that cinnamon?" she asked, crinkling her nose.

Trish took a small sip. She shook her head slightly. "Not cinnamon, but something very similar."

Candi shrugged. "Well, whatever it is, I like it. It's *very* tasty!" She took a huge drink, draining half the mug before setting it back onto the table. The warmth of the hot tea spread through her like a lover's embrace, leaving her content.

They ate in silence, not realizing how hungry they were. The barmaid refilled their bowls twice and their mugs once more. "I hope it is to your liking?" she asked with a smile.

"Delicious!" Candi stated. "Is this tea cinnamon? It tastes like cinnamon, but Trish doesn't think that it is. Is it? Cinnamon, I mean."

Trish frowned at her friend. "Slow down, Candi."

Candi's face went blank, and she frowned darkly. She put a hand to her lips and leaned back slightly. Trish blurred in her vision. "I... don't... feel so good."

"You probably ate too fast," Trish said.

Candi placed both hands onto the table and stood unsteadily. She shook her head, trying to focus, but the bar was spinning wildly. "No...!" She collapsed on the floor.

Trish jumped up from her seat. She swayed slightly. She looked from Candi to the barmaid. "What did you *do* to us?" Her eyes rolled up into her head as she reached for her sword; it never cleared the scabbard as she fell to the floor beside her friend.

Trish awoke with a start. She was surprised to find that she was in a room with two beds. Fortunately, Candi was in the other; sound asleep as though she hadn't a care in the world. Trish swung her feet to the floor and pushed herself up off the bed. Her mind was fuzzy, the room was spinning slightly, and for a moment she wasn't certain she could remain standing.

She eased back down on the thin mattress and blinked repeatedly, giving her head a little shake in an attempt to clear her vision. It seemed to be working. After a moment the fog cleared and so did her vision. She was able to stand steadily, and she walked to the door. She turned the knob expecting it to be locked. It wasn't. *At least they weren't prisoners!*

Candi groaned as she sat up in bed, pulling her knees up toward her chest. She rested her elbows on her knees and put the heel of both hands onto her closed eyelids and shook her head slowly. "I feel sick."

"Just take it easy for a minute, it'll pass."

Candi blinked. "Did they *drug* us?"

Trish nodded as she ran her fingers through her auburn curls. "I think so."

Angry, Candi slung her feet over the side of the bed and hopped up. Trish winced as Candi fell to the floor. "I told you to take it easy."

The blonde heaved her shoulders and slapped the floor with the palm of her hands. "This is so messed up. Why would they drug us? Are we prisoners now?"

Trish shook her head. "It doesn't appear so. The door isn't bolted from the outside and there's no one standing guard."

"None of this is making any sense."

Trish shrugged. "Well, as soon as you're ready we'll go down and get some answers."

Candi nodded. "Someone's got some serious explaining to do!" She stood and looked around the room. Surprised, she said, "We still have our weapons? Why go to all the trouble of drugging us and putting us up here like this if they weren't going to take away our weapons?" She frowned at Trish. "This is starting to like *really* freak me out!"

"I agree," said the redhead. "I think we should extend the olive branch, don't you?"

Candi frowned. "What do you mean?"

"Well," Trish said with a raised brow, "since they didn't really harm us, and we aren't truly prisoners, and not to mention the fact that they didn't take our weapons away, maybe we should go downstairs unarmed."

Candi couldn't believe what she'd just heard. "You're absolutely kidding, right?" She shook her head. "We don't *know* what they may have done to us while we were unconscious. Not to mention that we have no idea how long we've been out. They could've done some really *horrible* things."

Trish crossed her arms over her chest and lightly shook her head. "I don't think so." It was difficult for her to imagine anyone doing anything more horrible to her than what she'd already experienced since coming through the *Portal* to *Vespia*.

"Well," Candi said with a quick puff of air, "you can go down unarmed if you want to, but I think I'll go down armed to the teeth."

Trish sighed. "I need you to trust me on this, Candace. I honestly don't think that we're in any danger. If we go down there ready to fight I just think that we'll be making a big mistake. Like really *huge*!"

Candi sighed heavily as she shrugged. "Fine. But if I die, I'll so never speak to you again Patricia Morgan!"

Trish smiled. "Fair enough. You've got a deal."

The two friends descended the stairs side-by-side. They paused at the base of the staircase and looked around; the tavern was still pretty full of clientele. It looked as though little had changed. This time, however, they were largely ignored. The scintillating aroma of venison stew reached them and both were aware of their stomachs' protest. They *were* still very hungry.

"Take your seat," the barmaid said, "and I will fetch you each a bowl." She smiled. "How about a mug of ale this time?"

Candi nodded as she glanced at Trish.

"Fine," Trish said.

They made their way to the same table that they'd shared earlier and as Candi sat down, Trish touched her arm. "I'll be back in a sec."

Candi's eyes went wide, panicked. "Where are you going?"

"To get some answers," Trish said. She walked to the table shrouded in the shadowy corner of the barroom.

Trish placed both her hands on the table; it was difficult to see the tall man sitting in the darkness even from close up. "Mind telling me what all that was about?"

"Whatever do you mean?" the male said softly. Though she couldn't make out details in the darkness, Trish could *hear* the smile in his voice.

"You know *precisely* what I mean. I don't feel like playing your silly little games." Trish said with a slight edge to her voice.

The man sighed. "We do not get many visitors coming to us, especially from the west. We had to be certain that you meant no harm."

"So you drugged us? What did *that* prove?"

He chuckled softly. "I find it much easier to search one's mind while they are incapacitated. There is no deception while you are in a state of unconsciousness. Conscious thought evaporates, deception becomes impossible. We did neither of you any harm. Rest assured it will not happen again."

Trish crossed her arms. "Damned right it won't."

He indicated the table where Candi was sitting. "Your dinner has arrived. Eat and enjoy. We will talk afterwards. I will answer all of your questions."

Candi looked from the shadowy corner to her friend as Trish returned. "Well? Did you find out anything useful?"

Trish shook her head. "Not really. He promises to tell us everything after we've eaten."

Candi lifted her spoon and let it drop back into the bowl. She shook her head. "I'm *not* gonna eat this crap. Not after what happened last time." Her stomach protested. The stew smelled delicious!

"Don't be silly," Trish said. She quickly shoveled a spoonful into her mouth and swallowed. Tears sprang to her eyes. "Careful! It's hot!"

Candi scowled darkly as she crossed her arms over her chest. "I don't care."

Trish shrugged. "Suit yourself. If it helps, he said he wouldn't drug us again. You really ought to try the stew. It really is good."

Candi heard her stomach grumble. She pouted, taking hold of her spoon. "Fine, but I *won't* enjoy it."

After they had eaten, two tall elven men approached the table. They were quite different in appearance. One had normal skin while the other's appeared to have something resembling scales; not fishlike but more reptilian. "Allow me to introduce ourselves," said the man with the scaled skin. Trish recognized his voice from the shadowy corner. "I am Ansanthe Lael'dain and this is Enialirl Feanrenia. If you will accompany us, we will explain everything to your complete satisfaction."

Trish and Candi exchanged looks, neither was able to take their eyes from Ansanthe for very long. They followed them into an adjoining room where four other elves were waiting, one of whom was female. The light in here was much better than it had been in the barroom. They could see that *all* of those assembled had similar scaled skin; Ansanthe's was more pronounced. He made all the introductions. "This is Borrilis Tarneas," he indicated an older looking male elf with silver hair. The next two were much younger and had dark brown hair, which they wore tied at the back into ponytails. "Silvanil Hilion and Vaelreen D'arcentil." They bowed their heads slightly, amused smiles curving their lips. "And this is Celephia Vala'tenarii," he motioned toward a pretty blonde female, whose skin was the most normal looking. "Together we are referred to as *The Guardians*."

Trish arched a brow. "Guardians of what?"

Candi nodded with a frown. "And *what* are you? Elves? I've *never* seen elves with eyes like yours, and your skin…"

Ansanthe arched a brow. Celephia placed a hand on his arm and smiled warmly, her eyes bright and twinkling. "We have elven blood in our ancestry to be sure, but that is not all. We are known as *Drelkin*."

Trish shook her head slightly. "Drelkin?"

Celephia nodded. "That is correct. We share the bloodlines of both Dragons and Elves."

"So," Trish said putting the information together quickly, "that is why your skin is scaled."

Celephia bowed slightly. "Precisely."

Candi's eyes were wide. She resisted the urge to reach out and touch the woman's arm. "Wow," she said, clearly amazed.

Trish looked back at Ansanthe. "Guardians?"

He nodded. "Yes," he said, admiring her tenacity. "Since you are both relatively new to *Vespia* there is much of our history that you do not know. Dragons once flew freely throughout the lands. They were great, magical beasts without equal. Despite their majesty, or perhaps *because of it*, the other races feared them. They became hunted, nearly to the point of extinction. A change was needed. That is where the elves came in."

Celephia took up his tale. "The elves that made their home in the forests of the *Dragon Spire Mountains* have always been protectors of the *earth magic* like our cousins from *Serendil Brenatis*, and the *Fae*. We came to the conclusion that we had to act quickly to save the Dragons before they were gone forever. Ansanthe is a *Trueborn Dragon*. His blood, with its mystical properties, has enabled us to become *Drelkin*. Together, we guard over the *dragon eggs*, waiting for them to hatch. It is our hope that one day the great Dragons will be accepted and no longer feared."

Borrilis Tarneas nodded sadly. "I can only hope that I am still around to see it."

Ansanthe spoke briefly with Silvanil and Vaelreen. They nodded and quickly departed. Ansanthe smiled at Trish and Candi. "Forgive their hasty departure, but there are matters that need their attention."

Enialirl poured several crystal glasses of a fiery orange-colored drink; steaming vapors rose in the air. "This will warm you." At Trish's raised brow he chuckled softly. "And I promise, it will do you no harm."

Ansanthe raised his glass to his lips and drank, hoping to prove that they had nothing to fear. He smiled. "It is exquisite, I assure you."

Candi took a tentative sip. It was sweet to the taste but immediately warmed its way down as she swallowed. It reminded her of a mulled cider that her grandmother used to make on Christmas Eve. "It's delicious. What is it?"

Enialirl smiled appreciatively. "It is *Mulled Dragon Wine*; a favorite during this time of year."

Trish smiled. "I can see why."

Celephia raised her glass. "It is hoped that you will forgive our earlier transgression. We must take care when strangers walk amongst us. There are those that seek to harm the *Dragon Eggs* by corrupting them; Kaspian Altair is one of those. When you came to us from the west, we had to be sure of your intent. It would not be the first time that he has sent his agents against us."

Candi nodded. "This Kaspian Altair is an evil man. He holds one of our friends prisoner. Friends of ours are attempting to rescue her even now."

Borrilis shook his head, his brows furrowing. "Kaspian Altair is a formidable enemy, a very *Dark Mage* to be sure. He intends to employ nefarious means to taint the Dragon Eggs and turn them evil *before* they hatch. It is his goal to use evil dragons to conquer the lands of *Vespia*. With all dragons under his control, there would be no one to stop him."

Trish frowned and shook her head. "This is all very interesting, but I still don't see how it makes it right for you to drug us. We had done nothing against you. You risked turning us into potential enemies without even knowing us."

Ansanthe smiled sympathetically. "That is true. But we could not take the chance that you were acting under Kaspian Altair's orders. The *only* way we could be certain of your intent was to explore your minds. As I said before, in your unconscious state there could be no deceit." He glanced at Candi and then fixed his eyes upon Trish. "We now know your truths."

Trish locked eyes with him. She wasn't sure she liked what she was hearing. *What did he know? Did he know about her and how she had changed since coming through the Portal? And if he did, was she in jeopardy? She wasn't even certain what she was any more...*

"Suffice it to say that we view you as no threat to our cause," Ansanthe said reassuringly.

Candi smiled brightly. "Then you also know why we are here."

Celephia nodded. "You are searching for those that have taken your friend's infant brother."

"Wow," Candi said, "that's amazing!"

Borrilis nodded. "Sinnestra will not come here. She has likely returned to her own fortress within the *Demon Spires*. I believe it was an old dwarven fortress that she stole years ago."

Ansanthe finished his glass of the *Dragon Wine* and set the crystal aside. "Sinnestra can also be a very formidable foe, far worse than Kaspian Altair."

Chapter 50
The Darkwater Mines

Bekka was stretched out under a pine tree as she peered down at the entrance to the mines, it was little more than a cave opening in the side of the mountain; not at all what she'd been expecting. Two large Orc warriors stood on either side of the entrance as sentries; each was holding a massive battleaxe. Getting past them was going to be the hard part. She shivered. A light rain had been falling for the better part of an hour, turning mounds of snow into a slushy mess. It was bitterly cold. Her breath rose up through the pine boughs, like wafts of smoke. The slender pine needles that had fallen onto the ground were damp from the snow and rain, and they stuck to her skin. She remembered mornings like this back in *Midvale*; as she and her Dad were building snowmen in the backyard her Mom would greet them at the door with hot chocolate. *God, she would love to have a mug of cocoa right now!*

Taggarty touched her arm as he slithered up next to her, and whispered, "Are ye alright lass?"

She opened her eyes and nodded. "Yes. Why do you ask?" she answered softly.

He shrugged. "Well, I heard ye moan."

Bekka chuckled softly and shook her head with a smile. "I was just having a moment with my folks. We were drinking hot chocolate."

He gave her a bewildered look. "Don't know if I'll e'er understan' humans." He started crawling backwards. "We should get movin', time's a wastin'!"

Bekka mimicked his movements, joining Lightfingers and Taggarty in the little hollow below the ridgeline. She looked at the thief; worry suddenly clouding her eyes. He did not look well. "Are you alright, Darren?"

Beads of sweat covered his forehead, his complexion ashen. He nodded as he shivered. "I'm fine. Just cold."

Bekka put her palm against his forehead. "You're practically burning up!"

He pushed her hand away, an angry scowl on his face. "I *said* I was fine."

She glanced over at the dwarf but he seemed uninterested. She shook her head in frustration. "Honestly, Darren, you don't look well at all." If they were going to have any hope of saving Valoria everybody needed to be focused and on their A-game; their very lives depended on it. She had serious concerns about the thief.

"Here, lad," Taggarty shoved a flask of *Dwarven Firewater* against his chest. "Have a wee sip o' this," he winked. "It'll warm yer innards right quick."

Lightfingers smiled as he took a huge sip and handed it back. He coughed as the brew burned its way down to his stomach. "Wow. That's pretty potent stuff," he said hoarsely.

Taggarty took a huge sip. "Me own *special* brew t'is this!" he said proudly. He offered the flask to Bekka.

"God no!" she said pushing his hand away. She'd had enough *Dwarven Firewater* to last her a lifetime.

Taggarty shrugged. "Suit yerself lass." He took another huge swallow before he put it away.

Bekka couldn't help but notice that his eyes were tinged in red. *'Great!' she thought, 'I'm going to assault the mines with a drunk dwarf and an ill thief! What could possibly go wrong? God help us!'*

Taggarty swayed drunkenly as he approached the entrance to the mines. The two orcs eyed him with obvious contempt. The dwarf held out the flask. "Ah, 'ow nice! A couple o' friendsh ta welcome me home ta *Shilver Frosht!*"

They looked at one another and chuckled as the dwarf stumbled forward, almost falling. "You got wrong side of mountain, dwarf scum!"

Taggarty stopped and swayed alarmingly, his eyes growing wide. He tried to take a sip from his flask but spilt most of it down his long beard. "Tha' sho?" he shrugged. "Must'a taken a wrong turn shomewheres." He sighed heavily. "No matter; I foun' me a couple o' new drinkin' buddysh. Ye fellers got anythin' ta drink? No? Well 'ere, 'ave shome o' mine. I'll be 'appy ta share." He stumbled forward into the nearest orc cutting his stomach wide open with a sharp knife he had concealed in his sleeve. The stunned orc dropped his battleaxe and desperately tried to keep his guts from falling to his feet.

Taggarty staggered backwards and pointed. "Looks like yer friend ain't got the stomach fer it. Canna handle 'is liquor I reckon." He chuckled at his own joke. "No worries, tha' jusht leaves more fer you an' me!"

Before the other orc could react, an arrow glanced off the dwarf's helm and struck the sentry in his massive green thigh. Another arrow followed, striking him in the shoulder causing the orc to drop his battleaxe. Taggarty quickly threw his flask at the orc, hitting him on the nose. He grabbed his own axe and swung it up in a vicious arc; killing the orc before he hit the ground.

Taggarty whirled around angrily. "Damnation lass! Ye 'bout took me ear off!"

Bekka stepped through the trees. "Sorry!" She shrugged apologetically and shook her head. "I'm not very good with this." She held up the bow.

"Ye got tha' right, lass, but thar be no harm done, I guess."

Lightfingers sheathed his shortsword as he walked out of the forest to their left. "Guess you two did all the hard work without me."

"Damnation!" snarled the dwarf. He knelt down and picked up his flask, the last of the *Dwarven Firewater* had poured out and mixed with the orc blood on the ground. "Tha' t'was me last bit!" He looked around, scratching his head. "Where's the stopper?" He sighed heavily as he dropped the flask onto the dead orc's chest. "No good ta me now!" He scowled darkly.

"We'd best be moving," Lightfingers said, slipping into the mine entrance

Bekka was relieved to see that he seemed to be feeling a lot better than he had earlier. She glanced at the dwarf. "I thought you really were drunk."

He batted a hand in the air. "Takes more'n tha' ta incapacitate ol' Tagg ta be sure." He winked. "I'll not let ye down, lass. Ye can count on me!"

They followed Lightfingers down the wide entryway that seemed to be sloping downward, deeper into the mountain. Burning torches were mounted to the rock wall in iron sconces, enabling them to see a good amount, yet there were still pockets of darkness where the firelight failed to reach. They were surprised that the passage seemed so empty. "T'is a wee bit late in the day. Maybe they dinna man the mines after dark," Tagg whispered.

Bekka hated hearing that news. If that were the case then they likely wouldn't find Valoria anywhere around here; she was probably back at *Bitterwood Castle* or some other nearby campsite that they hadn't uncovered. This had been their best shot.

From not far off, but deeper in the mines, they could hear the *clang* of hammers striking steel chisels. The sound of rock crumbling followed. Lightfingers pointed down a passage that branched off to their left. "I think it is coming from this way." They moved as quietly as they could, their weapons drawn in case they encountered anyone along the way.

The passage they followed was fairly wide, giving them the opportunity to walk three abreast if they chose, but for now they moved in single file with Lightfingers in the lead. They kept as close to the rough-hewn walls as they could, careful not to injure themselves on the jagged edges of the uneven stone.

Bekka didn't like it. She felt as though the mountain was closing in on her as they went deeper into the mine. She was *certain* that they were running out of breathable air. Taggarty must have noticed her increasing discomfort. He placed a calming hand on her arm, giving it a reassuring squeeze. "T'is goin' ta be fine, lass," he whispered, hoping to ease her rising despair. She nodded curtly, not trusting herself to speak. The sooner they returned to the surface, the better she'd like it.

Lightfingers stopped and quickly hugged the rock wall. As the others joined him they noticed several miners hefting huge chunks of stone from the ground and loading it into carts. Three guards stood nearby, ensuring obedience. Bekka gasped. One of the guards was Valoria; she struck one of the miners with a leather strap. "We haven't got all night!" she snarled. "Pick up the pace or suffer the consequences!" The iron collar she wore around her neck glowed with a black and purple hue.

Bekka touched her companions on the arm. "Did you see that?"

Taggarty nodded. "Aye, she struck me friends the same way a'for she murdered 'em."

Bekka shook her head. "No. I mean did you see the way that the shackle around her neck glowed? I think it is controlling her, somehow. Val would never be so heartless on her own."

The dwarf scratched his chin. "Ye may 'ave a point thar, lass. Me brother 'ad one o' those around 'is neck too, when he attempted ta take me head off with me own axe. I ne'er 'ad the chance ta see if'n it glowed or na'."

"I bet if we can get the shackle off of her she'll be herself again."

"T'is worth a try, I suppose."

Lightfingers chuckled. "Getting her to cooperate won't be easy, and we'll have to deal with the other two as well."

"What do ye propose?"

The thief shrugged. "Whatever we decide, we'll need to act fast. We don't know how many others are nearby; we could easily be overwhelmed with superior numbers if they call for reinforcements."

Taggarty pointed at an oil lamp sitting on a pile of rocks. "Lass, reckon ye could hit tha' lantern wi' one o' yer arrows? It may cause a ruckus givin' us the time we need ta make our assault."

Bekka shrugged. "I can give it a try." She had her doubts. She had never been very good with a bow; her attempt to make the Midvale archery team had been a complete failure. She wished that Candi were here. She drew an arrow from her quiver and bit down on it as she nocked another to her bow. She took aim and fired. The arrow struck the rock with a glancing blow and ricocheted off to the right, striking one of the guards in the chest. He fell to the ground.

Bekka quickly fired another arrow and missed. *"Shit!"* She felt panic rising through her. She drew another from her quiver and nocked it on her bow. She took a deep breath, blew it out in a huff, and then took another breath and exhaled slowly. She let the arrow fly. This time she struck the oil lamp, knocking it to the ground. The oil quickly spread and caught fire; the remaining guard couldn't escape the bursting flames in time. In seconds he was a staggering inferno.

Valoria drew her sword and rushed Bekka, hatred etched across her face.

Chapter 51
Preparations

Han held Sinnestra in his arms as they stepped through the *Obsidian Gate*. He was relieved to see that Brother Dinurés was expecting him; he had two priests ready to take his mother to her bedchambers. She had lost a considerable amount of weight while they had been in the *Demon Realm*; he was concerned about her. She seemed *so* fragile.

Dinurés motioned for his priests to take Sinnestra from the young man's arms. He seemed unfazed that their time away had aged the boy so drastically. He was a man now. Han was well muscled and his shoulders were broad. He stood well over six feet tall. A smile appeared on his face. Han reminded the priest of the young man's father. He had a lot of Robert Kensington's features, which would undoubtedly cause the *Chosen One* to pause when they met face-to-face. That moment's hesitation could be her downfall. The dark priest could see an *intensity* in his eyes, fueled by his raging anger. Obviously Sinnestra's goal had been achieved but at what cost to her own health?

Han shook his head as he watched the priests take Sinnestra away. "Is there nothing that can be done for her? She grows weaker by the day. I fear that she does not have long. Seeing her suffer like this is almost more than I can stand."

Dinurés shrugged his shoulders. "Your mother knew the cost that she would have to pay by going through the *Obsidian Gate*. I tried to caution her against it, but she would not hear of it. She wanted to spend as much time with you as she could."

Han sighed heavily, his shoulders rising and falling in defeat. "I wish that I could do something for her... anything. I feel so helpless."

The priest nodded. "The only thing that you can do for your mother is to prepare to face her enemies. They will be coming to finish her off and to take away what is rightfully yours. You will be left with nothing."

He could see the vein in the young man's neck swell and throb with his growing hatred. His hands clenched tightly into fists. "They will *not* succeed!" Han spat the words. "I will destroy them."

Han glared at the dark priest. "Do whatever you can to prolong my mother's life." He flexed his fingers. "I need my mother to survive long enough to taste the heart of *The Chosen One*! My victory will be hers!"

Chapter 52
Dragonspawn

Borrilis looked at Ansanthe and placed his fist to his mouth, clearing his throat; he coughed. "I think it is time to take our guests downstairs."

Ansanthe nodded as he arched an eyebrow. He glanced at the young women as they continued to chat with Celephia. After searching their minds while they slept, he knew the humans were no threat to them at the present, especially the blonde. She had been *sent* to them for a reason. But the redhead was another story altogether. She carried within her the blood and power of their sworn enemies. She would need to be watched much more closely.

However, he knew at this moment she bore them no ill will. She was seeking the demoness known as Sinnestra and a companion who had taken a small boy. He knew this to be true. But after that had all been settled, would she return to *Dragon's Reach*? If she did, he would have to deal with her swiftly—she would know too much.

He turned to Borrilis who was watching him with an amused smile. The old Drelkin was wise beyond his years. He must have known what he had been thinking; but he said nothing. Ansanthe sighed as he placed a hand upon his friend's shoulder. "Perhaps you are right. It is time that we move forward with our plans."

Borrilis drew his brows together as if in thought. "I think that I shall let you and the others accompany our guests down to the *Sacred Chamber*. I am tired and not feeling well; perhaps I ate something that disagrees with me."

Ansanthe looked alarmed. "We can always do this another time."

"No," Borrilis said hastily. "There is no sense in that. Our guests need to be rejoining their friends. We should not delay them any more than absolutely necessary; it would only impede our own goals." He patted Ansanthe's arm. "I will be fine, I assure you."

"If you are certain?" Ansanthe said.

Borrilis walked up to the others and smiled charmingly. "It has been a most tiring day for me. I bid you all a good night." He smiled at Trish and Candi. "I only wish that I could see the looks on your faces, you are in for a real treat! Celephia, we shall talk more tomorrow."

Celephia bowed her head and smiled. "Rest well Borrilis."

Trish and Candi exchanged looks. Something was up.

Ansanthe rejoined them and forced a pleasant smile to his face. "It is time that our guests are taken below. Borrilis desires that their journey continue as soon as possible, and to that end, they need to enter the *Sacred Chamber*."

Celephia's eyes sparkled. "Of course." She slipped her arm around the blonde girl's own and gave her hand a little pat. "You are about to embark on a grand adventure, my dear! One like no other that you have ever taken!" Her smile grew. "I only wish that I could go on it with you!"

Candi blinked at her curiously. "I'm not sure that I understand."

Celephia chuckled softly. "Worry not, all will soon become crystal clear my dear girl!"

Trish drew her brows together as she gave Ansanthe a glare of uncertainty. "What is this all about?"

The tall Drelkin watched as Celephia led the blonde toward the double doors on the northern wall. "If your friend is whom we believe her to be, then she will soon be blessed like few others have ever been." He smiled. "Worry not. Neither of you will be harmed." He swept a hand in the air toward their companions. "Shall we?"

Trish took a deep breath and let it out slowly. She shook her head and started after the others. "I hope I don't regret this." She wished that she hadn't insisted upon leaving their weapons behind. Hopefully they wouldn't need them; but she had a bad feeling growing in the pit of her stomach.

The stone steps that descended steeply in a circular fashion hugged the rock wall forcing them to go down into the depths slowly. Glowing crystal shards protruding from the rock wall seemed evenly spaced, perhaps man-made, to keep the darkness at bay; whether natural phenomenon or deliberately placed, Trish was thankful for their presence. Without their golden glow to guide them along, Candi or herself could easily misplace a foot and slip over the side and plummet to their death. She could see her friend's descent in front of her; Candi seemed unfazed. Trish shook her head and continued to press her back against the smooth stone.

Celephia and Candi waited for them in front of a massive iron double-door. It was wider *and* taller than any Trish had ever seen. Etched on both panels was the image of a dragon holding a sphere. She exhaled loudly. "Wow! Talk about a workout!" She could feel the burn in her thighs; already she regretted having to climb back up the steep stonework. She glanced over at Candi and shook her head, her blonde friend was exuberant, full of enthusiasm, and she was actually bouncing on the balls of her feet. A fleeting thought flashed through Trish's mind of strangling the girl until all her energy was gone. She quickly squashed that thought. She would never intentionally hurt her friend. It was good to see that Candi hadn't changed too much from the girl she was on the other side of the *Portal*. Her boundless spirit could still drive you nuts!

Ansanthe stepped forward and placed his hand upon an indentation formed in one of the spheres held by the dragons. He spread his fingers wide. Glancing over at Celephia, he nodded once. She placed her hand into the depression within the other sphere and spread her fingers out just as he had done. The dent under their hands glowed with a bluish-white light. The eyes of the two dragon etchings illuminated with a soft green light. A slow rumble of stone filled the stairwell as the massive doors began to part, sliding sideways allowing them access to the chamber beyond.

Candi grinned at Trish as she wrapped her arm through her friend's. She leaned toward her and whispered excitedly, "I feel like Lara Croft!"

Trish couldn't help but chuckle. It did kinda feel like they were raiding an ancient tomb.

The rumble of stone stopped and the dust that had been stirred up settled and a massive cavity was revealed. Enormous stalagmites stretched toward the ceiling, which was shrouded in darkness, as equally impressive stalactites reached toward the floor of the cavern. Here and there the two had actually joined together, forming an hourglass shape of stone and calcite.

"This is amazing!" Candi said as she stepped forward. *"Oh my God! Oh my God! Oh my God! Are those eggs?"* She turned to face the two Drelkin, her eyes wide and her mouth dropped open.

Celephia smiled. "They are the future of our race."

Ansanthe nodded. "They are my siblings."

Tears formed in Candi's eyes as she slowly shook her head. She glanced at Trish. "Can you believe this?"

Trish ran a hand through her auburn curls and silently shook her head. Finally, she managed to speak. "There must be hundreds."

"Thousands!" Candi said stepping forward. She could see eggs stretching into the darkness in every direction. The floor of the cavern was littered with them.

Trish looked from her friend and studied their companions. Celephia seemed to have a hopeful look in her eyes, almost an eager anticipation, whereas Ansanthe remained impassive; emotionless. He was watching Candi carefully.

Candi could hear what sounded like an egg splintering; she seemed drawn to it. She scanned the dragon eggs at her feet but saw nothing but inert pods. Careful not to disturb any of them, she moved slowly, judiciously placing each foot upon the ground as she eased forward. The cracking grew louder.

Finally, she could see the source; a straw-colored egg was wobbling as its inhabitant chipped its way out from within. In awe, Candi slowly knelt with her hands on the top of her thighs and watched as what appeared to be a tiny claw emerged, followed by another. The claws tightened and pushed away a portion of the shell. The claws disappeared back into the opening and a small golden snout appeared. Tears of joy rolled down Candi's cheeks. *"Oh my God... how precious are you?"* she whispered softly as the tiny dragon snorted, causing a thin wisp of gray smoke to rise in the air from each nostril.

Candi turned to the others, smiling with delight, her cheeks wet with tears. "Trish, do you see how cute this dragon is?"

Trish couldn't help but smile back at her friend. "I think a puppy is cute, maybe even a kitten or a baby chick." She crossed her arms over her chest. "The jury's still out on baby dragons."

"How can you say such a thing?" She turned back to the baby dragon in time to see the top of the shell fall away. A tiny golden dragon sat up in the base of its shell, its wings spreading up and away from its back. With the flick of its tail it broke apart the last of the shell.

Candi leaned forward. "Hi there little fella. Welcome to the world!"

The tiny golden dragon stepped out of its shell and nudged her hand with its snout.

Celephia smiled. "It seems that you have made a new friend. Would you care to hold him?"

"May I?" Candi asked sounding surprised at the offer.

Celephia nodded. "Of course. He cannot stay here. If he is to survive, he will need to be taken upstairs. You can carry him if you like."

Candi cupped her hands together and extended her arms forward. The baby dragon cocked its head from one side to the other. Leaning forward it sniffed her hands and then climbed in, wrapping its long tail over her fingers. It curled up in her palms as though it was ready for a nap.

"Oh my gosh!" Candi said with a huge smile stretched across her face. She stood carefully, not wanting to disturb the little dragon.

Trish glanced around and found that Ansanthe was watching her closely as though he wanted to see her reaction to what was going on. She stared back at him, practically daring him to say something. He remained unruffled but he continued to watch her. Trish finally looked away, unable to tolerate his scrutinization any longer.

The climb back up the circular stairwell had not been pleasant for Trish. She could feel Ansanthe's eyes boring into her back as she made her ascent behind the others. The tiny golden dragon infatuated Candi. She continually made little cooing noises to the infant as she cuddled him against her chest. When the blonde started in with her baby talk it made Trish want to scream. The sooner they could leave *Dragon's Reach* behind, the better.

When they made it back into the room at the top of the stairs, Trish made a beeline for the door that led to the main barroom, pushing past the others. All she wanted was to get back up to their room, gather her things and just leave. She had had enough! But where would she go? Only two places sprang to mind: *Darkwater* or the *Portal.*

She paused at the door, her hand on the knob. Bekka still needed her help. Could she just abandon her and return home? Her hand started shaking. She couldn't go home like this. She would never fit in. She turned toward Candi and wiped the tears from her eyes. "We need to go. We've learned all we can about Sinnestra, it's time we got back to Bekka."

Candi frowned as she nodded. "Okay... We can go." She glanced at Ansanthe and Celephia. "Can't we?"

Ansanthe arched a brow. "Whenever you like. You are not prisoners here."

"Good!" Trish said. "We need to return to *Darkwater* as quickly as we can. Our friends will be waiting for us."

Ansanthe exchanged looks with Celephia. "That can be arranged, can it not?"

Celephia nodded. "Of course. I was hoping we would have more time, but we can make that happen if we must." She turned to Trish. "We can transport you to where you need to be."

Trish nodded curtly. "Good. Let's pack our things, Candi."

Candi smiled weakly. Reluctantly she handed the infant dragon over to Celephia. She had a look of disappointment in her eyes. "I'm sorry," she said, trying her best not to cry.

As the two girls left the room, closing the door behind them, the baby dragon let out a distressed squawk. Celephia arched a brow and looked at Ansanthe. "It seems that it is decided. She has made her decision."

He nodded as he placed a hand on the top of the dragon's head. "I believe that she has."

As Trish shoved the last of her things into the rucksack that they shared, she glanced around to make certain that they hadn't forgotten anything. Satisfied that they had everything of importance, she slung the bag over one shoulder. "Ready?" she asked her companion.

Candi nodded. "I guess so," she said, sounding morose.

Trish shook her head. "What's got you so down in the dumps?"

The blonde shrugged. "I just hate leaving when things were starting to get interesting, you know. I get the feeling that it would've been best if we were able to stay a bit longer."

Trish's green eyes went wide; she hadn't expected that. "Really? I would think that you'd be eager to get back to Bekka. She's gonna need us, you know."

Candi frowned. "I know. And we really should go. I just..." she shook her head. "I don't know."

There was a knock at the door. Trish frowned as she went to open it. "Who could this be?" She didn't want to delay their departure any longer than was necessary. It was going to be hard enough getting Candi to leave as it was.

Celephia smiled as the door was opened. "I wanted to see you before you left." She stepped into the room and handed a bag to Candi. "I brought you something that may be of use to you on your journey; food and things."

Candi smiled as she placed the bag onto the bed. "Oh, you

shouldn't have. That's really very sweet of you. Thank you."

"It is nothing, really. A few supplies that I thought would make things easier. No need to worry about them now." She turned and smiled at Trish. "Ansanthe has arranged your transport. We should go, he does not like to be kept waiting."

Trish smiled. "Music to my ears!"

Candi glared at her as she slung the bag over her shoulder; she wasn't thrilled.

As they stepped outside of the *Dragon's Maw Inn* the air was crisp and cold, they could feel the burn at the back of their throats as they breathed. A smattering of stars sparkled in the night sky. Ansanthe was nowhere to be seen: in fact, the street seemed to be deserted. Celephia swept her arm toward the side of the inn. "Your transport is this way."

When they rounded the corner they stopped in their tracks, not believing what they saw. A dragon with silver scales stood before them. On its back, just above the wings, was a two-seated saddle. Trish and Candi exchanged looks of surprise. "You've got to be kidding me!" they said in breathless unison.

Celephia smiled but kept her silence. Instead, the silver dragon spoke. "I assure you that I am not." It was Ansanthe's voice.

Celephia stepped forward. "We do not have horses. And even if we did, it is highly doubtful that they would survive the trek back to *Darkwater*. It is not practical for you to make the journey on foot. The safest way is for you to fly; it is also the quickest. Ansanthe wishes to take you personally."

Candi squeezed Trish's hand. "Can you believe this? We get to fly on a dragon!"

Chapter 53
My Enemy, My Ally

Bekka's eyes went wide as Valoria charged, bringing up her sword. Her grip tightened on her bow and she swallowed. She had never been a good match against her friend's skill; with only a bow in hand, she was doomed for sure. "Val! It's me, Bekka!" she said frantically as she held out her hands in a nonthreatening gesture.

Valoria slapped the bow out of her hands and then grabbed her roughly by her leather jerkin. Her lone eye flashed dangerously. "Well, now you die, *Bekka*!" She raised her sword, preparing to plunge it into the girl's gut.

Taggarty swung his battleaxe as hard as he could, striking the flat of the blade against the back of the warrior's head with a resounding thud! Valoria fell to the ground almost instantly. "Na' so fast!" he roared.

"Don't hurt her!" Bekka said forcefully as she looked down at her unconscious friend.

Taggarty shook his head. "I was trying ta keep her from killin' ye, lass. She'll 'ave a knot on her noggin but she'll be fine when she wakes." He knelt down and started to bind Valoria's wrists with a thin strap of leather. "This'll keep her from attackin' us right away. We canna be certain tha' the shackle truly controls her."

Bekka nodded. She glanced at the thief. "Your turn."

Lightfingers knelt down and examined the shackle around the warrior's neck; it appeared to be made out of stone similar to the rocks that the dwarf carried in his pouch. He glanced at Taggarty for confirmation as beads of sweat trickled down the sides of his face.

The dwarf nodded. "Aye, it be fashioned from the *Stones of Darkwater*, ta be sure. Be careful, lad. Tha' be powerful magic. If'n ye strike it just so wi' yer weapon it'll explode an' take her head clean off."

Lightfingers nodded. "Good to know."

"Whoa!" Bekka said hastily. "None of that!"

Lightfingers chuckled. "No worries." He laid his shortsword on the ground as he pulled his thieves' kit from a leather pouch attached to his belt. Despite the trembling of his fingers, he had the shackle unlocked and removed in a manner of seconds. The *Darkwater Stone* ceased glowing and went dark almost instantly. He sighed. "Now we'll see if it was controlling her or not."

"How do we do that?" Bekka asked.

He grinned. "Well, if she still tries to kill us when she wakes, it's a good bet that it wasn't the shackle."

Taggarty nodded. "An' until then, we keep her bound."

"Can we at least take her outside?" Bekka asked. "No telling when someone will be coming through here."

Lightfingers looked around, frowning. "What happened to the prisoners that they were guarding?"

Taggarty shrugged. "Beats me."

"They took off running when Tagg struck Valoria down. They're probably long gone by now," Bekka said.

Taggarty stroked his beard thoughtfully. "Let's hope they chose freedom o'er alerting more guards ta our presence."

"Why wouldn't they?" Bekka asked with a shake of her head.

Taggarty shrugged. "Sometimes folks act all crazy like."

Lightfingers lifted Valoria off the ground and placed her over his shoulder with a grunt. He staggered for a second but quickly regained his balance. "Somebody grab my sword, and let's get out of here."

Bekka stowed her bow and grabbed the shortsword off the ground. "Got it."

"Foller me!" the dwarf said as he headed back in the direction from which they had come.

Bekka allowed Lightfingers to go next. "I'll cover our rear." She was only too happy to be leaving the mines behind.

Moving hastily, they left the mine and managed to get to a secure spot in *Darken Wood* where they felt safe enough to stop and make a temporary camp. Valoria was still unconscious when Lightfingers sat her down against a tree. He sighed heavily as he flexed his arms over his head and stretched his back. His forehead was covered in sweat.

Bekka started gathering firewood, longing for the warmth that a fire would bring. She was cold despite the strenuous march they had completed leaving the mines behind. Taggarty shook his head as she stepped into the camp with an armload of branches. "Na lass, we canna afford a fire. The woodsmoke would bring 'em right ta our location quicker than ye can imagine."

She dropped her arms dejectedly allowing the wood to fall to the ground at her feet. "I hadn't even considered that."

Taggarty winked. "When ye live this kind o' life fer as long as I, ye learn ta think o' these things first. When I was but a wee lad just a startin' out on the adventurin' life, I thought o' me comfort first an' foremost." He chuckled softly at some memory conjured up. "I 'ad ta learn the hard way." He started patting himself down in search of his flask. He frowned remembering its fate.

"Mind telling me why I'm tied up?" Valoria asked with a slight hint of irritation in her voice.

Bekka looked at her friend. "Val, you're awake!"

Valoria winced. "I've got a splitting headache."

Taggarty averted his eyes. "Sorry 'bout tha'."

Valoria glanced from the dwarf to Bekka. "You going to untie me?"

Bekka arched a brow. "That depends."

"On?"

"Whether you're gonna try and kill me again, or not."

"Try to kill you?" Valoria frowned. "Why would I want to do that?"

"You tried to back in the mines," Bekka said crossing her arms over her chest. She cocked her head to the side, tapping her toe upon the ground. "What's it gonna be?"

Valoria shook her head. "I don't recall any of this." She shrugged. "What mine are you even talking about?"

"What *do* ye remember?" Tagg asked.

Valoria glanced at the dwarf. "I remember getting off the ship in *Dagmarth* as a prisoner." She frowned. "I remember a wizard, or some such, and a couple of big orcs holding me as another slapped a shackle around my neck. After that... I don't recollect anything."

Lightfingers looked at Bekka. "What do you think? She could be lying."

Bekka studied her friend. "Who am I?" she asked.

Valoria furrowed a brow as she looked at her. "You're Bekka."

Bekka put her hands on her hips. "I told you that earlier. Who am I to you?"

Valoria gave her a confused look and shook her head slowly. "Bekka... you *know* me. We're sisters."

Bekka pulled out her knife and cut the leather strap binding her friend's wrists. Her eyes filled with unexpected tears. She hugged Valoria tightly. "Thank you for coming back to me, Val. I've been *so* lost without you."

Lightfingers bent over and puked without warning. His legs wobbled and he couldn't stand. He fell to his knees. Taggarty looked at him. "Are ye alright lad? Ye dinna' look so good."

It was true; the thief's complexion had taken on an ashen

color. He tried to speak but couldn't. He turned his head and vomited again, dropping to his hands. His body heaved and he groaned miserably. He fell over, convulsing. He reminded Bekka of Bimini.

Valoria pulled away from her friend. "What's wrong with him?"

Taggarty began to search Lightfingers frantically. He found what he had feared; two holes in the back of the thief's leather, near the shoulder. He pulled at the holes with his fingers, ripping the leather with some difficulty. Two puncture wounds had ruptured his skin. The surrounding skin was red at the site, turning to a dark gray as it spread out across his back and shoulder. "Spider bite! The lad's been poisoned."

"How? When?" Bekka asked, eyes wide.

Taggarty shrugged. "It had ta 'ave been when tha' spider dropped on 'im from the tree. We should 'ave checked 'im over right then! All the strain musta pushed the poison into 'is bloodstream o'er time."

"Is there anything we can do for him?" Bekka asked, beginning to panic as she watched Lightfingers continue to thrash.

Taggarty nodded his head vigorously. "I've me last vial o' *sweetwater* in me pouch. It will counteract the poison, if'n we're na too late."

Valoria quickly searched through the dwarf's pouch and pulled out the vial of bright blue liquid. She handed it to the dwarf. "So, what do we need to do?"

The dwarf frowned as he took out his knife and lanced the wound between the two punctures. Surprisingly there was very little blood. Taggarty took the vial from the ranger and then bit the stopper off, spitting it onto the ground. He hastily poured about half of the *sweetwater* into the wound and then forced the vial to the thief's lips. "Drink, laddie! Be quick about it!"

Bekka helped to support the thief's head; his body was still thrashing wildly. Tears stung at her eyes. "Darren! You need to drink!"

It was hard watching their friend suffer knowing that it could very well be too late to save him. They watched as his eyes bulged and he clawed at his own throat, desperate to breathe.

Lightfingers' complexion was completely gray; the whites of his eyes had turned blood red. He sputtered as he tried to drink. "Keep it in, lad!" Taggarty demanded.

After a few minutes his convulsions eased, and he appeared to be breathing without difficulty. Bekka continued to cradle his head in her lap, tears rolling down her cheeks. She glanced at the dwarf. "Is he going to be okay?"

Exhausted, Taggarty sat back and drew up his knees. "Aye. I believe we acted quickly enough ta save him. He just needs ta rest a bit and gather 'is strength."

Bekka continued to watch over the thief as Lightfingers slept. His color was returning to normal. Valoria stepped up beside her and placed a hand on her shoulder. "You gonna be okay?"

Bekka nodded as she wiped away more tears; she couldn't seem to stop from crying. "I thought I was going to lose him, Val. I've already lost so much, I'm not sure how much more I can take." She sighed heavily. "I think I might be falling in love with him."

"You think?" Val said with a crooked little smile.

Bekka nodded. "Yeah. I don't know. Maybe." She wiped the tears from her cheeks and blew out a quick breath in a huff. "He saved me from the *Hellhounds* in *Freeport* when I went looking for you."

"Oh," Valoria said with just a hint of sarcasm. "That would have done it for me."

Bekka chuckled and slapped her arm. "Alright, so maybe I wasn't actually *in* love with him. But I *did* think he was kinda cute! Who knows what might still happen between us? I think he likes me." She smiled down at the sleeping figure. "When this is all over, I think I wanna see where this leads."

Valoria chuckled. "From what I know of Darren O'Leary there isn't a girl that he *doesn't* like. There was a time when I thought he and I had a chance at something special, but then I found him in the arms of another. I couldn't get out of *Freeport* fast enough after that."

Bekka gave her a look. "Are you saying he's a *player*?"

Valoria shook her head. "I do not know what that means.

Lightfingers O'Leary is certainly a lady's man. He will love you and then leave you, promising you the moon. When his eyes catch another, he'll leave you without explanation."

Bekka stared down at the thief. "You make him sound like a real prick."

Valoria arched a brow quizzically, "if by that you mean he can be a heartbreaker, then I would agree, otherwise I'm not certain I get your meaning."

Bekka shook her head, "it doesn't matter."

Valoria laughed, hugging her friend close. She shrugged. "Maybe he's changed."

Bekka nodded. "I hope so."

Taggarty coughed into his fist. "Methinks we should be headin' out o' here as soon as the lad is fit ta travel. Thar's na tellin' when they'll notice things 'ave gone awry back at the mines. We dinna' want ta face Kaspian Altair with just the three o' us."

Bekka nodded. "We do need to get back to *Darkwater*. Trish and Candi could be back there at any time."

"Trish?" Valoria said with a raised brow. "I thought my father had killed her."

"So did I," Bekka nodded. "It seems that she survived."

Valoria whistled. "Sounds to me like I have a lot of catching up to do."

"Yes, I guess you do," Bekka said. "I'll fill you in on the way."

Chapter 54
City in Chaos

Trevor stood on the bow of the two-masted schooner, *Gilly's Penance*, holding Lithania's hand as the sun was beginning to rise to the east of *Freeport*. He smiled at her; in the golden rays of the sun she was more beautiful than ever. It was almost as if she were glowing from within. She was carrying his child, so maybe she was. He couldn't remember ever being this happy.

She must have felt his eyes watching her. She gave his hand a slight squeeze and sighed as a smile curved her lips. "I thought you had wanted to see the sunrise."

He kissed the back of his hand, smiling. "My sun rises and sets with you, Litha." He shrugged. "Besides, the sunrise pales in comparison to you."

Lithania chuckled softly. "Oh my. Are you attempting to charm me?"

He laughed, giving his shoulders a slight shrug. "Perhaps."

"Well," she said, "it seems to be working."

He wrapped his arm around her and pulled her against him. "I am serious though. You are my life. I can't imagine myself without you." He placed his hand on the small bulge of her stomach, caressing softly. "Soon we are going to be parents."

He felt happier than he had any right to be.

She placed a hand over his and smiled. "I wonder *what* it will be."

Trevor chuckled. "A boy or a girl, I really have no preference."

Lithania eyed him curiously. "Are you certain of that?"

He nodded. "Absolutely. I'm an only child and always wanted a little brother or a sister. Either would've been fine with me. So it truly doesn't matter if our baby is a boy or a girl. I just want our child to be healthy and happy. And I think that I'd like a large family." He smiled after a moment of silence. "I have wondered about something though."

Lithania arched a brow. "You have piqued my curiosity."

Trevor's smile grew wider. He chuckled slightly as color slowly flooded his cheeks. "Well... I have wondered which of us the baby will look like."

Lithania turned away from him and faced the rising sun. A salty breeze blew through her hair and tugged gently at her garments. She cocked her head to the side and arched a single brow. "Indeed."

An hour later the *Gilly's Penance* moored at one of the long piers near the slums of the coastal city. Since the murder of De La'Corte, the city had remained in a state of upheaval, with various factions vying for control; the top two contenders were the priests of the Brotherhood wielding their power from the *Cathedral* and the mages from the Mage Quarter. Entry into, and departure from *Freeport*, was heavily guarded by abusive *Hellhounds* that still controlled the *City Keep*. In the days following the death of De La'Corte, it was proven that the orc *Hellhounds* couldn't hold onto their newly found power, and they were willing to fight for whomever paid the most. It was only a matter of time before the docks to the south of the city were included in this fight for total domination. But until that time, the slums were the safest option for privateer shipping to escape high taxation and the loss of goods brought on by the chaos running rampant throughout the city.

As Trevor and Lithania departed the gangplank of the *Penance* they were nearly knocked over as a throng of desperate people attempted to board the ship. It was all the ship's captain and crew could do to hold them off. Trevor took Lithania's elbow and guided her quickly through the frantic crowd. He didn't like the look of desperation he was seeing on the faces that confronted them.

"We need to get away from here as quickly as possible," Trevor said as he ushered her forward. His eyes were wide and fearful, alert to impending danger. The press of the crowd was beginning to fuel the tempers of the frantic citizens trying to make their escape. Trevor was worried that something terrible would happen to the pregnant woman at his side. He drew his sword. The sight of the weapon helped to keep others away for the moment. He couldn't be sure how long that would last.

"The Hellhounds are coming!" came a desperate cry of warning from somewhere within the mob to the north. It was accompanied by wails of agony and screams of panic and fear. The crowd began to run, in every direction; many were being trampled underfoot. Only Trevor's tight grip on Lithania's hand kept them from becoming separated.

In desperation to escape the riot that was taking place around them, they turned and started heading down a narrow street leading to the southeast as swiftly as they could. Even outside the walls of *Freeport* pandemonium was replacing all rationale and with it, hope was lost. The coastal city was in total chaos.

Trevor took Lithania by the hand and began to run through the twisted alleyways that made up the slums of *Freeport* with only one thing in mind, escape the insanity! Terrified screams sounded behind them with greater intensity. It conjured up visions of people being ruthlessly murdered on the streets; little did they know that was exactly what was happening.

The cold-blooded orc *Hellhounds* were swinging greatswords and battleaxes with malicious intent to all in their path as they made their way through the streets and alleyways. Wizards followed in their wake casting bolts of lightning from their fingertips that splintered through the air with jagged blue-white streaks that sizzled when they struck several hapless citizens in the back or in the chest, knocking them to the ground. They were carelessly trampled underfoot by those fortunate enough to escape the initial onslaught.

"We need to find shelter soon!" Trevor said as he tried a doorknob. He was breathing hard, on the verge of panic. The door wouldn't budge. He found two more that wouldn't allow him access before finding one that turned easily. He forced the door open and entered quickly, pulling Lithania after him into the small two-room hovel. Trevor bolted the door and then quickly looked into the adjoining room. The place was deserted. "We should be safe here," he said as he returned to Lithania's side.

She nodded as she took a seat at the small table. Her eyes were wide. She was not accustomed to so much noise and lawlessness. She looked at him with a furrowed brow. "What happens when whoever lives here returns? Surely they will not understand us being here. They might even bring the *Hellhounds* here to force us out."

Trevor sat across from her and held her hand on top of the table. He hadn't considered that possibility. His mind was reeling. He sighed. "We'll rest here for just a bit, give it a chance to clear up some, and then we'll move on." He looked her over as best he could. "You're not hurt, are you?"

She shook her head. "No, I am well. I have just never seen so much discord, especially in a city like this."

Trevor frowned. It kind of reminded him of when the Deceivers attacked *Serendil Brenatis*. He smiled, deciding it best to take her mind off their current situation. "Have you been to many cities before?"

She chuckled softly. "Admittedly I have not."

Trevor squeezed her hand as he stood. "You rest. I'll gather up some supplies." He placed some copper pieces onto the table and smiled at her. "For payment," he added.

They waited until much of the noise had died down before Trevor opened the door a crack. He peered outside but couldn't see much. He turned back to Lithania and spoke softly. "I'm going to have a look around. Bolt the door behind me and don't open it for anyone but me."

She nodded, rising from the table. "Be safe my love." She touched his hand as she stood beside him.

He kissed her cheek before slipping outside. "I will."

Trevor listened and was relieved to hear Lithania bolt the door behind him. He took a deep breath and blew it out slowly. Glancing up and down the street he spotted a shadowy figure stumbling along, moving toward him. He appeared to be checking doors much the same as Trevor had done.

Trevor moved to his left, stepping into the deeper shadows at the edge of the tiny house. He could only hope that he hadn't been seen. He waited as the sounds of the man drew closer. He was shuffling his feet along, not bothering to lift them and walk normally. He stopped in the middle of the street and seemed to stare right at Trevor. After a moment of indecision, the man wiped his lips with the back of his hand and then staggered onward. A moment later a jagged bolt of lightning lit the street in an instant flash of blue-white fire as it raced toward the man. It struck him squarely in the center of his back, propelling him forward. He fell, face first to the street, sliding forward another two feet before settling in a heap. Trevor took a step back, hoping that he had not been detected; the hilt of his sword scraped the side of the house. He froze.

The mage stopped in his tracks and peered in his direction. Trevor couldn't bring himself to breathe. After a long pause, the mage moved on. It was another minute before Trevor could breathe normally.

Lithania awoke with a start. There was a bizarre knock upon the door that she was unfamiliar with. She had fallen asleep at the table surrounded by darkness. Trevor had not yet returned and she had no idea how long he had been gone. She reached for her sword, sliding it slowly from its scabbard. She stood quietly as she turned toward the door.

Trevor knocked *Shave and a haircut* again. After getting no answer a second time, he rattled the doorknob. He spoke in a loud whisper, "Lithania! It's me! Open up!"

The door opened swiftly and she practically flew into his arms. "I was so worried about you!" her voice was thick with emotion.

He couldn't help but smile as her lips pressed against his. He placed his hands upon her waist and eased her back. "We need to be going. There is a wagon just to the south of here that is willing to take us away from the city, but we have to leave now."

She reached back toward the table and grabbed her sword and scabbard. Trevor gathered their knapsack and slung it over his shoulder. He took her hand and they quickly departed. A reddish-orange glow was making its way in the eastern sky as they began to pick their way through the slums. After the tumultuous noise of the previous day and night, the streets were now eerily quiet. A stray cat scampered ahead of hem, disappearing into a dark alleyway.

The early morning was cool; a light breeze blew through the streets from across the western sea. The smell of smoke hung thick in the air, and they could detect an occasional whiff of something else, burnt flesh, either human or animal; it was impossible to tell which. Distant cries could be heard in almost every direction, except to the east, where they were headed, but even then it was only a matter of time before the chaos caught up with them.

There was a single wagon waiting upon the southern road out of the dying coastal city. Trevor had been expecting to find several wagons; there had been five not long ago when he had made the arrangements. Sitting in the wagon were five men and two women. One of the men hopped down as he saw Trevor and Lithania approach. He motioned for them. "Quickly!" he said. "We must hurry! I was afraid you weren't going to make it!" He helped Lithania into the back of the wagon with the assistance of those onboard and then he turned to Trevor. "You did not say that your wife was expecting a baby. Even better that we leave now! You don't want to bring a newborn into the world amid all this chaos."

Trevor hopped into the wagon; his new friend did the same. They sat for a moment with their legs dangling over the back of the crowded wagon and watched as the slums began to fade into the distance. The man grinned. "I am glad to finally be leaving this place. I feel as though my fortunes are about to change!"

Trevor nodded; he had the same feeling. For a while there he had thought that he and Lithania would never get out of

Freeport in one piece. They still had a long way to go to make it to *Serendil Brenatis*, but his optimism had been restored; they had even made new friends along the way. He looked at the man beside him. "What happened to the other wagons?"

The man shrugged. "They didn't want to wait; but it is better this way. They would only slow us down. We don't need them. You'll see."

Trevor had liked the idea that there would be so many wagons going together. More people meant more safety. Now if they encountered trouble on the road there were only the nine of them. Still, it was better than he and Lithania travelling alone. There was safety in numbers; anything was better than just the two of them.

The hot, noonday sun beat down on them unmercifully. Trevor was glad that the wagon came to a stop, his muscles were starting to ache, and it would be good to stretch his legs. He hopped from the wagon and then turned to help the others down. He smiled as he held his arms up to Lithania. "How are you doing?"

She smiled. "As good as can be expected. It will take longer to get home this way. If we had horses, we could move a lot faster."

Trevor gave a slight nod. "I understand that, but I really like the fact that we are travelling with a group. Maybe once we get to *Schiff's Crossing* we can buy some horses and go on alone."

Lithania nodded. Squeezing his hand she whispered, "We do not know these people, they could be dangerous. We really know little about them. I think that we need to keep an eye on them."

Trevor allowed a chuckle to escape. "They are refugees from *Freeport*, just like we are. They wanted to escape the danger and go where it's safe." He looked into her eyes as he touched her cheek. "They are no different than us. Trust me. It's going to be all right, I promise."

Ultimately it proved a promise that he couldn't keep.

As they were getting ready to load back up into the wagon and depart, he and Lithania were struck over the head and knocked unconscious. When Trevor awoke, the wagon was gone, and so was Lithania. He had been left alone.

Trevor had lost a good deal of blood from his head wound, the front of his shirt was stained, but he felt okay. He touched his forehead with his fingertips; they came away sticky with blood, and it looked fresh. Obviously, he was still bleeding, but not as badly as he had been. Head wounds often bled worse than other wounds, and since he wasn't feeling light-headed, he assumed he would be all right.

He inspected the wound as best he could, probing gingerly with his fingers. He had a big knot on his forehead, but the wound itself was only a small gash, probably only an inch or so long. By the amount of blood on his shirt he had expected it to be far worse. He was lucky, and he knew it.

By the positioning of the sun, he could tell that it was already late in the afternoon. It would be dark soon. He wasn't familiar with the territory at all, having only traversed it once. There was no way that he would be able to see the wagon tracks in the deepening darkness. He would have to wait until morning. Now, it was imperative that he find shelter. The night would be extremely cold.

The wagon came to a stop. It would be dark soon. The two human women helped Lithania, who was bound at the wrists, to the rear of the wagon. Two of the bigger men helped her down. They were not gentle with her but took care to leave no lasting damage. The better shape she was in, the higher price she would fetch when she was sold. Elves were rare, a dying breed, there were not many of them left.

"What is the meaning of this?" Lithania demanded. Her head throbbed where they had struck her, and the pain was dulled. It was difficult to maintain her focus.

One man grinned savagely, she recognized him as the one who had befriended Trevor; the one who had ultimately betrayed him. "Simple. You are an elf. We plan to sell you." He glanced down at the bulge of her belly. "Two for one sweet price!"

Lithania arched a brow. "There is a flaw to this plan of yours."

"Oh?" he grinned. "I don't *think* so. You're not the first elf that we've bartered."

Lithania chuckled. "Oh, I am *not* an elf."

He grabbed her hair and pulled it away from her face, exposing her ear. "Not an elf, eh? Sure looks like an elf ear to me!"

Her eyes flashed dangerously. "You have *no* idea what you have here; what you have done." She laughed again as she scanned their faces. "I almost pity the lot of you!" In a flash of movement, she broke free from her bonds and the smiles left the faces of her captors.

As the last rays of sunlight painted the western skies a fiery orange and yellow, their terrified screams welcomed the night...

Chapter 55
Dragon Flight

Ansanthe, the dragon, waited until his two passengers were seated securely in the saddle before he spoke again. As Celephia buckled them in, he said, "It has been awhile since I last took to the skies; I shall try not to soar to high."

Speechless, Trish could only nod. She swallowed, finding it difficult to comprehend. *She was on the back of an actual dragon! Holy moly! She was about to fly!* For the first time in a very long time she found herself wondering if any of this were real. Since coming through the *Portal* she had been living in a nightmare world, or so it seemed.

Candi squealed in delight behind her. *"How cool is this!?"*

Celephia smiled. "I wish the both of you well."

Trish nodded, and as she was about to say something, the silver dragon dipped its head and then leapt into the air. She immediately felt the rush of cold air hit her in the face as the sound of leathery wings beat the air powerfully, taking them all higher and higher. She risked a look down and saw the ground fading into the clouds, or at least it appeared to, but she realized that they were the ones breaking through the wisps of clouds. "Oh my..." It was absolutely exhilarating!

Both girls sighed in awe as they broke through the last of the cloud cover and were greeted by the sparkling stars of the night. There seemed to be thousands of them filling the heavens, and the moon shown silver, full and bright in the western sky. It truly was a beautiful sight.

Candi leaned toward her friend and touched her lightly on the shoulder. "Do you think anyone will *ever* believe us?"

Trish shrugged. "I'm not even certain I believe this!" She couldn't keep the smile from her face.

Candi peered down toward the ground. "I wonder if we'll be able to see that wrecked ship from up here, the one with the zombies."

Ansanthe spoke. "The Winged Galleon is a myth. A ship such as that could never fly."

"Ha!" Trish scoffed. "And Dragons aren't real either."

"I see your point," Ansanthe said. "How did you come to learn of the Winged Galleon?"

Candi batted a hand in the air. "We spent the night in part of its hull on our way to *Dragon's Reach*. The next morning these zombie-like creatures attacked us. I think they were once *halflings*, but I don't know, really. They were just like Vincente described; if they hadn't been zombified."

"Interesting," Ansanthe said. "Where was this, exactly?"

Trish shrugged. "Somewhere between the *Bone yard* and *Darkwater*."

"We are nearing the *Bone yard* now." Ansanthe pulled his massive wings in close to his body and dipped his head downward. They began to descend rapidly. Finally, they leveled out about a hundred feet above the ground. They could see the skeletal remains of dragons as they approached. They quickly soared beyond the ancient remnants of the powerful creatures and out across the frozen tundra beyond.

"How far from this hallowed ground?" asked Ansanthe.

Trish and Candi both shrugged. "Somewhere in the Ghostlands," Trish said.

"Ah," Ansanthe said. "It is no wonder that it has not been found, strange and inexplicable things happen there."

"We just happened upon it really," Candi said.

"Yes," Ansanthe said without doubt in his voice, "but it is unlikely that you would find it again. The *Ghostlands* are not normal, not by *any* stretch of the imagination."

Candi frowned. "Nothing about this world is normal."

Trish shook her head in agreement. She definitely concurred with Candi's assessment; after all, she was living proof.

Ansanthe swiftly gained altitude. "We are above the *Ghostlands* now, it would be unwise to fly so close to the ground. I will see you safely to the other side; but know this: Terrible things inhabit those lands below. You are both fortunate that you survived intact. More things than undead halflings can be found there. Far more deadly things."

They could easily believe that. As they approached the *Ghostlands* they had begun to sense something was amiss. Candi remembered how the air had smelled when they had first gone into the *Vile Forest*. Rosa had said that it was the scent of *Evil*. She could smell it now, emanating up from the ground. She was thankful that the dragon had soared higher.

Death was there. Waiting...

Ansanthe set down in a wooded area. As Trish and Candi stepped down from the dragon's back, he seemed to shimmer. In less than a heartbeat, the dragon and the double saddle were gone; the tall Drclkin was all that remained. "We shall camp here," he said. "Tomorrow you can make your way to *Darkwater* on your own; it would not be wise for one of my kind to be seen there."

In little time he had a fire blazing up spreading its warmth throughout the small encampment. He opened a leather rucksack and passed around chunks of bread and cheese to his companions. They eagerly accepted the food; both were hungry. It had been some time since they had last eaten.

As the darkness deepened within the forest, it grew increasingly colder. Trish and Candi huddled together seeking warmth in their closeness. Trish marveled at how Ansanthe seemed unaffected by the frigid temperature. Perhaps his unique skin shielded him. He wasn't human, after all. That thought brought a smirk to Trish's face; she didn't think that she was any more either.

Chapter 56
Tales by the Fireside

Lightfingers held the door of the *Spilt Tankard Inn* open for Bekka, Valoria and Tagg; all of them were red-faced and cold. They entered and made a beeline for the crackling fire. Carandra Toshe filled four tankards with hot cider and quickly brought them as the four sat at a table near the hearth.

Taggarty squinted as he took a sip. "Thank ye lass, might ye 'ave somethin' with a wee bit more kick ta it?"

Bekka slapped his arm. "Don't be rude." She smiled up at the blonde hostess. "Thank you, Carandra. Would you have anything available to eat, as well?"

Lightfingers chuckled softly and winked at the dwarf. It was clear that he too, hoped for something a little stronger.

Carandra pushed a wisp of blonde hair out of her eyes. "My Taren managed to kill another buck today and a wild boar the other day, so I've a fresh batch o' venison stew on hand; or I can make ye some hot ham soup if ye'd prefer."

Bekka smiled. "The stew sounds divine."

Carandra smiled warmly. "I'll bring ye all a bowl then."

Tagg winced as he quickly drained his tankard. "About tha' drink lass?"

She nodded with a chuckle. "Aye. I 'ave wha' ye be wantin'. Let me fetch the stew first."

Carandra returned with a tray holding four steaming bowls of venison stew. The savory aroma reached them before she did, making their mouths water with anticipation. She placed a bowl in front of each of them and then placed wooden spoons to the side. She nodded toward Taren who was bringing two tankards of *Dwarven Firewater* to the dwarf and the thief. She turned her attention to the women. "Can I get ye ladies anythin' else? More hot cider perhaps?"

Valoria nodded. "Yes, please!"

"That would be great! Thank you," Bekka said.

Taggarty accepted the tankard eagerly. "Thank ye lad!"

Lightfingers lifted his tankard to the dwarf, and they clinked softly together in toast.

"Will there be anythin' else?" Taren asked

Taggarty shook his head. As the young man left, the dwarf leaned forward. "So, wha' t'is the plan? Surely the four o' us canna strike out ta face this demon lady wi'out help."

Bekka swallowed the bite of stew and then touched the cloth napkin to her lips. "Hopefully Trish and Candi will be rejoining us soon. That will add to our numbers."

Taggarty shook his head, he had been hoping for a bit more reinforcement; adding two more women to the mix wasn't likely to do a lot of good, not that they weren't capable of contributing something. His eyes grew wide. "Tha's it, then? Just the six o' us ta face a demon an' her army? Ye canna be serious!" He glanced from Bekka to Valoria and then shook his head in disbelief as he shot a meaningful glance at Lightfingers. He took a huge gulp from his tankard. "I canna believe wha' I'm hearin'!"

"I don't think Sinnestra has an army fighting for her," Bekka said. "From everything that I have heard it is just her and this dark priest. That's it. If she'd had an army with her, she would've most likely taken it to *Kensington Castle*; but she didn't. It was just the two of them. I'm not worried."

Taggarty finished off his tankard and slammed it down upon the table. "Weel, let me tell ye, she dinna' conquer *Silver Frost Keep* wi' just a single dark priest at her side. She woulda had ta 'ave an army ta boot ta o'erwhelm the dwarven fortress!"

"If I recall my history," Valoria said, "*Silver Frost Keep* was abandoned by the dwarves a hundred years or so ago. In order to maintain the fortress she would need some kind of presence there."

Bekka nodded. "Most likely but remember for the last several years she was dwelling in the City of the Spider Queen until we came along."

Taggarty tipped his tankard so that he could see inside. He frowned darkly and pushed it aside. "Weel tha' only seems ta prove me point. T'is only the six o' us against who knows 'ow many. This could vera well be the last thing we e'er do."

Valoria smirked. "You wanna live forever?"

"Weel, lass, I dinna 'ave ta live forever, long as I go out fer the right reasons!"

Lightfingers drank the last of his *Dwarven Firewater* and placed the empty tankard upon the table with a thud. "I for one have a lot more living I want to do!" He flashed a grin at Bekka.

She arched a brow as a slight smile curved her lips.

Valoria glanced at Bekka. "So where is the *Blade of the Spider's Kiss?*"

Bekka patted her rucksack. "I have it. When Lithania and Trevor decided to go back to *Serendil Brenatis*, they left it with me."

Valoria turned and smiled at the dwarf. "Well, there you go. Bekka was always destined to use the Drow blade against Sinnestra according to the *Prophecy*. It was only by chance that Lithania struck Sinnestra with it in the first place. Had Bekka wielded the weapon Sinnestra would probably already be dead."

Bekka rolled her eyes. "You make it sound *sooo* easy."

Taren brought over two new tankards of the Dwarven brew and two of hot cider. He placed everything else from the table onto the tray he carried. "Anythin' else?"

Taggarty shook his head. "Nah, lad. Methinks this'll be it fer the night."

"Good evening, then," Taren said with a nod as he took the tray toward the kitchen.

They sat in silence for quite some time. Taggarty propped his feet up on a chair next to him and stroked his beard as he sipped from his tankard. His eyes drew together in a frown, but he kept silent.

After Bekka finished her tankard of cider, she pushed her tankard toward the center of the round table. "I think I'm gonna turn in. We can formulate a plan in the morning, or just wait until Trish and Candi return. I don't really care. I'm tired. I'm going to bed."

Valoria nodded as she sipped from her tankard. "G'night, Bekka." She paused and then raised her tankard in a salute. "Thanks for rescuing me."

Bekka leaned in and gave her friend a hug. "You're my sister. I *had* to come for you." She kissed the top of Valoria's head. "I love you. Good night."

Taggarty had already finished his tankard of *Firewater* and was reaching for the one that Lightfingers had abandoned. "G'night lass. Pleasant dreams."

Lightfingers forced a yawn and stretched his arms into the air. "I think I'll call it a night as well." He got to his feet and followed Bekka.

After Bekka and Lightfingers had gone upstairs, Valoria looked at the dwarf over the top of her tankard. "Can you get us into *Silver Frost Keep* without anyone noticing us?"

Taggarty continued to stroke his beard as he cocked his head to the side in consideration. "Thar may be a way ta accomplish tha' now tha' ye ask. Thar be a dwarven metalsmith in the hamlet o' *Glynn* if'n he still breathes, tha' is. He is one o' the ol' timers, just a young man when Sinnestra invaded the *Keep*. He may know o' a way in tha' be fergotten. Think 'is name was Breegan or somesuch."

"Weren't you also from *Silver Frost?*" Valoria asked with a raised brow.

"Aye." He nodded. "But I was a wee lil' lad at the time, still clingin' ta me mother's skirt." He shook his head after a bit. "Thar's na' much tha' I recall 'bout the place. Certainly na' enough ta see us safely inside. This Breegan t'would be our best bet."

"We need to find him," Valoria said. "If he can help us find an easier way in it would greatly increase our chances of surviving this mess."

Taggarty waved his tankard toward the stairs. "Wha' 'bout the lassie? She goin' ta wanna take a side trip ta *Glynn*, ye think?"

Valoria nodded. "If it is going to improve our chances I believe she will. She's in no big hurry to throw her life away any more than you are."

Taggarty sat his tankard down onto the table with a long, drawn out sigh, it was still over half full. "Then I guess I should consider an early start fer tomorrow."

Valoria cocked her head to the side and allowed a thin smile to curve her lips. "I'm impressed."

Taggarty chuckled and he rolled his eyes as he slid the tankard back in front of him. "Heh, who am I kiddin'? Ne'er was one ta let good drink go ta waste."

Valoria chuckled softly and took a sip from her tankard. "Good. I never cared for drinking alone."

The dwarf eyed her thoughtfully as he stroked his beard with his free hand. "Looks like ye 'ave 'ad a rough life, lass. Care ta enlighten me 'bout it? I always did like a good yarn whilst I drank."

Valoria took a sip and sighed. She stretched out her legs, propping her feet up on the chair vacated by Bekka. "The scars on my face and back are all compliments of my loving father."

"Tarnation, lass! What would possess a man ta do tha' ta 'is own daughter?"

"Fear, I think," Valoria said with a shrug.

"Fear?"

Valoria nodded. "My father was Maragh." Taggarty's eyes went wide for a brief instant. He recognized the name; that was good. Valoria didn't feel like going into a whole lot of detail; it was far too painful. She chuckled softly; that kind of surprised her.

"Ye mentioned scars on yer back. Wha'd the bastard do? Beat ye wi' a whip?"

Valoria inhaled sharply at the remembered pain of the beatings she had received. She could feel the barbs digging into her skin, tearing her back to shreds. Maragh had very nearly killed her. She took another sip of the hot spiced cider. "You're familiar with the *prophecy* that claimed a *Chosen One* would kill my father?" At the dwarf's nod, she continued. "It was said that an infant would grow and eventually defeat him, but it did not say whom that person would be. So, my father set out to slay all infants he could find, starting with his own."

Taggarty frowned. "Ye could na' possibly 'ave been an infant when he started all tha' genocide."

Val shook her head. "Not me, I was fourteen summers old, but my sister was newly born."

"Ah." Taggarty's brows drew together. It was difficult for him to fathom that a man could be so cruel to his own kin.

"When I tried to stop him from murdering her, I managed to cut his cheek with a knife. I tried my best to kill him, I desperately tried to save my sister." She traced her own scar along her face. "He was infuriated and slashed me with the blade of his sword. It was a wonder that he didn't kill me then. Only the wail of my baby sister saved me; but it doomed her. After he killed her, he tied me up in his dungeon and whipped me with a bullwhip every day for a week." She shook her head as tears fell onto her cheeks. "I don't know what made him stop. Perhaps it was because there wasn't a spot on my back untouched by the whip. Or, even more likely, he had simply passed out from too much to drink. I don't know. The threat of the prophecy remained. He was desperate to prevent its fruition."

Valoria wiped the tears from her face. "After the beating he gave me, no one would stand against him. If he would kill one of his daughters and beat the other to within an inch of her life, they could only imagine what he would do to them. They feared him."

Valoria drained her tankard. "When I healed up enough, I left. I never saw him again until the day he died."

Taggarty finished his drink and shoved the tankard onto the table. He stroked his beard thoughtfully. "Tha' was when ye killed 'im."

Valoria nodded. "I had a hand it."

The old dwarf shook his head. "A lass shouldna' 'ave ta endure somethin' like tha'; especially at the hands o' her own da'. I canna even imagine wha' it musta been like fer one so young."

Valoria crossed her arms. "So, what's your story?"

He chuckled softly and shrugged. "Mine goes back a long ways. I was just a wee babe when Sinnestra invaded our home. Me ma and me da' snuck me an' me brothers out o' *Silver Frost* during all the chaos." He shook his head sadly. "They're all gone now. I am the last o' the line."

Lightfingers quickly caught up to Bekka before she reached her room. He smiled at her as he grasped the doorknob, preventing her from opening the door. "I never got the chance to properly thank you for saving me." A sly smile curved the corner of his lips.

She could feel her breathing quicken. "It wasn't just me. The others are the ones that truly saved you. If Tagg hadn't had the *sweetwater*..." she shook her head, remembering how close she had come to losing him.

He chuckled softly as he placed a finger over her lips. "If you hadn't given me a reason to fight, it wouldn't have mattered." He bent his head and kissed her softly. "I owe you my life."

The kiss left her feeling slightly dizzy; her brain seemed unusually fuzzy as she struggled against the wave of emotions that flooded over her. Blinking, she cleared her throat. "I... I think we should just call it a night. Tomorrow's going to be a busy day. I'm tired and you must be exhausted!"

He leaned in for another kiss. "I just wanted to show you my appreciation."

She forced a yawn, raising her hand over her mouth, blocking her lips from his. "We'll talk more tomorrow. Promise." She found the doorknob and twisted it, feeling the door swing away from her. She slipped into the room, closing the door behind her. As she leaned against the door, she heard his hand slap the wall softly in frustration. She held her breath until she heard his footsteps recede.

Chapter 57
An Unexpected Find

Candi and Trish awoke to find that Ansanthe was already gone. Unattended, the fire was now nothing more than glowing ember. "Wow," Trish said, "I guess your friend isn't much with 'goodbyes' huh?" She wasn't mad that he was gone, but she wasn't happy either. He could've at least added a bit of wood to the fire before he departed. When she was cold, she was absolutely miserable and cranky; it didn't take much to set her off.

Candi scowled at her friend as she tried to bring warmth to her own body by briskly rubbing her upper arms. "He probably didn't want to risk being seen in the daylight. A dragon taking flight might cause a ruckus."

Trish chuckled. "I suppose." She sighed and grabbed her knapsack. "We should probably be going if we want to reach *Darkwater* by lunchtime."

Candi put a hand to her stomach as it growled noisily. "Is there any way we can get there in time for breakfast? I'm absolutely starving!"

Trish laughed. "I'm afraid not." Her eyes grew wide as she pointed toward Candi's rucksack. "Did that just move?"

Candi screamed as she quickly high-stepped toward her friend. She stared at her bag with growing fear; the flap of the bag was moving. "You think it's a snake? I *hate* snakes! Or raccoons! Those critters give me the creeps!"

Trish scowled darkly. "Stop being such a baby! It's *your* bag, you need to deal with it!"

Candi shook her head and stepped around Trish, grabbing her and using her as a shield. "Nope! Not gonna happen! I told you that I don't like snakes! Or bugs! Or..." she pointed at the bag, "... or *whatever* that is!"

Trish sighed as she drew her sword, "Fine. I'll handle it." She tried to take a step toward the bag, but Candi was still clutching her in a death-grip and refusing to budge. "You need to let go of me so I can move."

Candi whimpered. "I'm scared!"

"You need to let go of me so I can handle this."

Candi sighed heavily. "Fine. Just please be careful." She released her grip and practically shoved Trish forward.

Trish turned and glared at her blonde friend. "What the Hell?"

Candi shrugged. "Sorry! I didn't mean to!" She swallowed and pointed at the bag. "Please, don't hurt whatever it is!"

Trish ran a hand through her auburn hair. "I don't know how you've managed to live through everything you've gone through on this side of the *Portal*! You're such a coward, Candi. I mean, seriously!"

Candi stiffened. "I am *not*!" Her chin rose defiantly. She was angry with her friend but more at herself, than anything. *Why was she acting like this? She could handle whatever had crawled into her bag! She didn't need Trish to protect her! What was it about being around Patricia Morgan made her revert back to her old self, she wasn't that weak follower anymore. She had changed! She was Candace Anderson 2.0 for crying out loud!*

She swallowed her fear and quickly stepped around Trish and knelt in front of her bag. She took a deep breath, shook her hands vigorously in the air, and grasped the flap. She could do this! She would prove she wasn't a coward! She opened the bag without further hesitation.

"Oh my God!" she said, clearly astonished.

"What is it?" Trish asked. She couldn't see; Candi was blocking her view.

"Hey little fella!" Candi almost cooed. "How'd you get in there?"

Trish stepped around Candi so that she could better see what was going on. She stopped suddenly, her eyes growing wide as her friend pulled the baby golden dragon out of the knapsack. *"What the Hell, Candi?"*

Candi scooped the golden dragon into her palm, the dragon's long tail wrapped around her wrist, clearly content to stay in her hand. Candi frowned at Trish. "I didn't have *anything* to do with this!"

Trish sighed in exasperation. "Well, we can't keep it!"

Candi held it close to her breast, protectively shielding it with her other hand. "We can't leave him out here all alone. We have to take him with us! He'd never survive on his own."

Trish shook her head and rolled her eyes. "Whatever!"

Trevor awoke shivering; the small fire he had built to keep warm had finally died. Fortunately, it had remained burning throughout the night, keeping him from freezing to death. But now he was beginning to feel the cold seep back into his bones. It would be daylight soon and he would be able to track the wagon. He thought about waiting until the sun rose, but really, there was enough light to see by already; it wasn't the pitch-black it had been most of the night. He quickly gathered his sword; he had held onto it while he slept and kicked dirt over the ash contained in his firepit. Better to be safe than sorry.

His stomach grumbled in protest, but there was very little he could do about that at the moment. They had taken his rucksack when they left him unconscious. He was really surprised that they hadn't just killed him or at the very least, taken his weapon. They had left him to die. They didn't see him as a threat, clearly. Well, he would just have to prove them wrong.

He could see the deep ruts in the ground left behind by the wagon's passing. They were heading eastward, toward *Schiff's*

Crossing. He began to run in that direction. The sun was beginning to rise far to the east; like a guiding light, it beckoned.

After a while, the wagon tracks began to turn toward the northeast. They were evidently looking for a better place to make camp. Trevor could see a clump of trees that seemed to hug the southern base of the *Red Hills*. He had no choice; he had to follow the wagon if he had any hope of finding Lithania.

As he jogged along, he tried to recall what he would be facing. There were five men, not counting the driver of the wagon, and two other women. They all had various weapons. Freeing Lithania wasn't going to be easy. He had to make certain that whatever he did, that she and the baby remained safe.

He smiled. The baby, *his baby*, hadn't even been born yet, but he was already thinking of the child as if she had! *She? What made him suddenly so certain that it was a girl and not a boy?* He chuckled softly. He could picture a little girl with dark brown, curly hair and softly pointed ears and almond shaped eyes. A mini version of her mother!

He could see the wagon, hidden among the trees. He quickly darted into the foliage and trees nearest him, hoping to lose himself in them before he was spotted. He had to maintain the element of surprise; their lives depended upon it! Careful not to make a sound, Trevor moved through the small forest, sneaking stealthily up to where they had made their camp.

He froze.

Something was wrong!

Bodies lay scattered about, their faces hideously frozen in agonizing death. Some had weapons drawn as though to resist whatever had attacked them, but no blood coated the steel of their blades. Others appeared to have been caught completely unaware. All of the dead had empty eye-sockets, which Trevor thought was peculiar. Their noses were torn and bloody, almost as if something had pierced their nostrils violently.

"Oh my God!" Trevor said as he stumbled into the campsite. He quickly looked around at the dead bodies hoping his worst fears wouldn't be realized, he wouldn't be able to take it if he found Lithania among them.

Whatever had attacked the camp had either taken Lithania

with them when they left, or she had somehow managed to escape. Her corpse was not among the dead. That gave him a small glimmer of hope.

The horses were still picketed nearby. They seemed skittish and frightened. Trevor frowned, only three of the horses were present; there had been a fourth. He quickly searched the ground and found tracks leading through the trees toward the east. *Had Lithania taken the horse?* He certainly hoped that she had.

He pulled up the stakes and mounted one of the horses. He had to follow the trail, hoping it would lead him to Lithania; but he refused to leave the extra horses behind. Whatever had attacked the camp might come back and this time around the horses might not be so fortunate.

Candi put the golden dragon back into her knapsack and gently tied the flap closed, but it was loose enough so that the dragon wouldn't feel like it was going to be suffocated. She could only hope that he wouldn't draw any attention to himself once they got to *Darkwater*. He would be difficult to explain.

Trish wasn't happy. She tried to convince Candi to leave the dragon behind, but the blonde flatly refused. "It's just a baby," Candi had said. She repeated her reasoning, "It can't survive out here by itself. We *have* to take it with us."

"It shouldn't even be here!" Trish complained. "It should've stayed back in *Dragon's Reach*!" She shook her head. "I don't know what Celephia was thinking. This had to be all her doing!"

"Wait, what?" Candi said, startled. "You think Celephia had something to do with this dragon being in my pack? Why would she do that? I don't understand what her reasoning could've been."

"Nor do I," Trish said. "But it is the only explanation that makes sense. She's the one that brought the bag to you when we were fixing to depart. She had to have placed the dragon inside."

"I hadn't even considered that," Candi said.

They stepped out of the forest and headed toward *Darkwater*, the sun rising up into the sky behind them.

Candi and Trish could hear the sharp *clang* of Bran's hammer strike upon cold steel from somewhere in his smithy. Though they hadn't seen the big man yet, his presence was known.

Trish rolled her eyes as they walked past the barn where he had his shop. "I hope we don't have to stay in this place for very long. If that man does this every morning, I won't be able to stand it!"

Candi chuckled. "It isn't early morning, Trish. It's almost noon already."

Trish touched her temple with the tips of her fingers and rubbed. "Still, I'm getting a headache." She winced. "I would *kill* for some Tylenol!"

Candi ran a hand through her blonde hair and scrunched her brows together. After a moment of contemplation her face brightened and she snapped her fingers. "I have a solution for that, but you probably wouldn't like it very much." She smiled coyly. "Lady Rosa taught it to me."

Trish shook her head. "No. I'm not interested. It probably involves ingesting tree moss or something else equally as gross!"

Candi chuckled. "No, it's nothing like that. I wouldn't make you ingest anything horrid." She grinned. "You take houseleeks, earthworms and a flower. Blend them all together to make a paste and then spread it all upon a bandage; you then wrap it around your head and after a several hours, *tada*! your headache's gone!"

Trish scowled darkly. "You're kidding, right?"

"No. Lady Rosa swore by it."

"Why am I not surprised?"

They walked around to the front of the *Spilt Tankard Inn* and found Carandra Toshe sweeping the wooden porch. She smiled at them. "Ah, I see tha' ye made it back! The others are just sittin' down ta some stew. I'll fetch ye a bowl if'n ye want ta clean up first. Same rooms as before."

Trish smiled. "Thank you, Carandra. That sounds nice."

Bekka saw her friends enter the inn and she jumped up from her seat and quickly ran to give them both a hug. "You're back!" she said enthusiastically.

Trish took a deep breath, enjoying the tantalizing smells that filled the inn. It was good to be back in civilization once again. She returned Bekka's warm hug and then rubbed her briskly upon the back. She then slid her knapsack off her shoulder and handed it to Candi. "Won't you be a dear and take our gear upstairs?"

Candi nodded. "Sure. No problem." There was a hint of irritation in her voice. She was already getting tired of Trish's overbearing attitude. They weren't in high school anymore. She wasn't at her beck and call, following her commands without question. Those days were over! But she understood what Trish was saying, she needed to get the golden dragon upstairs before anyone noticed. She just wished Trish had handled it with a little more finesse. *That* made her chuckle. Subtlety was so not in Trish's wheelhouse! So, with a quick smile at Bekka, Candi fell back into her old routine of simply doing Trish's bidding. "Save me a seat!"

Trish wrapped her arm through Bekka's and steered her toward the table where she had been sitting. "So, tell me all about your efforts to save Valoria!"

Candi placed the knapsacks onto the bed and quickly opened the flap of hers to allow the dragon to escape the burlap bag. "Hi fella! You can come out now; we're here. I'm gonna go downstairs and get you a bite to eat. What does a baby dragon eat, anyway?" She shrugged. "Don't worry. I'll find something." She smiled as the dragon cocked its head at her. "You've gotta stay here and be good though. I'll try not to be too long." As if understanding, the tiny dragon curled up against a pillow and tucked its snout beneath a wing.

"Ooh! You are just *so* cute! Yes, you are!" she gushed. She hated to leave the baby dragon alone, but she didn't have much choice in the matter. Trish could only cover for her for so long; eventually Bekka would come upstairs to check on her. And then she would discover the golden dragon.

Candi wasn't really concerned how Bekka would react toward the dragon. She trusted her more than she did Trish— especially lately. Ever since Trish had been reunited with the group it had been obvious that she wasn't the same girl she had been prior to coming through the *Portal*. She had changed. Trevor had mentioned that the girl had been pregnant and that the baby was Cleve's.

That alone had sent the alarms sounding in Candi's mind. She had been present when Cleveland Montgomery's ravaged body had been found on the stone slab in the *Vile Forest*. Trish and Cleve had been separated after coming through the *Portal*. The baby couldn't possibly be his! I*t had to be a Deceiver's!* Both Mrs. Kensington and Lady Rosa had said that Maragh had stabbed Trish in the stomach. Surely that would've killed the baby. *But had it?*

Regardless, Trish was *not* normal. She had been *changed* by the events that had happened to her. *But what did it really mean?* Candi had seen what she did onboard the *Reaver*. What happened to those men was violent. It made Candi shiver just thinking about it. It was like something out of a horror movie.

Candi took one last look at the small dragon before she closed the door behind her. Its golden eyelids drooped heavily, and finally closed. She needed to make an appearance downstairs and then make some excuse to get back up to her room. She was starving, and she had no doubt that the dragon was as well. Babies were always hungry; fortunately, they slept a lot as well.

Carandra was just setting a bowl of stew onto the table for her when Candi sat down. The others were already finishing their luncheon. Bekka smiled at her friend. "Everything okay?"

"Uhm... sure. Why wouldn't they be?" Candi said. Trish rolled her eyes but kept her silence.

Bekka's brows drew together and her smile seemed to widen slightly. "You are *so not* a good liar, Candi. You never have been." She reached across the table and put a hand on the blonde's arm. "Out with it."

Candi shot Trish a nervous look. She swallowed the bite of stew that she had in her mouth. "I... I just haven't been feeling all that well since we left *Dragon's Reach*." She shrugged. "That's it." She slipped her arm out of Bekka's grasp and stood. "I'm not feeling too well. I think I'll go and lie down." She quickly ran from the table and back up the stairs.

"Candi, wait!" Bekka called out to her.

"Just let her go," Trish said. "She's really not well."

Bekka looked at her friend and sighed. "So, you gonna tell us what happened in *Dragon's Reach*? I've already caught you up on everything here."

Trish spooned a chunk of meat and potatoes into her mouth. She shrugged. "There isn't much to tell. When we got there, we were told that nobody matching Sinnestra's description had been through there. Nor had anyone with a severely wounded shoulder, nor anyone toting a baby." She shrugged. "We couldn't really call anyone a liar without proof of some kind, so we came back. We were hoping you had better luck." She glanced at Valoria. "Obviously you did."

"I'm just a wee bit surprised ye came back so soon," Taggarty said with a watchful eye. "T'is quite a ways ta *Dragon's Reach*. A trip thar an' back should take a bit more time, I would think. Especially since I dinna see ye come in wi' your horses."

Trish glared at the dwarf menacingly. "So, what is it that you're saying, exactly?"

You could feel the tension in the room. Bekka decided to diffuse the situation. "Don't worry about Tagg, he's had a bit to drink." She tried to kick his shin under the table. Had his legs been normal sized, she wouldn't have missed. Instead she struck the leg of his chair, pushing it askew; causing him to spill his drink onto his chest.

"Wha' in tarnation was tha' fer?" he roared.

Trish shook her head as she chuckled.

Candi opened the door and entered the bedroom. She quickly closed it and turned around. She was about to tell the dragon that she had managed to bring it a chunk of bread, but she stopped short. A young girl was sitting on the edge of the bed; the golden dragon was gone. "Who are you?" Candi demanded. "And what are you doing in my room?" She was afraid to mention anything about the dragon.

The girl had curly blonde hair that extended past her shoulders; it was a more golden shade than Candi's. She wore a long blouse that had ornate swirls upon the sleeves, a thin belt at her waist and leggings that matched the color and design of the top. "My name is Ellisandra." Her voice was soft, sweet and melodic. "I am here because you brought me here."

"I did no such thing!" Candi said taking a step forward. She didn't know *who* this girl was, but she was clearly lying.

Ellisandra smiled, clearly amused. "Of course you did. I am Ansanthe's sibling. I came here with you and the other woman with red hair, Trish, I believe."

Candi shook her head. "I'm confused."

"You told me to remain here, and you would bring me something to eat. Did you? I am very hungry."

Candi looked down at the chunk of bread in her hand. "I brought this... but..."

Ellisandra took the bread from Candi's hand and took a bite. "Thank you."

Candi nodded as she sat upon the edge of the bed. Her eyes were wide. She ran a hand through her hair. "I don't believe this."

Chapter 58
The Journey South Begins

Trish knocked on the door before she opened it. She wanted to give Candi ample time to hide the dragon. She paused for a moment and then opened the door and slipped quickly inside. "You *really* need to work on your lying skills, Candi. You are absolutely the worst liar I know."

She turned and stopped abruptly, seeing that they were not alone. "Oh, you have company. Who's this?"

Candi gave her a weak smile. "This is Ellie. You probably remember her as the golden dragon."

Trish blinked, her eyes going wide. "You've *got* to be shitting me!"

Candi laughed as she lightly shook her head. She was still having difficulty believing it all. She stood up from the edge of her bed and looked at Trish. "What are we going to do? We can't keep her, can we?"

Trish drew her head back and blinked. "Keep her? She's not

some puppy that followed us home! No, we *can't* keep her!"

They both turned their attention to the girl, staring as though she were an apparition.

"My place is here, with Candace," Ellisandra stated.

Trish ran her fingers through her auburn hair and crossed the room. She sat upon the other bed and sighed as she shook her head. "What do you mean your *place* is with Candi?"

"I go where she goes. I belong with her," Ellisandra said simply.

"You *belong* with her?" Trish shot a look at her friend. "Mind explaining this to me?"

"Evidently it has been foretold that she and I would be bonded together," Candi said. "At least that is what she told me. It's some kind of *Drelkin prophecy.*" She shrugged. "It's like I was *chosen.*"

"What the heck does that even mean?" Trish was having difficulty with this news.

Ellisandra smiled patiently. "There is a prophecy told among the Drelkin that a human girl from a distant land would come among us. With her assistance, the Dragons would be welcomed back into the world and would no longer be forced to dwell in secrecy deep within the *Dragon Spires.* Candace is the *Chosen One.* I heard her calling to me before I hatched. We are bound together. We belong together, now and always."

Candi sat across from Trish on her own bed. She placed her hands onto her lap; her fingers fidgeting. She smiled at her friend weakly. "Just call me *Khaleesi.*"

Trish practically snorted. "Yeah. No. You are not Queen nor the *Mother of Dragons.*"

There was a knock at the door and Trish and Candi's eyes grew wide. Before either of them could get up and rush to see whom it was; the door opened. Bekka came in and closed the door behind her. "Hi guys. I just figured I'd... *oh*! You've got company." She gave them a curious look. "Who's this?"

Candi and Trish quickly exchanged glances. Candi shook her hands in the air nervously. "I can explain."

Bekka had a bemused smile on her face as she crossed her arms in front of her. "Do tell."

Candi looked pleadingly at Trish. "Can you tell her?"

Trish rolled her eyes. "No, Candi, I cannot. She is bound to you, not me."

Bekka shook her head and frowned. "What do you mean she's *bound* to her?"

Trish crossed her arms. "I'm not saying another word about this. She needs to tell you herself."

Candi looked as though she were about to break down and start crying. Bekka moved to her friend and placed a hand on her shoulder. "Oh, Candi, there's no reason for you to get so upset. It's me, Bekka. You can tell me anything. You know that."

Candi sniffled. "I... I know. It's just... it's just that I don't even know how to explain this without it sounding like completely crazy!"

Bekka smiled. "Start from the beginning."

Bekka had sat patiently as Candi spoke. The blonde girl had a tendency to ramble and had to be prodded to stay on topic every now and then. When she had finished, Bekka remained silent for several minutes, just staring at Ellisandra thoughtfully. Finally she said, "Sooo you can turn into a dragon?"

Ellisandra smiled. "No. I am a dragon; I can turn into a girl."

Bekka lowered one brow. "There's a difference?"

Ellisandra nodded. "There is."

Bekka chuckled softly. "Point taken." She sat beside Trish on the opposite bed. "If you were just born a few days ago, then why do you look like you are about thirteen years old already?"

The corner of Ellisandra's mouth curled upward. "I was not born, I was hatched. Dragons age differently than do humans. We are one of the *ancient races of Vespia*. Our lifespan is far greater than any of the others."

Bekka nodded. "Candi claims that Ansanthe is a Drelkin and that he is your sibling. So are you a Drelkin or a dragon? I'm just trying to wrap my head around all of this. It's a lot to take in, all at once."

"I am a dragon. Ansanthe has my bloodline flowing through his veins. He is my brother, several thousand times removed you could say."

"Wow," Bekka said softly. She looked at Trish and then at Candi and Ellisandra. "So, you are *bound* to Candi. What does that mean, exactly?"

"It simply means that from this point on our paths are the same. Wherever she goes, so too will I."

"What if she decides to go home, back through the *Portal* to her own world? Will you go there too?"

Ellisandra looked at Candi. "I cannot."

A tear fell from Candi's eye and rolled down her cheek. "Oh, Ellie... I could never leave you!"

Bekka sighed. "I need to consider what all this means. We'll talk more later."

Ellisandra put a hand on Bekka's arm. "What more is there to talk about? I will not be separated from Candi."

Bekka studied the girl for a moment. *Was there a threat hidden in her words?* It was only now that she noticed that Ellisandra's eyes were not perfectly round; her pupils were like those of a cat. She smiled. "We may be going into dangerous territory soon. I cannot be responsible for the life of a young girl."

Ellisandra smiled slyly. "Good thing I am a dragon then."

Bekka chuckled softly. "Good point." She placed a hand on Ellisandra's own. "Let me inform the others. If they agree then you can come along with us."

"And if they are not in agreement? What happens then?"

Bekka studied the girl for a moment. She shrugged. "Then I guess you'll stay behind."

Ellisandra shook her head slowly. "I will *not* be separated from Candi. We are bound together. It is a bond that cannot be broken so easily."

"Look," Bekka said, "this is a violent world in which we live. You know that to be true. Your race was hunted to near extinction. I can't be responsible for getting you killed. If the others agree that you can come along, then I will go along with their decision. If they refuse, then you must stay. It'll be up to Candi to decide what she will do."

Ellisandra looked into Bekka's eyes. "It would be a mistake not to have me along. I can be of some use. I will prove my worth."

"A dragon, ye say?" Taggarty scratched his bearded chin. He found a crumb of bread in his whiskers and he freed it. He studied it for a second and then popped it into his mouth. "I thought the last dragon 'ad died years ago. Thar be a graveyard littered wi' their bones beyond the *Ghostlands*. I've ne'er e'en seen a live beastie a'for."

Lightfingers arched his brows. "This could prove very interesting, to be sure."

Bekka looked at Valoria. "What do you think?"

Valoria shrugged. "She wants to come along, I say we let her."

Bekka sighed. "Ellisandra said she would prove her usefulness to us."

Taggarty nodded. "Weel then, lass, I say tha' we give her the chance. She could give us the upper hand should we be needin' it."

Valoria nodded her agreement. "Our numbers are few. There's no telling how large a force Sinnestra commands. A dragon could help to level the field." She cocked an eyebrow. "At the very least a dragon might be useful in a fight with a demon."

The thief nodded. "Valoria makes a good point. Going up against Sinnestra will not be an easy task. Ellisandra could prove beneficial."

Tagg seemed to agree.

"Alright," Bekka said. "We'll leave at first light."

Bran Toshe and his son Taren had hitched a team of horses up to a wagon; they had it waiting outside the *Spilt Tankard Inn* when Bekka and her companions stepped outside. Taren went inside at his mother's summons and returned a short time later with two large knapsacks stuffed full of supplies. Carandra had grown quite fond of the group of adventurers and hoped to satisfy their needs.

Bekka gave Carandra a warm hug. "I don't know how to thank you other than to pay you." She held out a leather pouch for the woman to take; it was full of gold and silver coins.

Carandra refused to accept the payment. "Ye may 'ave need o' your money once ye reach *Glynn*. Keep it with ye. We can settle up another time."

Bekka shook her head. "We can't take your wagon and horses without paying you; it just wouldn't be right."

Bran wrapped a massive arm around his wife's shoulder. "Cara an' I 'ave spoke of this. Ye can reserve payment fer when the dust settles."

With tears filling her eyes, Bekka hugged them both. "Thank you."

Chapter 59
Marren's Generosity

Trevor reached *Schiff's Crossing* almost two hours before sundown. Marren Schiff and his son's ferried him across the *Stebin River*. The old man looked at him with a broad, friendly smile that showed he had more than a few missing teeth. Trevor tried to recall if the man had been missing them when he made the crossing from east to west; he couldn't be sure. Marren nodded. "Good thing you got here when you did, we were about to stop for the night. Been a busy day."

Trevor frowned. "Did you ferry across an elf? She was riding a horse. We became separated and I need to find her. It's important."

Marren Schiff seemed reluctant to disclose any information. Who could really blame him? Trevor was looking pretty rough; his shirt was still bloodstained and dirty. He shrugged. "Lots of folks been through here lately. They pay their fare I don't pay them much attention."

"Look, the elf maiden is my wife and she's very pregnant.

The people we were traveling with attacked us and we got separated. They left me for dead and took her with them. I found them all dead near the *Red Hills*, but Lithania, my wife, wasn't among them. I'm worried about her. Please, she doesn't need to be traveling on her own."

Marren studied him intently. Finally he nodded. "Yup. I ferried her across about two hours ago. She decided it was best if she pushed on toward the east. Said she was goin' to *Serendil Brenatis*." He scratched his grizzled chin. "I thought the Elven Tree City was destroyed a while back. Guess I heard wrong."

"I need to catch up with her as quickly as I can," Trevor said frantically. "A pregnant woman should have someone with her. She's going to have my child, I *need* to be with her!"

Marren Schiff shook his head. "That horse o' yours is spent. You'll not catch up to her on that. Tell you what I'll do; I'll take your horse in trade if you can add another fifty silver to sweeten the deal. The horse you'll get will be faster than the one she's been riding, an' a whole lot fresher too."

Trevor checked his pockets; his coin pouch was gone, stolen. He hadn't thought to check the corpses that he found; he was in such a hurry to find Lithania. He frowned darkly. "I don't have any money; it was taken from me."

Marren grinned after another minute of studying Trevor. He chuckled softly. "Alright. I think I can go ahead and make the deal with you anyways. Seein' how you're about to become a father. We'll call it a Papa discount."

Trevor smiled with relief. "Thank you, sir. That is very kind of you. I'll find a way to repay you. Promise."

As the raft docked at the eastern pier, Marren instructed his sons to secure the craft for the night. He looked at Trevor. "Can I at least convince you to stay the night? It will be awfully dark soon."

Trevor shook his head. "I really need to head out. I won't be comfortable about her being out there alone. I have to find her."

Marren nodded. "Alright. Why don't you go pick out a horse and saddle it up; I'll pack you some supplies to take along. I won't have you going after your pregnant elf maiden without giving you adequate provisions. Your friends helped me out of a bind; this'll go towards repayment."

Trevor shook his hand. "I'll be sure to let them know that your debt has been paid in full."

As the last rays of sunlight faded beyond the western horizon, Trevor mounted his horse and turned toward the northeast. He could tell that the stallion had been in a barn too long and was eager to run. He nudged the horse with a final wave over his shoulder. He could see Marren Schiff raise his hand and then drop it; he then had to turn and give his undivided attention to his mount.

Chapter 60
The Vale

Bekka was being jostled to and fro as the wagon continued along; it was almost enough to rock her to sleep. Sleep remained elusive, the aching muscles throughout her body kept her uncomfortable. They had been travelling in relative silence since they left *Darkwater* several hours earlier. The road was muddy and covered in slush, greatly slowing their progress. They had all expected to be farther along than they were.

Taggarty reined the horses to a halt as they approached a crossroads. They could either continue to skirt along the edge of *Darken Wood* as they travelled southward, or they could head further east into *The Vale* where it was rumored powerful druids lived. He glanced at Lightfingers who was sitting beside him.

Lightfingers pointed toward the east and shrugged.

Valoria had been watching their back trail. "We are being followed by a sizable force."

Ellisandra hopped over the side rail of the wagon. Candi

grasped for her but couldn't stop her. "What are you doing, Ellie?"

The girl smiled. "We need to know who it is that is following us, and if they mean to do us harm." Before anyone could object further, Ellisandra leapt into the air and transformed into a golden dragon—she was already twice the size she had been the last time Candi had seen her in this form. She flew up into the air and circled back in the direction from which they had just travelled.

I see them! Candi heard the dragon's thoughts in her mind. It was almost as though Ellisandra was next to her, speaking. Only it was different, somehow; more ethereal. *It is a small army, maybe thirty in number. There is a mage with them. They appear to be tracking us.* Ellisandra's method of communicating was different than Ansanthe's had been while in dragon form. He *actually* spoke out loud—Ellie seemed to be using *telepathy*.

Candi quickly relayed Ellisandra's *thoughts* to the others. She cocked her head to one side, and after a moment spoke to Bekka. "She wants to know if we want her to stop them."

Bekka looked at Valoria. "We don't know if they plan us any harm. We can't just attack them."

"Sounds ta me like it be Kaspian Altair. If'n he be the one trailin' us, he means ta do us grave harm, ye can count on tha'," Tagg said over his shoulder as he kept the wagon rolling.

Valoria nodded her agreement. "Altair has most likely already discovered your interference at the mine. He will be after revenge. He is not one to trifle with."

"There are ways to eliminate that threat," Lightfingers said.

"So what? We just tell the dragon to kill him and his men?" Bekka was obviously struggling with this course of action. She looked at Candi and Trish for support. "I can't condone any of this. Those men likely don't have a choice. They're probably all wearing those collars like the one Val wore. We *can't* just kill them."

Trish put a hand on Bekka's arm. "This is the world in which we now live. It is violent and unforgiving. We must strike them before they catch up and attack us. Taggarty and Lightfingers will most likely be spared the horrors that the rest of us will be forced to endure." She glanced at Candi. "Tell Ellisandra to do whatever she must to stop them."

"No!" Bekka said. "We *can't* murder them."

Trish squeezed her arm and shook her. "Do you *want* to be raped by a blood-thirsty army?"

Candi looked at Bekka, a horrified expression on her face. "What do I do?"

Trish glared at her. *"Do it!"* she demanded harshly.

Bekka closed her eyes tightly, forcing tears to roll down her cheeks and she gave a quick nod.

Tears fell from Candi's eyes as she spoke to the dragon in her thoughts. *'Stop them. Do whatever it takes.'*

It is done! The dragon swooped out of the sky toward the unsuspecting army, breathing fiery death down upon them.

Bekka looked back and saw the blazing cone descend from the heavens and spread upon the ground. She covered her mouth with a hand and spoke in a whisper. "What have we done?" Candi gave her friend a hug and sobbed on her shoulder. She couldn't bring herself to look back despite the fact that she had been the one to tell Ellisandra to attack the army.

Bekka slipped out of Candi's embrace. She glared at Trish and then at the dwarf. "Well, I hope you are all happy now." She wiped her tears from her eyes and then crossed her arms over her chest while she silently brooded.

Taggarty glanced over at Lightfingers who was still sitting silently beside him. The dwarf's eyes went wide and he exhaled a huge breath; some things were best left unsaid. There was no sense in pursuing the topic further; it would only aggravate the matter, causing it to fester like an open wound. Besides, what was done was done. It was already too late to change anything.

The Vale was surrounded on three sides by water; few trees were in the area, save for the huge oaks that grew near the *Lake of Tears, Dread Lake* and along the *River of Sorrow*. The heart of *The Vale* was filled with bright flowers and tall grass that were all noticeably barren of snow. It was almost as if spring was eternal here. Dryads and Druids were reportedly the only inhabitants of this area. They kept a watchful eye over the hearty oaks that they called home, protecting them with powerful magic. Taggarty had never seen a dryad before but he had definitely heard stories about them.

More than a hundred years ago, when Sinnestra had conquered *Silver Frost Keep* and forced the dwarven clans to flee, some had fled south of the *Demon Spires* and settled just north of where *Glynn* now sits. Some of the dwarven woodsmiths had found tall, sturdy oaks at the heart of *The Vale*, perfect for building their homes and businesses.

They began to cut them down without any concern of *who* or *what* might dwell within the wood. The stories claimed that Alalia, a powerful dryad, pleaded with the leader of the dwarves, Jokreak Drakethane, to spare the massive oaks, but he denied her. With nowhere to turn, Alalia pleaded with her cousin, Ilaira, a water nymph with considerable powers, to come to her aid. After Jokreak and his men had built their homes and settled in the village they called *Marndoranhal*, Ilaira summoned her magic and flooded the town, drowning the dwarves. *Marndoranhal* now lies at the bottom of *Dread Lake* according to legend. To this day, dwarves fear great bodies of water.

Whether or not the stories were true, Taggarty couldn't say. He did try to avoid going out on the water. Crossing a stream was enough to leave him cold and sweaty. He couldn't swim, nor did he have any desire to.

Taggarty steered the horses that pulled the wagon toward the southeast to a point where the stream from *Dread Lake* poured into the *River of Sorrow*. There, the crossing was shallow enough that it would permit the wagon to ford to the other side with little threat. They followed a faint trail through the tall grass, littered with rock and dirt. The wagon jostled and creaked as the horses ambled along. "Perhaps we should take a wee bit o' a break, stretch our legs an' 'ave a bite ta eat. This be a good spot fer the beasties ta nibble upon the grass."

Candi hopped down from the bed of the wagon as it came to a stop. She scanned the sky wondering where Ellisandra was now. It was as if the dragon had just vanished. Candi frowned. She hoped nothing terrible had happened when she attacked the army. *Had Kaspian Altair managed to mount a counterattack?* The silence in her mind was deafening; already she had grown accustomed to the dragon's thoughts, but now there seemed only to be emptiness. It was unsettling. *'Ellisandra... Ellie... where are you?'*

There was no response from the dragon.

Valoria climbed down from the wagon and scanned the trail ahead of them. Bekka smiled at her. "I know that look."

A small smile curved the corner of the ranger's mouth. "It would be wise to scout ahead. I think I'll take a look around."

Bekka took a step toward her. "Want some company?"

Valoria bowed her head. "If you want."

Bekka looked at the others. "We're going to take a look and see what is up ahead. We'll be back."

Lightfingers hopped down from the wagon seat. "I'll come along."

Trish glanced from Candi to Bekka. "I'm gonna check our back trail. See if I can spot anything."

Candi had a worried look on her face. "I'll go too, I *can't* just sit here!"

Taggarty climbed into the back of the wagon. "Ye lassies do wha' ye need ta do. I'll just stretch me limbs an' take a lil' nap."

A cool breeze blew through *The Vale* as everyone set out upon their tasks. Before long, the dwarf was snoring heavily, the horses nibbling grass contentedly. The sun beat down, warming everything it touched with a comforting glow. The blades of grass swayed as the yellow flowers danced with the red and blue. Everything was peaceful and serene.

And then it wasn't.

Ellisandra fell from the sky and slid upon the ground, a spear sticking through her left shoulder. The impact of the dragon striking the ground startled the horses and they reared up, uprooting their stakes and panicked, they took off toward the east at a swift run. Candi and Trish had seen the trajectory of the dragon as it streaked across the sky and Candi quickly turned and followed; Trish continued toward the northwest.

Candi began to run toward the cloud of dust that was rising up from the ground. *"Ellisandra!"* she shouted frantically. *"Ellisandra, are you okay?"* Tears sprang from her eyes.

Trish could see about a dozen or so warriors moving in their direction. Behind them she could see a bearded man with flowing robes carrying a staff coming toward them. "Shit!" she said. She turned and started following Candi back toward the wagon.

"There!" Valoria whispered as she pointed toward the oak trees that lined the stream. "Did you see that?"

Bekka had seen the movement. She smiled. She was getting much better at all this *outdoorsy stuff*! She nodded. "Uh huh." She glanced at the ranger. "What was it, could you tell? It *couldn't* be what I thought I saw!" Impossible! It appeared to Bekka like a person with *bark* for skin—and *grass* for hair; but *surely* that had to be wrong. It just didn't make any sense.

"If I am correct," Valoria whispered softly, "it was a *Dryad*."

"A Dryad? What's a Dryad?"

Valoria chuckled softly. "Dryads are tree spirits. They inhabit mainly oak trees. This valley used to have thousands of oak trees until the dwarves were driven out of *Silver Frost Keep* and decided to build their homes nearby. The Dryads fiercely protect the remaining trees with powerful magic."

Lightfingers had heard of the woodland creatures but had never actually seen one.

"So the village we are going to, *Glynn*, is the dwarven village you spoke of?" Bekka asked.

Valoria shook her head. "No. The village of the dwarves was destroyed long ago. Legends claim that it is at the bottom of *Dread Lake*." She shrugged. "But who knows if those stories are even true? If they were, you'd think you would see stumps of all the oak trees that were cut down littering *The Vale*. But it is only grassland as far as you can see."

"Should we be worried about the Dryads?" Bekka asked, scanning the woods.

"I think we will be okay as long as we remain respectful and do no harm to them or the trees. We should go back to the others and let them know that we are not alone; that we are being observed. I do not want them to inadvertently anger the Dryad. That would not be good for any of us."

As Candi ran toward the golden dragon she feared that Ellisandra was dead. She hadn't moved since she crashed down upon the ground. Through her tears Candi couldn't even tell if the dragon was still breathing; her vision was so blurred. "Ellie! Please don't be dead! Please!" She looked at the dwarf who was already at the dragon's side. Swallowing her fear, she asked, "Is she dead?"

Taggarty shook his head. "Na, lass. The beastie still lives. See?" He pointed to the chest that still rose and fell with each breath. The dwarf placed both hands around the shaft of the spear. "I need ta pull this out o' her shoulder so's we can stop the bleedin."

As he pulled the spear from the wound the dragon roared in pain. Her eyes opened and she glared at the dwarf angrily. Snarling, she bared her massive teeth. Taggarty's eyes went wide. He dropped the spear and raised both hands into the air, taking a step back. "Easy lassie... take it easy." He glanced at Candi. "She may need ta revert back ta human form so I can bandage her shoulder an' stop the blood flow. It'll make things a might easier fer sure."

"Do as he says, Ellie," Candi said in a soothing voice. "Tagg just wants to help you. He's sorry if he hurt you, but he had to remove the spear from your shoulder."

Ellisandra closed her eyes and then shimmered, transforming into human form in just a few seconds. Her shoulder started bleeding profusely. Taggarty rushed forward. "We need ta get the bleeding stopped quick, a'for she bleeds out! Put yer hand on the wound an' apply pressure whilst I get me bag from under the wagon seat."

Candi had to use both hands to cover the entrance and exit wounds of the spear. It wasn't easy to maintain constant pressure, and every time she let up, the blood would continue. She was beginning to panic. "Hurry Tagg!" she urged frightfully.

The dwarf jumped down from the wagon and by the time he got back to where Candi and Ellisandra were, he was fairly winded. His cheeks had a ruddy color as he exhaled and quickly sucked in air again. I won't be doin' nobody any good if'n I keel o'er."

He opened a pocket on the side of his bag and pulled out a grayish substance that he quickly smeared over both sides of Ellisandra's wounded shoulder. He then pulled a small jar out of the pack and dug out a good bit of what looked to Candi to be moss. He divided it into two equal portions and applied it over the top of the other, sticky item. He then went back into the bag and grabbed some bandages. He handed them to Candi. "Wrap it tightly o'er the wounds."

Candi did as instructed, while she was doing so she asked, "Was that moss you used?"

Tagg nodded. "Aye, t'was, an' a'for tha' I used cobwebs. Combined together they make a fine poultice. It'll ward off infection too. Handy stuff, tha'."

She smiled at him. "Where'd you learn to use all that?"

He chuckled softly. "I been in me fair share o' scrapes. If'n ye live the life I do, ye learn 'ow ta survive."

Bekka, Valoria and Lightfingers returned riding the horses that had been frightened off when the dragon fell out of the sky. "Did you guys lose something?" Bekka asked with a grin. When she saw the bandages on Ellie's shoulder, her eyes went wide. "What happened to her?"

Candi pointed at the spear lying in the grass. "Someone from Kaspian Altair's army threw that into her shoulder. If it hadn't been for Taggarty she'd probably be dead. He saved her."

Lightfingers went about harnessing the horses back to the wagon. "We should leave as soon as we are able."

Valoria nodded. "Agreed."

Taggarty scratched his bearded chin. "Tha' red-headed lass isna' back just yet. She went ta check our back trail."

Bekka glared at the dwarf and then at Candi. "You both just *let* her go?"

"Whoa!" Candi said with a raised hand. "We were more concerned about Ellie than we were about Trish. She's a grown woman; she can take care of herself. Besides, I seriously doubt we could've stopped her anyway. She's pretty head-strong when she gets something stuck in her mind."

Tagg nodded. "Tha' be true enough. 'Sides, it might be a good idea ta make sure tha' Kaspian Altair isna' comin' up behind us."

Valoria looked toward the northwest. "On that we are in agreement."

Bekka looked at Ellisandra with concern. "Will she be able to travel in the back of the wagon?"

"Aye," Taggarty said with a nod.

Lightfingers had finished with the horses, and now he bent down and picked Ellisandra up with ease. He carried her to the wagon and with some assistance from Candi and Bekka, he got her lying down and as comfortable as possible. "If we leave now, we should be able to make it into *Glynn Wood* before it gets too dark. We can make camp there and then ride into the village in the morning."

Candi looked at Bekka with concern. "What about Trish? We can't just leave her behind."

Bekka sighed. "You said it yourself, she's a grown woman; she can take care of herself. I don't like being in this place any longer. There's no cover; we're in the open, vulnerable."

Candi placed a hand on Bekka's arm, giving it a firm squeeze. "Trish is our friend! What if she encounters Kaspian Altair or his army? What if she's hurt? We can't just leave her!"

Bekka was suddenly irritated. "What would you have me do, Candace? Risk everyone else's life for her? What about Ellisandra? She's weak as it is."

"We can't leave Trish," Candi said emphatically. "Not again! It wouldn't be right!"

Tears stung Bekka's eyes. "Don't do that, Candi! Don't try and make me feel guilty. It won't work. Trish made her decision. She knew we couldn't wait long. This is *not* on me! She did this!"

"Bekka," Candi pleaded, "she's our friend."

Bekka whirled on her, angry now. "*That is not our friend!* Trish was killed by Maragh; I don't know *who* or *what* that is!"

Candi stepped back; her eyes were wide, filling with tears of sorrow. She shook her head slowly. "How can you say that?"

"Seriously, Candi?" Bekka said.

The dwarf cleared his throat loudly. "Weel, tha' is a moot point now. 'ere she comes, yonder." They all turned and looked to the northwest. They could see her familiar red hair blowing in the gentle breeze that swept through the valley as Trish trotted toward them.

Trish stopped twenty feet from the group and put her hands on her hips. "Looks like you were fixing to leave me behind." She sounded slightly aggrieved.

Candi turned and glared at Bekka before running to give Trish a hug. "I for one am glad you're back!"

Chapter 61
Lithania

Trevor could see the glow of the campfire reflecting off the rocks and trees near the base of the *Griffin Peaks*. He hoped it was Lithania, but he couldn't be certain. He was tired and hungry; his mouth and throat were parched. He needed rest and he needed water; he had dropped his canteen somewhere along the way. He must've fallen asleep in the saddle.

He eased his horse forward slowly. "Hello the camp!" he called out hoarsely. It sounded like a croak to him, certainly not the voice he was accustomed to hearing. Still, it seemed to carry in the peacefulness of the night.

Relief flooded over him when he heard Lithania's voice answer. "Trevor?!" He smiled happily, almost falling from the horse as she rushed toward him.

Lithania reached out her hands to steady him. "Careful!" she said.

He practically fell into her arms, hugging her to him tightly. Tears formed in his eyes. "I thought I'd lost you!"

She kissed his cheek. "I thought you were dead, or I would've gone back for you. All I could think about was getting home."

He pushed her to arm's length. "What happened? I found the camp... I saw the dead bodies..."

"We were attacked and in the confusion I managed to get away. I was *so* scared!" She led him into her camp. "I think I cried all the way to *Schiff's Crossing*."

They sat by the fire, arms wrapped around one another as though they were both afraid to let the other go. Lithania rested her head on his chest. Trevor ran a hand through her hair. He frowned, lost in thought. "Litha," he said softly. "I... I saw those corpses." He could feel her stiffen in his embrace, but he continued, "They were hideous. Their eyes were gone, and it seemed as though something went through their noses. What attacked you? What kind of monster could do all that?"

She was silent. All he could hear was the snapping and pop of the pine logs in the fire. He waited patiently for her to respond, though it felt as if he were sitting on pins and needles. He could only imagine what had happened at the slaver campsite. He felt her stir against him.

Her voice was soft, tentative. "I do not know what it was. Something came at us from the darkness, but I do not know what it could have been. They had me bound and blindfolded, I do not know why, but they did. I heard a ferocious growl, slashing and screams. At first, I believed it was a bear, but it could not have been, not with the injuries you described. The camp was total chaos. One of the men forced me onto a horse, I think he intended to flee with me. They were going to sell me into slavery and I guess he believed that now the profit would be his alone. But he too was slain. My horse was frightened and it took off, saving me from the same fate as the others. I managed to free my hands along the way and remove my blindfold. I have *never* been so frightened." Her hand rested on the hilt of her dagger strapped to her thigh.

Trevor kissed the top of her head and tightened his embrace. "Ssh, my love. It is okay now. We're together again."

Lithania raised her head and pressed her lips against his. She smiled as she kissed him; she shifted her body, her fingers wrestling with the ties of his breeches...

Chapter 62
Rosa's Warning

They had made camp deep within the alders of *Glynn Wood* as a light rain drizzled down through the trees. Taggarty and Lightfingers had rigged a tarpaulin above the back of the wagon so that Ellisandra could rest in peace with Candi by her side, Trish was sleeping there too. Valoria had wandered away from the camp in the direction from which they had entered the wood, wanting to stand a vigil throughout the night. Bekka sat alone by the fire, a thin blanket wrapped around her shoulders as she leaned against the smooth trunk of the red alder. The dwarf had stretched out beneath the wagon, his battleaxe resting on his chest. He was snoring robustly, oblivious to his surroundings.

The aroma of the burning alder logs was sweet. The logs twisted, shifting and crackling as they burned. Bekka closed her eyes and inhaled deeply. She was tired; it had been a long day. When she opened her eyes, she saw Rosa sitting across the fire, jabbing the burning timber with a blackened, pointed stick. Bekka blinked, not believing her eyes. "Rosa?" she said in disbelief. "What are you doing here?"

The old woman batted a hand in the air. "Of all de tings you could ask, *dat* ees vhat you start vith?" She looked at Bekka with narrow, wizened eyes. "I *know* dat you can do better!" She chuckled softly.

Bekka sat up, rolling her head about her neck; she could hear the cartilage pop. *This couldn't be real. She had to be dreaming!* She tried to force herself to awaken; but still she saw Rosa sitting across from her. *Had she finally lost her mind?*

The old Gypsy woman shook a finger at her. "You 'ave not progressed! Vhat 'ave you been doing vith your time? Adara, you *need* to prepare yourself! Sinnestra ees ready for you! She 'as corrupted your brother's mind. She 'as taken 'im to another realm vhere time ees not de same as here, he ees now much older. Han ees a grown man and he believes dat she ees 'is true mother! He vill destroy you eef you are not prepared! He 'as only hate for you in 'is heart. You must be ready to keel 'im!"

Bekka shook her head. She was having difficulty believing any of this. *How could Han be a grown man? He was just a baby! This was beyond crazy!* "Rosa, I cannot fight my brother. I can't kill him. I won't!"

"Bah!" Rosa batted the air again. "Den you 'ave lost already!"

"Don't say that, Rosa." Bekka jumped to her feet. "We are family. I cannot fight him. There *has* to be another way."

Rosa shrugged, seeming to puzzle over something. "I tink dat Han vill seek de *Timestones*. Dey are 'is only chance to save 'is mother, to save Sinnestra," she corrected quickly upon seeing Bekka's face. "Eef he finds dem, den *all* hope ees truly lost!"

Bekka blinked. "*Timestones?* What are these stones?"

Rosa sighed heavily. "Dey can grant you de ability to change vhat 'as already come to pass but dey may not even be real; dey could be leetle more dan a myth." She shook her head. "I 'ave never seen dem. But I 'ave heard stories."

Bekka's mind was churning. "These *Timestones* ... if they can be used by Han to alter time and save Sinnestra, can they be used to bring back the dead?"

The old Gypsy shrugged. "Dey are rumored to 'ave strong

magic power. Dey can alter time and events dat 'ave 'appened. I suppose dat dey can be used to bring back de dead, to prevent dem from dying." She gave Bekka a dark look. "Sometimes eet ees unwise to change one's fate." She pointed at Bekka and stared at her with her eyes narrowed. "De cost of using dark magic can be *very* high. You should not tempt fate in dis vay. Eet could be very dangerous! You could lose more dan you gain."

Bekka ran a hand through her hair. If she had these *Timestones* could she use them to bring back everyone that she had lost? Could she somehow save them? Rosa claimed that it was dark magic and that using the stones could be dangerous and likely came at a high cost. *Was she willing to pay the price to save her friends and family?* "Rosa…?" She had so many more questions.

The old Gypsy woman was gone.

Had she ever truly been there?

Chapter 63

Breegan Dalmurnin

They were up and ready to break camp as the first rays of golden sunlight filled the gaps in the tall alder trees. Taggarty kicked dirt over the smoldering embers of the dying fire, causing smoke to rise up in feeble protest, as Lightfingers hitched up the wagon. Candi stretched her arms over her head from the bed of the wagon and was all smiles. She reported that Ellisandra had made a miraculous recovery to the delight of them all. It no doubt had to do with the dragon blood that flowed through her veins.

Bekka pulled Valoria aside; she kept her voice low, not wanting the others to hear. "What can you tell me about *Timestones*?"

Valoria shook her head. "Never heard of them. Why do you ask?"

Bekka blushed. She glanced around to make sure no one was listening; everybody seemed preoccupied preparing to break camp and move on. "Last night I had another visit with Rosa. She spoke about them to me."

"What are you saying? Like in a dream?"

Bekka nodded. She found it difficult to make eye contact with the ranger; she was aware of how crazy she sounded. "Kinda like that, only I *wasn't* dreaming."

"I see," Valoria said. Lady Rosa had once told her that she suspected that Bekka had *the sight* like her mother; so this news didn't really sound as far-fetched as it otherwise might. Rosa had told Valoria to trust Bekka's *visions* when she had them. "Did Rosa tell you anything useful concerning these - what did you call them - *Timestones*?"

Bekka hesitated. "Well," she took a deep breath, "she said they were *dark magic*, and using them could come with a pretty stiff price."

Valoria placed a hand on Bekka's shoulder. "*Dark magic* is not something you should be playing with."

"Lady Rosa said that Sinnestra had somehow taken Han to another realm where time passes differently. Now my baby brother is supposedly a grown man." She shook her head. Hearing it out loud even sounded crazy to her! "Rosa suspects that Han might try to use the *Timestones* to alter time and save Sinnestra." Bekka searched the warrior's face. "We cannot allow him to succeed. We have to find these *Timestones* before he does."

Valoria studied her friend intently. "And what do you plan to do with them if we are successful? Destroy them?"

Bekka shrugged as tears sprang to her eyes, she wiped them away with a frustrated swipe of her fingertips. "I don't really know, to be honest. I thought about maybe saving everyone we've lost. You know, bring them back."

Valoria squeezed Bekka's shoulder. "I know how tempting that sounds, but I must really caution you against it. *Dark magic* can be deadly. You can wind up doing more harm than good. I honestly believe that fate cannot be changed."

Bekka raised her hands into the air, a helpless expression clouding her face. "Well it probably doesn't matter. I was hoping you knew what these stones were; what they looked like, where they might be found." She wiped the tears from her cheeks. "But you're just as clueless as I am."

Valoria nodded. "Maybe that's for the best. We manage to

get into enough trouble without involving ourselves with *dark magic*."

They arrived in the tiny hamlet of *Glynn* about two hours later. The first building they came to was the smithy. Taggarty walked up and waited as the dwarven blacksmith plunged the glowing horseshoe into the bucket of water. Steam rose in the air with a prolonged *hiss* from the water. "Excuse me, lad," Tagg said. "Could ye perhaps tell me where I might find a feller by the name o' Breegan?"

The young dwarf looked at Taggarty with a furrowed brow; he glanced at the others curiously. "Wha' business ye got wi' 'im if'n ye dinna mind me askin'?"

Taggarty chuckled softly, but it was without humor; it seemed to be a subtle warning, somehow. "Tha' be our business, mind ye. Best ye na' go stickin' yer nose inta it. Who are ye, anyway?"

"Weel..." said the young dwarf with a grin, "I'm Orin. The man ye seek is me da' an' if'n ye want me ta tell ye where ye can find 'im, maybe ye can make it my business too."

Taggarty chuckled heartily as he slapped the younger dwarf upon the shoulder. "Vera well laddie! Vera well! We only want ta ask yer da' a question or two. He may know another way inta ol' *Silver Frost Keep*, one tha' others know nothin' 'bout."

The young man nodded as he pulled the horseshoe out of the bucket and put it into a crate with several others that he had already completed to his satisfaction. "Aye, me da' knows tha' place better than any other, I suppose." He squinted. "But he hasna' spoke o' it in many a year." He studied Taggarty for a moment. "He may be willin' ta speak wi' ye."

"Weel then, lad," Taggarty tucked his thumbs into his belt, "whcrc might I find 'im?"

"Da' is usually out back 'round this time," he said with a nod over his left shoulder.

Taggarty had to squint in the darkness to see the door at the back of the smithy. He pointed with a fat, stubby finger. "Yonder?"

"Aye."

Taggarty stepped around the young man as he started pounding upon another shoe. He found the door handle in the darkness as the firelight from the smith's forge danced upon its smooth surface. He pushed the door open and was blinded by the sunlight reflected off the waters of the eastern bay of the *Sea of Dagmarth*. He blinked several times and raised a hand to his brow, searching for Breegan as the others joined him.

They saw a well-worn path cutting through the brush along the shoreline and followed it. They found the old dwarf sitting upon a large rock staring off across the water, one hand resting upon his knee, the other held a pipe to his lips; a ring of smoke floating up around his head. Taggarty glanced at the others and then spoke, his eyes returning to the dwarf. "Breegan? Breegan Dalmurnin? Tha' be ye?"

The old man gave a barely perceptible nod as another smoke ring floated into the air about his head; he remained silent. The top of his head was nearly completely bald, only a few thin, sparse strands of white remained. The hair along the sides and back of his head was long and flowed in gentle waves over his shoulders.

"We've come from *Darkwater* ta ask ye a few questions 'bout *Silver Frost*. We be needin' a way in—wi' out bein' seen."

The old man turned his head slightly and pulled the pipe out of his mouth, smoke seeped from the stem. "Tha' so?" he said simply.

"Aye," Taggarty nodded. "We be meanin' ta rid the place o' tha' demon bitch Sinnestra."

"Tha' so?" came the dwarf's only reply.

After a long moment of silence, enough time for Taggarty's skin to turn red with rising anger, Breegan said, "Then ye be needin' a way in wi' out bein' seen, I 'spect."

"Tha's wha' I said!" Taggarty sputtered angrily. Valoria put a calming hand upon his arm and shook her head as Bekka stepped forward.

"Sinnestra has my brother. I plan on getting him back." She withdrew the silver coffer from the pouch she carried. She held it out for the dwarf to see as she opened it. "This is the *Blade of the Spider's Kiss*, the Drow weapon said to be the *only* thing that can kill her."

Breegan's eyes widened as he looked upon the blade nestled

within the black velvet. He reached out a trembling hand to lightly caress the *Blade of the Spider's Kiss*. To Bekka's surprise the Drow blade glowed as it had when she held it in her hands—as it had when Lithania first wielded it against Sinnestra all those months before! She looked at the old dwarf with astonishment lighting her eyes. "How?" she asked.

A lone tear escaped the dwarf's eye and rolled down his weathered cheek and into his grizzled beard. "T'was I tha' forged this blade wi' me own two hands!" He shook his head. "I ne'er thought I'd see it again." He looked up at Bekka. "Ye must be the *Chosen One*, eh?"

Bekka nodded silently. She had spent many months hating that phrase, but hearing it spoken by this old dwarf didn't bother her at all. She looked into his eyes with renewed intensity. "Will you help us?"

Breegan studied her for a long time and then glanced back at the *Blade of the Spider's Kiss*. He closed the coffer and returned his eyes to hers. He nodded as he puffed on his pipe, blowing another ring of smoke into the air. "Aye," he said.

The sun was sinking low in the western sky, painting the far horizon with a warm glow of red, orange and yellow. They sat outside of the *Water Barrel Tavern* where the tables and chairs were placed to take advantage of the setting sun. Fomrelsia Dalmurnin, Orin's wife, an unusually large and robust woman for a dwarf, ran the *WBT*. Her hair was braided and tied at the back into a thick bun. She was obviously very fond of her father-in-law and seemed quite protective of the aged dwarf, never straying too far from him.

After she had cleared away the last of the supper from the table, she looked at Breegan with a concerned eye. "Ye should come inside an' chat by the fire a'for ye catch cold."

"Nah," Breegan scoffed, "it will be another hour or so a'for the air chills me bones. Be a dear an' fetch me tobacco pouch. Ye'll find it in the drawer beside me bed." He grinned at her and gave her a wink as he shooed her away with his hand. "Off ye go!"

After she had gone inside, Breegan chuckled softly. "She's a good lass, takes better care o' me than I do. T'is probably why I still breathe instead o' pushin' up daisies."

Taggarty nodded. "I know the type; me brother 'ad 'isself a fine woman like tha'. She was far better than either o' us deserved." He chuckled at some forgotten memory. "She was always a givin' me the evil eye. Threatened ta beat me ears wi' a wooden spoon if'n I kept takin' Dussin wi' me on my 'hair-brained' adventures as she called 'em.

Threatened Dussin too. Ne'er did any good though, he always follered me. I think he feared I'd git in o'er me head if'n he dinna." Taggarty sighed. "Dussin would still be livin' 'ad he listened ta her this last time."

"Weel," Breegan pointed to the north with the stem of his pipe, "if ye all go ahead wi' yer plans ta o'ertake *Silver Frost* tha' be more o' ye tha' willna' make it. Sinnestra uses dark magic. Tha' is 'ow she took the *Keep* all those years ago."

"But you know a back way in," Bekka said. "That should help us some."

Breegan nodded. "Aye, but it isna' wi' out perils o' its own, lass. An' thar be no tellin' wha' kinda shape e'erythin' is in now due ta neglect."

"We'll take our chances," Valoria said.

The old dwarf studied Valoria with a measured gaze. He nodded. "Aye, an' I believe ye can handle yerself better than most by the look o' ye. Ye 'ave taken a walk o'er the bridge an' into the fire as it were."

Breegan accepted the tobacco pouch from the cute little blonde girl that came skipping up to him. "Thank ye, Annalise!"

His granddaughter hugged him tightly. "G'night, Papa. Ma says I 'ave ta go ta bed, but I wanna stay up wi' ye."

He kissed the top of her head and patted her bottom. "Best mind yer ma lil' one."

"She said you should come inside too!"

"Weel, first I'm goin' ta 'ave me a smoke, since ye went ta all tha' trouble ta fetch it fer me, then I'll be in. Off wi' ye."

She nodded; her blond curls bouncing as she stepped away from him. "Okay, Papa."

He was silent as he filled his pipe with the tobacco. Satisfied, he struck a match and lit the pipe, puffing smoke from the corner of his mouth. The pungent aroma of the burning tobacco filled the air with a scent of sweetness and a hint of spice all at once that was as pleasing as it was relaxing.

Darkness claimed the sky and the shadows seemed to close in around them. They talked well into the night, with Breegan detailing all he could recall about the secret way into *Silver Frost Keep*. Then, when the chill in the air became too much for his bones - he suffered badly from arthritis - they went into the *Water Barrel Tavern*. Still puffing upon his pipe, the old dwarf asked to see their weapons; he made it clear that he didn't like what he saw. "Nah," he shook his head, quickly pointing out defects in the craftsmanship of each weapon, "these willna' do. T'is no small feat tha' ye've not all been keeled a'for now. Yer weapons be pitiful!"

Taggarty took obvious offense as he jerked his battleaxe away from the older dwarf. "I'll 'ave ye know tha' this t'were me da's own. It served him well fer more'n a hundred years!"

Breegan met Taggarty's banter with a voice equally as powerful. "Tha' so? An' I bet he used it when he was keeled too!"

"Aye!" Taggarty said heatedly. "But not a'for he spilt 'is enemies' own blood ta be sure!"

"Weel," Breegan said with a spread of his hands, "all I'm sayin' is tha' weapon is too heavy and cumbersome ta do any real benefit when yer life depends on it!"

Taggarty frowned. "Aye, but ye get used ta the weight o' it after a wee bit."

Breegan chuckled slapping Taggarty on the shoulder. "Aye, but ye shouldna' 'ave ta is all I be sayin'! Look, I realize it 'as real sentimental value ta ye, bein' yer da's own blade. But sentiment will get ye pushin' up daisies." He pointed to the edge of the blade. "See those chips...? An' this one 'ere? See the way it be cracking a wee bit? It willna' be long a'for yer axe shatters completely leavin' ye a holdin' just a splintered piece o' wood."

Breegan stroked his beard thoughtfully for a moment. His eyes twinkled brightly. "Come ta the smithy first thing in the morn. I'll get ye all fitted up proper wi' some better weapons." He looked at Bekka. "But yer Drow blade canna' be beat, lass," he said with a wink.

Chapter 64
New Weapons

Breegan puffed on his pipe as the others finished their morning meal to break their fast. He studied them thoughtfully and finally he spoke. "When are ye plannin' on headin' fer *Silver Frost?*"

Bekka glanced at Valoria and swallowed the last bite of egg she had in her mouth. "I'd like to go over the route to this secret entrance into the *Keep* one more time. Once we're comfortable that we can find it, we'll be leaving. The sooner we face Sinnestra the better."

Breegan nodded as a circle of smoke floated lazily into the air above his head, followed by another. "Weel," he said with a twinkle in his eye, "t'is na' somethin' tha' ye can easily find on yer own, na matter 'ow detailed a description I give ye. Oh, I can tell ye 'ow ta find it, but ye likely ne'er will. But I can surely *show* ye where it t'is."

Fomrelsia had been clearing away the empty plates from the table; she stopped suddenly and glared at her father-in-law.

"Ye'll na' be showin' them nothin' old man! Yer place is 'ere wi' yer family! An old man such as yerself ought na' be wanderin' 'round in the ice an' snow! Yer adventurin' days be long gone!" She looked at her husband. "Orin! Talk some sense inta yer pa, please! If na' fer 'is sake, then do it fer yer wee daughter!"

"Da…" Orin said, feeling the weight of his wife's words.

Breegan slammed the palm of his hand onto the table. "If'n these fine folks be goin' ta *Silver Frost Keep* ta rid it o' tha' demon bitch, then I plan on goin' too! I've lived a long life. A good life it 'as been too. Now, I love ye all dearly, but it is time tha' I went back ta me home!" He stared across the table at his son. "This is somethin' tha' I need ta do, lad."

Tears welled up in Orin's eyes and he slowly nodded. "Aye, I suppose tha' it t'is."

Fomrelsia burst into tears as she placed the tray of empty plates onto another table. She grabbed a handkerchief from a pocket of her apron and ran from the room. Orin cleared his throat. "I should see ta her." He got up and followed his wife out of the room.

They sat in silence for several minutes as the pleasant aroma of pipe tobacco continued to fill the air. Finally, Breegan tapped his pipe against the edge of the table, emptying the chamber of ash onto the floor. He tapped the residual embers with the ball of his booted foot. "If ye will accompany me ta the smithy, I'll show ye those weapons I spoke o' last night."

As they stepped out of the tavern they were greeted to the joyful sounds of birds chirping away high up in the treetops. The morning sun was already rising in the eastern sky, beginning to warm the frosty air. Dew sparkled upon the ground, like tiny diamonds scattered about. A gentle breeze carried with it the scent of damp moss and tree bark, as it mingled with the heavy fragrance of the salty sea. Spring was still likely a month away, but it was a promising start.

Bekka smiled as they walked along. "I love the smells of this place. The freshness of the forest and the saltiness of the ocean blending together seem so relaxing."

Trish chuckled. "You're kidding right? All I smell is the brine coming up from the ocean. It's positively nauseating."

Ellisandra twirled in a joyful circle. "I have never smelled the sea before! I think it is absolutely lovely!"

Trish rolled her eyes.

Candi giggled as she watched Ellie's delighted dance. "You amaze me!" She was happy to see that Ellisandra's shoulder wound seemed completely healed. Her recovery had been truly remarkable, nothing short of miraculous!

Once inside the smithy, Breegan opened a door that they had not noticed on their first visit to the shop; it was cleverly hidden by stonework. A set of stairs descended into the darkness and a musty odor rose up to greet them from the long closed off room. The old dwarf struck a match and lit a lantern as he beckoned them to follow. The steps were narrow and steep forcing them all to take great care in their descent; the dwarves however, seemed less troubled than the others.

At the base of the stairs stood a massive iron door without a handle of any kind. At first glance there seemed to be no way of opening it. Breegan handed the lantern to Valoria. "If'n ye'd be so kind, lass." As she took the lantern and held it aloft, the old dwarf reached into his shirt and pulled out a necklace that held a rather large, thin piece of metal with a pentagon shape to it. He detached it from the chain and then pressed it into a matching indentation centered on the door, giving it a slight twist to the right. He quickly removed the 'key' and refastened it to the chain around his neck. He slipped it back into his shirt as the sound of gears turning could be heard in the confined space. The metal door began to sink into the floor, revealing a well-lit room beyond. Breegan had a twinkle in his eyes as he grinned. "This be where the magic 'appens!" he said, rubbing his hands together briskly.

Taggarty let out an appreciative whistle. Inside the surprisingly large room was a treasure trove of weapons and armor. A forge sat centered upon the far wall; it hadn't seen use in decades, dusty cobwebs, long abandoned, stretched across its opening.

Breegan lit his pipe. "Go on," he encouraged as smoke rose in the air, "take yer pick."

Valoria picked up a longsword that had immediately caught her eye. She pulled it from the black scabbard with great care. The pommel glistened brightly in the light of the room; the sword's grip was blackened leather and seemed made for her hand, the blade itself was a blue-black color. The weapon was incredibly light. "What kind of steel is this?" she asked.

Breegan's eyes sparkled. "Tolvarian," he said.

She gave him a sharp look. "*Tolvarian?*" she was almost breathless.

He chuckled. "Aye, lass. Ye heard me correctly. Tha' sword be known as *Shadowfall.*"

Taggarty's eyes went wide and he whistled again as he hefted a battleaxe from its perch on the wall. The coloring of its double blades was the same blue-black as the sword. "I thought *Tolvaria* was na' but a myth!"

Breegan blew a series of smoke rings in Taggarty's direction; they burst upon his chest. "Tolvaria is na myth; I've been thar me self a time or two."

"*Deathbringer,*" Breegan said, blowing out a puff of smoke, "be the name o' tha' axe. Ye can hear its *deathsong* as ye wield it."

Taggarty sliced forward and back again, holding the battleaxe single-handed. "Weel I'll be, ya could knock me o'er wi' a feather from a downy chick!" he said appreciatively; Something akin to *angelic whispering* sounded as the blade cut through the air.

Candi selected a red bow and a quiver of finely crafted arrows. Breegan gave her a wink and a nod. "Ye 'ave a fine eye lass. Those are pure Drow artistry. The arrows be capable o' piercing stone wi' out splinterin' an' the bow itself will bend but na' snap. T'was a gift from the *Spider Queen* herself."

"Then I can't take it," Candi said as she started to return it.

"Bah!" Breegan said gruffly. "It needs ta belong ta someone tha'll truly appreciate it. Take them wi' me blessin'."

Candi smiled. "If you're sure."

"Aye, lass." He turned his attention to Trish. "What'll ye 'ave? Surely somethin' 'as caught yer eye?"

Trish crossed her arms over her chest. "I'm good."

"Suit yerself," he said with a shrug. He turned to the thief, "Wha' 'bout ye?"

Lightfingers placed his hand on the hilt of his shortsword and shook his head softly. "I think I'll stay with what I've got. She's served me well enough."

Breegan gave them all a long look as he puffed on his pipe. "Now, as ta the payment fer these fine weapons. All tha' I ask o' ye is tha' ye leave yer old ones 'ere. I'll be a one day meltin' 'em down fer use in somethin' else." He gave Taggarty a steady look. "Tha' goes fer yer da's battleaxe too, sentimental value or na."

Taggarty took his old battleaxe from his back and sighed heavily. He placed it upon the table, giving it a loving pat. He seemed reluctant to leave it behind.

By noon they were out of *Glynn* following the western road. For a while Annalise and her friends followed the wagon, skipping and laughing as they waved goodbye. "Come back, Papa! Travel safe!"

Breegan had a profound sadness wash over him that seemed to cloud his bright eyes as he rode upon the wagon seat next to Taggarty. "I'll likely ne'er see her again," he said as he returned her wave.

"Ye'll see 'em again," Tagg said feeling the sudden rush of emotion flood through him.

When the road split, they took the northern branch. Breegan waved a hand toward the other route. "Beyond the western ridges lay the *Outlands*, wild country tha'. A harsh land peopled by tough folk. Ye 'ave ta 'ave yer wits about ye at all times, e'en when ye sleep or yer likely ta na' be seein' the light o' day."

Tagg nodded. "Been thar a time or two, me self. Came close ta na' survivin' the ordeal. Some'ow we took a wrong turn an' found ourselves in the midst of *Drovar* territory. Came away wi' more an' a few scars."

"What are the *Drovar*?" Candi asked. She had been sitting behind them, listening to their tale.

Breegan lit his pipe and blew out a puff of smoke. "Some folk call 'em dark dwarves. They be a fierce lot, ta be sure." He shook his head. "Ye dinna' want ta get involved wi' their kind, especially a pretty lass such as yer self. They *do things* tha' just ain't right." He seemed to shiver.

"Oh!" Candi said fearfully. "Well, how do you tell them apart from other dwarves?" she wondered.

Breegan chuckled without humor. "Oh, ye'll know 'em when ye see 'em, na mistakin' 'em, tha's fer sure."

Taggarty nodded. "They be a bit smaller than yer average dwarf, wi' beady lil' eyes the color o' blood tha' kinda glow in the darkness. Fierce bastards they are."

"Aye," Breegan said in agreement. "Thar be stories tha' claim tha' ol' Kaspian Altair is the only man ta be on friendly terms wi' the Drovar on account o' he barters wi' 'em. Sells 'em the pretty lasses that' he captures. He 'as no use fer 'em. He claims tha' they be too fragile and canna' work in 'is mines."

Candi eased further away from the two dwarves no longer interested in the conversation they were having about the dwarf-like Drovar. She hoped never to encounter them; they sounded absolutely horrid! *Vespia* was a strange world populated by fantastic and strange—and *deadly* creatures. She scooted closer to where Ellisandra was napping, seeking comfort. She placed a gentle hand upon the girl, wondering if she were dreaming pleasantly; she had a smile on her lips.

Trish had been listening to Candi and the dwarves' conversation with her eyes closed. She knew that the talk of the Drovar had unsettled the blonde. Candi had always been easily frightened. Bekka claimed that Candi had changed drastically since coming to this side of the *Portal*, that she was stronger, more confident. If that truly were the case, Trish didn't see it. Candi had reverted back to her old routine of being just a follower in her company.

She watched the blonde as she absently caressed Ellie's back. "You know," Trish said softly, barely more than a whisper, "you can always go back through the *Portal* with me. We can go home."

Candi jolted, her fingertips leaving Ellie's back in mid caress; she hadn't thought that Trish was even awake. "I thought you were asleep."

Trish shook her head. "I've been listening to their conversation. But you should think about it," she said softly. "You and I can go home. We don't have to stay here."

Candi had a longing look in her eyes; as though she were considering what Trish was offering. Ellisandra stirred beside her. She glanced at the golden-haired girl and sighed. She looked at Trish and shook her head. "I can't go back. Not now. I have Ellie."

Trish practically snorted. "Don't be ridiculous, Candi. The girl can turn into a dragon. It won't be long before she grows tired of you. And when she does, she'll simply fly away. You probably won't ever see her again."

Tears formed in Candi's blue eyes and rolled down her cheeks. "Why would you say that? Why would you try to hurt me?" Trish could be *so* cruel sometimes!

Trish chuckled softly. "I'm not trying to be mean, Candi. I'm just pointing out the facts. Ellie is a dragon; she's going to want to be with her own kind. She belongs here. *Vespia* is her home. We can go home, too. We don't belong here. Don't you see that?"

Candi could feel the anger rise within her. Trish was wrong! "What about Bekka? Are we just gonna leave her behind?"

Trish sighed heavily. She reached out and placed a hand on Candi's knee. "We'll help Bekka with her fight against Sinnestra, but after that, there's nothing really to keep us here."

Candi shook her head. "I won't leave Bekka. I won't leave Ellie either."

Trish sat back with a shrug. "Suit yourself, Candi. I plan on going home."

Valoria, Bekka and Lightfingers had been riding ahead of the wagon, scouting the area. They stopped near a wooded spot close to *Dread Lake*. They dismounted and led their horses to the lake where they dipped their heads for a refreshing drink. Bekka shivered. She couldn't get the story of the dwarven village out of her head, she certainly couldn't bring herself to drink from the lake; no matter how refreshing it seemed. Valoria looked at her and laughed. Bekka slapped at her friend's arm. "Don't tease me!"

"Had you not heard the tale of *Mardoranhal* lying at the bottom of the lake you would be drinking from its refreshing water alongside your horse, none the wiser," Valoria said with a knowing grin.

Bekka scrunched her face and shivered again. "You're probably right, but I just can't bring myself to do it now. I wouldn't even want to swim in the lake; I'd be afraid that a long-dead dwarf would grab my ankles and pull me down to its murky depths."

Valoria laughed. "I'm sure it's just a story. It probably isn't even true."

Lightfingers arched his brows. "Oh, it's true enough, believe me."

Bekka shivered again. She took a step back from the water's edge. "I don't care."

"Yet you are perfectly willing to go up against Sinnestra, a demoness that you *know* is real."

Bekka gave her a lame smile. "You can't fight what you can't see. It's about picking your battles, I guess."

Lightfingers grinned but kept his silence.

Valoria looked around appraisingly. "This would make a good spot to camp for the night. If you want to ride back and get the others, I'll get started on setting things up. Maybe set a few snares."

Bekka nodded. "That sounds like a pretty good idea. We can get an early start in the morning and make it back to *Darkwater* sometime tomorrow afternoon, if all goes well."

Valoria handed her the reins to her horse. "Take my horse as well, Trish may want a break from the wagon."

"Good idea."

"I'll come along," Lightfingers said.

Taggarty halted the wagon as Bekka and the thief rode up. He gave them a concerned look. "Trouble? Where be the ranger?"

"She's setting up the campsite; she sent us back to lead you there. I brought her horse in case anyone wanted a break from the wagon."

Trish jumped over the side of the wagon. "Claim!" She took the reins and quickly mounted the horse; clearly not interested in giving anyone else the opportunity.

As they started off again, Trish gave Bekka a long look. She frowned, not knowing how to begin. Bekka smiled. "Something on your mind, Trish?" she asked.

Trish nodded, strands of auburn hair wisped across her face in the light breeze. "As a matter of fact, there is. I've been talking with Candace lately."

Bekka could sense that there was more. She was surprised

by Trish's seeming reluctance to say exactly what was on her mind, that was a problem she'd never had in the old days, back in *Midvale*. "Oh?"

Trish nodded. "I asked if she wanted to go back home."

Bekka felt like she'd just been stabbed with a white-hot poker. "What do you mean, *home*?" She somehow got the feeling that Trish wasn't referring to *Kensington Castle*. "You mean through the *Portal, home*? That home?"

Trish chuckled. "I do; back through the *Portal*. Home, home. Face it, neither of us truly belong here."

"I was born here," Bekka said.

Trish reached out her hand and touched Bekka's arm. "I get that, I do. But this is Candi and me that I'm talking about. We don't belong here. I mean, you are certainly welcome to come back with us, if you want. I'm sure we could work something out."

"You mean someplace for me to live, since my parents are both dead?" Bekka asked a little curtly.

"Look," Trish reached out to Bekka, "I didn't mean to upset you. Honest, I didn't."

Bekka took a long, slow breath. This whole idea about them returning through the *Portal* kinda stung. She could feel the tears threatening to come. That was the last thing she wanted right now; Trish to see her cry. She hadn't expected this; not yet. "Sooo... when is this all gonna happen?"

"Well, as it turns out, Candi refuses to leave. She doesn't want to desert you, or Ellisandra for that matter."

"You want me to talk to her? Convince her to go back?"

Trish swept her red hair behind her ear as she shook her head. "No, not at all. Besides, I don't think you could. She is devoted to the two of you. But I think that I want to go back. With Cleve gone there's nothing really to keep me here. Besides, I miss civilization." She paused, letting it all sink in. "Nevertheless, I won't go until after we've rescued your baby brother from Sinnestra. Once we've dealt with her, I want to return home, to *Midvale*."

They rode along in silence, keeping pace with the wagon. A cool breeze blew from the west. The sun was hanging low in the western sky, beginning to dip beyond the distant mountains. The air was fresh, soothing. Finally, Bekka looked over at Trish, "You're not the same person that came through that *Portal* all those months ago. You've changed. We all have; but you, I think, most of all. You've said it yourself."

Trish chuckled. "Yes. I have changed. *A lot*. I admit it. But that doesn't mean I can't go back; leave all this craziness behind. I can forget all about it," she snapped her fingers, "just like that."

"Bullshit," Bekka said with a laugh. "You're delusional if you think you can just forget everything that has happened. I know I can't. I won't. We've all lost someone, some of us more than others. I was stabbed by Maragh, almost killed; and if I'm not mistaken, so were you." She stared at Trish. "Mom and Lady Rosa said you were pregnant at the time. You've said yourself how that experience changed you, though you've never been clear as to what extent. How can you tell me that you can simply forget it all? Especially after some of the things you've done?"

Tears clouded Trish's green eyes; she quickly wiped them away. "I'll never forget any of it, that's true. But staying here on this side of the *Portal* only keeps it fresh in my mind and I don't like it. I miss my family. I'll help you get your brother back, but after that, I'm going home. I'm afraid that if I remain here, I'll lose whatever humanity I have left. That scares the *Hell* out of me!"

"There may be something that we can do that'll change everything," Bekka said after a moment of silence. Rosa came to me in a dream and told me about *Timestones*. Supposedly they can be used to alter time so that events can be changed. She said that it is the darkest of magic and could be risky."

"*Timestones...*" Trish said thoughtfully. "Crap like that never turns out well in the movies."

Bekka nodded. "Tell me about it."

By the time they got to the campsite, the sun was already gone from the sky. The reddish-orange glow above the distant mountains was only a sliver, blending with the deep purple and black of the coming night. In the heavens, stars could be seen between the gaps in the clouds. Valoria had done well in their absence. Two rabbits were roasting over the firepit and several nice-sized trout were already frying in a pan.

Trish and Bekka dismounted and picketed their horses in an area where there was plenty of grass for them to nibble upon. Lightfingers had been following some distance behind, giving the girls a chance to talk. Taggarty and Breegan stopped the wagon and unhitched the two draft horses, picketing them with the others. Candi and Ellisandra climbed out of the wagon and yawned and stretched. It was good to be back on solid ground. Everyone was tired and hungry. Tomorrow promised to be another long day.

Chapter 65
Betrayal Dawns

Trevor could see the glow of the lanterns from *Serendil Brenatis* high up in the tall trees of the forest as they approached. The sun was quickly fading, dipping below the jagged peaks of the *Stone Pike Mountains*. He smiled over at Lithania. "We're almost there," he reached out to her and squeezed her hand. "Are you excited to see Aloena again?"

Lithania grunted in response.

He couldn't get over the feeling that something was troubling her. Ever since they had ridden through the northern pass at the eastern edge of the *Griffin Peaks* he had noticed a drastic change in her mood. Now, the closer they came to the elven tree city, she seemed to grow even more somber. Finally, he couldn't take it any longer. "Is something wrong?" he asked with a furrowed brow.

She glared at him, giving him a look that clearly said he was going down a slippery slope, a very dangerous path. He ignored it. "I wish you would just tell me what's bothering you. I can't help you if I don't know what's troubling you. *Talk* to me, Litha."

She abruptly reined in her horse. "You want to know what's *bothering* me?" she snapped. Her eyes burned with fire, surprising him. At his nod, she continued. "To begin with, I am miserable on this beast. I am very pregnant, and I think our child is also uncomfortable being jostled around on the back of this horse as much as I. We are going back to *Serendil Brenatis*, where I suspect we will be greeted with far less enthusiasm than you obviously expect. Aloena will *not* be happy with me for taking off as I did. Nor will she be pleased that I did not return sooner. I suspect that she will be absolutely *livid*. And then there is Elanthor, he will not be delighted about me being pregnant with *your* child. He has always been against *half-breeds*, there are many among my people that are. You know how he feels about you, about humans in general."

Trevor sighed. "All good points. But I think that you give Aloe too little credit. She will be thrilled to see you again and ecstatic that you are fixing to have a baby! And furthermore, I think that Elan and I are getting along a whole lot better now. His time as co-leader of the elves has brought a certain *wisdom* to him. He has grown. I really think that he will be happy for the both of us."

Lithania sighed as she shook her head. "I can only hope that you are right. Forgive me. I am truly very sorry. It is just my body adjusting to the pregnancy. I am in a foul mood. I feel bloated, and I know my feet are swollen. They hurt. I am miserable. It is not fair to blame you for any of this." She shrugged. "But somehow I do."

Trevor blinked. "Oh." He remembered how his Aunt Sarah was when she was pregnant. His Uncle Mason had to walk around on eggshells the entire time she was carrying the baby. Her hormones were out of control. She would be happy and smiling one minute and sobbing the next! Trevor looked at Lithania and smiled. "I'm sorry. I'll try to be more understanding."

"That is all that I ask," Lithania said with a smile. She started her horse moving. "I am cold. Let us get this over with." She placed her hood over her head and pulled her cloak tighter. A cool breeze blew through the forest as they rode along. Only the crickets seemed to be in a joyful mood.

Looking up into the canopy of the tall trees, Trevor could barely see the hidden sentries watching as they passed underneath. They were easier to spot if you knew where to look. He couldn't resist the urge to wave. He had no doubt that their presence would be announced long before their arrival in the elven tree city. Both Aloena and Elanthor were determined to not allow the city to fall under siege again without advanced warning.

They dismounted at the foot of the wide staircase that led up into the trees, an elven runner ran out and retrieved their horses and led them away. Trevor reached out and took Lithania's hand and gave it a reassuring squeeze. "Ready?" he asked. He could scarcely see her nod beneath the hood that she wore; her face was nearly completely hidden by the fabric.

Elanthor met them at the top of the first landing. "Trevor! It is good to see you! We were so afraid that you had been killed by the Deceivers!" He glanced at Trevor's companion. "I see you brought a friend!" He didn't wait for a response; he quickly ushered them along. "Come, Aloena will be so happy to see you." He had a grin on his face as he led the two of them up to the highest tier of the tree city. "I think you will be surprised!"

They turned to the right at the top of the stairs and went about midway down the boardwalk. Elanthor rapped a fist upon the door and pushed it open. "Aloe, Trevor and a friend are here!" he quickly stepped to the side so that those that followed could enter the room.

Trevor saw that the blonde elf maiden was tending to a patient. She turned and smiled at him. "Trevor, it is good to see you are alive and well!" Smiling, Aloena stepped to the side so that Trevor could see the woman lying in the bed.

Trevor froze.

Lithania was lying in the bed, she had bandages upon her head and right arm; but it was clearly she. He blinked in disbelief, taking a faltering step backward he bumped into the figure beside him. He turned and looked at her. "How is this even possible?" he asked. He had a strange feeling rising up through his core.

Aloe had a sad look on her face. "We went searching for the both of you when you did not return. We found Litha, badly burned and near death in what was left of the *Vile Forest*. We brought her here and have been doing our best caring for her since then. It has been touch and go but her strength has surprised me."

Trevor looked at the woman by his side. He pointed to the bed. "If *that* is Lithania, then who...?" But he already knew.

The deceiver flung an arm around him and pulled him roughly against her body; the blade of her sword was at his throat in a flash. The flurried movement caused the hood to fall away. Both Aloena and Elanthor gasped as they saw Lithania holding Trevor hostage; their eyes went to the *other* Lithania that had been badly injured and was lying in the bed.

Elanthor quickly reached for the sword that was leaning against the wall. "Trevor! You have brought a Deceiver amongst us!"

Trevor could scarcely believe what he was hearing—let alone what he was seeing. If the figure lying in the bed was truly Lithania, then the woman who now held a sword to his throat *couldn't* be! The full realization of all that had occurred struck him like a ton of bricks. He felt ill. *"Oh, God... What have I done?"*

The memory of his intimacy with whom he thought was Litha flashed through his mind.

"Do not be fooled by them!" Lithania's voice whispered in his ear. *"Do not let them deceive you, my love! You know who I am! You saved me from the fires that burned the Vile Forest! I am having your child!"*

Trevor felt like he was living in a horrible nightmare.

He was being forced to back out of the room. *"She has either deceived them all, or perhaps they are Deceivers as well!"* Lithania's voice continued. *"We must leave this place! We must take our child to safety! We were wrong to come here!"*

Trevor's eyes filled with tears. He remembered how the *Blade of the Spider's Kiss* had not glowed when Lithania held it at *Kensington Castle*. Somehow the weapon had known that the elf maiden was not what she seemed. It could not be deceived as they all had been. He closed his eyes tightly. "You're right, Litha! I won't allow their deception to harm you or our child!"

They were out on the boardwalk now. He felt the sword leave

his throat. He turned toward Lithania and smiled. "Give me the sword, I'll protect you both."

Lithania allowed Trevor to take the sword from her grasp. She cupped his cheek in the palm of her hand. "I love you, Trevor!"

He wrapped his arms around her and kissed her lightly on the lips. "I know," he said. In the next instant he flung the two of them against the railing. It was flimsily tied and with their combined weight it broke away easily.

Aloe and Elanthor ran to prevent them from falling but it was too late. As they reached the edge of the boardwalk, they could see their bodies lying broken and entwined upon the forest floor. The visage of Lithania seemed to shimmer and fade away, replaced by the gray-mottled skin of the Deceiver. In death, the illusion was shattered...

Chapter 66
Visions of Timestones

Bekka was always a little saddened by the school day coming to an end on Friday afternoon, but not this time. She was eager to get back home and enjoy a nice, home-cooked dinner with her parents. Her mother had promised a nice pot roast with mashed potatoes, brown gravy with carrots and celery; Bekka's favorite. It was good to leave *Vespia* behind. Now, after she'd used the *Timestones*, it was as if it had never happened; it was as though it had only been a bad dream. *A nightmare.*

She pulled her math book out of her locker and tucked it with her history text into her backpack. She *still* had homework to get out of the way before she could really enjoy the weekend. She slammed her locker closed and twirled the combination dial to secure it until Monday. She smiled as she saw Candi and Trish flirting with Cleve and Jacob at the far end of the hallway, waiting for her. Trevor was there too. He was watching her. She passed Ginger Whitney and Scott Thompson, they were hanging all over one another, talking about the Carnival out on

Miller's Farm. She smiled, knowing that they were now safe as well.

As she walked down the hallway, she heard the distinct sound of horses' hooves pounding upon the tiled flooring of *Midvale High*. They were coming up fast behind her. Turning, she saw Maragh swing his sword at her, she felt the biting sting as it slit her throat, her mother's necklace came off in her hand, both were covered in blood—*her blood!*

Bekka awoke with a start, kicking out from under the bedroll. She could see the others were soundly sleeping; it had been nothing more than a dream. She hadn't used the *Timestones*. They had not yet faced Sinnestra at *Silver Frost Keep*. She rolled up her bedding, no longer interested in sleep. She couldn't be certain whether she had just experienced another vision, or if it had simply been a horrible dream.

Was it a warning? Was something telling her that if she attempted to use the mystical *Timestones* her efforts would prove fruitless? Rosa had told her in no uncertain terms that use of the stones was dark magic and the cost would be high. Was this what it meant? Would she be the only victim if she were to use the *Timestones*? Would everyone else survive? Could her sacrifice save everyone else? It was something to consider.

If she used the *Timestones* and it was as though she never come through the *Portal* in the first place, what else would be changed? If she hadn't gone to the Carnival out on Miller's Farm, both Ginger Whitney and Scott Thompson would still be alive—she wouldn't have been there to drop the snow cone all over Ginger's blouse, so she wouldn't have been wearing Bekka's jacket. Trish, Candi and her would not have gone to see the Gypsy fortuneteller at the Carnival, either. So the old woman would not have disguised her scent with the onyx dust. Nobody would have gone through the *Portal* and been transported to *Vespia*; Cleve's cousin Jacob would still be alive and so would Cleve. Her parents would not be dead.

But what else would be altered?

Would Valoria manage to go up against her father? Would Sinnestra still sit on the throne of the *Spider Queen*? What of the *Band of Steel*? Would Vincente and the other Roma that had lost their lives still be alive? And what of Rosa?

Would Bekka's sacrifice save them all? Was that possible?

It made Bekka's head spin.

Lost in her thoughts, Bekka stared at the dying embers of the campfire as the others began to stir around her. The first rays of sunrise were painting the eastern sky with a red and gold hue. The dwarves were harnessing the horses back up to the wagon. Ellisandra had morphed back into a dragon and was scouting what lay ahead. Valoria was nowhere to be seen.

Trish frowned at her friend as she added more wood to the fire pit so that breakfast could be prepared. "How long have you been sitting there?"

Bekka blinked, shrugging. "I... I couldn't sleep."

"You could've kept the fire going, though," Trish admonished her. "Instead of letting it die."

"Sorry," Bekka said softly. "I didn't even think about it."

Candi glared at the redhead. "Lighten up. Bekka has a lot on her mind."

Trish shook her head. "If you're gonna sit up by the fire, you might as well add a log or two to keep it going. A little bit of consideration for everyone else would be nice, it's all I'm sayin'."

Candi placed a hand on Bekka's shoulder as she sat beside her. "She's just got a stick up her butt, ignore her." She pulled Bekka against her. "What's on your mind? Anything I can help you with?"

Bekka shook her head. "No, I'm fine. But Trish is right. I should've paid more attention to the fire. It's a chilly morning."

Candi batted a hand in the air. "Bah! The sun's coming up and it is chasing the chill away. Before long we'll be hot and sweaty."

Bekka scrunched her nose and chuckled softly. "That sounds appealing."

Trish sat across from her friends. "So, you wanna tell us what's got you so troubled? Maybe we can help."

"Who says I'm troubled?"

"Come on, Beks! Candi and I are your best friends. We know you. So come on, spill the beans; I bet you've been thinking about those rocks." She frowned. "What did you call them? Time-rocks, or something?"

Bekka grinned. *"Timestones."*

"Whatever," Trish said. "So, let's hear it. If you talk to us about it, we can help. That's always been the case with the three of us. We share our problems and our concerns, and we find a solution."

Candi nodded. "She's right, you know. We've always helped each other, but we can't really do that unless we share." She gave Bekka's shoulder a little shake. "So, what is bothering you sweetie?"

Bekka sighed. "Well, I was considering using the *Timestones* to change the way things have played out. But I had a dream, or a vision—I don't really know which; I don't even know if I was asleep or awake at the time. It's given me a lot to think about."

"What are these *Timestones*, anyway?" Candi asked.

"Dark magic," Trish said. "They can allow you to go back in time and change things."

Lightfingers frowned darkly. "*Timestones* aren't even real, are they? I've heard old tales about them over the years, but always dismissed them as childhood stories."

"Well, real or not," Candi said raising her brows. "I hate to be like the geeky one, but I have to just say, that for every action there's an equal and opposite reaction. I think it's a law, or something."

Trish waved a hand at Candi as she rolled her eyes at Bekka. "So says the science nerd."

Candi frowned. "I'm just saying that we need to consider what can happen. Is it worth the cost of trying to change things? Maybe these things were *supposed* to happen in the grand cosmic scheme of things. If that's truly the case, then changing them might not even be possible. We could only be making things worse!"

Bekka nodded. "I know. Everything you've said, I've already considered. I still don't know what to do. Besides, it really doesn't matter at the moment. We don't have the *Timestones*. We don't know what they look like, or where we can find them. It's just got me thinking about them, that's all."

Candi had an uneasy look. "Trish said they were dark magic; does that mean that they aren't safe to use?"

Bekka's left brow rose slightly; she couldn't meet the blonde's gaze. "There could be a price to pay for their usage."

"What price?" Candi asked, not liking any of this.

Bekka shrugged. "I don't know."

Candi's eyes grew wide. "*What?* You don't know, but you're considering it anyway? I don't like the sound of this, really I don't." She looked across the fire at Trish. "What about you? Are you okay with any of this?"

Trish glanced at Bekka and then at Candi. She shrugged. "It's not my call."

"Seriously?" Candi couldn't believe what she had just heard. She looked at Bekka. "It sounds really dangerous to me."

Bekka nodded. "I know, I know. But it may be our only option in the end." She still had a lot to think about. The good thing was that she had time.

Candi stood abruptly. "Just so you know, I don't want any part of it. Using dark magic can damn your soul, especially if you don't have any idea what the Hell you're doing!"

"How would you know that it'd damn your soul? How could you possibly know that?" Trish asked.

Candi rolled her eyes. "Oh come on! We've all seen it happen in the movies!"

"That's just Hollywood!" Trish laughed.

Candi placed her hands on her hips. "That may very well be the case but," she turned her attention back to Bekka, "I know that Rosa always cautioned against using dark magic. If Rosa said to not do it, then that is good enough for me!"

"Well," Trish said with a smirk, "Lady Rosa is the one that told Beks about the *Timestones* in the first place!"

"*What? When?*" Candi asked, completely taken by surprise at this revelation.

Bekka's eyes had started to water. "She came to me in a vision before we arrived in Glynn."

"A vision?" Candi said. "And what did this phantom Rosa say in this vision of yours? Did she tell you to use the *Timestones*? What were her exact words?"

Bekka remained silent; she just stared at the blonde. She didn't like feeling like she was on trial. Trish spoke, "Give it a rest, Madam Prosecutor!"

Candi glared at the redhead as though she were offended. "No. I want to know what Rosa said." She glanced back at Bekka. "Did she tell you to use the stones or not?"

Bekka swallowed. "She cautioned against it. She said that Han might try and use them to save Sinnestra."

Candi gave her a quizzical look. "But Han is *just* a baby for Pete's sake!"

"Not anymore," Bekka said with a sigh. A tear rolled unheeded down her cheek.

Candi sat back down by her distraught friend. "What do you mean 'not anymore'? I don't follow you."

Bekka stood. "Evidently Sinnestra went through some dark portal to another realm where time passes differently. Han has grown up there. He's a man now and he thinks that Sinnestra is his mother. He wants to save her. Rosa says he will try and use the *Timestones*."

Candi blinked, looking at Trish. "Unbelievable!"

Trish shook her head slowly. "We have to stop him. We can't let him use them to save her."

"I know," Bekka said. "We have to find them and destroy them if we can or use them ourselves."

Taggarty grabbed Breegan's arm as they finished hooking the draft horses back up to the wagon. "Did ye hear wha' they've been discussin'?" he inclined his head toward the campfire.

Breegan shook his head. "Na, me hearin' ain't wha' it used ta be."

"They said somethin' 'bout *Timestones*. I was wonderin' wha' they might be."

"*Timestones*, ye say? Hmph, heard stories 'bout 'em when I was but a wee laddie. Ne'er seen 'em me self. Heard they were dark magic, 'bout the darkest ye can get."

"Sounded ta me like Sinnestra may 'ave Bekka's brother use 'em ta save her."

Breegan ran a hand over the top of his head. "Weel, we canna' let tha' 'appen!"

Taggarty nodded. "Aye, tha's wha' I thought." He gave Breegan a steady look. "We best keep the fact tha' we know 'bout these stones ta ourselves fer now."

"Aye."

Valoria returned to the campsite with half a dozen trout. She handed them to Taggarty. "This was all I could manage."

"Twill 'ave ta do. I'll fry 'em up and we can all 'ave a wee bite a'for we head out."

Ellisandra rejoined the group in human form as they were breaking camp. "I did not see any sign of Kaspian Altair or his army. Perhaps they have returned to their fortress to lick their wounds." There was a hint of pride in her voice.

Candi shook her head. "I really don't like you flying off like that; not after what happened the last time. You might not be so lucky."

Ellie shrugged. "We needed to know what was up ahead. I made sure that I flew high enough to where they could not strike me." She placed a hand on Candi's arm. "Do not worry about me. I can take care of myself."

Candi wasn't happy with her reply. "Like last time?"

Chapter 67
The Obsidian Graveyard

Between *Darken Wood* and *The Vale* they had an unexpected find; it hadn't been this way when they had traveled south. The grassland was charred and puddles of hardened obsidian were scattered everywhere. Here and there weapons and armor could be seen lying abandoned upon the ground.

"What is all this?" Bekka asked as she rode alongside Lightfingers.

"It has to be the result of Ellisandra's attack on Kaspian Altair and his army," Valoria said.

"But what is with all the black puddles? It almost looks like melted glass."

Valoria shrugged. "Maybe each one represents a soldier in Kaspian's army. He uses *Darkwater Stones* to create them. Maybe this is all that remains after a fire-breathing dragon attacks."

Lightfingers nodded. "That certainly sounds reasonable." He glanced over at Taggerty, "Like the stones you carry in your pocket after killing Kaspian's men."

Taggerty nodded soberly, "Aye lad."

Bekka shook her head. "I guess so. I mean, I know when you strike one down with a weapon all that is left on the ground is a handful of stones; no corpse. But that is only if they were created by the *Stones*. Surely he had other troops, besides." She couldn't stop the shiver that ran through her. "This place gives me the creeps."

"Would you prefer to see a bunch of charred skeletons lying everywhere?" the ranger asked with a raised brow.

Bekka's face scrunched. "Oh God, no! Absolutely not."

Valoria chuckled softly. "I didn't think so."

"In my world they call this *'Dragonglass'*. It was used to kill white walkers on the *Game of Thrones*."

"I did not know you had dragons on the other side of the *Portal*."

"We don't," Bekka smiled. "Except in fantasy stories. The *Dragonglass* was used in a television show to defeat some really bad enemies; it was about the only way to kill them."

Valoria shook her head. She was trying her best to follow Bekka, but she was having considerable difficulty. "I'm not sure I understand. What is a television show?"

Bekka laughed, rolling her eyes. "Well, a television is a little box that you sit in front of and watch..."

Valoria raised a hand in the air, cutting her off. She shook her head. "Forget I even asked. It sounds like a colossal waste of time!"

Bekka laughed. "Oh, it is, trust me. But it can be entertaining."

"I'd rather be outside in the fresh air."

"Television had its moments!" Bekka said defensively.

"Oh," Valoria said with a grin, "I'm certain that it did."

"I think it might be fun for you to see the other side of the *Portal*!" Bekka said.

Valoria shook her head. "I'd never fit in. I'd be like a fish out of water. Besides, I have difficulty enough navigating my own world without everyone's stares. It makes me uncomfortable."

"Well," Bekka said with a dreamy smile, "it would be fun to see your reaction to everything, anyway."

Valoria shook her head and chuckled. "I saw enough of the other side when we first met. Some of the garments you were wearing..."

Bekka laughed.

Lightfingers had grown silent. He didn't particularly like Bekka talking about life on the other side of the *Portal*. Perhaps he feared that she might decide to go back, leaving him behind. He wasn't sure that he liked that idea. *She was unlike any woman that he had ever known.* He didn't want to lose her.

Chapter 68
The Return to Darkwater

It was late afternoon when they reached the bridge going into *Darkwater*; the breeze was cooler now as they crossed the *River of Sorrow*; already the warmth of the dying sun was beginning to wane. Smoke from various chimneys was rising into the brisk air. The inhabitants were beginning to settle in for the evening.

Taren Toshe greeted them with a curt nod as he offered to tend the horses. The young man said little but was otherwise friendly. Bran, his father, had already ceased work at the smithy for the day; but they knew that the *clang* of his hammer would sound at first light. Trish jokingly referred to him as *'Rooster'*. Carandra greeted them at the door of the *Spilt Tankard* with a welcoming smile. "Come! Come," she said, "take a seat by the fire. I 'ave a nice vegetable soup ta warm ye up from the inside." She winked at Taggarty and Breegan. "An' I'll fetch ye both a mug o' *Firewater* as well."

Taggarty grinned appreciatively. "If'n ye were na' already

spoke fer, I'd try an' steal ye away me self!" He winked at Breegan. "A fine woman tha'."

"Aye," Breegan acknowledged. "As fine a woman as me own daughter-in-law Fomrelsia!"

"Aye," Tagg agreed with a nod.

Lightfingers chuckled as he followed them inside.

After their meal had been cleared away, and their tankards refilled with their drink of choice, they sat around the hearth listening to the crackle of yew logs burning. Breegan struck a match and lit his pipe, blowing his customary rings of smoke into the air about his head. With a sly grin he sent one toward Trish; it was *somehow* fashioned in the shape of a heart. When she glared at him, he chuckled softly. "Always 'ad me a soft spot fer gingers," he said with a wink.

"Careful, ole man," Trish teased, "I might be more than you can handle."

His cheeks turned rosy. "Weel now, dinna' tempt me lass! I always wanted ta die wi' a smile on me face!" He chuckled robustly, slapping his knee. "I might surprise ye a wee bit!"

Trish rolled her eyes. "Smoking is bad for you, I don't like it. It makes you stink and I don't approve."

Breegan seemed a bit put out. "Bah," he said.

Bekka cleared her throat. "I hate to interrupt your playful banter, but I was wondering when you think we should get started for *Silver Frost Keep*? I'd like to get through the *Demon Spires* before another snow falls."

Breegan nodded as he sent three smoke rings into the air above his head. They grew larger as they rose, and each one that followed the first went into the middle of the one before. Finally, the single enlarged ring of smoke burst apart on the beamed ceiling of the tavern. "Aye, lass, tha' would be most prudent. If'n ye like, we can start out in two days' time. Tha'll give us the opportunity ta gather wha' supplies we might need. Perhaps ye might be able ta talk young Taren into drivin' the wagon fer us. When we strike out upon the path through the *Spires*, we willna' be a needin' the beasties any longer; he can return wi' 'em so's they na' be lost in the wild."

Bekka nodded. "I'll certainly speak with his mother and see if she is agreeable. I hadn't really thought about what would become of the horses; I guess that I assumed that we'd have them all the way to the Keep."

He chewed on the end of his pipe. "Tha' willna' be possible. The trail we must foller through the *Demon Spires* is a wee bit treacherous even in the springtime. It'll likely be twice as bad now."

Taggarty stroked his beard thoughtfully. "Hmph," he grunted. "Thar be no tellin' wha' shape the trail be in. Ye 'ave na' traveled it in a hundred years or so. Could be many a thing tha' alter it. Wind, rain, ice an' such."

Breegan raised his brows as he blew another smoke ring. "Aye, tha's so." He chuckled softly. He tapped the ash out of the pipe's chamber and smothered it underfoot. He pulled out his pouch and began to tamp the tobacco into his pipe. He pulled the drawstrings on the pouch, closing it. He offered it to Taggarty. "Smoke?"

Taggarty shook his head and raised his tankard into the air. "Nah. I prefer ta 'ave a nice, stiff drink."

Breegan shrugged as he put the pouch into his pocket. "Suit yer self, lad." He struck a match on the arm of his chair and held the flame over his pipe. He drew the fire down into the chamber by sucking upon the stem; finally thin curls of smoke escaped his lips. He shook the match out and tossed it into the fireplace where it was quickly consumed by the flames. Holding the pipe with his teeth he laced his fingers together over his chest and closed his eyes. He propped his feet onto a wooden footrest in front of the hearth. Occasionally he would puff on his pipe sending clouds into the air. After a while he seemed to have fallen asleep.

Bekka was the last of the girls to go upstairs to bed; the others had all sporadically disappeared after dinner. It had been a long, tedious trip from *Glynn* to *Darkwater*, and they were facing another in the following days. Everyone was exhausted.

Taggarty rose from his chair, belched, and then staggered off in search of more to drink. Breegan opened one eye and saw that he had been deserted, but he didn't seem to mind. In no time at all he was breathing deeply and softly snoring.

The following day seemed to fly quickly by. Carandra and Bran had no problem with Taren driving the wagon to the base of the *Demon Spires*, and then returning with all of the horses after dropping the adventurers off. It would also give him the opportunity to hunt and bring back game for Carandra to cook.

The other supplies that they needed for their journey were found at the various shops in *Darkwater*; which consisted mostly of foodstuffs, warmer clothes and the like. They required very little; they weren't preparing for a prolonged siege of *Silver Frost Keep*. It wasn't like they needed supplies to outfit an army, there were only seven of them. With any luck at all, they would enter the fortress, maintain the element of surprise, find Sinnestra and do what needed to be done.

It sounded easy. Simple plans were often the best. They had a better chance of success. But what they were proposing was anything *but* simple. There were too many unknowns. They weren't even certain that this 'backdoor' into the Keep remained undiscovered by Sinnestra and her army; they could have found it years ago and eliminated it altogether or simply posted guards upon it. Nor did they know how large a force Sinnestra commanded; they could easily find themselves overwhelmed. And this was all dependent upon whether they actually made it inside the fortress. The route to *Silver Frost Keep* was undoubtedly treacherous; they could perish before they ever arrived at their destination.

These thoughts weighed heavily upon Bekka, keeping her from much needed sleep. They were leaving *Darkwater* at first light; it was already well past midnight. She dressed and went outside, hoping the fresh air would help to clear her mind. As she stepped out of the front door of the inn, she found Valoria standing at the edge of the porch. She was staring off to the north, at the rugged peaks of the *Demon Spires* rising above the distant trees beyond *Darkwater Lake*.

Bekka chuckled softly. "What's the matter, you couldn't sleep?"

Valoria shook her head. "No, but I see that I'm not alone."

Bekka crossed her arms over her chest. "I've been thinking about what we're about to do, and I wonder if it really is what we *should* be doing. We've lost so much chasing after Sinnestra, I'm just not sure if it's even worth it."

"She needs to pay for all that she has done. She has murdered people that we know and love, she's kidnapped your baby brother—robbed you of his childhood. You have not seen him grow to adulthood; your bond with your brother has been stolen. We *have* to stop her."

Bekka sighed. "I know."

They were silent for a long time, both staring off into the night. The crescent moon shone brightly in the night sky. A few stars could be seen, sparkling like glimmering diamonds upon a sea of ebony. Finally, Bekka broke the silence. "I keep having visions, nightmares really, about the *Timestones*."

"Oh?" Valoria said. She studied her friend, waiting for her to continue.

Bekka nodded. "Each time I use the stones, it never ends well. If I use them to change the past and save everyone, then I get killed. Maragh comes through the *Portal* and kills me. Either I get killed or everyone else does. It doesn't seem to matter, really."

She shook her head. "In one vision I tried going back to the point where Lithania first struck Sinnestra with the *Blade of the Spider's Kiss*, and that ended horribly. Sinnestra killed Candi and Vincente and then you and finally me." Tears fell from her eyes. "It just doesn't seem to make any difference. It seems that every scenario in which the stones are used, it never works out like I want."

Valoria shrugged. "I don't know. Maybe you should abandon all thought of using the *Timestones*. Evidently you are having these visions so that you can see that it is pointless to attempt it. I mean, something is obviously trying to tell you not to use them; You change some things hoping to make the outcome better but fate always intervenes making things worse than before."

Bekka nodded. "I know. But Rosa told me in that first vision where she told me about the *Timestones*, she said Han was going to seek them out in order to save Sinnestra. What if he is successful?"

"So what are you saying?" Valoria asked, turning to face her. She leaned up against the porch rail and crossed her arms; it was cold.

"We can't use them, obviously, but we can't allow my brother to either. We have to stop him; destroy the *Timestones* if we can."

"What happens if Han tries to stop us?"

That had been what troubled Bekka the most. If Han stood in their way, they would have to deal with him. *Could she do what was necessary? If she couldn't get Han to see reason, would she be able to prevent him from using the Stones to save Sinnestra?* Bekka sighed, shaking her head. "Then I guess we do what we must."

Chapter 69
The Demon Spires

Taren Toshe returned his mother's hug, it seemed that she would never release him from her tight embrace. Bran had to gently pry his wife from their son. "Let 'im go, Carandra. They need ta be goin'; they will na' wait for 'im."

Once separated from her tall son, she covered her mouth with trembling fingers. "Take care o' yer self, Taren. Come back ta me, ye hear?"

He nodded, blushing. "Aye."

He glanced at his father as the big man gripped his shoulder with a powerful hand. "Take na chances, ye hear? Ye'll 'ave chores ta tend ta once ye return. Only hunt if'n ye spot somethin' right away, dinna' waste time. Remember, if ye go lookin', trouble will likely find ye!"

Taren nodded. He glanced toward the wagon; Breegan was already starting to slap the reins to get the horses moving, following along behind Lightfingers, Valoria, Bekka and Trish, who were all on horseback. "I know, Pa," he said hurriedly.

He turned to leave but hesitated and quickly stepped back and kissed his mother one last time. "Be seein' ye both!" He sprinted after the rolling wagon and jumped in the back. He dangled his feet over the rear of the wagon and waved at his folks. They had both descended the porch steps and were waving with their free hand; their other arms were wrapped around each other for support.

Candi smiled at Taren. "You have very sweet parents."

He nodded with a grin. "Aye, tha' I do!" He glanced at Ellisandra who was sitting up front with the two dwarves, and then smiled at Candi, "Wha' about yer sister and ye, where are yer folks?"

Candi laughed. "Oh, Ellie isn't my sister."

He had a shocked expression on his face. "I thought ye were; ye both 'ave the same light hair. Dinna' tell me tha' she is yer daughter then; ye dinna' look old enough ta 'ave a bairn o' tha' age."

Candi placed a hand on Taren's arm and giggled. "Oh, no. That isn't it either. Ellie and I are... well, it's complicated."

He frowned. "I'm na' sure tha' I understand."

Candi smiled. She glanced toward Ellisandra and then looked at Taren. "I guess that you could say we are friends, but it's more than that, really. Somehow we were fated to be together." She shook her head. "I guess I don't understand it very well, either." Her eyes suddenly went wide. "I certainly can't explain it very well."

She frowned. She didn't know how to make him understand, especially since she, herself, didn't fully grasp it. She couldn't expect him to understand that Ellisandra was hatched from a dragon egg a short time ago and now appeared as a teenager. Nor could she explain their unique bond. She couldn't tell him that Ellie could morph into a dragon whenever she wanted; the fewer that knew that the better.

She turned and watched Ellie sitting between the two dwarves. They were having a conversation that she couldn't hear, but evidently the girl was entertaining both men; she had them laughing.

Candi shifted her position in the wagon so that she was now sitting beside Taren on the edge of the wagon. She swung her feet in the air, back and forth, as they dangled above the ground, with no real purpose. She tried her best to explain. "I guess you could say that Ellie and I kinda look out for each other. We protect one another. We are friends, but more than just friends, if you know what I mean."

Taren frowned, lightly nodding his head. "Kind o' like family?"

Candi smiled. "Yeah, something like that." She nodded. "We're family."

The road north had not seen much use in recent months, and it was barely perceptible beneath the mounds of snow that had fallen. Valoria, Lightfingers, Trish and Bekka were riding abreast of one another, taking it slow, so that the wagon could easily follow.

A light northern wind was blowing across *Darkwater Lake* making the air seem even colder. Their exposed skin was starting to ache from the extreme chill in the frosty air. They adjusted their clothing so that they could hide behind the collars of their coats and the scarves that they wore in an attempt to keep warm. Little more than their eyes were exposed, but there was nothing they could do about that. Bekka and Trish longed for a pair of ski goggles, but that comfort was of another world.

The going was painstakingly slow and miserable.

The biting air off the lake was intense. Candi and Taren moved to the front of the wagon and huddled together behind the dwarves; Ellisandra joined them, burrowing her body beneath the thick, fur blankets that they had brought along. Sensing the girl's need for warmth, Candi pulled her close against her body; she could feel the coldness of Ellie's hair against her face.

They continued this excruciatingly slow pace until mid-afternoon. They stopped near a grove of trees that was far enough away from the lake so that they were no longer pelted by the frosty breeze and bits of ice blowing across the turbulent water. Neither they, nor the horses could go any further without rest.

Bran Toshe had insisted that Taren load a couple of hay bales into the wagon. His foresight was now greatly appreciated by everyone. The grass was completely covered in snow, and what little was exposed was not enough for the horses to eat. They set up camp in an area that required very little clearing of snow and ice. The thick canopy of the trees had prevented the snow from accumulating in mounds; there were small drifts here and there, but nothing of any great worth. It had also kept out the sunlight, so there was very little grass to be found anyway.

Breegan lit his pipe. "T'would be best if'n we remained 'ere until the morrow. We can get a fresh start in the morn."

Valoria nodded. "How much farther until we're forced to go the rest of the way on foot?"

He stroked his beard. "Weel, tha' depends," he said with a shrug as he looked around. "We'll need ta cross a couple o' streams tha' lie in our path a'for we get ta the footpath leadin' ta the backdoor o' the Keep. From tha' point we can go on foot and willna' need the beasties, so the lad can take 'em home."

Lightfingers broke apart one of the hay bales and tended to the horses. Then he spread some hay upon the ground and placed their bedrolls on top, the ground, free of snow, was still nearly frozen; the hay helped to keep the cold from their bodies.

Taggarty went through the wooded area with his axe and returned with a couple of armloads of firewood. He dropped his load near where Valoria and Lightfingers were building the firepit and went back for more. After several trips, they had enough timber for a nice bonfire, which everyone seemed to appreciate. Even the horses appeared grateful.

The remainder of the day passed slowly. Taggarty made several more trips into the wooded area around them to ensure they had plenty of firewood for the night. As cold as it was during the day, they were all painfully aware that it would grow even colder as night approached.

Throughout the night Valoria and Lightfingers did their best to keep the bonfire going, taking turns so that they could attempt to get some sleep; neither did. Despite all the care that had been taken to keep everyone as warm as possible, their efforts seemed futile. No one slept very well; it was just too cold.

They awoke the next morning shivering and miserable. They moved stiffly about, breaking camp and preparing to leave. No one was in a good mood, tempers were short; the gray rock seemed sheer and uninviting, impassable. Undaunted, they loaded up the wagon, mounted their horses, and pushed onward.

They had left the road, which went up through the *Northern Pass*, behind. They noticed that the mounds of snow weren't quite as deep the closer they got to the *Demon Spires*; likely because the great mountain range served as a buffer from the storms blowing from the north. The going was much easier; the horses were not having to strain quite as much as they had been previously.

By late afternoon they had reached the first river that flowed out of the *Spires*. Valoria looked at the three companions beside her. "We need to find a suitable place for the wagon to cross."

Bekka nodded. "Okay, but I'm not certain what I should be looking for, exactly."

Trish grinned at her. "Someplace that's not too deep."

"Duh!" Bekka said, giving her friend an incredulous look.

Lightfingers chuckled softly with a shake of his head, but otherwise kept his silence.

Valoria started her horse across the river, but she could tell almost immediately that this place was far too deep. They couldn't afford for the wagon to start floating downstream; if that were to happen, it would surely be lost. She turned her horse and continued along the riverbank. Finally, she found a spot that looked fairly shallow. Riding four abreast, they easily crossed the river. "This will be a good place for the wagon to cross over."

They crossed back to the other side and waited for the others to join them. Seeing the river, Taggarty had a worried expression on his face. "I hate ta be the feller tha' brings ill tidings, but this'll na' work fer me. I dinna' think tha' I can cross the river 'ere."

Lightfingers frowned. "This is the perfect spot. It's shallow enough so that the wagon won't get swept away, and there's enough river rock in the bed so that you shouldn't get stuck. Trust me, this will be easy."

He shook his head adamantly. "An' I'm tellin' ye this isna' good! I willna' make it across!"

Breegan rolled his eyes. "Can ye na' see tha' he be terrified? Water absolutely scares 'im!"

Taggarty's face turned a beet red. "Na, tha's na' it. Water doesna' scare me!"

Breegan narrowed his eyes at him. "Then wha' t'is it tha's got ye all puckered up like a kitten?"

Tagg was absolutely furious now. "Like a wee kitten, ye say?"

"Aye! A wee lil' kitten!"

Taggarty tightened his hand in a fist and shook it in the other dwarf's face. "Old man or na', ye watch yer mouth a'for I give ye a whippin' like ye've ne'er seen!"

"Oh? Is tha' right? I'd like ta see ye try!"

Bekka couldn't take it anymore. "Enough! Cross the damned river before it gets dark!"

Taggarty crossed his arms over his chest in defiance. "Na' until I get me an apology!"

Breegan snatched the reins out of Taggarty's hand and snapped the hindquarter of the draft horses. *"Hey ya!"* he yelled, getting them moving. Before Taggarty could do anything about it, the horses plunged into the river and took them across without any difficulty. Afterward, Breegan tossed the reins into Taggarty's lap. "See 'ow easy tha' t'was?"

Valoria dismounted. "We'll make camp here and get a fresh start in the morning. I've had enough for today."

Breegan climbed down from the wagon and headed off into the woods with his axe, mumbling something about gathering some firewood. Taggarty stroked his beard as he watched him go, an angry glare in his eyes. He was still angry with the older dwarf that much was clear. He climbed down from the wagon seat and went to unharness the draft horses.

Ellisandra joined Taggarty with an armload of hay, which the horses couldn't wait to get at; they started nibbling it before she could set it down. "Guess I should have brought more!" she said with delight in her eyes and a huge smile on her face.

Taggarty found it difficult to stay in a sour mood with such enchanting company. He was quite fond of Ellie. "Aye, lass. The beasties 'ave worked up an appetite ta be sure. I'll give ye a hand wi' tha'."

Her smile spread even wider as she bounced on the balls of her feet. "That would be great, Tagg!"

Valoria smiled at Candi and indicated the pair tending the horses with a nod of her head, "Looks like Ellisandra has worked her magic on him."

"What do you mean?"

Valoria raised her brows. "I thought for a moment there was going to be trouble between the dwarves. Taggarty looked as though he were ready to chop Breegan into little pieces. I believed he was going to follow him into the woods and we'd have to come to the rescue before they managed to actually hurt one another."

Candi nodded. "And you think they're over it now, simply because of Ellie?"

"I certainly hope so. We can't afford to fight amongst ourselves. Our numbers are too few as it is; we don't need to increase our disadvantage."

Lightfingers began clearing a spot for the fire pit, but it wasn't easy finding rocks that weren't already frozen to the ground. He had to chip around most with his knife in order to free them. He quickly found that this task was bringing some much-needed warmth to his body.

Bekka followed Breegan into the woods, figuring that there was safety in numbers and no one should really be going off on their own. Besides, they were going to need another bonfire to keep warm through the night, and two could carry more wood than one. She just silently hoped that they wouldn't encounter anything along the way.

It quickly became clear that the old dwarf wasn't out looking to gather firewood; he had passed by some prime logs that would've been perfect. Bekka frowned. "What are you up to?" she whispered softly to herself. She briefly thought about calling out to the dwarf but decided against it. Instead, she decided to simply follow him. She had to move fast; he already had a fairly good head start on her. She could just see him up ahead of her, a dark figure moving through a sea of white.

It was impossible to move silently through the wooded area. The snow had a layer of frost upon it that crunched loudly whenever she took a step. So it was no great surprise to her that she found Breegan waiting for her with his arms crossed over his chest as he puffed on his pipe. There was a sparkle of amusement in his eyes as she approached. "You caught me," she said. "I thought you were gathering wood for tonight's fire, and I was going to help you." Her breath floated in the air like billowy clouds.

"Wha' gave ye tha' impression, lass?"

Bekka narrowed her gaze at him "You did. I heard you mumble something about gathering firewood."

"Oh," he said with a chuckle that caused smoke to seep past his lips. "I dinna' think anyone t'was payin' me any notice."

"So," Bekka asked, trying to catch her breath, "what *are* you doing out here, then? You're obviously *not* looking for kindling."

He glanced around casually. "Oh, I was just a lookin' 'round. We be vera close ta where we need ta be. I was hopin' ta find a familiar landmark. I figured if'n I could find the waterfall, then I could find the cave. Thought tha' we could shelter in there fer the night; it'd be a wee bit warmer."

Bekka looked hopeful. "Will this cave lead us to the back entrance of *Silver Frost Keep*?" Her eyes darted around the woods.

Breegan chuckled as he blew a smoke ring toward her. "It'd be a start."

Bekka was beginning to feel the biting cold; just standing around in the snow wasn't helping. "Well, let's see if we can find this cave of yours before we both freeze to death." She smiled at him. "We should probably hear the waterfall before we actually see it, don't you think?"

Breegan took another look around, scanning the area for something—*anything*—that looked familiar. It had been too long ago, almost a hundred years; small saplings then, were now towering trees, storms had reshaped the land causing rocks to shift and slide. Nothing was the same anymore. He could only hope that they could stumble upon the waterfall; that was likely to still exist much as it had. "Aye," he said. He pointed to the west. "We need ta get back ta the river; it'll guide us ta the fall."

Bekka didn't care which direction they went, just as long as they started moving. She was cold. Her throat and lungs seemed to burn with every breath she took; fingers and toes were starting to numb. *How long before we have to worry about frostbite?* she wondered.

After trudging through the snow in what they hoped was westward, they finally found the river. After a while they came to a point where the river branched off in both directions. "Which way?" Bekka asked.

Breegan shrugged. "I dinna' recall crossin' the river but once. I think we should foller it east," he pointed off to his right. Bekka hoped that he was remembering correctly. She *really* didn't want to have to cross the river on foot, and they'd have to in order to follow the western branch.

It was hard to hear much of anything as they made their way along the riverbank. Between the rushing water and the crunch of snow underfoot, very little else was perceptible. But still, Bekka strained to hear a waterfall as they went along.

Finally, they reached a small lake, or a pond, with a towering waterfall at the far side. Bekka's smile felt frozen upon her face; but she didn't care. She grasped Breegan's shoulder excitedly. "We found it!"

They stood staring at the water falling from high above, sending massive ripples across the lake as it cascaded down. Bekka estimated the drop to be at least a hundred feet but would not have been surprised to discover that it was more. It was hard to believe that they hadn't been able to hear the loud cacophony of the water plunging down the mountain. As they moved forward, they could hear little else.

As they made their way to the opposite side of the lake where the waterfall was located, they had to climb over huge boulders and fallen trees that had nearly rotted away. It wasn't easy, but eventually they made it. Bekka could feel the heat returning to her body as they scrambled over the rough terrain.

The spray coming off the waterfall as they followed a narrow dirt path along the side of the rocks pelted them. They had to take great care as they navigated the water's edge; the ground was muddy and slick. One false step and they would slide down the slope and into the turbulent water at the base of the waterfall. Twice Breegan almost slipped, causing Bekka to stop in panic, if the dwarf fell, she wouldn't be able to save him without help.

After several more mishaps, they made it behind the waterfall safely. Bekka was surprised that neither of them had arrived behind the falling curtain of water without getting completely soaked. For that, she was thankful. The immediate area behind the waterfall was partially lit by the refracted sunlight; she could tell that the cave was fairly large and went back into the mountain a good distance; but just how far, she couldn't tell. The depths of the cave was shrouded in pitch-black.

Breegan struck a match and held it aloft as he searched the ground. Bekka was surprised that he was able to light the match; she had thought it would be too damp, but it obviously wasn't. He pointed to his left. "Hand me tha' torch, lass. Quickly!" The flame was getting close to his fingertips.

Lying just a few feet away was a thick limb with a tapered end. The fat end had a piece of cloth wrapped around it. Bekka scooped it up and held it toward the dwarf. Breegan managed to get it lit just before he was forced to drop the match. He took the torch from Bekka and held it out in front of him as he stepped deeper into the cave. He seemed to be searching for something, and Bekka remained silent, not wanting to break his concentration as she followed close behind.

Breegan aimed the torch down and to his left, over the top of what seemed to be a gaping hole in the floor. "Careful where ye walk, lass. One wrong step an' it can be yer last in this lifetime!"

Bekka leaned forward and tried to see the bottom, but the torchlight wouldn't penetrate the murky depths. "How far down do you think it goes?" she asked.

The old dwarf chuckled softly, the firelight dancing in his eyes. "All the way!"

Bekka quickly straightened. *What kind of an answer was that, anyway?* She frowned at the dwarf. He ignored the look she gave him and continued to walk deeper into the cavern; the torch swinging slowly left to right in front of him, lighting the way.

The path they followed through the rock twisted and turned, sometimes it seemed to double back, but it nonetheless continued deeper into the mountain. They barely noticed that the path had begun to ascend, rising ever so slightly. Eventually they could see daylight ahead of them. Without the need for torchlight, their pace quickened.

They shielded their eyes from the bright light of the sun as they reached the mouth of the cave. The opening in the side of the mountain here was nowhere near as large as the one behind the waterfall. "We need ta be headin' back," Breegan said. "The sun will set soon, an' we need ta get the others ta the cave a'for it gets dark."

It took them nearly an hour to make it back to the group. Taggarty gave them a stern look when they arrived, empty-handed. "Where 'ave the two o' ye been? We were afeared tha' ye'd gotten yer selves lost! An' 'ow come ye dinna' have any firewood wi' ye?" He shook his head in disbelief.

"We found a cave that is better suited to make camp," Bekka said quickly. "It's warmer there. We can get a fresh start from there in the morning." She glanced at Taren. "This will be as far as the horses can go."

Taren nodded. "I'll stay wi' the horses an' head back in the morn."

"You should come with us. It'll be too cold for you here all alone," Bekka said.

"Dinna' worry 'bout me. I'll make do wi' the hay an' the fur blankets. I willna' leave the horses to fend fer themselves."

They said their goodbyes and went about dividing what remained of their food supplies. The sun was beginning to sink behind the high peaks of the Demon Spires by the time they had finished.

By the time that Breegan and Bekka led them into the cave, darkness had fallen.

They had gathered wood as they walked to the cave, and in no time at all Lightfingers had a blazing fire going, spreading warmth and a fiery orange glow around the cavern. As they settled in, Bekka told them about the path that they would follow in the morning, and she cautioned them to be careful where they walked, as there were seemingly bottomless pits scattered here and there.

Lightfingers pulled Bekka away from the others and grinned. "I've missed your company. If I didn't know better, I'd think you were avoiding me."

Bekka smiled up at him, her eyes sparkling with delight. "You're not getting rid of me that easily."

He kissed her softly on the lips. "I certainly hope not."

Candi sat near the fire, a sad look in her eyes as she rested her chin upon her knees. "I hate the fact that Taren is alone out there. I would hate it."

Trish smiled at her sympathetically. "He'll be fine. He's probably done this sort of thing thousands of times."

"Not like this," Candi said sullenly. "Not so far from home."

"Would you have felt better if someone stayed with him?" Trish asked.

Candi nodded. "I would've stayed with him, but I have to think about Ellie." She glanced at the girl who was already fast asleep.

Trish shook her head slowly as she got to her feet. She started putting on her warmer clothes. "What are you doing?" Candi asked, raising her head from her knees.

"I'm gonna go keep Taren company."

"You're not serious!"

Trish smiled. "I am."

Bekka and Lightfingers rejoined the others. Bekka looked at Trish, frowning. "What are you fixing to do? You can't go out there, it's pitch black outside! You could get lost, or hurt, or worse!"

Trish chuckled softly. "This won't be my first time wandering around in the woods at night. I'll be fine." She was certain that there was *nothing* out there in the dark that could frighten her, maybe once upon a time, but not anymore; the night no longer held any fear over her.

"Trish!" Bekka said firmly. "You can't go! We leave here first thing in the morning."

The redhead shook her head and chuckled. "Do what you have to do, Beks. I'm going to spend the night in Taren's company so that he isn't all alone on the mountain." She gave a little wink. "I'm doing it so Candi will feel better."

"I won't let you go out there!" Bekka said, quickly standing.

Trish gave her a smirk. "You *can't* stop me, Beks. I'm going."

"We won't wait for you," Bekka said in a final attempt to convince her friend to stay.

"I'll be back before you leave," Trish said as she slipped out into the night.

Valoria had been exploring the cave. She joined Bekka's side. "Where is she going?"

Bekka shrugged. "She's going to keep Taren company."

"You want me to follow her?" Valoria asked.

Bekka sighed. "No." She looked down at Candi. "I hope you're satisfied."

Candi's eyes went wide. "Me? This wasn't my idea, Bekka."

The horses began to stomp nervously and snort as they pulled against their reins. Something was frightening them. Taren had been sitting by the fire, bundled in fur blankets, trying to stay warm. He looked off into the darkness hoping to see whatever it was that had startled the animals, but he couldn't see anything. He had been staring into the dancing flames of his campfire and now he was night-blind. He cursed himself; he knew better.

He stood, tossing the blankets aside as he drew his sword. "Who is there?" he asked, stepping boldly forward.

Trish chuckled softly as she saw him standing there. "Take it easy with that thing, before you hurt someone."

He turned to his left and saw her stepping through the trees. She made no sound that he could hear as she walked up to him. "What are ye doin' 'ere? I could 'ave hurt ye!"

She chuckled again, the light of the fire dancing in her green eyes. "Not likely."

"Ye should be wi' the others," he tried to protest, but he wasn't very convincing.

Trish wrapped an arm around his shoulder as she pushed his sword aside. She pulled him against her body. "You look cold," she said softly.

He nodded, shivering at her touch. "It is a vera cold night."

She nibbled at his earlobe, smiling as his body quivered in her embrace. "I know how we can get warm."

His eyes widened and he stepped back, trying to distance himself from her. He stumbled and fell down, hard, landing upon the fur blankets. He swallowed as he stared up at her.

Trish smiled, and bit at her bottom lip. "Have you ever been with a woman?" she asked as she began to undress.

Taren swallowed, nodding as he watched her. "Y-yes! I 'ave 'ad plenty o' women."

He didn't sound very convincing.

Chapter 70
An Arduous Journey

Taren Toshe awoke to find that Trish was already gone. There was no sign of her anywhere. She had slipped off in the wee hours, just as quietly as she had come. He grinned at the thought of her in his arms, her kisses upon his skin, her gentle touch... *He shook his head. Had it been real, or was it a dream?* He could still smell the fragrance of her auburn curls, their softness against his cheek. He could only hope to see her again.

He gathered his clothes; she had practically ripped them off him. They were scattered all over the camp. The morning air was crisp and cold. He dressed as quickly as he could, pulling bits of straw from his tangled hair.

He couldn't stop smiling.

As Trish stepped into the cave, the others were just packing up their bedrolls. "Good morning!" she called out, smiling. "I see you haven't left me behind just yet." She felt warm and glowing; almost giddy.

Bekka glared at her. "How was your night?"

Trish gave her a devilish smile and winked. "Better than yours, I'm sure!"

Candi gasped sharply. "Patricia Delaney Morgan! *You didn't!*"

Trish giggled. "Well we had to do *something* to keep warm."

Bekka's eyes grew wide. "You took advantage of that poor, sweet boy?"

Trish rolled her eyes, placing her hands on her hips. "Oh puhlease! You're beginning to sound like my mother."

Bekka snapped her mouth closed. She glanced at Candi in disbelief. Candi just smiled and shrugged. "Not what I expected to happen!"

Bekka shook her head. "But how could you? He's just a boy."

Trish gave her an incredulous look. "He's only a year or two younger than we are. Besides, if he didn't live in some backwater town in the middle of nowhere, he'd already be married and probably have two little rug rats of his own, by now." She glared at Bekka pointedly. "This *isn't* back home. Besides, he enjoyed it every bit as much as I did!"

Bekka crossed her arm. "I bet he did."

A wicked smile appeared on Trish's lips. "You're just jealous because I got laid and you didn't. When is the last time you got any, Rebekka Lynn Kensington?"

Bekka practically growled at her friend. "We *don't* have time for any of this nonsense!" she stomped off angrily, joining the dwarves, Lightfingers and Valoria.

Trish looked at Candi and raised her brows, her eyes going wide. "I think I struck a nerve!"

Candi crossed her arms over her chest. "You think?"

They followed the same path through the cavern as Bekka and Breegan had taken the day before. By the time the golden rays of the morning sun began to paint the sky with an orange glow, they stepped out of the cave. The air was crisp and cold, and it burned the back of their throats as they gulped it in; but they didn't care, it was far more refreshing than the dank, musty smells of the cave.

A thin trail wound up the side of the mountain and, after only a brief pause to take in the beauty of the rugged, snowy landscape, they pressed onward. Trish and Candi walked together just behind Ellisandra and Taggarty. Valoria and Bekka followed Breegan and Lightfingers who were leading the way up the pathway. Candi smiled at Trish and gave her head a little shake. "I still can't believe that you had sex with Taren."

Trish frowned. "I don't see why everyone is having such a hard time with it." She shrugged. "It was consensual, it's not like I forced myself on the poor boy."

Candi quickly put a hand on Trish's arm. "Whoa, hold on a second. No one is saying that you *seduced* him, or anything like that."

Trish snorted as she glared up ahead at Bekka. "Well, some people could've sure fooled me."

Candi followed her gaze. "No, I'm sure Bekka doesn't either. She just thinks that you may have taken advantage of him. That's all."

Trish gave her a side-glance. "Is that what you think too?"

The blonde shrugged, frowning. "I don't know what to think. But it really doesn't matter, does it? So, you guys *did it*. Big deal. He'll probably remember it for the rest of his life." She smiled. "You gave him something to remember you by. It's really kinda sweet."

Trish chuckled softly as she put an arm around Candi. "I love you, girlfriend. Really, I do."

They were silent for some time after that. Finally, Trish said, "I didn't go down there with the intent of having sex with Taren, despite what everybody may believe. I was truly worried about him being there alone with just the horses to keep him company. When you expressed your fears to me, it got me thinking. I thought it was a real shitty thing for us to do, abandon him like that. It wasn't right. And, if we don't survive this battle with Sinnestra, which we likely won't—I mean, she *is* a fricking demon—I didn't want that to be one of my final acts in life."

"I wish you wouldn't talk like that," Candi said. "We're gonna make it through this; you, Bekka and me. We'll survive this somehow. We have to."

Trish grinned. "Well, if we don't, at least I got laid beforehand."

Candi slapped her arm. "You are so bad, Patricia Delaney!"

Trish shook her head. "I really wish you'd stop with the middle name. No one needs to know that. Besides, you promised."

Candi blinked. "Oh come on! We were in first grade when I made that promise!"

Trish nodded. "Yeah, but a promise is still a promise."

Candi's eyes went wide. "I'm sorry. I didn't mean to. I just forgot."

"Do you even remember why I told you my middle name in the first place?" Trish asked.

Candi frowned, then her face brightened as she recalled. "Of course I do! To make me feel better."

Trish nodded in agreement. "And why was that?"

Candi shrugged. "I... I can't recall."

Trish chuckled. "Someone wore a dress that day and forgot to wear any panties."

Candi paled suddenly. She slapped Trish's arm. "Oh my God! I completely forgot all about that! I must've blocked it out of my mind!" She nodded. "I remember now. My Mom used to dress me for school. She had to, every single day. That particular day she was distracted cuz she and Dad had a big fight. She forgot to put my underwear on me. I tried to tell her, but she wouldn't listen. I guess her mind was still on the argument she'd had. I don't know." She chuckled softly, shaking her head. She looked at Trish in amazement. "I can't believe you even remember that!"

Trish sighed. "I've never told anyone. You made me promise."

Candi gasped, placing a hand over her mouth. "We made a pinky-swear!"

"Yup! Sure did!"

Candi wrapped her arms around the redhead and held her in a tight embrace. Her eyes were wet with tears. "I love you Trish! I'm so glad that you came back to us!" She paused. "I just wish you'd change your mind about going back through the *Portal*. I don't want to lose you! We still need you. We'll *always* need you."

Trish sighed heavily as she returned Candi's hug. She refused to have this conversation again. She knew how Candi could be. She wasn't going to stop until she wrestled a promise out of her. Trish wouldn't make that commitment. She wanted to go home. If Candi wanted to keep them all together, then they both could go back to *Midvale* with her. There was nothing to keep either of them here except for the few friends that they had made. But the fact of the matter was, Sinnestra could very well kill them all. The only way that their deaths could be avoided was if they went through the *Portal* now, instead of continuing down the path they were on—or up, in this case. But she knew that wasn't about to happen.

Finally, Trish forced them apart. "We're falling behind, we'd better catch up or Bekka will be all over us!"

Candi reluctantly turned and started walking. "Something's up. They've stopped," she said. She strained to see what was going on, but really couldn't see much of anything. As they neared the group it became obvious. A good-sized portion of the mountain had fallen away; a gaping chasm separated them from the remainder of the path.

Breegan shook his head. "Weel, tha' be the end o' the line fer us! We'll ne'er get across tha' span," he pointed to the rocks above the chasm, "they look as though they'll fall away at any second." He gave the others a dark look. "I guess we'll 'ave ta sneak in through the front door o' the Keep; or abandon the quest altogether."

"There is another way!" Ellisandra said.

All eyes turned to her.

She smiled. "I can get everyone across. It will take some time, but it is certainly better than just giving up."

Breegan chuckled. "I appreciate yer enthusiasm, lassie, but thar is na way tha' ye can get us across unless ye 'ave a magic spell or some such." He chuckled again. "You're just a wee lassie."

"Hmph!" Taggarty glared at the older dwarf; he was obviously still a little miffed at him. "Methinks the wee lassie can get us all across."

Breegan rolled his eyes and puffed on his pipe. "Ye've lost yer mind, 'ave ye? Thar be no way," he pointed a stubby finger toward Ellisandra, "tha' lassie can get us across ta the other side!"

Taggarty nodded. "Show 'im, lass."

Ellisandra pushed passed the group and jumped into the chasm before anyone could stop her. She immediately transformed into a golden dragon. She grabbed Breegan by the shoulders with her talons and ferried him across the gorge effortlessly. The look on his face said it all.

Taggarty slapped his knees as he laughed robustly. "Now wha' ye got ta say 'bout wha' the wee lassie can do?" He was laughing so hard that he actually plopped down on his backside and continued to chortle, tears springing to his eyes.

Flabbergasted, Breegan watched as the great dragon scooped up Taggarty and dropped him on the other side of the chasm and returned to the group, picking up Trish and Candi. She repeated the process until they were all back together.

Taggarty slapped Breegan's pipe against his chest. "I believe ye dropped this when yer mouth hit the ground. I figured ye might need a smoke!" He chuckled again as the old dwarf sputtered in response.

After several minutes, Bekka touched Breegan's shoulder. "Are you going to be all right?" Valoria smiled as she walked past. She was going to scout up ahead while they waited for the old dwarf to regain his composure.

Breegan rubbed the top of his bald head as he stuck the pipe back into his mouth, biting upon the stem. He puffed, but no smoke came. Frowning darkly, he searched his pockets for his matches. When he found them, he struck a match and held it over the chamber of his pipe with a trembling hand. Finally he was able to relight the tobacco. After a few deep drags on the pipe, billowy smoke swirled about his head as he exhaled. He smiled weakly up at Bekka. "Aye, lass. Thank ye."

He glanced at Ellisandra who had returned to her human form. "So, ye're a dragon, are ye?" He shook his head. "Weel, I've just 'bout seen it all now!" He chuckled softly.

Ellie hugged him close. "I hope that I did not frighten you too badly. That was never my intent."

"Aye, lass, I know," he patted her softly on the back.

When Valoria returned to the group she informed them that

the way ahead looked fairly clear. So they gathered their gear and started off. The path was starting to become even steeper than it had been, in less than two hours they were breathing hard and utterly exhausted. With nowhere suited to set up camp, even for a brief respite, they were forced to either take a break where they were or continue on.

The ice-covered path narrowed on the side of the mountain and they were forced to press their backs against the icy rock wall and side-step as they made their way along. This only served to slow their progress even more. They had to walk with greater care upon the slippery slope. They desperately needed a break.

"How much further until we reach this 'backdoor' that you've been telling us about?" Valoria inquired.

Breegan's eyes grew wide and he scratched the side of his head. "Ye 'ave ta remember, I was just a wee young un when we fled the Keep all those years ago. My mem'ry isna' wha' it used ta be." He shrugged as best he could. "I wish I could be more reassuring."

"So, wha' yer sayin' is, ye 'ave no bloody idea!" Taggarty said heatedly.

Breegan shrugged again. "Weel, t'was a hundred years ago! I canna' be expected ta remember e'er lil' detail," he snapped his fingers together, "just like tha', now can I? We was runnin' fer our vera lives. E'eryone o' us was scared we was gonna die a'for we saw the light o' day. T'was pitch black; nary a star in the sky, nor the moon to guide our way along. The wee bairns were all a wailin' an' we did our best ta keep 'em all quiet so's the demon bitch an' her army wouldna' discover us." Tears filled his eyes at the memory of that long-ago night.

Everyone had grown silent, reliving that night with the old dwarf. It had been difficult to listen to the harrowing tale of the dwarven exodus from their home. They had been frightened, certain that death would find them at any moment. And death *had* come for many of them. Yet, with no other option available to them, they continued on. In the end, most of them had survived.

Taggarty stroked his beard thoughtfully. "Perhaps it would be best if'n Ellisandra flew along the trail and scouted fer the entrance. Maybe she could find it an' give us a better idea."

Ellie nodded eagerly. "I can do that! I would just need to have some idea of what I was searching for. Is it easy to find? How will I know it when I see it?"

Breegan sighed heavily as he wiped the tears from his cheeks. "Aye. This path should only continue ta rise a tad more, an' then it should level fer a good ways a'for descendin' again. Eventually ye'll find a spot where the trail just seems ta end. It should be at a sheer wall. 'bout fifty feet up is a narra' openin' in the side o' the mountain. It could just be a thin crack or some such."

Ellie nodded. "That should be enough for me to find it." She touched a hand on Candi's arm. "I will keep in contact with you and let you know what I find."

Candi reached out and squeezed her hand. "Be careful!"

She smiled, her eyes bright. "I will!" She stepped off the narrow path and plummeted down, almost instantly she transformed into the golden dragon. She beat her powerful wings and took flight, soaring upwards, and then continuing, she flew above the path.

Candi watched her as she grew smaller and smaller the further away she flew. The path high above turned to the right and soon, Ellisandra had disappeared completely, the sound of her leathery wings beating the frigid air, fading. The group had remained pressed against the sheer wall of ice as they silently watched the dragon's flight. Now, they continued to side-step along.

I see the entrance! Ellisandra said in Candi's mind. *It is just as Breegan said! It is not that far.*

Candi grinned. "Ellie's found the entrance. She says it isn't that far away!" This news seemed to buoy everyone's spirits, and though they were tired, they picked up their pace and ascended the trail with renewed energy.

Almost an hour later they were on level ground and the going was much easier, and even better, the path widened considerably. They could see the dragon flapping its massive wings, seeming to hover in place several hundred feet up ahead. When they reached her, they could see that the rest of the path descended at a fairly steep angle. The real problem was the ice that covered it; they were afraid that they wouldn't be able to make the descent safely.

"How much rope do we have?" Valoria asked.

Taggarty shook his head as he peered down the pathway. "Na' enough ta see us safely down."

Lightfingers sighed as he glanced at Bekka. "All that ice will make it too dangerous for us. Maybe we should have Ellisandra carry us down."

Trish shook her head. "There's no time, we are losing daylight too quickly." It was true; the sun was rapidly sinking beyond the rugged peaks of the *Demon Spires*.

Candi's eyes went wide as a thought occurred to her. "What if Ellie melts the ice?"

On it! Stand back! Ellisandra flew in a half circle above them and then streaked along the downward path, breathing a cone of fire as she descended. Even from the safe distance where they stood, they could feel the intense heat rising up. You could hear the ice crack and splinter as it began to melt away.

Valoria stepped to the edge and tested it with her foot. She didn't slip. "It's safe, but we need to go now." The snow above the path was now showing signs that it too, was starting to quickly thaw. If they didn't move quickly the entire mountain could come down on them.

They descended as rapidly as they could, and the steepness of the incline helped to some extent. The hard part was going to be stopping at the bottom. Fortunately, the path flattened out at the end with twenty feel of level ground before the sheer rock wall. Ellie waited at the bottom for them, back in human form.

The sheer rock wall that rose above them was almost ten feet high. They could see hand and footholds cut out of the face of the stone; navigating it was easier than it looked. As they reached the top of the wall, a small ledge jutted out at the base of a two-foot wide opening in the mountain, squeezing in wasn't the easiest, but it was manageable.

Taggarty lit the torches he had crafted the night before and had stored in his pack. He handed one to Valoria. They found themselves in a cavern that was close to fifteen feet wide, and about twice as deep. Breegan pointed to the darkness that lay ahead. "Thar be a set o' stone steps yonder! They will take us ta the hidden door into the Keep."

Bekka stared into the dark shadows where the torchlight wouldn't reach; she couldn't help but feel that they were so close to reaching their goal. Somewhere within the fortress above them, were Sinnestra—and Han. She looked at those around her knowing how exhausted they were and admittedly she was too. She wanted nothing more than to press forward and finish this, but was it fair to her friends? She wasn't certain.

Valoria had been watching her, sensing her desire. She had a crooked little smile on her face. "Copper for your thoughts?"

Bekka laughed. Her mother used to ask if she'd trade a penny for what she was thinking; the thought made her smile. Her eyes watered unexpectedly and she quickly wiped the tears away. *Now was not the time for this sentimentality!* She sighed heavily, shrugging. "I want so much for this to be over."

Trish and Candi joined their side. "Well," Trish said, "let's do this."

"Now?" Bekka asked sounding surprised that they were willing to continue without rest.

Candi nodded. "No time like the present."

Lightfingers shivered, not liking the cold. "The sooner we can get back to civilization the happier I'll be!"

Taggarty chuckled. "We all be tired, t'is true enough. Me Da' always said tha' we could rest when we was dead." He rolled his shoulders. "I been a hankerin' ta try out me new battleaxe fer some time now." He reached back and took hold of *Deathbringer* and readied the weapon with a practiced flourish. The whispers of its angelic *deathsong* caressed the air.

Breegan swung his torch toward the darkness that lay ahead of them. "Tha' demon bitch 'as sullied this place fer far too long. I say it be time we remedied tha'!"

Tears welled up in Bekka's eyes as she looked at each of them. "Well, what are we waiting for?" She took the *Blade of the Spider's Kiss* out of the coffer and it immediately began to glow brightly.

Chapter 71
Silver Frost Keep

Breegan led them forward, his torch beating back the dark shadows as he held it aloft. They had left their winter coats behind and donned their armor, ready for battle. They found the stone steps leading upward and began their climb. Thirty feet above the cavern floor the steps ended at a rock wall; there was no door. "This canna' be!" the old dwarf exclaimed.

He turned and faced the group, shaking his head in confusion, "I dinna' understand wha's 'appened. I was certain tha' we was on the right path!"

"Weel," Taggarty said, sounding frustrated, "clearly ye were mistaken. Maybe thar be another set o' stairs?"

Breegan shrugged. "I dinna' think so, but thar has ta be."

Trish shook her head. "Maybe Sinnestra found this opening and sealed it off so it couldn't be used."

Ellisandra stepped forward and examined the wall. She turned and smiled at everyone. "No! This is it!" Turning back to the wall she took a confident step forward and disappeared completely.

Lightfingers chuckled softly. "Well I'll be damned!"

Valoria smiled. "It's just an illusion." She walked through the wall, pulling Bekka by the arm. The others followed. After they had all stepped through the illusory rock wall they turned and studied the wall; it appeared to be an ordinary interior wall of the castle.

Breegan tossed his torch at the wall, and the torch was suddenly gone. He scratched his head in amazement. "Weel, I'll be!"

Candi looked at Ellisandra. "How did you know it wasn't real?"

Ellie shrugged. "I guess my kind can see through simple magic if we concentrate hard enough."

Trish and Bekka exchanged looks with Candi. "That's good to know," Trish said with a smirk.

Valoria looked at Breegan. "Where to?"

The old dwarf shook his head. "I dinna' know fer sure. But fer the moment thar is only one direction in which we can go."

It was true. Other than going back through the illusory wall, the corridor stretched out in front of them; there appeared to be stone steps rising upward into darkness some fifty feet away.

"Do ye recall wha' lies at the top o' those stairs?" Taggarty asked.

Breegan shook his head. "Been too long, an' me mind isna' as sharp as me battleaxe." He started walking. "But thar is only one way ta find out."

"Aye," Taggarty said as he started after him.

The risers of each step were not that high, and each tread was narrower than normal; obviously made for dwarven feet and not human. Twice Candi almost stumbled. Trish shook her head. "Take them two at a time, you won't have as much difficulty."

Candi skipped the next stair tread and found it quite a bit easier to navigate up the stone steps. "Thanks."

A double door stood at the top of the landing. Breegan pressed his ear against it. After a second or two he eased his head away and looked at the others that were starting to group up around him. "I dinna' 'ear anythin'."

Bekka held the Drow weapon in her right hand; with her left she turned one doorknob while Trish turned the other. With a nod, they pushed the doors open, allowing the dwarves to slip inside. They stepped into the corridor, but this one was nearly twice as wide as the one below, and certainly better lit. Torches burned in wall sconces at even intervals; it was otherwise empty.

Taggarty's eyes narrowed. "Left or right?" he asked.

"Both," Bekka said, "we can't leave anything to chance."

Valoria gave her an angry look. "I don't like splitting our forces."

Bekka nodded. "Normally, I wouldn't either. Sinnestra could be anywhere. I have a sense that we are swiftly running out of time. We have to cover as much territory as we can, as quickly as we can. Tagg, take Trish, Valoria and Ellie and go that way," she indicated to her right with a nod of her head. Breegan, Candi, Lightfingers and I will go left."

Valoria shook her head. "I still don't think this is very smart."

Candi was about to voice her objections to being separated from Ellie, but Bekka spoke first. "Candi and Ellisandra seem to be able to communicate telepathically at great distances. If either of us finds anything, we can let the other know." She squeezed Valoria's arm. "You need to trust me. This is the best way."

Valoria looked at Ellisandra, still skeptical. "Can you communicate telepathically while in human form?"

Ellisandra nodded. "Yes."

Valoria sighed, giving in. "I hope that we don't regret this." She drew her sword and followed along after Taggarty and Ellisandra who had already began to move off down the corridor.

Candi watched them as they drew further away down the corridor; her eyes glued to the back of Ellie's head. *'Be safe!'* she said in her thoughts.

I will watch after them, do not worry.

Candi smiled as she turned back to Bekka, Lightfingers and the old dwarf, they were already a good ten paces away. She had to run to catch up to them.

Taggarty glanced at Trish and Ellie as they reached the end of the corridor. A set of stone steps descended into the depths of the fortress. "Guess we go down," he said.

Valoria nodded, shifting her grip on the hilt of her sword. She glanced over her shoulder. "Lead the way. I want to join the others as quickly as we can."

Taggarty began to navigate the circular steps. "Aye. Watch yer step as ye go."

At the bottom of the stairs a short corridor opened to a large, round room. It was nearly empty except for a wooden table set near the entrance, and a massive stone archway of black rock in the room's center. Torches were evenly spaced around the circular room, illuminating the obsidian rock of the arch with a fiery glow.

Taggarty shrugged. "Looks like a dead end."

Trish seemed drawn to the archway. "It's beautiful, in a creepy sort of way." She looked at the handprint that seemed carved into the stone. "Is that *blood*?" she asked as she extended her fingertips toward the indentation.

Ellisandra quickly stopped her. "Don't touch it!" she warned.

Trish paused with her fingertips less than an inch away from the stone.

"What is it?" Valoria asked.

"*A Demon Gate.* T'is what Sinnestra used ta gain access ta our world. T'is 'ow she was able ta defeat the fortress defenses. She attacked from wi'in the Keep; they ne'er 'ad a chance." Taggerty explained.

Trish dropped her hand to her side. "Do you think it still works?"

Ellie nodded. "As long as the blood remains, I think it can be easily activated; allowing passage through the arch." She shook her head. "No telling where it leads."

Valoria looked at her. "Do you think we need to go through to find Sinnestra?"

Ellie slowly shook her head. "I do not think that would be wise."

"Strange," Bekka said softly, "It's almost as if the entire place is deserted." They had gone down several corridors, twisting through the fortress and each new one was just as empty as the one before. They had tried several doors, all were unguarded, unlocked and unoccupied.

Lightfingers shook his head. "This isn't right. This place should be crawling with Sinnestra's men."

Several of the rooms had shown signs that they were inhabited recently, but nothing gave them any clue as to where the people had gone, or when they had departed. They were simply abandoned.

Candi cocked her head to the side, as though trying to hear something nearby, something barely discernable. She frowned. "Ellie reports the same for them. They've not found anyone, nor have they heard anything that would indicate someone was close. She says that they found some sort of *demonic gate* that Sinnestra may have used to gain access to the fortress."

Breegan stroked his beard. "Tha's interestin' ta be sure."

Bekka nodded. She had the feeling that Ellisandra's suspicions were accurate. "I think it leads to where she is originally from. That's probably where she took my brother to raise him."

Candi looked at her. "Do you think we need to go through that thing to find Han?" she didn't like the sound of that.

Bekka shook her head. "No. I think they are both here, on this side. Somewhere."

Breegan had been chewing on the stem of his unlit pipe; he took it out of his mouth and pointed. "Methinks down yonder corridor be the throne room. Surely we'll find someone thar."

Lightfingers nodded as he cautiously led the way.

As they turned the corner, they found the corridor widened even more; it was now double in size. They were relieved to see that this new passage was relatively short. Some thirty feet away was another set of double doors that seemed to go all the way up to the ceiling, or nearly so, which was well beyond twenty feet above them. *Why would dwarves build doors that were so tall?* To Bekka, it didn't make any sense.

Breegan pointed toward the doors. "Thar it be! The throne room o' *Silver Frost Keep!*" he spoke reverently.

Candi frowned. "Why isn't it guarded? You'd think that a sentry or two would be posted outside."

Lightfingers swallowed, crinkling his nose. "I smell a trap."

Bekka chuckled softly. "You'd think we would've seen someone by now." She shook her head. "But everywhere we've looked, it's been empty." She had a sinking feeling that they were too late.

"Do ye think tha' demon bitch 'as departed?"

Candi bit at her bottom lip. "Or maybe she's dead already and everyone just abandoned the Keep."

Bekka sighed as she drew up her shoulders. It was hard not to feel a measure of discouragement. "We'll never know until we get in there."

As the four of them approached the doors they heard the sound of grinding stone. The doors were slowly sliding open. They hesitated for a moment and watched, tightening their grips on their weapons; Breegan held his battleaxe in front of him with both hands, Bekka held the *Blade of the Spider's Kiss* out, away from her body, as Candi nocked an arrow to her bow. Lightfingers readied his shortsword. They just needed an enemy...

As the doors opened wide enough for all four to pass, a blast of frigid air burst out accompanied by a brilliant blue flash of light. Bekka was momentarily blinded. She quickly shielded her eyes with a raised hand; warmth seemed to emanate from the Drow weapon as its glow brightened momentarily. "What the heck was that?" Bekka asked; but there was no answer forthcoming from the others. She glanced at Candi and gasped sharply.

Candi, Breegan and Lightfingers had a hand raised in the air to shield their eyes; but neither was moving. They seemed completely frozen in place. Panicked, Bekka touched Candi's arm. "Candace?"

Nothing.

She tried the dwarf. "Breegan?"

Bekka looked fearfully at the thief. "Darren?"

The response was the same. They all stood like statues, unmoving, not even seeming to breathe. Bekka heard throaty, feminine laughter coming from the other room. Seeing that she could do nothing to help her friends she turned toward the throne room and stepped inside.

She could see Sinnestra sitting high upon her throne. Bekka cocked her head to one side as she stepped forward; she arched a brow as she considered the demoness. Sinnestra seemed different than she remembered. In all the visions Bekka had had in which Sinnestra appeared, she seemed to contrast with the one that was now before her. *This* Sinnestra resembled something *weaker*...

Her alabaster skin seemed grayer, somehow.

Bekka's eyes locked upon the wound on Sinnestra's shoulder; it hadn't healed. It looked putrid; infection had spread down her arm, up her neck and across her chest. Dark circles were under her eyes; she looked positively ill. She must have been in an extreme amount of agony

Sinnestra rose from her throne and slowly descended the dais. "Have you come to finish me?" she asked. Her words seethed with hatred.

Bekka walked toward her, slowly. The *Blade of the Spider's Kiss* seemed to glow brighter with each step. It was almost as though it knew what was about to happen. As if it wanted to fulfill its own destiny.

Bekka saw the Dark Priest moving to stop her. She whirled to face him; ready to do whatever it took to prevent him from stopping her. Sinnestra spoke sharply. "Leave us, Dinurés! Do not interfere!" she commanded, her voice sounded strong and powerful, not weak and feeble.

The Dark Priest hesitated, turning slightly toward Sinnestra, but not daring to take his eyes completely away from Bekka; he was no fool. "Mistress...?" he asked, sounding uncertain.

"Do not make me repeat myself!" Sinnestra roared angrily.

Bekka could see the priest tremble. He undoubtedly feared Sinnestra a great deal. She almost laughed. *Shouldn't she as well?* But she didn't.

Dinurés almost stumbled as he regained what little composure he had remaining. He glanced at Bekka as he passed by; his eyes were definitely fear-filled.

To Bekka's surprise, Sinnestra tossed her sword upon the floor. It clattered and slid out of reach. And then she did the truly unthinkable. She dropped to her knees and holding her arms out to her sides, she closed her eyes. "I am ready."

Bekka stopped. *What trick was this? What was she doing?* They were less than a foot apart. She raised the *Blade of the Spider's Kiss* high into the air, ready to strike the demoness down. From this distance she couldn't miss. There would be no glancing blow like Lithania had delivered all those months ago. This time Sinnestra would die. "Have you any last words?" Bekka asked, her words filled with anger, and hate. She wanted this. *Vengeance would be sooo sweet!*

Sinnestra slowly shook her head. "No. I am ready. End this."

Bekka spread her legs apart and prepared to strike. But she hesitated. She blinked slowly and then lowered the Drow weapon and stepped back. "No. I won't kill you."

Sinnestra's eyes flew open, and then Bekka could see her confusion turn into anger and rage. It only made her smile.

"Finish me!" Sinnestra hissed.

Bekka shook her head, taking another backward step. "No."

Sinnestra was seething with outrage. "Your mother was braver than you! She at least had the courage to fight me! Finish me you coward!" she spat the words. "Finish me!"

Bekka turned from the demoness, a smirk on her face as she started to walk away. "You're dead already."

Sinnestra screamed at the top of her lungs as tears fell from her eyes. "Finish me, you coward!" She fell to her stomach, crying. "Finish me!" She screamed again, still sobbing.

As Bekka continued to walk away, she could hear Sinnestra's final whimpers. "Please... finish me... please..." Her words were replaced by anguished sobs.

Bekka stepped out of the throne room and saw that the others had returned and that they held the Dark Priest as prisoner, he was kneeling in front of them, his hands securely tied. Miraculously Candi, Lightfingers and Breegan were no longer frozen statues, but they each wore looks of utter confusion and were shivering almost uncontrollably.

"We're done here," Bekka said as she looked at Valoria.

Taggarty placed a firm hand on the Dark Priest's shoulder. "Tell her wha' ye told us."

Bekka sighed. "Han's gone after the *Timestones*," she said with certainty.

The priest blinked in surprise. He looked up at her in confusion. "How did you know?"

She studied him for a minute before she responded. Finally she said, "That isn't important. I think you know where he's gone. You're going to tell me, or I promise your death will be very painful, and it will come very slowly. Tell me what I need to know, and you can go."

He seemed totally confused, but he knew he had no real choice in the matter. "The *Timestones* are in *Tolvaria*. He plans to gather them and use them to save his... to save Sinnestra. That is all that I know."

Bekka nodded. She cut the leather straps that bound his wrists. "Go, before I change my mind."

The Dark Priest quickly stood and ran down the corridor.

Trish stared at Bekka for a moment and then stepped away from the group. She threw the dagger she had strapped to her thigh, impaling the priest in the back. He fell dead upon the floor, sliding another three feet, leaving a trail of blood in his wake.

Bekka glared at Trish angrily. "I gave my word!" she said.

Trish shrugged. "Well I *didn't* give mine!"

Candi reached out and touched Bekka's arm with chilled fingers. "So what do we do now?"

Bekka looked them over. "I guess we go after Han. We go to *Tolvaria* and find these *Timestones* before my brother does. We cannot allow Han to use them."

Trish shook her head. "Not me. I'm done."

"Trish!" Candi said. "You have to come with us!"

Tears filled Trish's eyes. She shook her head again. "No. I'm going home." She looked at Bekka. "I'm sorry."

Bekka nodded. She flung her arms around her friend and hugged her tightly. She kissed the side of her head. "It's okay. I understand."

Chapter 72
Lithania

Lithania stepped out onto the boardwalk as the golden rays of sunlight began to rise above the distant *Eagle Peaks*. She paused in the doorway, her eyes going to the repaired section of railing where Trevor and that *thing* had gone over. Elanthor had done a good job with the replacement, and once it was sufficiently aged by the weather, you'd never know that it had been rebuilt. She shook her head. No, that wasn't true. *She would always know!*

There was a slight chill in the air and she felt it most on her right arm, the right side of her neck and jawbone, where the burn scars were exposed. She had miraculously survived the fire that had burned the Vile Forest and the attack by the Deceivers. Ironically, the fire had saved her from certain death. Very few survived their attacks; most were left as a shattered corpse.

Lithania closed her eyes tightly as memories returned to haunt her. She was not whole, she knew. The Deceiver had stolen a part of her; a part she could never get back. She had been left for dead, the Deceiver certain that the fire would finish her. *It almost had!* Even now she could feel the intense heat of the flames that fought to consume the forest around her. *It still seemed so real!* She could feel the snake-like tendrils of the Deceiver forcing their way into her. She tried to fight back, to resist, but the Deceiver was much stronger than she was. She was going to lose her battle to survive, and she knew it. Exhausted, she decided to give in and accept her fate. She dropped her arms to her sides, her right landing within the nearby flames. *That alone, had saved her!* She found it difficult to breathe; her lungs felt as though they too were on fire...

She forced her eyes open, stumbling forward, she pressed against the railing. Dropping her cane, she gripped the top rail tightly with both hands, until she felt her balance returning. Tears stung at her eyes. It seemed that every time she closed her eyes the memories of that night returned to haunt her. It made sleep difficult to come by. And when it did come, it was always fleeting. She was exhausted.

She bent and retrieved her cane from the boardwalk, she could scarcely walk without it; her right leg had been badly burned as well. She continued toward the Central Tree Lift, finding it made getting to the ground much easier than the wide stairs that had been built into the trees, but even it was hard on her.

She grunted painfully as the lift came to a stop upon the forest ground; it always seemed to come to a jarring halt that shook through every fiber of her being. It had likely always been like that, but it was much more noticeable after she was injured. The only other choice would be to leave the trees and live upon the ground but Aloena wouldn't have any of that, she knew. Aloe wanted her to be where she could keep an eye on her easier. *Was she afraid that she would disappear on them again?*

She had nowhere else to go.

Lithania closed the door to the tree lift and turned to the right. She followed a worn path that twisted through the trees and shrubs. As she limped along, she passed only a few elves, most were probably still sleeping. Those that were out were probably heading out to relieve the various watches located throughout the forest. She couldn't help but notice the way they looked at her as they passed; her burns seemed to make everyone uncomfortable. She tended to ignore them as best she could. She wasn't interested in their opinions of her. She had done what she did in order to save them. She could hold her head up high. Their judgment of her was irrelevant.

She left the well-worn path and began to follow a faint trail that wound through the trees. The terrain here was slightly rougher for her to traverse. She had to take greater care navigating this part of the forest. Small beads of sweat had broken out on her forehead by the time that she stepped into the small clearing where the grave was located, and her breathing had become ragged. Wincing, she eased down beside the grave and traced her fingertips over the wooden marker that bore Trevor's name.

The ache in her heart would likely never heal. Had she not gone to destroy the Deceivers, he would still be alive. It was obvious that he had loved her or at least whom he *believed* her to be. He had chosen her over Bekka. Tears rolled down her cheeks, unheeded. "I am so sorry, Trevor," she whispered.

She sniffled as she wiped her nose with the back of one hand and plucked grass from the mound of earth that lay in the center of the small clearing with the other. "I am sorry that I was not here to greet you when you came," she chuckled softly. "Father always said that I often acted without thinking. Had I waited I would be happy now."

She sighed heavily, shaking her head. She kissed her fingertips and then placed them upon the marker that bore his name. *"Ihl amon teres. I will always love you, Trevor."*

Epilogue
Midvale

Trish Morgan stepped out of the pond, completely soaked to the skin. "Well, *this* is just great!" she said to herself. It was cold, but she was immediately pleased to discover that there was no snow on the ground. But in reality, that brought her very little real comfort. She rubbed her hands briskly along her biceps, hoping to bring her some warmth; it had only a slight effect.

She turned and gazed back toward the pond from which she had emerged hoping she might still see the shimmering mist above the dark waters, indicating that the *Portal* back to *Vespia* was still open. She sighed as she shook her head; it looked perfectly ordinary, nothing like it had that night that they'd all gone through. It was already too late for her to change her mind. Not that it had been a consideration, but it was always nice to have options.

She started through the forest after getting her bearings; an acute sense of direction had always been one of her many strong suits. That thought made her chuckle. After several minutes of picking her route through the trees she emerged on the wide-open area of Miller's Farm where the Carnival usually set up. It was bare. Tall grass and weeds were sprouting up everywhere.

She glanced up at the sun, it had begun its descent, ready to give up the day as night beckoned. It was already late in the afternoon; if she picked up her pace, she might reach the outskirts of *Midvale* before the sun fully set. She chuckled to herself as the thought entered her mind that she might actually make it home in time for dinner. That made her smile. A home-cooked meal sounded delightful!

A big German Shepherd startled her as it came bounding towards her in the tall grass. It was barking and growling, warning her that this was his territory and she shouldn't be here. Trish stopped walking, not wanting to give the dog any reason to attack. She raised her hands in the air, waist high, and spoke in a soft, soothing voice. "Hey there, fella, how you doing? You're such a good boy, yes you are!"

The dog snarled, baring its sharp canines, the hair on its back bristling. She could see that the animal was set to attack. It clearly was not interested in making friends. Trish spread her legs, bracing herself for the inevitable. "You *don't* want to do this," she warned. "Be a good boy and run along. Shoo!" she batted her fingers in the air.

The dog leapt towards her but stopped in mid-air as long tentacles shot from his prey and impeded his flight. Another tentacle flew toward the dog's open mouth and shot down his throat. He yelped once before all sound was squelched from his feeble protest.

Trish wiped her mouth with the back of her hand as she left the corpse of the dog lying beside the dirt path. "Stupid dog," she said with a shake of her head. A small smile curved her lips.

As she walked along the dirt road, she could see a car heading her way, dust billowing up behind the automobile. It slowed as it got near her and she stopped, waiting for what would come next. To her surprise it was a local sheriff patrol car.

In the fading light of the afternoon, the officer turned on his blue and red flashing lights. He knew immediately that something was amiss...

"Breaking news," the announcer said to the camera, as he shuffled through papers he had just received. "Patricia Morgan, one of the Midvale teens that had gone missing last October, after two others were found brutally murdered near the Carnival grounds out on Miller's Farm, has been found. Morgan disappeared along with five other teens. She is reportedly safe, and currently being tended to at Midvale Memorial Hospital. Police state that a patrolman found the girl just outside of the city's limits, late this afternoon. Currently, she has no memory of what has happened over the past nine months, and police are still questioning her for more details. Five other Midvale teens are still unaccounted for. Two suspects are still being sought in this bizarre case: Julia and Robert Kensington, parents of one of the missing teens. Their abandoned car had been found at the Carnival on the night the teens disappeared. Foul play is suspected. Anyone with more information is encouraged to call the Midvale Police Department at the number on the bottom of your screen.

In other news..."

Read more of Bekka's continuing adventure in *The Quest for the Timestones: The Chronicles of Vespia Book 3.*

Maps

Eastern Vespia

Freeport

FREEPORT
CAPITAL CITY
MAP LEGEND
1 - GREAT LIBRARY ARCANUM
2 - CATHEDRAL
3 - MAGIC QUARTER
4 - WAREHOUSE DISTRICT
5 - CITY KEEP
6 - BUSINESS DISTRICT
7 - SLUMS
8 - TWISTED OAK TAVERN
N
W
E
S

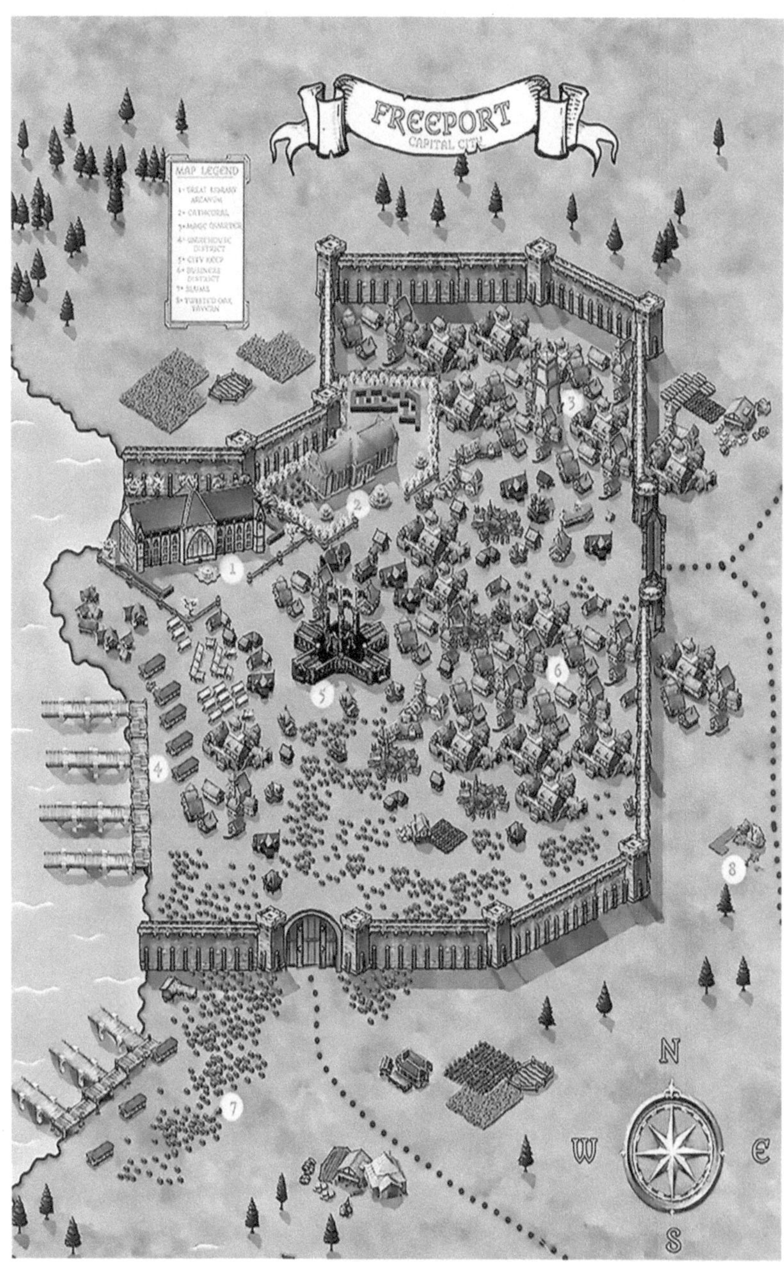

Sea of Dagmarth
DEMON SPIRES
NORTHERN PASS
THE BONEYARD
DRAGON REACH
THE GHOSTLANDS
BARRIER PEAKS
BITTERWOOD CASTLE
DARKWATER LAKE
DARKWATER
LAKE OF TEARS
DARKEN WOOD
THE VALE
RIVER OF SORROW
DREAD LAKE
SARN FOREST
THE BLACK BOGG
GLYNN FOREST
DAGMARTH
GLYNN
SEA OF DAGMARTH
N
W E
S
THE NARROWS
PERIL ISLE
FREEPORT
FREEPORT BLUFFS
SEA OF VESPIN

Dagmarth

LAKE OF TEARS
BARRIER PEAKS
BARRIER PEAKS
ISARN FOREST
RIVER OF SORROW
DAGMARTH
THE BLACK BOGG
SEA OF DAGMARTH

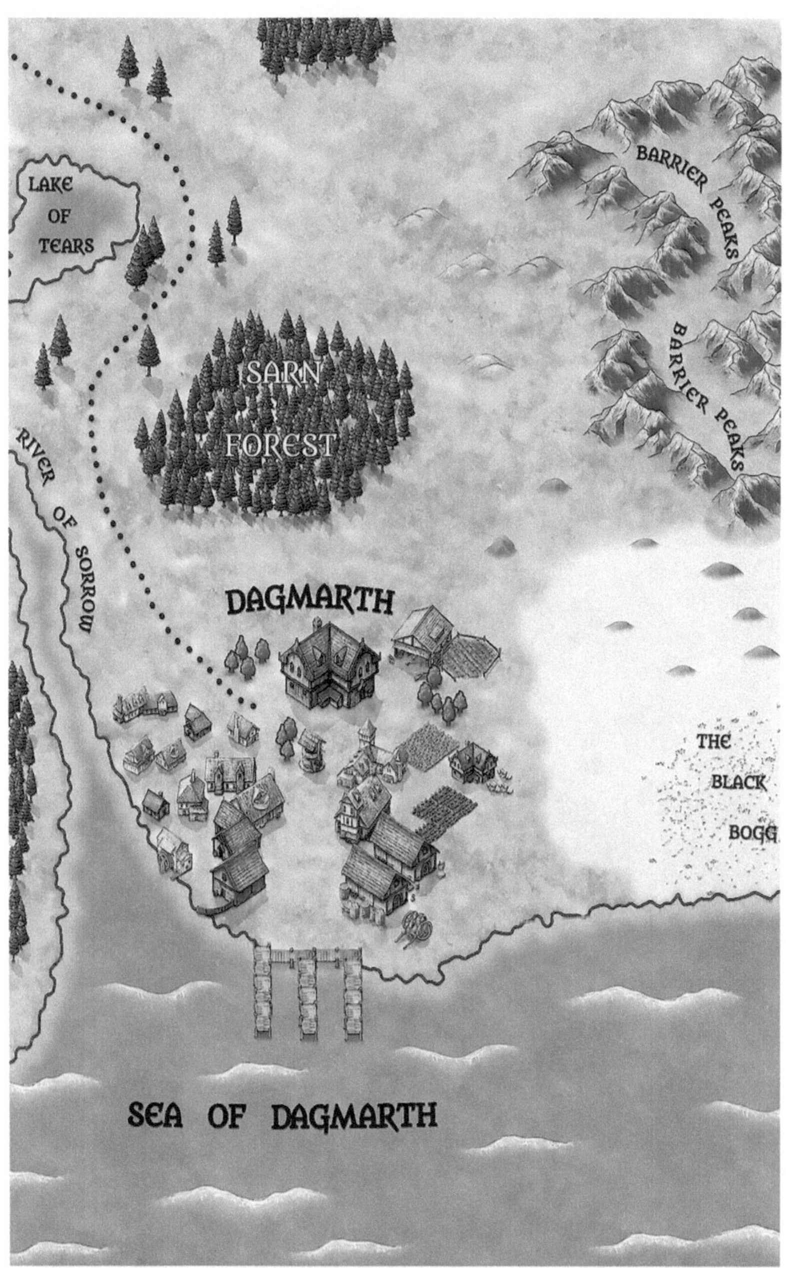

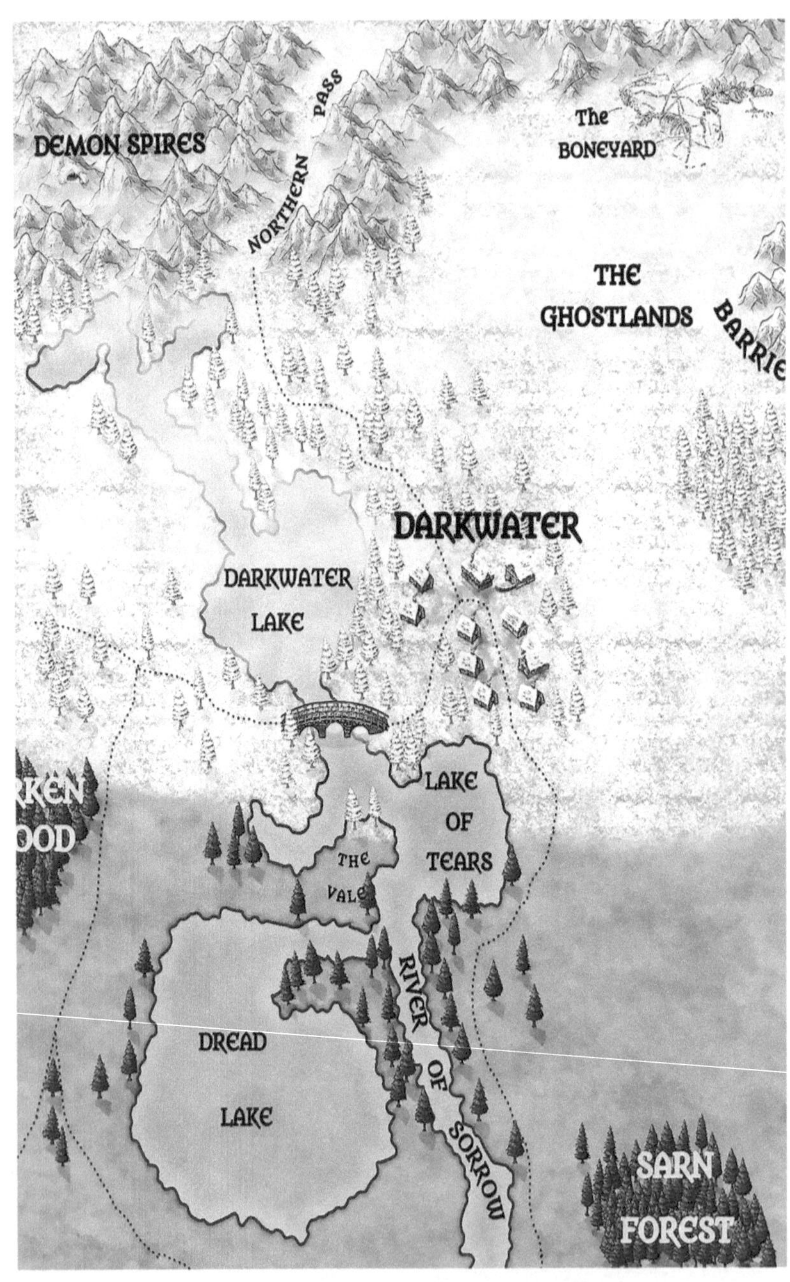

DEMON SPIRES
NORTHERN PASS
The BONEYARD
THE GHOSTLANDS
BARRIE
DARKWATER
DARKWATER LAKE
RKEN OOD
LAKE OF TEARS
THE VALE
DREAD LAKE
RIVER OF SORROW
SARN FOREST

DRAGON
SPIRES
DRAGON'S REACH
DRAGON
SPAWN RIV
BARRIER PEAKS
DRAGON SPAWN RIVER
SILVERMIST PEAKS
THE
EMERALD FOREST

About the author

Born in Kermit, Texas in 1960 and raised all over the Great American Southwest. He graduated High School from an American boarding school in Mallorca, Spain in 1978. He spent the next twelve years serving in the Navy. Diagnosed as an insulin-dependent diabetic, he was forced to change careers and begin work in the construction industry as a Union Pipefitter where he often worked at the Kennedy Space Center. He dreamed of being an author from a very young age and was always scribbling away in a notepad that he carried in his pocket. *The Chosen*, his first published novel is proof that 'Dreams don't have to stay that way.' He currently lives in Satellite Beach, Florida with his wife, daughter, and granddaughter, along with two precious Maltipoo pups; Bandit and Patches. *Sinnestra's Fury* is his second novel in The Chronicles of Vespia series. Tom says, "Another dream of mine is to see my books turned into Motion Pictures!"

http://www.tomhornauthor.com